Published by Nexgate Press © 2016

Dedicated to my wife, Amber (Wonder Woman).
You are amazing.

FEDERAL
UNDERGROUND

Penn Mitchell's Ancient Alien Saga

Book 1

Jeff Bennington

COPYRIGHT

Published by Nexgate Press, 2014. Edited by Streamlined Editing. Cover and interior formatting by Jeff Bennington.

ISBN-13: 978-1537647852

ISBN-10: 1537647857

Acknowledgments

I would like to extend a big thank you to those who have helped me over the last few years as I formulated this series, beginning with my gun guys, Steve Hovermale, Bill Crawl, and Brad Doak (a voracious Sci-fi fan) who offered valuable feedback to this horror/supernatural writer. I'd also like to thank Katherine from Streamlined Editing for the multiple read-throughs. Your careful eye is much appreciated. And how can I forget the thousands of readers who nominated this book into the Kindle Scout program. I am eternally grateful for your support and faith in me, and this book. I can't tell you how much I don't want to disappoint you! Likewise, I owe a huge debt to the Kindle Press team for taking this book on. Although the print version is not a KP publication, the eBook and audio rights are Kindle Press publications, and I couldn't be more excited about that.

Finally to Amber, Caleb, Levi, Asher, and Anna: My crazy existence would be mighty dull if I didn't have you. I love you all so much.

Jeff Bennington

Chapter 1
Genesis

"The Nephilim were in the Earth in those days, and also after that." Genesis 6:4 (JPS 1917)

November 1, 1942, Archuleta Mesa, Southern CO

"Move it, Wheeler! They're coming!"

Sergeant Raymond Clark squirmed through the cavity in the murky rock, frantically shoving Marcus Wheeler forward until the surveyor fell into the clearing on the other side, landing with a thud. Raymond turned, wiping beads of sweat from his eyes, and blindly shot his Colt 1911 three times into the dark tunnel. The bullets whizzed a hundred feet and a cluster of moist limestone shattered, spraying a triad of mineral dust. He waited to hear a body hitting the cave floor, but there was only a blaring echo of the three-round blast.

Menacing voices cried out in the distance and grew louder by the second. Somewhere, deep within, he could hear the strange clicking and hissing that had tormented his geological team for weeks. Whatever those things were, they were moving fast. The eerie sounds that seeped from the tunnel rock had terrorized two of his five teammates. Raymond and Wheeler chose to brave the cavernous system, a decision that Raymond would always regret. With the exception of the two government contractors and the Lieutenant Colonel (who led from above ground), the team had abandoned their posts the day before. They had been gripping their ears, unable to stop the deafening shrill inside their brains.

The rat-like scampering that was barely audible a few hours prior had escalated into a stampede. When Raymond first heard the light footfall and clicking sounds that came and went like an apparition, he thought they had stumbled upon a new species: giant ants or arachnids, perhaps. But when they found a glass radar panel and other high-tech gadgets in a cave that looked like a highly advanced mission-control room, the general consensus was that it must be the Germans. But as Raymond wedged himself through the rocky hole, he knew these *beings* were not ants or Nazis. Far from it. They were deceptive, intelligent, and now they were coming.

When he turned back to make his way into the cave, an energy pulse of some kind hit the rock inches from his leg and he felt a static charge envelop his ankle, racing all the way to the back of his neck. *Oh, God,* he thought, panting. He plopped through to the other side and began to run as fast as he could up the narrow tunnel, a passage as round and smooth as a glass tube. He thought of his family: his wife, Lydia, and their four children, Ray Jr., Marla, Richard and Peter, not a one of them more than ten years old. Would this be his legacy? Would he see them again? Would he make it home for another Christmas with Granny Clark? She didn't have much time left, but probably more than he did, or so it seemed. He imagined the terror and gore that would befall him, and then he questioned what kind of man would die like this—afraid, tormented—eaten alive.

Justifiably terrorized, Raymond ran out of the tunnel and into the larger, lighted cave opening where he immediately found Wheeler bent over and hyperventilating. The surveyor was breathing so hard that he couldn't explain what was happening. Lieutenant Colonel Walter Hyberg and the two scientists, Emerson Smith and Eugene Zondervan, gathered around Wheeler with looks of concern and confusion.

"Take cover!" Raymond shouted, bursting from the darkness that trailed behind. His voice blared in the immense talus cave, their heads pivoting in his direction. He could barely see Wheeler and the other three men as his eyes adjusted to the natural light.

They looked like ghosts morphing into a solid form as he raced toward them.

Lt. Col. Hyberg opened his mouth, but there was no time to speak.

"Take cover!" Raymond screamed again. "We're under attack!"

Wheeler eagerly nodded his head in agreement, pulled out his Colt and clumsily began loading the weapon.

"Get ready to fire. They're right behind me," gasped Raymond as he slid behind a large stone. Age-old dirt billowed in his wake and his body smacked against the backside of the rock.

"Who's firing?" Lt. Col. Hyberg asked. His six-foot-four frame crouched down, holding his pistol at the ready. He surveyed the gloom, then commanded Eugene Zondervan, the geologist from the Army Corps of Engineers, to hit the ground. "Pull that goddamned rifle off your back, Geo, and take aim."

Hyberg shuffled toward Raymond. "How many are we talking about, Sergeant?"

Raymond turned to his right, shaking, breathless. "I don't know, Sir. S-s-sounds like a herd of cattle... I took fire, Sir. It wasn't a bullet."

"What the hell was it?"

"Electricity... or something else... I don't know."

"Dear God in heaven," Hyberg said, his pistol momentarily sinking toward the dusty earth.

"Look," Zondervan shouted, pointing toward the tunnel.

Raymond peered over the rock and felt his heart sink. Dozens of emerald lights surged from the depths of the cave like lime soda bubbling out of a bottle. A luminous discharge barely missed Raymond, deflecting off the rock with a wave of electricity. The herd was coming and the beasts were armed. He fired back, blindly pointing over the stone.

"Shoot at the green lights!" Hyberg commanded. "Fire! Fire! Fire!"

Bursts of greenish light exploded at Hyberg's feet. He maneuvered near a cleft in the rock, nearly unloaded his weapon, and one of the green lights tumbled to the pebbly floor.

Guns boomed. Electrical pulses burned the dirt and rock surrounding Raymond, leaving red-hot scars wherever they came to rest. He wiped a wisp of dark hair and sweat from his eyes and then slid behind the protective boulder, shaking.

Wheeler shrieked when he took a direct hit. His severed left arm fell to the ground only inches from where Raymond had hunkered down. Blood pooled at Raymond's feet. Wheeler staggered, hysterically reaching for his lost limb, hemorrhaging. He turned toward Raymond, eyes rolling back into his head, and then toppled over the stone. Raymond jerked back in shock and fear. Another blast hit Wheeler's back and blood sprayed across Raymond's face. Instinctively, Raymond lifted his Colt and fired four more rounds at the green dots and three more lights dropped to the glassy floor.

Zondervan returned fire until his right hand exploded into a miasma of flesh and blood after taking a direct electrifying blast. Crying out with a shrill howl, he dropped his gun and gripped the bleeding nub.

Hyberg snatched up Zondervan, dragging him to safety with his left hand while shooting two more rounds into the darkness. A pulse of energy snagged a hunk of Hyberg's thigh, but he kept shooting. Raymond reloaded, and the blasts from within abated.

Wheeler lay silent. Zondervan cried in agony.

Doctor Emerson Smith, the team physicist, fired his Springfield rifle with crazed eyes. Boom. Boom. Boom. A final electrical burst rushed so close to his head that his thin white hair stood on end, but he kept firing even though he was out of ammo. Click. Click. Click.

Raymond shot another round and watched the last green light fall.

"Hold your fire!" said Hyberg, limping as he set Zondervan's half-dead body beside Raymond.

Smith continued pulling the trigger. Click. Click. Click.

"I said hold your fire, Smith" Hyberg repeated, glaring at the physicist.

Smith, an aging physicist and government contractor, held his rifle with white-knuckled terror. His entire body was shaking and his pants were soaked from pissing himself. Raymond stood up, approaching the scientist with caution. Smith noticed the movement and jerked his weapon toward Raymond and resumed firing. Click. Click. Click. Click.

Raymond moved closer, speaking softly, methodically as trained, carefully nudging the barrel to the left and then yanked the gun out of Smith's hands.

"They're gone," said Raymond. "For now." Smith stared right through Raymond, his chest pumping, veins filled with adrenaline.

Raymond looked at the war zone that had unfolded before him, a place of wonder when they arrived only three weeks earlier. Assigned to the U.S. Southwest Pacific Division to locate suitable atom bomb test zones, Lt. Col. Hyberg's team had stumbled upon a geological and scientific discovery with the potential to change the trajectory of the human race, advance civilization a hundred years in the blink of an eye, and possibly re-write history. The beauty of their find, however, had gradually lost its luster while they removed their spoils: "typing boards" as they called them, biologically sensitive weaponry, a highly advanced energy source applied to small devices throughout the facility, and ecological or possibly biological lighting systems. The glass-like walls would immediately glow purple when they were touched, lighting several feet in front and back when contact was made, and then dim several seconds later as they walked on.

The discovery was glorious and each of the five men, hand-selected for their specialized fields, spoke openly about the ramifications as they sat around the evening campfires that Sergeant Raymond Clark had routinely prepared. Raymond's prayers were finally answered. He dreamed of the riches that would follow. He'd have enough money to put his children through college and move Lydia off the Army base and into a real home of their own, closer to Granny, where the children could grow up in one place, a hometown where the boys could hunt and fish; he and Lydia could put down roots. But Raymond's dreams waned with each passing day. The creepy screams and insect-like tapping that never materialized but always seemed to claw their way into his ears left each man haunted, caring less about fame and fortune and more about survival. Do your duty. Follow orders. Retrieve the technology, and report your findings directly to Major General Murphy Ward Simpson, Chief of Engineers, who was currently in flight with a material recovery Battalion to witness his subordinates' claims firsthand.

The team was first alerted when Zondervan discovered what appeared to be Native Indian remains in the mouth of the cave. After further investigation, the Army engineering team found a scene that looked like a massacre: dozens of skeletons, scattered weaponry, and deep within the tunnel, small, non-human bones with strange objects still bonded to their bony hands. The weapons lacked triggers, biologically fixed to each creature. Their new orders were to collect as much evidence and materials as possible.

When General Simpson arrived two days later, on November 3, 1942, the Army Corps of Engineers immediately began the process of annexing the Archuleta Mesa outside of Dulce, New Mexico. The Department of Defense still controls the area today.

Chapter 2
Murals on a Wall

December 17, 2006
New York City

Agent Liz Ramsey awoke to her phone vibrating on her nightstand. She sluggishly rolled her feet off the bed. The phone buzzed once more and she read the name on her screen: Shanna.

She answered, "Good morning, Shan."

"Morning," replied Shanna, Liz's partner and best friend.

She looked at the time on her phone: 4:17 am. "It's a little early, don't you think?"

"Not at all. We're moving on Project Steward right now."

"Okay," Liz said with a yawn. "What's going on? Did Tango make it home?"

"Sweetie, Tango made it home and he's parked in the rear of the De Carver Youth Center. We're here now. Tried to call you, but—"

"Damn it! What's the status?" Liz set her phone on speaker and scrambled to her walk-in closet. She put on her slacks and dress shirt, and tightened her black leather belt.

"Tango's parked at the loading dock, so we haven't seen the delivery yet. But get this; we've got about six or seven high-profile donors who happened to stop by this morning."

"Buyers?"

"We think so. It's a who's who convention."

"State or Fed?"

"Both. It's a goldmine and the price of precious metals is going up every second because we're still mining luxury vehicles at ground zero."

"Anyone I'd know?"

"Mitch Sizemore, among others."

"Right… Maryland Assistant Prosecutor…figures we'd see him. Keep talking. I've got you on speaker." Liz fluffed her shoulder-length hair with baby powder, pulled it into a ponytail, and put on her FBI-labeled cap.

"I've heard that there's one or two movie execs, someone from the military, and a luminary from your alma mater… But I'm a block away, Liz. I'm only getting reports every five minutes. There's probably been other pervs show since my last update."

"Daniels?"

"I haven't heard."

"What about Harper?"

"He showed up at three and unlocked the joint… looked like shit."

"Is he our handler?"

"Looks that way… Listen, Liz… the Boss is on the line right now… Hang on…"

Liz strapped on her side holster and shoved her Glock in the leather nest. She grabbed her field jacket and badge while slipping on a pair of black walking shoes and then headed to her car.

"Shan. Don't go in yet," begged Liz.

"Too, late. He's giving a five-minute countdown."

"Shit! I'm leaving now. Be there in ten if the traffic gods care at all."

"I'm sure they do," Shanna replied. "See you in ten."

"See you in nine."

Liz hung up, and sped away from her Mid-Manhattan apartment, heading for 9th and 37th, a strategic location with a direct exit out of Manhattan via The Lincoln Tunnel, and then it's off to the races; New Jersey, Philly, and Chicago were a short road trip away, and so were the billions made each year in the body business. Human trafficking across the country had escalated in recent years, and the De Carver Youth Center was merely a blip on the FBI's radar until Liz managed to stumble upon a hot lead.

After she'd discovered Jinnie two years ago, she committed herself to putting away as many pedophiles as possible. Jinnie was eleven years old. She was from Lansing, Michigan, but Liz found her in a basement in Queens—locked in a cage. She found the girl while searching the home of David Espeznas, a previously convicted pedophile, who—after serving a miniscule sentence— was back on the streets.

While investigating the Espeznas' home, Liz and her team found what they were looking for, which was the computer linking David to an online kiddie-porn ring that spanned from California to New York to Louisiana. They found the IP addresses of sixteen men and one woman. Within hours, FBI Field Offices across the country were given names, addresses, and warrants. With the exception of two runners, all were captured, arrested and convicted. As expected, David caved under pressure and leaked a name: James Tahlski. The name seemed insignificant at the time, but Liz later discovered that James, a small-time thug and pimp, had connections to a foster family that was previously associated with a family services rape investigation. It was this foster family that led to information regarding the De Carver Center. At the time, Liz's daughter, Angie, was fourteen years old, so finding Jinnie, a beautiful, happy little girl, ripped from her home and used for God knows what, was like taking a punch to the gut. The girl was locked inside a steel cage, no bigger than four feet by four feet, with a dog cushion for a mattress; she was filthy, nearly malnourished, and heavily sedated. Her dark eyes looked terribly wounded.

Liz remembered taking her in her arms and feeling the emotional detachment emitting from Jinnie. When Liz escorted her out of the house, she felt a heaviness crashing down on her like she'd never known. She never forgot that day, and as she raced to the De Carver Center, she wondered if she'd find another Jinnie.

Liz had worked in the violent crimes division since she first joined the Bureau, but Jinnie's case was the worst she'd seen. The acts committed against this poor girl were unfathomable. But what really sparked Liz's interest was when Jinnie stated that David Espeznas never touched her sexually. She claimed that he paid very little attention to her until it was time for her to "go on a date". At that time, he'd take her out of the cage, lock her in the bathroom until she bathed herself, and then he'd give her something pretty to wear. That's when he drugged her with fresh juice and drove her someplace fancy, and other places that were frequently dark and scary. Her story seemed common until she mentioned the caves. Jinnie tried to describe where she was taken, but Liz just couldn't get enough details. There were others, Jennie said. "...lots of others, underground".

That was a tipping point for Liz. She knew there was more to the tens of thousands of children who go missing every year. She knew the kids weren't all victims of the creepy man down the street... not every day... not thirty thousand a year. She suspected that there was something bigger, something organized, structured and protected. Her team usually nailed the small-time pervs and individuals at the bottom of the food chain, but they were only fool's gold compared to what she was after.

When she arrived at The De Carver Youth Center, the parking lot had been taped off, and a paddy wagon was filled with alleged sex offenders. She took note of the luxury vehicles in the parking lot and wondered how the hell these wealthy, respected men can live such disgusting lives and not throw themselves over the Brooklyn Bridge.

She looked inside the wagon, guarded by two NYPD officers, and recognized a few faces. A graying, heavy-set man turned away.

"Good morning, Senator," Liz said, smiling at the retired politician. He had dropped out of his eighth-term race when an alleged sex scandal between him and a senatorial page broke in the Washington Post.

Liz looked at the young, handsome, affluent lawyer from The Old-Line State. "How you doin', Sizemore?"

Mitch Sizemore, who was seated closest toward the door, sneered and turned his handcuffed hands toward Liz, flashing his middle finger.

She scanned the others and immediately recognized Dirkus Harper, the Center's Director. His thin, normally well-groomed hair was tangled in knots, and his face pale and wrinkled. He usually cleaned up a little better. "How's business, Dirk?" Liz asked, feeling a bit sick to her stomach. "Times are tough these days, eh?"

"Go fuck yourself," snapped Dirkus. His brow twisted with hate. His filthy white dress shirt hung out of his pants, stained from resisting.

"Looks like you've got that well in hand, Dirk." Liz shifted her cap and said, "Have a nice day, fellas." She nodded at the officers and hurried under the crime tape. She realized that although these dirtbags were in a world of shit, most wouldn't pay what they owed society and the lives they'd ruined. Her time working in New York's FBI Crimes Against Children Unit had taught her that. Some could afford bail and easily flee the country. The others would plea-bargain their way into less than a nickel in the pokey, or hire a top attorney that would inevitably find a loophole somewhere.

Liz walked into the large, privately endowed youth center, and she felt an extreme sense of accomplishment. Vincent, her ex-husband, would be proud. He was a CIA agent on assignment in Saudi Arabia and was scheduled to return to the States by Christmas. She knew very little about his work because Vince refused to tell her. He always said it was better that she didn't know, and Liz understood. They had chosen careers in the world of secrets and agreed a long time ago that they'd rather discuss other things when they were together; things like Angie and family life. It didn't take long, however, before a breaking story about international affairs got Vincent talking. And although it frustrated her, Liz couldn't resist commenting on the latest criminal case that hit the headlines. Far too often they'd catch themselves talking about everything except what was real, what Vincent really did, and who they had become. Their conversations circled around true intimacy like an eagle watching from on high, but they never came in for the kill. Liz hurt deeply because of it. Vincent wouldn't budge. He'd almost get there and then fly away—leaving Liz empty and longing. So as time trudged on, the lovers morphed into something like associates, comfortable with the distance that had wedged itself between them. Still, years after their divorce, Liz longed to share the news about the bust.

She had warned Vince that she was on the verge of a major shakedown. When they received reports that a few high-profile suspected sex offenders had frequented the De Carver Youth Center, she knew they'd hit the jackpot. Within days, Liz and Shanna were able to connect a Family Services incident report with the center and before they knew it, they'd stirred up a hornet's nest.

Liz walked through the glass doors at the front of the facility. The reception area was well lit and the walls were covered with poignant murals that told the story of broken homes, addiction, living on the street, and ultimately hope and healing, painted by some of the center's most talented boys and girls. Then in the midst of the chaos, she noticed an agent kneeling beside a young boy who was sitting against the wall, sobbing into both hands. Liz almost missed it—another story for the mural.

Beyond the foyer, she walked through a huge gymnasium that housed two half-court basketball courts, gymnastic mats equipped with parallel bars and rings, and plastic barrels filled with dodge balls, Frisbees, you name it. Although there were no kids playing in the gym that morning, the smells of fun and armpits lingered in the air.

State and federal agents walked in and out of the gymnasium, creating a line that resembled an army of ants coming and going. Each worker entered with empty carts or two-wheeled dollies but left with something of value: weapons, money, computers, boxes, and documents of every sort.

Liz fell in line and entered a narrow hallway with school-like rooms on each side. The doors had large signs overhead indicating the activities that took place: ART, MUSIC, PHOTOGRAPHY, and GENEALOGY.

At the end of the hall, which was much darker than the entrance, gray double doors were wedged open, exposing the shipping and receiving area. Her sense of achievement had waned, and she imagined what she'd find beyond the doorway. She began hearing the muffled sounds of children crying, Agents consoling, and cameras snapping. Inside, dozens of children huddled together en masse, sitting cross-legged. She watched their little bodies and scared eyes, and covered her mouth with her left hand, forcing herself to pull her shit together.

Her heart felt heavy. She wanted to cry, to kick Harper's teeth in, but this was not the time or the place. She'd learned to save her tears for the drive home. It was always the same routine—let it out before she walked through the front door, because life went on no matter how screwed up the world was. Dinner needed fixing, her daughter needed a mother, and if she had a free moment before going to bed, she needed to escape into a good book and a full glass of wine.

Only a few feet away from the open semi-trailer where the kids were exchanged for cash, Shanna gingerly wrapped a blanket around a little blond-haired girl wearing nothing but an oversized t-shirt. Liz's partner was so petite that she could almost pass for one of the children, but she bent down with a clipboard in hand and asked the girl a few questions. Each time, the girl shook her head or nodded, but never spoke—a worst-case scenario. The damage was done. This was a raw shipment, but as they say in the body business, *There's no such thing as damaged goods in human trafficking. If they're still breathing, they're still salable.*

"How many are there?" Liz asked.

Shanna looked at Liz, paused, her dark eyes glassed over. "Thirty-seven."

Liz felt a knot turn in her gut. She couldn't help but think about Angie. Her daughter was sixteen now, and these boys and girls appeared to range in age from nine to fourteen years old. She pried her eyes away from the little blond and approached her boss, Special Agent Ted Gilmore, who supervised the New York Violent Crimes Against Children Division. He stood in the middle of the docking bay with one hand holding a clipboard against his hip and the other balled into a tight fist that pressed against his lips. He turned toward Liz as she approached and she noticed the rage in his eyes.

"Are they all hot?" asked Liz, referring to whether they'd been in the market long. If they had, then she was most likely standing in a room full of pre-pubescent rape victims, a sickening thought.

A large man in both height and girth, Gilmore turned and said, "I think so. Here…" He handed the clipboard to Liz. "You got your pick of the litter."

"Thanks, Boss. I appreciate the busy work, but I want to know who hasn't been arrested yet. I counted three Jaguars, two Lexuses, one Rolls-Royce, two Mercedes-Benzes, and one Bentley. That's nine perps, and I only counted eight heads in the meat wagon. So…where's number nine?"

Gilmore ran his hands over his meticulously trimmed, short hair, took a deep breath and said, "Just fill out the paperwork, Agent Ramsey. I'm not in the mood for your heroics."

Liz knew it was going to be a long, emotionally draining day for everyone, no less her boss, so she let it go and bit her tongue for the moment.

"I need you to follow up on these kids," directed Gilmore. "If the parents and guardians will consent to

SOEC kits, we might get lucky and pluck out a few more spokes from the wheel."

"I'll do what I can. The state's already backed up. You know that."

Gilmore took an impatient step forward and said, "Then give 'em hell. We need those rape kits before we run out of time." He turned and walked away.

Liz cased the room and found a sad little black boy sitting on the outer perimeter of a circle composed of five other kids in similar condition. They looked sad— five beautiful children most likely hand-selected by their buyers. She bent down and began to fill out the questionnaire, recording statements and making observations. One down. Thirty-six to go.

Chapter 3
Basecamp

From the desk of: General Murphy Ward
Simpson
13, November 1942

General Dodson,

    I am pleased to inform you that Lieutenant Colonel Hyberg's report regarding the strange objects found near the Archuleta Mesa have been confirmed and will be of great interest to the War Department. After examining the findings at the location in question, I have seen for myself the magnitude of this discovery, including the intricate tunnel systems, audio interference, and other advanced gadgets allegedly created by the unidentified beings. Because of the incredible nature of these discoveries, I believe it would prove beneficial if you and your superiors make arrangements to visit the location as soon as possible. Not only have we stumbled upon devices that appear to have been developed by a race far superior to our own, my men have encountered and taken fire from the beings who we believe live in the underground dwellings. There were casualties, Sir. The threat is real and we remain on high alert. Fortunately, we have preserved the body of one of the beings we killed in the scrimmage; the others were taken the night following the firefight by (I presume) the surviving clan, leaving no evidence of their existence. Fortunately, the corpse is small in stature and fits comfortably in an icebox.

Sir, I believe these creatures are highly intelligent, not only because of their advanced instruments but because they seem to know where we are at all times, stirring fear in the heart of our soldiers with a form of psychological warfare (that we can discuss in detail at a later date). They are deceptively dangerous and highly protective of their tunnel systems. Our current strategy is to expand our basecamp near the caves outside Dulce, New Mexico and hold our position until you visit the site for yourself.

Regards,
General Murphy Ward Simpson

Chapter 4
Off Limits

December 17, 2006, 10:44 am.
De Carver Youth Center, New York City

Liz moved on to child number seven, an eight-year-old boy from Nebraska who'd gone missing three months ago. His name was Philip. Covered in freckles and topped with a rusty mane, Liz wanted to take him home and keep him safe, but he had a family and he wanted to see them. He was a talker and explained the process of his abduction. Apparently he was stolen right off his bicycle while riding home from a friend's house. Transported over the course of two weeks in car trunks, steel cages, and grouped with more children with each passing day, he recalled days without food, scarce water, and few bathroom breaks. Philip had no idea where he was taken, but he mentioned a dark, dirty place where people in white suits poked at him and took all kinds of samples. After that, he was shipped from one sicko to another, some fancy (his words), some nasty. He relayed the details of his abuse, details Liz had heard several times beginning when she was a graduate student, studying Psychology at Penn State. When the boy had shared everything he knew, Liz passed him on to a Family Services worker and stood to stretch her legs when her cell phone rang.

Vincent—Thank God.

She walked out of the loading dock.

"Hey, Vince. Where are you?"

"On a flight to JFK," responded her ex-husband, his voice deep and exhausted.

"So soon?"

Vince laughed. "Yeah, I know. Four weeks is a cake walk after Iraq."

"I'm just glad you're safe."

"Glad to be back. But listen, I can't talk now, there's a rabbit hole in *Denver* that I need to sniff out before I come home."

"Figures," Liz said coldly. "Angie was looking forward to seeing you."

"Like I said, I can't talk. The hole's pretty deep. Tell my Angel I love her, will you?"

"Sure. I always do," Liz said with a hint of sarcasm.

"Liz. We've talked about this."

"That doesn't mean she deserves to be caught in the crossfire, Badger. She loves you."

Liz rarely called Vince by his code name, a private name she gave him when they were planning their wedding sixteen years ago. Vince had a reputation for being extremely fierce, not only while he served as a Navy Seal, but in every aspect of his life. "I'm not going to waste time on anything if I can't give it two hundred percent," he'd say. And he made that promise to Liz as well. "I've never failed my team. I've never failed a mission, and I'll never fail you," he assured her just before he opened the box to her engagement ring, and just before she said yes. She was already pregnant with his baby, his angel; how could she refuse his proposal?

"Listen. I should be home in thirty-six hours and after that, they're shipping me out again. I don't know where. All I know is I'm putting in the plumbing somewhere near the Mediterranean, and I think it's connected to us here at home. That's why I'm shopping in Denver."

"What? We're in the middle of a war in Iraq. Why would they send you there?"

"Liz? Really?"

"I'm sorry. You can't blame me for asking."

"And you can't blame me for connecting the dots. Playing pin the tail on the donkey in my line of work can bite me in the ass."

"What are you saying? Are you in danger?"

"Possibly. Tell Angie I love her."

"Vince?"

"See you soon."

"Don't hang up."

Click.

"Badger?... Badger!"

The only reply Liz heard was the dial tone. She cleared her phone and thought, *Oh my God. What's going on, Vince?* She stood stock still, trying to make sense of what he had said. *What the hell are you doing in Denver?*

Liz turned when she heard arguing in the art room. She walked to the door and stole a look through the sidelight. Gilmore was talking with two white-haired men. One thin and clean-shaven, the other, older and balding with a well-trimmed fully white beard, both dressed in crisp black suits and handcuffs.

What the hell?

She turned the knob and six eyes shot across the room. If looks could kill, she narrowly escaped death. "Ted?"

"Get out, Liz. This doesn't concern you."

Shocked, Liz stared at Gilmore in disbelief. This *did* fucking concern her. "Two perps confined in the art room—on *my* case—*is* my concern, sir."

Gilmore rushed toward Liz, taking Goliath steps. "Get out and close the door. Now!" If she didn't know any better, she'd swear he was using his body to block her view of the two men in question.

"Who are they?"

"Get out."

"What are they doing in there?"

"*Out!*" Gilmore said, pointing toward the door.

Liz peered around his body, sneaking one last glance before he came any closer, snapping a mental picture of their faces. "Why aren't they with the others?" she asked, resisting his outstretched arms. Within seconds, she found herself pushed out of the classroom, with her boss closing the door as he exited.

Liz fumed, feeling the heat rising to her neck and face. She didn't need the stress. "I demand to know what's going on in there!" she said with gritted teeth.

Gilmore leaned close and gripped her shoulders, faking a smile as a team of agents walked past.

"Get your hands off me!"

"Lower your voice, Liz," said Gilmore, calmly, releasing her. "This is a stressful situation, and you'll have to pull yourself together."

"Pull myself—?" She realized what he was doing, and just as quickly agreed to play his game. "Who are they?" she whispered. "Who the hell—?" She could hear her mother's voice, *temper, temper, temper.* "Who are they?" she said calmly.

Gilmore looked away, probably making sure no one was close enough to listen. "I can't tell you."

"This is ludicrous. Obviously you can. It's your *job.*"

"Not this time. You can have the rest, and I hope to God we find more of those ass-wipes, but you can't have these two. They're..."

"They're what?"

"They're off limits."

"Off limits?" Liz could hardly stand still; her hands shook, anxiously expressing her irritation. "Off limits? Since when is anyone off limits?"

"Since we walked into something that is way beyond your pay grade."

Liz shook her head. This wasn't making sense. "What the hell does that mean, Boss? Are they foreigners? God, that wouldn't even matter..."

"It doesn't matter," replied Gilmore, shaking his head. "In the next five minutes, I'm going to escort these two men to their vehicle, and they're going to drive away, unharmed, and they will not be investigated. Do you understand?"

Liz peered down the hall and glanced at the children who remained in the room. "No." She turned back and looked him square in the eyes. "Enlighten me."

Rather than grab her shoulders, he gripped her with a stern gaze instead and lashed out with a quiet intensity. "Listen to me, Agent Ramsey. If you interfere in this matter, you'll put this entire project in jeopardy. *All* of those men will go free. Every ounce of evidence will be thrown out. You and I will both lose our jobs, if not disappear, and the Agency will experience a shakeup the likes of which you've never seen. We're *that* fucking deep in hog shit. Do you understand what I'm trying to tell you?"

Liz reluctantly said nothing and carefully studied each man's face as the Special Agent led the mysterious duo out of the room. They looked cool and relaxed, almost plastic. Something about their eyes seemed off, void of emotion. As bad-ass as she felt at the time, she had an eerie suspicion they were studying her as well. She stepped aside and watched two men, probably the bearings in the center of this wheel, walk free.

Chapter 5
Negotiations

From the office of: General Murphy Ward Simpson

21, November 1942

General Dodson,

I realize you are a man with many responsibilities and with the war effort, the demands on your time have increased exponentially. Nonetheless, it is imperative that you visit this incredible site north of Dulce. We have now encountered these beings face-to-face and have begun what could only be described as dialogue, although few audible words have been spoken. Apparently they can read our minds and understand our written language. It seems they are trying to negotiate the return of their fallen brother (the one in the icebox), but what they are willing to give in return is unclear at this time. They have gestured that we follow them down into the cave (beyond our secured position we call point A), but my men and I have decided to forgo that option until we have a full battalion to serve as reinforcements. At this point their agenda is unclear, as are their total numbers.

In addition to the men and supplies needed for a full excavation beyond point A, it is my opinion that we will need linguisticians, scientists, archeologists, engineers, and physicists. We have quarantined a single cavern and removed hundreds of devices and other unknown tools, plaques, and documents that seem to be of great value to the beings, of which we have reason to believe are submissive to a ranking breed if you will. Their superiors have not shown their faces, but from a distance, they appear larger in stature and appear ominous (in my opinion) if it is even possible to discern such a trait. They show little emotion and appear as interested in retrieving their tablets (riddled with indecipherable writings) as the dead body in the icebox. As a result, our negotiations are becoming increasingly tense.

In conclusion, I hope you see the urgency and possibilities of this matter. Your assessment, visit, and consideration are highly valued and profoundly anticipated.

Regards,
General Murphy Ward Simpson

Chapter 6
Badger

December 18, 2006, 1:15 pm
Denver International Airport

Vincent hurried out of the jetway and headed for the Jeppessen Terminal. He had planned to meet with Bruce Warnill, his mentor and retired CIA brass, who had taken a consulting position with the newly formed Department of Homeland Security's Intelligence and Analysis Department. Bruce claimed to have information that Vince would find extremely compelling. Vince scanned the open aired, tent-like area near the fountain and quickly noticed his aging friend sitting on a bench. Bruce walked with a cane; he had a thin band of gray hair that horseshoed around his head and his spotting skin sagged around his eyes. Vincent noticed a small bag near his feet. His friend didn't say anything about traveling, which was odd considering the old man's knack for covering all the details.

Vince, a tall and dark-complexioned man with a hint of Egyptian blood in his veins, ideal for middle-eastern covert ops, walked toward his friend and they embraced. He assumed they'd talk somewhere in private, but Bruce assured Vince that the background noise from the fountain made the perfect location for what he wanted to share.

"Thanks for coming, Vinny. I hope I haven't disrupted your holiday plans."

"Ah, don't worry.... We'll make do."

"I wouldn't ask you to come if this wasn't an extraordinary circumstance."

Vince put a hand on Bruce's shoulder, gripping affectionately. He adored the man. Had a tremendous amount of respect for his many years of service and vast knowledge of global events. "Have you ever known me to dodge the extraordinary?" Vince said, smiling.

Bruce looked at Vince, his tender eyes contemplative, reflecting Vince's grin right back at his younger cohort. "No... never. I always regarded you as among the best in the Agency. Speaking of which, how's Elizabeth and your little girl these days?"

"Liz is doing just fine," he said matter-of-factly. "Said her unit made a big bust yesterday. And Angie just turned sixteen. Not so little anymore." Even as the words rolled off of Vince's tongue, he wished he could give Bruce more, like the details a regular father would know: her favorite color, book, or band. But all he had was surface intel about his ex-wife and teenage daughter. The CIA had made a distant and calculating human being out of him, but he still longed to be close to Liz and spend more time with his baby girl, regardless of their decision to end the marriage. He longed to know Angie, who she really was, what really wound her clock, but there wasn't time–not enough, anyway.

"Glad to hear it, Vince. You must be proud."

"Couldn't be more," Vince said mechanically.

Bruce smiled, patting Vince on the thigh as he stood up, laboriously pressing his weight on the cane and Vince's knee. "Let's get a cup of coffee, shall we?"

Vince reached for Bruce's elbow and assisted. "Sure," Vince said. "My treat." Bruce took hold of the small rollaway carry-on and pulled it along.

As they walked to a Starbucks kiosk further into the terminal, Bruce said, "Did you know some of the agents took bets on when you and Elizabeth would get divorced?"

Vince sneered. "Pfft. No. I didn't."

"Always behind your back," added Bruce.

"I'm not surprised."

"You were too enterprising to notice, focused on the job at hand. You had a dedication that seemed to be lacking in many of your contemporaries."

"Well, there were some that managed to *overstep* from time to time."

"That's putting it lightly," Bruce said sharply.

A young barista took their order and Vince paid the bill. When the kid walked away to prepare the drinks, Vince turned toward his mentor and said, "You're losing me, Bruce. What does any of this have to do with Denver International? Or the price of rice in China?"

"Everything, my friend. Minus the rice."

The barista handed Vince two coffees. Black. He grabbed the drinks and handed one to Bruce.

"Okay... I'm all ears."

Bruce hobbled toward a string of murals on the wall. The images were a grotesque depiction of infanticide and toxic gassing overseen by a Nazi-like soldier; all of which Vince thought had no place in a public building. Bruce glanced at the images and said, "I'll be blunt. They're forcing the apocalypse."

Vince thought of the horse standing at the entrance of the airport, red eyes glaring and hooves striking. "The Pale Horse?"

"Yes."

Vince understood the prophecy—The Pale Horse—the angel of death that would usher in the coming atrocities foretold by Judaism, Christianity, and Islam.

"I thought the DoD had everything under control?"

"It appears we were wrong."

"How do you know? What's going on?"

"DHS is adjusting their plans. They're bringing in others—Russian, French Foreign Legion, Aussies—to enforce what our soldiers are refusing to manage underneath."

"What the hell's going on, Bruce? I thought we've signed treaties with those things."

"We have. But agreements are fragile. Only paper. One slip on either side and everything changes."

"So what's changed?"

Bruce paused. "The terrestrials. They want more."

"As usual. So what's our response?"

Bruce chuckled. "I sat in a closed-door meeting last week with DOD, FEMA, and DHS officials—among other intelligence agency leaders—and they named ten Regional Commanders. There weren't any nominations, congressional oversight, or public input—"

"Whoa, whoa, whoa... Regional Commanders? Of what?"

"The ten quadrants... Ten new zones, initially set up by FEMA for emergency management, but the divisions are meant for something more. They're already putting the infrastructure in place, and preparing for resistance with all branches of the armed forces, UN troops, and the National Guard."

"That's impossible."

"It's not impossible, Vince. It's unfathomable. But that's exactly what's going to happen. If they come out of their hole all hell's gonna break loose, and you and I both know that Joe Schmo isn't going to like those things ruling over his shit."

"Should we be discussing this here?" asked Vincent.

"Indeed. It's perfect. It's the heart of the new Capital—the Mile High City. Why do you think they put that creepy pale horse out front for everyone to see?"

"Okay. Okay. Wait... Hold on... What's your part in all of this, Bruce?"

Bruce ran his hand across the Nazi figure on the mural. "Commander. Region Three. Keep the uprising in check."

"Holy Christ. You can't be serious?"

"I'm dead serious."

"Damn it! How does that help us?"

Bruce smiled. "It's perfect."

"Perfect?" asked Vince, imagining Bruce's face on the wall. "Do tell."

"I may be old, Vincent, but I have a Trojan Horse of my own."

"And what horse is that?"

Bruce paused and turned toward Vince. "You. You're my colt."

"What's that supposed to mean?"

"It means I'm asking you to take over what I've started, to use their rules against them. The assets are in place... counter measures calculated. But there are very few men who have the skills and wherewithal to handle a large-scale resistance."

"I'm afraid to ask, but exactly how deep are you in this?"

"I'm all in."

"Jesus, Bruce."

"I, I've done things, Vince. Privately. Things I'm ashamed to admit. But it was the only way I could prove myself... the only way to work myself into their system."

Vince glanced over his shoulder, feeling a little paranoid and reducing his tone to a whisper. "I mean... How can you be on their side? This isn't what we agreed upon."

Bruce took a sip of his coffee, his baritone voice penetrating the space closing in on Vince. "Do you love your daughter?"

"Yes. You know that," Vince replied with a hint of annoyance.

"Do you want to see her grow up? Get married? Have children of her own?"

Vince imagined Angie's life flashing before his eyes—the birthdays, college, wedding, babies. "I think you know the answer to that," Vince replied, tenderly contemplating Angie's future.

"I do... And that's why I've prepared everything: documentation, strategies, contingencies... all for you. I need you to learn *everything* I know to counteract what's happening. But you have to decide today. Things are taking shape quickly. If you choose to walk away, I'll take what I know to the grave and there will be little anyone can do to stop what's coming."

"Which is?"

"It's all in the files."

Vince groaned, "Bruce... What are you getting me into?"

Bruce smiled. His aged eyes gleamed with excitement as if this would be his last hurrah.

"Fair enough," said Vince. He took another sip of his coffee. "But tell me... What's the end game here? If you're infiltrating, how am I going to change anything on my own?"

"You're not alone," Bruce said chuckling. "I've been planning a secondary course of action since I was in the service, and it's time to activate it."

"That's what I'm doing? Activating your secret plan?"

"Yes."

"And if I accept this so called plan that we never talked about—?"

"If you accept, we'll continue to work together. So don't worry. It's not like we're cutting ties. You'll still have my full support, but the stakes will be higher if something goes wrong. We'll talk less and you'll lead everything on your end. If you make a mistake, you're on your own."

Vince stood up, quietly contemplating.

"If you hesitate, it's all over," reiterated Bruce. "You'll incorporate everything you know about psychological warfare, covert operations, team building, guerrilla warfare, whatever it takes. And I'm certain this will be your final assignment. You'll never go home again."

Vince thought for a moment. *Final assignment. I've heard that before.* He'd learned over the course of his career that plans don't always turn out as expected, and a final assignment was always a possibility, but, in fact, the term was code for a pat on the back and a brief vacation in Maui.

He realized long ago that he'd have to take a role in resisting what the government had been feeding the public. He saw their lies firsthand. He obeyed CIA orders without question because that was his duty, his way of life. But he also took his oath seriously, the oath to protect and defend the United States of America from enemies both foreign and domestic.

The question wasn't if he'd accept whatever Bruce had in mind. The question was if he was ready to do it. He had a daughter. And there was Liz. He couldn't be married to her; he had too little to give, but he still loved her, and he believed that she felt the same way. It was sad really; two lovers separated by their career choices and mere continents most days. He was proud of her, wanted to share her joy and sorrows to a point. But in reality, he knew he was alone—the Agency and his commitment to his work made damn sure of that. And there was that callus—a thick scab on his heart that prevented genuine, real intimacy. Not that he didn't want to fully give himself to her, as if he thought in those terms, but if he did it would've been a sincere feeling.

There was love, and there was reality, and the reality of his life revolved around the CIA—the harder the mission, the better. Each assignment had become his drug, and like any addict, no matter how much you really love your family and want to break the habit for their sake, the narcotic beckons.

Vince struggled with his priorities. Every Agent did. But the idea that he'd take part in a covert operation against his own government went against everything in his being. It was one thing to obey out of duty, to turn a blind eye to the internal crimes, half-truths, and blatant lies he witnessed every day. But it was his participation in the lies that brought him to this point. The very thing that made him excellent allowed him to see the evil in it all, despite his training. The CIA managed to mill his sensitivities down to a nub, but they couldn't erase his integrity. They couldn't hide the fact that something sinister was treading below the surface of everything that happened in Washington—their operations—their policies—the unanswered questions. It was his inquisitiveness that led him to Bruce in the first place, reminding him of the old cliché—curiosity killed the cat.

"It's the only way—if you think our way of life is worth dying for."

"I do…But the terrestrials? I thought we had them under control?"

"Not any more than usual," Bruce said matter-of-factly, laboring to catch his breath. "They're entrenching and deceiving more of the brass every day. They're not just humanoid, you know; there's something supernatural about them."

Vince didn't know that. With his limited knowledge of the underground creatures—the downed craft and technology in exchange for human resources—he knew the government would exploit them sooner or later, which was the reason he and

Bruce would meet in private; to discuss the latest intelligence in the matter, to assure their families' safety in case the world ever turned on its ass.

"If the DoD can't keep them in check, they'll be forced to shut everything down and declare Martial Law," said Bruce, his voice shaky. "But there are factions, as you know, among the DoD brass. Some are sympathizing with the terrestrials, almost deifying them."

"Like Gods?" said Vince. "You've got to be kidding me!"

"Some believe they're too powerful. They're too advanced, they'll tell us. They believe that when the dust settles, they'll justifiably rule over us."

"So what? The DoD's going just bow down and give them control?"

"Yes; that's what some of them want. Some of them think they're above us. Spiritually. Others want to eliminate them. But the factions are growing stronger. They not only want the US, but the world to unite for a common purpose... a new time... a fresh start where religion and all our differences become immaterial. They'll re-write history. They'll redefine what it means to be human, convincing the world that we've finally connected with our space-brothers and -sisters."

"Bruce. This can't be happening."

"It's been the goal since the dawn of time. The great deception."

"What do they want?" asked Vince.

Bruce gripped his hands together, nursing his arthritis, and said, "Our souls, among other things, but it's mostly our souls they crave."

"I don't understand," said Vince. This was getting far deeper than he imagined.

"It's the one thing they lack," replied Bruce. "It's what makes us immortal. Without it, they're stuck in this shit hole."

"Then why would the DoD work with them? Why protect them if we have something so valuable?"

"Oh, I suppose for the same reason anyone sneaks scraps to the enemy. Power. Wealth. Pleasure. There's always a trade-off. Only takes a few rotten apples at the top of the tree to bring them all tumbling down. And that's when they'll realize they were deceived…"

"And the cycle starts all over again?"

"Exactly," affirmed Bruce. "The fruit is tempting, but when it smells like money and sex and power, the last thing you think about is your sins."

Bruce appeared to be in physical pain, but Vince knew the ache was emotional anguish more than anything. He'd seen the "CIA stare" numerous times, the wrinkling of the brow and dead eyes, a look of anger that couldn't be directed at anyone because no matter how hard you scrutinized the system, there wasn't really anyone to blame. It was a sinister, living, breathing system, an unidentifiable, faceless force driving humanity over a cliff. You can't touch it. You can't stop it. You can't punch it in the face. All you can do is dive into its elusive flames and hope your flesh provides enough water to extinguish a fraction of the inferno.

But here, with his friend, he could identify the enemy, put a name on the face of evil that had hijacked global leadership. The elusive force that made the world go crazy was not complicated at all. It was elementary. They were gray, deceptive, terrestrial beings. Serpents. Devils. The illness corrupting our global system was an ancient race hidden from the public, and from our history books.

The thought cemented his decision.

"What do you need me to do?" said Vince, coldly pushing his emotions aside.

"Die," said Bruce matter-of-factly, shocking Vince with a single word. "I need you to die. Today."

Vince returned his gaze back to his mentor. "Is that all?" he said, with a snicker.

"Yes," said Bruce.

In a moment of silence, Vince considered the cost and assumed Bruce was doing the same.

"Together," said Bruce. "We'll sacrifice. The few for the many. Collateral damage."

"Martyrs?" said Vince. "Isn't that what you really mean?"

Bruce cleared his throat. "If that's what you want to call it."

"That's quite an entry fee."

"It is," said Bruce. "I've always said martyrdom is an acceptable tax for true patriots."

"Yes, Sir; it is."

Vince looked at his old friend, wondering if he put too much trust in him. He thought about Liz and Angie and everything he'd give up if he took this course of action. Memories of Kansas, growing up on the farm, special ops, and the agency whipped through his mind like a twister, stirring up debris and emotions he'd rather keep buried.

The CIA had schooled Vince in the art of emotional numbing, making the decision to join Bruce a logical choice rather than an emotional one. As much as it pained him to drop out of life, he felt obligated to fight those who would destroy life as he knew it—enemies so entrenched within the matrix of bureaucracy, they were completely off the grid. And that's where this battle would take place.

Bruce slid his bag next to Vince's leg. "If you're in, you'll need this."

Vince sat quiet and still for what seemed like minutes, until he forced out the words, "I'm in."

Bruce smiled expectantly and said, "Excellent."

"I gather you were expecting a yes from me."

"I did," said Bruce. "But I wouldn't bring you to this point if I wasn't fully prepared to launch."

"And when do we do that?"

"Now. If you're ready."

Vince looked at the mural. He paused to consider all that he'd miss, ignoring the ache that attempted to rise in his throat, and said with only a slight hesitation, "I am."

"Okay then." Bruce smiled momentarily. "Go to the men's room across from the fountain where we met. Enter a stall, and open the bag. You'll find a yellow jumpsuit. Put it on. There's a map that'll lead you into the lower levels of the airport, baggage handling, maintenance, etc. Study the map, and follow the route indicated without veering. Answer only to those who call you by the name indicated on your phone. It'll change randomly, so keep a close eye on the screen identifier. I'll help Liz with your funeral preparations."

Chapter 7
Davenport

June 12, 2008
Arriba Science & Technology Underground Auxiliary

Sergeant Major William Davenport thumbed through the old documents. Knowledge was the path to survival down there; the top-secret files were cherished and protected at all costs. He studied the archives diligently and kept them under lock and key 24/7. The desire to understand his mission—the real mission behind the mumbo jumbo typed up in his official orders—fed his power and position like an iron forge. And each memo filed over the course of fifty years emboldened his pursuit of truth and the secrets he found with each new document. He turned the page and continued reading.

From the office of: General Murphy Ward Simpson
26 December 1942

Davenport loved the beginning. It reminded him of the stories his father would tell about the second Great War. He could picture every uniform, star, and stripe, and the good old boys who played each role— reminded him of the toy soldiers he used to tinker with. And it all happened while the rest of the world was busy killing each other, completely unaware what this small band of soldiers discovered in a forgotten and irrelevant desert. General Simpson's memos were always worth re-reading.

General Dodson,
I hope this letter finds you and yours well and in God's good favor. The troops and equipment you sent made for a wonderful Christmas present. Although we'd all like to go home to see our families, I feel we should continue our work as long as our boys are fighting overseas. For it seems the battle beneath our soil is raging as well as the war beyond our shores. As I previously informed you, we have made significant headway in our talks with the creatures beneath, although we now use a different name that more

accurately describes the beings—Grays, although they call themselves something like Nef-a-lem. As a result of these negotiations, we have established two more checkpoints (Point B and Point C) in the tunnel systems with only minor altercations with a few of the more aggressive creatures. The checkpoints were secured at the additional cost of human and other life forms, but our differences were resolved with the help of linguistics.

Our communication team has discovered that the beings are in need of certain elements and materials no longer available to them such as (gold, boron, and other trace elements) and that they are willing to share their technology in exchange for these items. We are not only encouraged by this, we are excited to deliver these "gadgets" to the War Department as we see military and civilian applications that you could only imagine. We see these efforts as our contribution to the war and sincerely hope they can be used for the cause of freedom here at home and abroad. As always, I will keep you abreast of our victories and...

Sergeant Major Davenport stopped reading the minute his phone rang. He listened intensely and hung up in a fury. He quickly put the pile of letters in the manila folder and slipped it back in the slot where he'd found it. After he locked the cabinet, he hurried out of his office and bustled down the hall to pay a visit to the site's head of security, Carlos Alverez, but he wasn't there.

Davenport returned to his office and grabbed his radio from his desk. "Alvarez... report."

"Go for Alvarez."

"This is Sergeant Major Davenport. What the hell's going on on Level Three?"

"We're apprehending a rogue, Sir."

"A rogue what?"

"Electrician."

"Is he the one we suspected?"

"No, Sir. She's female. She's running, but we're going to head her off in mechanical."

Davenport heard shooting. Pop. Pop. Pop.

"Damn it!" Davenport ran out of the room, lugging his extra hundred pounds with him. He headed toward a stout electrical cart driven by his personal security guard, who'd been waiting outside smoking one of those hippy-ass organic cigs. "Sergeant Franks! Take me to Level Three."

"Yes, Sir," yielded the burly southern soldier.

"Are you armed?" asked Davenport.

"Sir?"

"Are you packing heat?"

"Yes."

"Good. Get us to the cargo elevator as fast as you can!"

Sergeant Franks pressed the pedal, and sped through the underground military base, departing Level One—Central Command. After dropping one level in the elevator, Davenport called Alvarez again. "What's your twenty, Alvarez?"

"We've apprehended the suspect south of the second-level IT room."

"Excellent. Hold your position; I'm around the corner."

Franks wheeled through the main cargo tunnel on Level Two: Facilities, where everything was concrete or rock, holding the level above with huge stone pillars. They passed Boiler Room One through the dimly lit structure, D-2 compressor block, a medium-temp chiller room, and approached the powerhouse, home of a massive underground electrical power grid that webbed through several layers beneath the surface. Only a few electricians knew where the energy source came from, and two of them had died back in 1979 after the main cables were installed.

Davenport saw a crowd of military and contract security guards circling someone in an orange jumpsuit. The captive was lying face-down with hands zip-tied. The Sergeant Major pointed toward the group and Franks stopped as soon as they arrived.

Davenport hurried toward Alvarez, a chiseled Marine and head of contract security. Alvarez had served three years as an assistant to his previous boss "Radar", until the man mysteriously disappeared. Naturally, Alvarez was handed the reins valued at an additional twenty-five thousand a year. He gladly accepted.

"What's her name, Alvarez?" asked Davenport, still huffing.

"Fedlesworth, Sir. Sandy Fedlesworth."

Davenport's lips smacked when he looked down at what he considered a traitor. He crossed his arms, took in a slow, deep breath and exhaled for all to hear. He realized some time ago that doing so gave his decision making an appearance of strength, control, and ultimately wisdom, even in moments when he had nothing to offer. But the tactic worked and helped advance his career. He squinted his eyes, knowing that the soldiers were watching, waiting for his instructions when he said, "What did she do?"

"Video surveillance caught her working in a restricted area—Sector 32, in the executive conference room. Two of my men, Chirkoff and Prevot, investigated. She refused to show her work orders. When they attempted to escort her to HR, she ran."

The Sergeant Major looked at the men in his presence. *A good team. Loyal. Disciplined.*

"Why did she run?" asked Davenport. "What was she doing?"

"Installing a sensor of some kind?" replied Alvarez.

A sensor? That's new. "Get her up," instructed Davenport.

Chirkoff and Prevot, recruited from UN security forces, lifted Fedlesworth from the concrete floor and faced her toward the Sergeant Major. Blood had dried under her nose, and a reddened scratch gouged the side of her face from where she'd been pinned down. Otherwise, she appeared to be a rather fit, clear-eyed worker. Her dark hair was cut short, almost looked like a boy at first glance, but that couldn't hide her natural beauty—olive tone, silky chocolate eyes that seemed quite inviting, even in the midst of distress.

Davenport studied Sandy before speaking. He found he'd get better results if he addressed people at their level, and Davenport believed all men and women were ranked according to level, grade, and DNA, so he studied their eyes, looking for strengths and weaknesses. And he liked what he saw in this sweet little confectionary. She had strengths and assets—nice assets—and vulnerabilities, but mostly weakness as far as he could see.

The Sergeant Major removed his gold-rimmed glasses and glared at the prisoner. "What's the sensor for, Sandy?" he asked quizzically, squinting his small gray eyes that could turn warm or cold in an instant.

Sandy didn't respond. She turned away.

Davenport motioned to Chirkoff, and the guard gave a swift punch to her kidney. She squawked and winced, her back crooking as if a gale force had suddenly thrust her forward.

"Sandy, please... Just tell me what you were doing in that conference room. Without work orders, you're clearly in violation of your contract. You'll be terminated or taken up on charges if you don't give me an explanation immediately."

She looked away, eyes glassed over with pain.

The Sergeant Major inched closer, heels clicked, hands folded behind his back. "I'll tell you what, Mrs. Fedlesworth, if you answer a few questions, I can probably arrange for you to be moved to a different department, maybe a group under a little more scrutiny. You can keep your job. You can feed your family and all that good stuff. But you have to be truthful."

Sandy sighed. She shook her head, jaw squared.

Davenport gave Prevot a nod.

Prevot opened his expandable police baton and whacked it across the back of her thigh. Sandy fell to her knees, stealing short, pain-filled breaths, silently protesting with a warped brow.

"Listen, Fedlesworth. I'm not playing games here. The rules are simple: Do your job, quickly and quietly. It's a basic process." Davenport crouched down and asked, "So what are you up to?"

Sandy lifted her head, "What you're doing is wrong," she said. She locked on Davenport's eyes, her supple chest huffing rapidly. The Sergeant Major matched her gaze, remembering that it was possible to charm a snake by not blinking.

Davenport put his glasses back on and said, "You don't have any idea what you're talking about, Sandy. You're not a security analyst. You're an electrician. A sparky. Pull the wires and make 'em hot. That's your job... not this, whatever you're involved in. Now, tell me what you were doing in that room or there will be serious consequences."

Davenport stooped down, hands clenched behind his back.

Sandy lifted her chin, her mocha eyes weak but undeterred. "Never," she said. "There are too many of us, Bill. We won't let this continue..." She managed to laugh, which really pissed off Davenport. "Funny thing is, you need us. We don't need you."

The bitch was pulling rank. Goddamned smartass. Sergeant Major William Davenport wasn't about to let a worker-bee call him out in front of his men. Aside from the security risk, this bee needed to stop buzzing, an example set. He turned his back, took a few steps and called for Alvarez.

Alvarez moved on command and stood beside Davenport.

The Sergeant Major put his arm around Alvarez, squeezed his shoulder and said, "I need you to take these men back to the upper deck. No one talks."

"Yes. Sir. Would you like me to escort Mrs. Fedlesworth out of the facility?"

Davenport shook his head. "That's not necessary."

"But, Sir—I—"

"Get your men, Alvarez, and get upstairs."

Alvarez looked confused. He couldn't possibly understand how complicated these matters can get. Bees need to be tended and their hives smoked out. It's the only way to prevent mutinous behavior. Alvarez would learn, too, Davenport supposed, so long as he kept up the good work and did as he was told. Secrets are passed only to obedient, trustworthy suck-ups. The beaner wasn't there yet, hadn't been tested, so he wouldn't get the privilege of watching the Sergeant

Major work his magic—not this time, anyway. Maybe later.

Davenport turned to Alverez and cocked his head, motioning him to exit.

Alverez saluted the Sergeant Major and turned.

"Don't bother writing a report, Alvarez. This never happened."

Alvarez stopped for just a moment and said, "Right," and continued on.

"Franks. Come with me. And bring her tool pouch."

Alvarez gathered his men and they retreated to the top floor.

Davenport paused a minute or so, considering how he'd handle little Sparky. When he'd thought of an appropriate deterrent, he grabbed her elbow, lifted the electrician to her feet and led her down the hall toward the powerhouse.

Franks followed.

"You know, Sandy, we have to be very careful who we allow on this site. There are security risks—terrorists abroad and on our soil."

Sandy tugged her elbow out of the Sergeant Major's hand, grunting in defiance.

The big man grabbed her and squeezed harder than before, causing his words to come out forced and fragmented. "Been all over the world, Iraq,

Afghanistan, Panama, and there's one thing I've learned that's helped me survive..." Davenport stopped walking momentarily, waited for Sandy to ask a question, and then continued. "I've learned that you don't defend with a defense. You keep your offense up at all times. You see a threat and you squash it. Run into a hazard—eliminate it. And I'm sure you think you're doing your duty, fighting the good fight, a valiant cause. It probably is. But it's in vain. I'm sure you realize that by now. Or you will, soon enough."

Davenport pushed Sandy forward, shoving her toward the powerhouse doors, and into a large room buzzing with the sounds of electrical current flowing like a raging river.

"You're looking for power in the wrong place, Sandy!" said Davenport, shouting over the loud humming. "It's not here in the underground. It's not in Washington, the Fusion Centers, FEMA camps, or the tunnels you've been constructing for how long now...?"

Silence, as expected.

"Hold her still, Franks!" Franks grabbed Sandy by her elbows. She tried to resist, but he outsized her three to one.

Sandy had a look of horror on her sweaty face. Davenport liked that. He liked the sound of terror coming from a vulnerable little honeybee. Turned him on sexually.

"What are you doing?" she asked.

The Sergeant Major approached the switchgear boxes that lined the powerhouse room, several rows, thirty feet long. Each panel delivered 15,000 or more volts that powered process waste, industrial chillers, living quarters, sub-panels, hundreds of miles of lighting, sewage pumps; just a small part of the fully functioning underground military base. This was Davenport's city, underground though it may be, and it was his to use however necessary as long as he accomplished the ultimate mission—secure the area, complete construction of the subterranean structure, and maintain healthy communication with the visitors below. When the process hiccupped, he took it personally.

Davenport pulled a large disconnect handle down, turning the power off that fed a remote area of the grid. Disregarding the red and black placard warning him of the dangers inside the cabinet, he opened the heavy gray door, keeping his distance as the panel swung open. Speaking with his hands, he directed Franks to turn Sandy around by spinning his fingers. Sergeant Franks, no less than six-foot-three and two hundred and forty pounds, shook her into position, exerting his physical dominance.

"Please. Don't do this."

"Hand me two of her zip ties," said Davenport.

Franks complied.

Davenport reached in the cabinet, and slipped the wire ties in the lower, non-energized portion of the switch box, leaving two plastic cuffs ready to receive her thin wrists, assuring that whatever was fastened to the copper plates would instantaneously explode when the "ON" switch is pulled, like a hotdog plugged into two hot wires. SPLAT! Her conductive flesh would never know how much like an Oscar Mayer Wiener she'd become. But whomever she was working with would know. As ugly as it would get, the message would be crystal clear.

"Oh, God... please don't!"

"See there, Mrs. Fedlesworth," said Davenport, ignoring his prisoner's pleadings, pointing inside the cabinet. "That's power. *That's* what you're looking for, isn't it? Fifteen thousand volts of pure kick your ass and lay you out like a downtown hooker. A lightning bolt in the closet is what that is. Ever been struck by lightning?"

Sandy shook her head, fear written all over her eyes, eyes that seemed to notice a patch on the shoulder of the Sergeant Major's dress coat, a red patch with a black circle surrounding an embroidered pentagram made of golden lightning bolts.

"No, you haven't," he said directing her eyes back at him with his fingers. "The chances are one in thousands, but you're not here to talk about statistics are you? You're here to talk about power. So let's talk. Let's talk about *you* and *me* and the powers that govern us."

Davenport eyed his prey, and the electrician continued resisting, uselessly kicking and carrying on like most bitches do.

"Come on. Please. God."

"God?" Davenport studied the electrician, working to keep from laughing out loud. "Jesus, Sandy. Are you that old school? After all you've seen here?"

"You will be judged, whether you want to believe it or not."

The Sergeant Major laughed. "Do you have children, Sandy?" He already knew the answer because he confirmed or denied each applicant's security application. He would never allow his facility to be overrun with deviants. Apparently he missed that she was a Holy Roller, but he vaguely recalled that children were mentioned in the final stages of her security screening.

Sandy turned her eyes away, refusing to answer his question.

"It's a simple query... I'm not going to hurt them. Christ, what do you think I am?"

"Yes," Sandy said, answering the initial question.

"Thank you," said Davenport. "Boys?"

"Girls. Two."

"Oh, how sweet," Davenport said with a disingenuous smile. "I have a daughter myself. What are their names if you don't mind me asking?"

"Madison... and... and K-Kaylen."

"Very nice... Are you married?"

"Yes."

"I'm sure you are. Happily, I presume?"

"Yes," Sandy replied, tears falling down her face.

Davenport fell in love with her eyes. God, they were beautiful; like two chocolate coffee treats; eyes he could look into for hours. Unfortunately, they had a sour-candy center and their sap was leaking all over his floor. "I'm sorry to hear that. I'll be sure to send your family my condolences."

"No. Please," said Sandy, as her knees gave way and her hands began shaking.

"No? You should have thought of them before you flirted with treason... here, of all places. It's too late. School is in session." Davenport pointed at the switchgear box, eyes rolling impatiently, raising his voice but slowing the delivery. "When you think about the power in this panel you may think, '*wow* what a force'. And that's good. That mindset will keep you alive in your trade. But, I see fifteen thousand volts as something much different. I see it as a motivational mechanism. And I think you need to be motivated."

"No," Sandy said, shaking her head.

"I'm going to give you what you want, Mrs. Fedlesworth."

"No. Please don't."

"You want to know what kind of power you're dealing with? Fine. I'll show you what you're up against!"

Sandy pleaded desperately, uselessly attempting to back away and out of Franks' grip.

Davenport stepped directly in front of her. "You want to know what you're fighting? Want to know if the conspiracies are true? If a black government faction is feeding Americans to little green men from Mars? Is that what you think?"

"Please," she begged. "No..." she said with a whimper.

"Well take a look, Sandy. Take a really close look." Davenport stepped back and instructed Franks to stuff her inside and lock her hands in the plastic fasteners.

Franks did as he was told. Sandy's resistance was futile. Davenport's voice boomed.

"You're going to find out how much power we really have," said Davenport, preparing to close the panel door.

"Wait!" said Sandy, giving Davenport the reaction he was hoping for: resignation.

"Stop! I'll talk!"

Chapter 8
The Cost

Franks shoved Sandy into Davenport's office and she fell to the floor, whimpering.

Looking at Franks, Davenport snapped, "Guard the door."

Franks nodded and walked outside.

Davenport locked the door and turned around. He smiled expectantly now that he had her where he really wanted her. "Thank you for your willingness to cooperate, Sandy," he said as he walked around his desk. "I know you're in an awkward position, but I can help you. Really. Here..." Davenport pointed to the chair in front of his oak bureau. "Have a seat."

Sandy roused to her feet and sat down with her hands zip-tied.

The Sergeant Major opened a drawer and presented his ASEK survival knife, opened the blade and said, "I'll be gentle," motioning her to twist around. She did, and he put the blade between her wrists and cut the zip tie off, sneaking a glance at her ass as she sat down.

Satisfied that she was a little more comfortable, the Davenport sat in his high-back chair and let her fears simmer a moment before he said anything. He'd been through this before and had learned to toy with these traitors' emotions. When beads of sweat accumulated on her forehead, making her ripe for questioning, he tossed a pad of lined paper and pen in front of her and said, "I want names and hierarchy."

The paper smacked on the table and Sandy jerked in her seat. She then reached for the pen and paper, her hands and body trembling.

Davenport waited for her to begin writing; she delayed, as expected. As soon as the ballpoint touched down, she hesitated. After she repeated this several times, Davenport abruptly pushed his chair back and hurried back to Sandy.

He wouldn't repeat the command, expecting full and immediate compliance.

Sandy started writing upon his approach, scribbling something, but it was too late. She needed to learn to obey orders. He grabbed a handful of her soft brown hair and forcefully jerked her head forward and back. She cried out, but Davenport ignored her plea.

He held her there a few seconds, feeling pleasure from her pain until he thought she got the point. Then he shoved her head forward, sat back down in his chair and repeated the instructions.

"I want names and hierarchy."

Sandy began scribbling again, her hand quivering more than before. "I can't do that... I... I only receive orders from one person."

Davenport took a deep breath and said, "Write his name."

Sandy stalled and Davenport jumped to his feet. She briefly attempted to escape, but he was already at her side, pulling her head back, knife at her neck, gritting his teeth and growling in her face. "Give me his name, Sandy, or you'll give me something else." He looked into her chocolate morsels and began rubbing the tip of his knife over her breasts. Aroused by the fear in her eyes and her quaking body, he peered at the blade and then further down.

"Last time. I want a name."

"Okay! I'll do it."

Sandy reached for the pen, straining as Davenport gripped her hair. She wrote: Marcus Wheeler.

Davenport lifted the pad of paper and returned to his chair. He read the name. "Who is this?"

"A carpenter. You probably don't know him."

"What department?"

"Finish. Doors and trim."

Davenport stood still, staring at his captive. "Uh, huh. I see."

Besides security and drilling, Davenport had eleven other direct reports, including four construction and several engineering subordinates. Of the four construction managers, Tim Bledsoe oversaw the carpenters. Davenport knew Tim well. They'd go drinking on occasion at the Desert Inn in downtown Dulce. Bledsoe had all sorts of problems including a nagging wife and tradesmen who weren't worth a damn. That worked out perfectly for Davenport because he had a habit of befriending men who were less than he, especially men who wouldn't stop talking. And Bledsoe had plenty to say about his two finish carpenters, Hicks and Blithe, two of the laziest sons-of-bitches in the union. They took the phrase "give 'em an inch and they'll take a mile" to a whole new level, milking jobs for twice the time it should take to complete. And Bledsoe should know, he was once a union carpenter before he took the supervisory position. Like most of the government contractors, turnover was high. Many went missing. A few quit. Some went crazy.

As far as Marcus Wheeler is concerned, using his name was a big mistake. Nobody knew the base's history like Davenport. He studied the reports—knew all about the explorations and excavating that took place back in the '40s. Was told long ago how important it was to understand the genesis, the mistakes that had been made, and to get a firm handle on the guidelines between humans and the visitors.

Davenport had reached his tipping point. If Little Miss Candy Eyes wasn't going to be honest with him, she'd get a full body ablation back in the powerhouse, or she'd have to give up that cute little ass on a regular basis. Either way, Davenport would get what he wanted out of her. It may take time, but she'd talk. They always do.

"Nice try, Sandy."

"Wait... maybe it was—"

"I've never heard of him."

"Oh, Yeah. Jim... Jim something—"

"Take off your clothes."

"Wait."

"Now!"

Chapter 9
Alvarez

Carlos Alvarez reported to Sergeant Major Davenport's office as commanded. This would be his first real test. The boss was well known for gauging his subordinate's devotion by assigning tasks that would assess moral boundaries, or more precisely, determine if they had any. Alvarez expected this. He'd anticipated it from the beginning and planned to prove his willingness to conform to the Sergeant Major's program. Trust came in phases with Davenport. It always had, and Alverez was well equipped to meet his demands.

Alvarez learned about discipline and patience in East L.A. when he was just el niño. His 16- and 17-year-old uncles were patriarchs in that Hoyo Mara gang. He was destined to join them when he turned twelve, although he was eager to enlist at ten. But Mama wouldn't allow that. He was just a child. He needed to grow strong and learn how the streets worked from the safety of his home, under his mother's watchful eye. She needed *un vengador principio y honorable*, not a sociopath. Two or three more years and she'd cut him loose, passing her little bebé into the hands of her cousins Santiago and Miguel. They'd raise him right, teach him the art of murder, the only craft he needed to avenge his father's untimely death.

Gabriel Alvarez, Carlos's father, had had dreams that transcended his living conditions, dreams that aligned with his family traditions. Sent to live with his aunt Maria in The Hole, Le Hoyo Maravilla, as a child, he was completely disconnected from his extended family living in Tijuana. Their only link was the Church and honor. Gabriel's father, an aging carpenter, had big dreams, too, but a back injury prevented him from realizing his ambitions of teaching his son the family trade. So he sent little Gabriel to live with his sister in East Los Angeles. Maria honored her brother's wishes that the boy would receive an education and that she would steer him toward an honorable trade. Having exceeded his father's dreams, graduating with honors, young Gabriel married his high school sweetheart and was accepted into the East L.A. Carpenter's Union apprenticeship—Local 3321. Two years later they had a son, Carlos Manuel Alvarez. Then on a tragic summer day in 1989, Gabriel was misidentified by a carload of boys on a mission to establish the newly developing boundaries between the stoners and gangbangers. He was shot so many times he was practically cut in two. It was from that moment on that Carlos's mother committed her life and her son's life to killing the bastards who murdered her husband.

Alvarez learned a craft, all right. Knives. Guns. Automatic. Semi-automatic. Machete. Hand-to-hand combat. When he'd terminated the surviving men on his mother's list, he left L.A., joined the Marines to escape the memories, and to finally honor his grandfather's wish: live an honorable life. The blood in his veins wasn't filled with murderous thoughts; they were constructive, a vessel of righteous anger waiting to combust. The Marines would fuel his flame. They'd hone his skill set, steer him in the right direction, and he'd kill only those who deserved it. Butchers on a global scale deserved the same fate as his father's assassins. Living the gangbanger life had never suited him. He despised it, actually. But the Marines had a purpose he could get behind: *Support and defend the Constitution of the United States against all enemies, foreign and domestic... So help me God.*

Sounded respectable.

People are people wherever you go, so changing his address didn't really keep him from murderers; in fact, the opposite was true. Entering the Marine Corps put him square in the middle of men hungry for blood. When he was fighting Al`Qaeda in Afghanistan, he'd seen more rag-headed boy rapists and wife beaters than he thought possible. Eight years later when he received an honorable discharge, he took a job with a private security contractor that kept him on US soil. He thought he'd seen his last mass murder, slaughterhouse, and cult leader. Dulce, New Mexico, he thought, sounded like the safest place on Earth. God's country. Warm temperatures. Great pay.

Alvarez couldn't have been more wrong. Within his first year underground he'd seen so many dead bodies he figured he was better off in L.A., but he couldn't leave the base. He was tired of running. It was time to stay where he was needed. Sometimes he wondered if those battles overseas were fabricated—all about feeding the war monster. It ate money and shit young soldiers all over the desert. But the battle *underground* was real. It mattered. It had real consequences here at home, because an enemy like that on our territory should be squashed, not influencing the miilitary. His orders to escort Sandy Fedlesworth to the Archuleta Mesa Medical Department would only reinforce his desire to see this war to the end.

There was no need to knock on the Sergeant Major's door. Sandy had walked as far from Davenport's office as she could manage. Franks had given Alvarez her location over the two-way radio and was keeping a close eye on her whereabouts. She sat on the stone floor, arms wrapped around her knees, cold, trembling. Blood had smeared across her mouth and dried, and mascara stains ran down her cheeks with sharp black lines turning toward her ear from when Davenport dragged her across the floor. The orange jumpsuit was torn and zipper broken, her hands clenching at the remaining material that covered her nakedness.

Alvarez found her sitting behind a concrete pillar and helped her to her feet as she limped toward the medical cart. Franks nodded from across the path, and Alvarez did the same. Words weren't necessary at the time. Alvarez knew what was going to happen to Sandy when he left her with Davenport. Sandy got caught, plain and simple. There wasn't anything he could do to help his friend. Everyone knew the consequences of defying Davenport's orders. This was *his* show—*his* world. He was the direct link between the rarely present Department of Defense brass and those living below Level Four, the red line, approximately three-quarters of a mile below the surface. Cross the red line without a scheduled escort from both sides, you're dead. Cross Davenport once and you'd never do it again. With too much riding on the bases' effectiveness, Davenport was given extreme latitude, a free pass. And he abused those liberties to the fullest extent.

Franks turned away and returned to keep guard over Davenport. Although Alvarez and Franks communicated an unspoken understanding, words would come later—bitter, angry words. So would the tears—plenty of them. Sandy collapsed onto the cart and Alvarez shuttled her to the Medical Department, arm wrapped around her shoulder to keep her steady. He was so tempted to slit Davenport's throat then and there. He wanted to shove his pistol so far up the Sergeant Major's ass that he'd shit hollow-point bullets for a week. But that wasn't the time for *vengaza,* vengeance. Sandy needed medical attention. She and the others needed to debrief, to figure out what went wrong. Everyone in the resistance was taking risks. Sandy understood and accepted the dangers. Same with Alvarez. Same with the others. They needed to assemble and talk things through before someone did something stupid, endangering years of work. If someone overreacted, there would be a bloodbath. Families would be taken out, women and children sold wholesale. Things would get ugly, fast.

•••

Alvarez's electric cart moved swiftly and quietly through the concrete tunnels, observed by dozens of security, tradesmen, engineers, military officers, and civilian laborers who busied themselves with daily routines. Their many ranks and levels of security clearance varied, but the only constant was that no one knew a formal, structured resistance existed except those who were involved. No one said a word; they were as secretive as the Freemasons, maybe more so. Outside of closed doors, no one spoke of the atrocities that occurred under the Earth's surface, allowing their clandestine operation to remain virtually unknown. These men (and occasionally, women) watched Sandy being paraded through the underground base with little sentiment. Beyond the emotional numbness that came with the occupation, they were paid to be silent, a job they did well, as predicted in their personality tests and psychological profiles. What happens in Dulce, stays in Dulce. That's why they were offered their positions in the first place. They were all hand-selected, willing to complete an assignment at all costs, highly dedicated, task oriented, result- and cash-driven personalities.

On the main floor, a manager wearing khaki pants, blue dress shirt, and only slightly dirty steel-toed shoes watched Sandy pass and quickly averted his attention back to one of his subordinates. Injuries, brawls, and near misses were standard fare. Further down the tunnel, a pack of electricians carting three or four long sticks of conduit stopped walking and glared at Alvarez and his sickly passenger. One waved casually, unassuming. Another smiled and quickly locked his eyes on Sandy when he recognized her as one of their own, realizing that something terrible had happened. He elbowed the guy to his right in the arm and soon they were all staring with interest. When the cart passed, the electricians resumed their duties, assuming the details would come later.

James "Truck" Donaldson, a thin heavy-equipment operator and ex-four-hundred-pound alcoholic, was watching the electric cart as he steered his transportation vehicle down the winding path to the bottom of the "Dome". The arched cave served as Grand Central Station where all equipment and motorized vehicles were stored when not in use, and where all Dulce workers began their descent into the ever-increasing web of tunnels spanning as far as two states away before connecting to another hub. With a diameter of about two hundred yards and one hundred feet below the surface, the scaled walls were illuminated with large mobile lighting systems evenly dispersed around the perimeter, giving the quarry-like chamber a flaming glow across the bedrock. The burrow looked like something you might see in an Indiana Jones movie, wowing new and seasoned workers alike. The top was domed for structural surety.

Truck always wondered if they'd paint a mural up there; something like St. Peter's Basilica featuring the creatures Moses wrote about in The Old Testament—the Nephilim. On certain days, a crepuscular ray would sneak in through a fissure in the rock, creating a spiritual experience for those who had made the underground their place of worship. Truck thought it was a sign from God when that happened. Judgment, that's what that was. He'd seen the light. He knew.

High above to his left, Truck observed Alvarez and Sandy driving on the road that circled the Dome, the main drag leading up to the central offices and personnel checkpoint. He hit the brakes to get a better look. The electric engine slowed irritably, the air brakes exhaled, and twenty passengers jerked forward when his vehicle came to a sudden stop. Clothed in orange jumpsuits, a security marker indicating that they were all cleared to work in Levels One through Three, Truck's passengers were already dirty, coughing, and as usual, mindlessly considering the exhaustion the next several hours would bring. All of the tradesmen wore blue hardhats. The managers wore yellow. Common laborers wore white. Every detail was about visually categorizing and safeguarding, including jumpsuit color-coding.

Truck removed his hat, ignoring the cursing and coarse jokes about how many equipment operators it takes to drive a bus, and watched Alvarez' yellow cart zip by like a shooting star. Sandy slouched forward.

She was too far away for Truck to see her alleged wounds and emotional scars. Luke Martin, one of the site's electrical engineers, assured him that she was in bad shape. She had stayed true to her oath and paid the price. Truck looked on with respect, anger, and resolve. Davenport would pay for what he'd done, but all in good time. Like the others in the resistance, Truck was patient and long-suffering.

Chapter 10
Gone

October 2, 2009 - New York City

Penn Mitchell had begun to believe New York City wasn't nearly as bad as he'd thought when he left his tiny home in Twinsburg, Ohio. He sat on a bench in the middle of Washington Square Park, watching the maple leaves sail downward. The smell of fallen foliage and the warmth of the midday sun seemed to make his problems disappear, at least for the moment. He shifted his eyes and watched an army of pigeons soaring up and over the Arch, alerted by their happy coos and fluttering wings. He admired their freedom to come and go as they pleased. He often felt like a bird in a cage, trapped by the four walls of his college classes and father's home, where he studied as little as possible. He longed for that fowl-like freedom to fly at will, to discover who he was or the meaning of life, venturing down streets and subway routes that needed exploring. After all, New York City was no little bird's nest. It was the Grand Canyon to a small town nineteen-year-old like Penn.

We're all like caged animals, he thought, assembling a poem in his head, something he'd do often without thinking. *We live and breathe, do as we're told. Skin when we're young, bones when we're old.*

He grinned in satisfaction at his lyrical assemblage until he heard someone coughing a few feet away under the Hangman's Elm. He turned and watched a silver-haired black man feeding peanuts and sunflower seeds to the birds and squirrels, calling them by name.

"David?" the man called, inviting a bird that swooped down from a tree overhead. The man reached out, holding a seed pinched between his fingers. The bird soared downward, clutched the tasty treat in its talons and flew away. Smiling, the man reached into his bag of goodies and said, "Where are you, Maxine?" Penn looked around, bright-eyed, wondering what creature would come next. While Penn waited, a black squirrel ran under his park bench and onto the old man's lap. The man smiled, gave the squirrel a nut, and it pranced off into the robust landscape nearby until she was summoned again.

Penn looked at the man and wondered what inspired him to care for those little creatures. Must've taken years to develop that kind of trust. He thought about his own life and wondered if he could trust anyone so big and dangerous if he were a squirrel. But then he repeated the poem in his mind... *We live and breathe, and do as we're told. Skin when we're young, bones when we're old.* Penn chuckled and nodded approvingly when the old man caught his eye.

The wind stirred in the branches overhead and the bustling students, chess players, and tourists came and went. As overpopulated as New York could be, he felt surprisingly alone, which he didn't mind at all. Penn felt content, enjoying the solitude. He closed his eyes and listened to the throng of footsteps, honking cabs and busy sounds of the city. New York wasn't anything like Ohio. You could actually hear yourself think in Ohio. Hell, you can hear the corn grow back there.

Penn never wanted to move to New York City. Not at first, anyway. He felt insecure, too small for such a big place. When he'd won the prestigious Zimmerman Literary Award as a high school senior, opportunities had abounded. His dad lived in "the Village", so he figured he'd try his hand at NYU, a top-twenty writing school, get a feel for big-city living, and spend some long-overdue time with his estranged father. Richard V. Mitchell was a generally cold businessman who seldom had a free minute, even before the divorce. But like many times before, there was always hope that he'd finally become emotionally available.

So far, no such luck.

Penn had a heck of a time adjusting to the Big Apple and had struggled to write anything worthwhile in his creative writing courses; he was completely uninspired, to the shock of his advisor and himself. He considered dropping out. He thought about heading north to join one of those crab ships he'd seen on television. Skipping town was a very tempting proposition. The only thing that held him back was his friend Lu Chi, an Asian American from Chinatown who was highly motivated and dangerous. He drilled Penn on the virtues of an education, in human terms, unlike his judgmental father.

Penn was supposed to meet his friend at the park. Apparently Lu had hit up some chicks who wanted to party later on and being that it was Friday, Lu would never take no for an answer, so Penn reluctantly agreed.

Turning away from the old man, he heard Lu call his name from the other side of the commons. He watched his hyperactive friend displaying his acrobatic skills, running on the fountain edge and then jumping into a front flip followed by a reverse aerial. Sometimes he'd show off with a no-hands cartwheel, but only if there were enough of a crowd. Lu's black hair fluffed out like a skirt over a street vent, and he strolled right back into his excited walk as if nothing ever happened, smiling at Penn as he approached.

"Wow, Lu," Penn said, standing to his feet, applauding. "Why don't you lay out a hat and take up a collection?"

Lu grinned sheepishly. "I've thought about it, but..."

"Well, you should try it sometime. You'd probably make a lot of money."

"A..." insisted Lu, counting the points with his fingers. "I don't care 'bout that. And B. It's fun." Lu plopped down on the park bench where Penn was sitting. "You still coming tonight?"

"I suppose." Penn sat down and looked out at the crowd. "I'm not big on dating blind."

"Well... you can keep your eyes open. They're pretty girls. Another reason to stay in school."

Penn laughed. "Oh, my gosh, Lu, you're so green."

Lu shrugged and smiled. "Come on. I'll introduce you. The girls work at the Starbucks over there," Lu said, pointing to the east side of the square.

Penn wasn't feeling it, but he consented. He stood up, threw his backpack over his shoulder and said, "Alright," but he was thinking, *whatever*.

They made their way through the crowd, toward the coffee shop near Loewe Theatre. When the two young men left the Park and stepped on the perimeter sidewalk, a man wearing a devil mask opened the sliding door from inside a black van and called Penn's name. Penn's first thought was that he'd walked onto a movie set, but he noticed there were no cameras. Then as quickly as he could turn away, a black cube sprung out of the guy's hand like a spring-action play tent made for kids, only the thing was about ten feet long on all sides and the bottom was open, allowing the cube to cover him without any trouble. It totally enveloped Penn, extending from the van to the edge of the sidewalk. Penn heard Lu call his name, but he couldn't respond. He stood in complete darkness, surrendering to vertigo. Then a forearm gripped his throat, and a thick, dry hand cupped his mouth.

He could feel someone wrapping something around his feet, and then his hands. In an instant, Penn was bound and gagged, but there was nothing he could do. It happened too fast, too skillfully. A black sack was thrown over his head and a drawstring tightened. Within seconds, he felt his hurried breath warming inside the pouch. He tried to resist.

He kicked.

He twisted.

He moaned in vain.

By the time he grasped what had happened, he was already carried away and thrown into the back of the van. The door slid shut, and the tent remained on the sidewalk like modern art capturing the interest of the passersby. They gawked at the piece, fascinated by the deeper meaning of its simplicity and intense blackness, all while the van drove away unnoticed. There were no markings on the vehicle. No plates. No description of suspects. All that remained at the scene was Penn's denim backpack lying on the dirty concrete. Penn felt a sting in his neck, fought to remain conscious, and fell asleep.

Chapter 11
Prodigal Son

Three months later - January 3, 2010
Twinsburg, Ohio

Rainwater streamed out of the gutter and into Penn's shoes. Lethargic and numb from the cold, raindrops stung his face, waking him from a deep sleep. Penn raised his head off a concrete step and wondered how he came to be sprawled out on someone's front porch in the pouring rain.

He sat up and pulled his legs close to his chest while his eyes came into focus. Breathing a cloud of cold air, he grunted and felt a severe pain in the back of his head. His shoulders ached terribly, too, and he could barely move on account of his stiff muscles. Thunder boomed in the distance, rattling the aluminum door that he found himself leaning against.

Where am I? What day is it? It could've been morning, noon, or evening for all he knew; the sky was dreary, but not nearly as foggy as his thoughts.

Stumbling to his feet, he crossed his arms, warming his skin, and then looked around. The place looked familiar—a quaint little street. The houses were small and well-groomed, minus the puddles and mud and dirty water spraying when dingy cars drove by. The little brick house across the street even looked like Debbie "does Twinsburg" McDaniel's house. Had to be. He'd stared into the front left window more than a few times. Saw more than he'd planned, but everything he'd hoped for. Yeah, he knew that house. A simple examination of the structure confirmed it.

When he realized where he was—his mother's home—he tried to open the door, but it was locked. After warming his hands with his breath, he knocked and called for his mom. No one answered. *She must be at work*, he thought, and then he shivered, feeling a sensation he'd never felt before. He'd throw up any minute if it didn't stop. His breathing felt labored and heavy. And if he didn't know any better, he'd swear his legs and hands were shaking; not from the cold but from something else, something that had gone terribly wrong with his body.

He lifted the floor mat and grabbed the spare key his mother faithfully left for emergencies. The brass key seemed to weigh a hundred pounds. Felt like he had a gold brick in his hands. He stood up, a little too fast, and then leaned against the edge of the door, feeling dizzy, nearly losing his footing. Fumbling with numb fingers, he managed to unlock the latch. It opened, squeaking as it always did, and then he collapsed, landing hard on the Linoleum entryway.

•••

"Penn... Wake up... Penn!"

Somewhere in the shadows of his mind, Penn heard someone calling. Someone was shaking him violently enough to force him into consciousness.

"Penn, can you hear me?" The voice sounded comforting. Penn's eyes opened, blinded by an overhead light. The figure knelt down, pressing a wet cloth to his forehead.

"What happened? Are you okay? Where've you been?" asked the woman kneeling beside him.

He raised his head, slowly, lifting himself up with his elbows. "Mom?"

"I was so worried about you... You've been gone so long! Nobody knew what happened." Penn's mother looked him over, her eyes filled with concern. Her hands busied themselves, inspecting for cuts, bruises, and other signs of injury. Penn looked at her round face and familiar curly hair, although it seemed a touch more silver from when he last saw her.

"Mom... I-I haven't a clue how I got here."

Gripping the cloth on his forehead, he stood up and walked over to his mom's old country couch. She walked beside him, instinctively assisting, arms wrapped around his waist. The cushion seams were frayed, the red canvas worn thin from twenty years of sleepless nights, but as much as Penn complained about it when he was younger, it never looked so good in that tired and nauseous moment. His mother laid a lion-print blanket over his shoulders, and his dripping wet body plunked down on the cushions. The blanket felt welcoming; it had always comforted Penn like he was one of its cubs warmed by the powerful beast's mane.

"What day is it?" he asked, grunting from the ache in the back of his head.

"It's January third... What's wrong, dear? You're shivering."

"You mean, October third?"

"No, sweetie," she said, turning her eyes back to her son, apparently satisfied that she'd completed her examination of his extremities. "It's Sunday, January third. You've been missing for three months. The Police and University Security, not to mention your friends, have been looking everywhere for you. We thought you were murde—." She threw her hands over her mouth, stopping herself from speaking, or crying, which didn't make any sense to Penn.

Carol sat down beside her boy on the couch and studied his appearance. The bags under her tired green eyes looked puffier than before. Darker. Her hands caressed his face like she did when he was a boy, and it felt calming. He could barely feel her touch; his mind was too busy piecing together what she was saying. *Gone three months? That's not possible... I was at school yesterday—or just the other day—which was it?* He couldn't be sure. He couldn't remember. He felt backward—frazzled—like he'd walked into a classroom wearing nothing but his underwear, a dream that he'd had more than once, but not as often as that persistent night terror with his teeth crumbling apart in his mouth for no good reason. Now that one scared the living shit out him. It would wake him up with cold sweats. And yet all of this seemed just as much a dream as any nightmare he'd had in the past.

"I missed you," his mother said, tenderly stroking his back.

Penn could smell his mother's salt and pepper hair, medicinal as always, snapping him out of his thoughts.

"Mom," he said, hesitating, turning his eyes down, and unsuccessfully recalling the past. "I don't remember anything. I don't understand. I think I was hangin' with Lu in the Square... and then... I was here on the porch... How can I lose track of three months?"

"I don't know, sweetie. We'll figure it out. You'll see. I just met the detective working your case... to see if they had any leads."

"Leads? What do you mean? I'm right here!"

"Penn," she said, shrinking back. "You disappeared three months ago and everyone's been searching for you. Even your father." Her chin started to quiver and her eyes swelled up with tears. "Oh, sweetheart, I thought you were dead." She threw her arms around her son, but she couldn't prevent the tears from pouring out. Like the storm raging outside, her heart thundered against Penn's chest.

No way, he thought. *No frickin'way.*

Penn hated to see her cry—always did—so he held her close. Her body started shaking, rattling Penn's nerves. She felt smaller, thinner, like she had lost twenty pounds or more, reminding him of the pain she went through back in the day, the only other time he'd seen her so thin, so distraught. When *Dick* decided to leave, he did everything he could to make life miserable for her, delaying court dates, payments, and affection to his son. Penn never understood the drama and tears. He knew dad was being an ass, and mom cried a lot, but the man was always like that even when he lived with them. This talk about missing three months was ludicrous. Totally not cool.

"It's okay, Mom. I'm here. I'm back. You don't have to worry anymore," Penn said, wishing she would stop crying.

He felt one of her tears splash on his arm and then wiped one from her cheek with his free hand. She pressed her face into his shoulder and spoke with a muffled voice. "I love you, Penn! I'm so glad you're home. I can't tell you how scared I was to lose you."

"It's okay... Mom... It's okay," Penn said, unable to connect with her. Nothing made sense. *How could I lose three months? It's not feasible.*

Then the thought occurred to him: maybe it was real. Maybe something did happen. He remembered sitting in the Park, although the exact day remained fuzzy. He remembered talking with Lu, and something about a couple of girls, and then... and then...

Penn stood up and dropped the blanket, hurtling over the coffee table. He could hear his mom utter a grunt of confusion. He burst through the front door and walked out to the front yard. Rainwater beat against his face, soaking him all over again. The big Maple Tree didn't look nearly as large as it used to, especially with the leaves gone, which was what he needed to see. The water felt so cold against his cheeks. *It must be less than forty degrees. The leaves are gone... and raked or blown away. The calendar. Check your calendar.*

Penn ran back inside, looking for his cell phone, stuffing his hands into his pockets but found nothing.

"My phone... Where's my phone?"

Carol stood up. "It fell out of your pocket, dear. I put it on the counter and plugged in the charger."

He ran into the meager dining room, picked up the phone and looked at the date. He had to see it for himself.

January 3, 2010.

Penn stood still, thinking so hard he thought his brain would explode. *What in the hell happened to me? Nothing. Nothing happened. I remember the old man. And Lu Chi, and the girls, and the van... shit... the van! Then what? Then WHAT?*

He looked at his mother and his eyes drifted away. She had returned to the couch, sitting with her hands in her lap, watching him anxiously. For some reason, he remembered that she used to tell him that his father loved him so much, but he just needed to get away for "a while", to clear his head. Seeing his mother sitting on the couch, her face expressing her tormented heart, reminded him how she'd stare while he waited for his father to show up on weekends. He waited and waited for *a while* to come, but it rarely did. For the next two or three years, his father would visit on Christmas and Penn's birthday, garnishing him with gifts, assuring him that one of these days they'd be a family after a while. Penn believed him for the longest time, but he lost trust eventually. The visits soon became over the phone conversations that grew cold and impersonal. He couldn't wait for the call, but he couldn't wait to say goodbye either.

Penn turned back to his mother. "So, you said Dad knows?"

"Yes. It was on the news," she said, sniffling. "I should call him. Tell 'im you're back."

Unreal, thought Penn. *Back from what?*

The pain that hammered in his head morphed into fear and dread. *If I've been gone for three months, where've I been? What happened to me? Who brought me here?* His mind raced with questions—more than he could handle. He lay back on the couch, closed his eyes, and tried to concentrate, to focus on the moments before he woke up. *Come on, Penn. Think. Think. Try to remember.*

•••

A week later, after dealing with the authorities and their many questions, he began to have terrible nightmares. Each day became a battle. He warred against his body, physically drained, the shakes slowly dissipating as a fever burned whatever drugs had been injected into his system. At night, he dreamed. Visions of ferocious creatures ate at his thoughts; flesh-eating beings chased and chewed and devoured everyone in sight. He'd dream of children being enslaved, swallowed whole by the grotesque monsters, locked behind bars, fetuses floating in huge test tubes, spinning and turning as they dangled from a biologically engineered umbilical cord. Although he couldn't decipher his nightmares, he remembered hearing humans screaming—millions of them so terror-stricken, so ear-piercingly loud that you'd think the Jews were frothing out of the bowels of Sheol to settle the score with Hitler once and for all.

The dreams continued to haunt him until he started writing them down. The NYPD and the FBI eventually left him in his mother's care, satisfied that he probably went on a psychosomatic trip, well on his way to schizophrenia. *He's a nut case*, they said. *Close his file.*

The dreams remained, always ending the same. Someone or something would chase him through strange tunnels and caves until they cornered him. Then just before it attacked, whatever *it* was, he'd wake up, wheezing and sweating.

Penn began writing ferociously one morning, compelled to record his night terrors if only to force himself to recall his bizarre dreams for entertainment purposes. Believing his disappearance had re-inspired his literary creativity, he threw down some of the craziest thoughts he'd ever had. His imagination went wild. It was as if he could paint his dreams with words, brushing in colors, phrases and textures with such intensity that he'd work himself into a sweat simply by the act of typing. But it wasn't just writing. He was reliving those terrible imaginings, those painful night terrors; unknowingly healing whatever wounds had scabbed inside his tormented mind. A new soul had been born in the wake of whatever had happened to him. The young Penn Mitchell had died in those hallucinations, gnawed to death by the uncertainty of whether he'd been the victim of some horrendous calamity, or if he'd actually been in the underground— but that was impossible.

He couldn't go back to school. His life as a student had ended and something new had sprung up in its place. A victim? No. There was no evidence that he'd been victimized; only thoughts that had translated into text. There was no reason for his post-traumatic stress syndrome, yet he was a ticking time bomb, constantly on the verge of an anxiety attack. His mother wouldn't allow him to return to college anyway; not until she was satisfied that he was well. And he clearly was not.

Mentally tortured, his only escape was when he opened his laptop. Writing had become an addiction, a fixation, an obsession. There was a strange world orbiting his thoughts—a strange world indeed.

So he wrote.

Day and night, and into the early morning hours, Penn typed away, weaving a maddening yarn. Shower—be damned. Hygiene—overrated. Cleanliness was evil, a waste of time.

The mantra that a writer should write what he knows had no place in his newly discovered existence. Passion fueled this tale. Intuition ruled the day. A living breathing reality had taken residence in his consciousness, and it needed to reveal itself before it could escape, before it collapsed on itself. The thing was a monster: fierce, ugly, yet incredibly intriguing, not to mention absurd. Page after page he typed. Morning after morning he recorded an incredible storyline. It played out in his mind like a movie, a script with plot, place, and purpose. The actors seemed real, as if he knew them personally. Whatever had spun out of his gray matter, these nuggets of trepidation, had converged into a horrific tale.

•••

Four months after his return, after twelve or more manic hours each day, Penn had written his first novel. He named it, *Federal Underground*. Two months later, after detailed self-editing, he presented it to his advisor and sympathetic professors. A year later, *Federal Underground* was published with the help of the university—a novel from the mind of the NYU student who had disappeared for three months, and who had unknowingly appeared on the front page of The New York Times on three separate occasions over the course of his absence, and a fourth upon his return. He couldn't have had a better platform guaranteeing immediate literary success if he had paid a million-dollar publicist a million-dollar retainer.

Chapter 12
Strawberry Fields

A year and a half later. - August 10, 2012
Central Park, Manhattan, NY

Liz had grown addicted to her Saturday afternoons in Central Park, where she'd feast on a new book every weekend. She rode her bike from her Carnegie Hill apartment to Central Park, usually in Strawberry Fields, and spread a blanket in the shady grass. She lay flat on her belly, sipped on her Raspberry-Green-Tea Frappuccino and flipped the book open. Bikers buzzed by, runners raced through the path, and children's laughter echoed in the peripheral. When she'd settled into her cozy retreat, she blocked out the noise—save the tweets of the birds and unavoidable sounds of the city—and focused on her literary furlough.

At the time, Liz was thirty-nine and had served a total of thirteen years with the FBI, excluding two years of bereavement after Vincent's death. Grieved by her loss, she left her field agent position and took a desk job, analyzing and entering data. Somehow the thrill of working for the FBI had diminished. The Bureau had become less of an adventure, and more of a chore; a job she no longer thrived upon, but rather, tolerated. She didn't need the work. She needed to keep her mind on other things. So when she opened the book Shanna had given her for her birthday, *Federal Underground*, she expected a thrilling afternoon filled with mystery and adventure, an imaginary world that would replace the adrenaline rush she once lived for. She opened the pages and began reading, rapidly flipping through Penn Mitchell's words. But instead of a thrill, she got a jab in her gut that burned like a red-hot bullet.

My codename is Badger X. I can't tell you who I really am because I spent twenty-four years, nearly all of my professional career, serving these United States of America. I served in the CIA, and served well...until I was killed—or so my superiors thought. I've never shared my story with anyone, until now... When I returned to the United States, I was approached about working on an information gathering task force. The men who spoke to me were not from the Agency, and yet they possessed a power over me that I couldn't resist, and reeked of malevolence. They had the power to control my thoughts, to dictate my behavior and that of my peers. They forced us to perform their will... It was then that I knew something was terribly wrong... I

*had to go into hiding in order to keep my family safe...
We had learned that the government was secretly
relocating its power base from D.C. to Denver... I had
heard rumors... I knew they had infiltrated our
government... they are not what we thought... We were
deceived... I'm compelled by my conscience to
disclose...*

Liz couldn't believe what she was reading. As
unlikely as it seemed, she couldn't help notice the
similarities: Vincent... Badger... CIA... Murdered...
Denver. *Impossible.* She shrugged off the
ridiculousness of her assumption, that the character
bore any resemblance to her ex-husband, and kept
reading.

*When we discovered they'd infiltrated the highest
ranks of the Department of Defense, I felt hopeless for
quite some time, wondering if my peers or
administrators were working with them—or God help
us, were one of them. When I met the men and women
working underground—the resistance—I knew I'd
made the right decision... If you know what's going on,
they give you three choices: obey, die, or watch your
family die with you. I chose to fight... to live... to save*

the rest of you from what's on the horizon... they're evil, deceptive... What they have planned... it isn't good...

Liz couldn't put the book down. She read all afternoon and continued late into the night, completely immersed, tuning out everything around her. She couldn't believe the book passed as fiction; there were details and highly top-secret information that civilians shouldn't know about, especially a wet-behind-the-ears, twenty-year-old, first-time author. She scribbled notes in the margins, highlighting facts and the answers to questions she'd often asked, or wondered about. It no longer mattered if the protagonist resembled Vincent, her deceased ex-husband; the question was: Where did Penn Mitchell get his information? And burning in the back of her mind, the thing that mattered most: How did Penn know so much about Vincent?

She recalled a few circumstances at work when strange men would abruptly whisper something in Gilmore's ear or hand her boss a mysterious packet stamped in red: "Top Secret". He never revealed the content of those conversations. Naturally that bothered her. It was discouraging that there were so many things she didn't know, documents she'd never read, secrets circulating of which she was not important enough to be briefed. She recalled the strange men Gilmore let go several years back at the youth center. She never saw them again, but their presence always bothered her. And for the longest time, she resented him for banning them from her investigation.

On the rare occasion when the underground military bases were brought up at the Bureau, whether by chance or intentionally, the topic was abruptly changed. The discussion of classified facilities had always been a proscriptive subject and she never understood why. Like other top-secret information she was not privy to, she let it go, because in her world intelligence was introduced on a need to know basis. She understood that. It made sense. There's something respectable about honoring high levels of trust. That was her life, and more so in Badger's covert CIA world. Talk about secrets. He must've been neck-deep in confidentialities. Yet, on that day, she held a copy of a tell-all narrative—written by nobody special, a kid no older than her own daughter—a book that revealed secrets she'd only dreamed of knowing.

When she finished, she set the book down on her bed where Vince used to sleep. For some reason it seemed dangerous—painfully disclosing a man she thought she knew—or a bomb, ticking, waiting to take out the masses. The book lay there, a small but mighty force with the power to implicate or deceive. This was no ordinary tale; she knew that. But after reading the author's biography on the back cover, she also knew Penn Mitchell couldn't have come up with all of the facts on his own. Perhaps *Penn Mitchell* was just a front, a pseudonym. The name rang a bell for some reason. Maybe he was a public figure, a young celebrity. Maybe he had an inside track. She needed information. She needed to meet this kid, to speak with him, to discern his intellect and maybe even conduct a background check. Either way, she needed to do something about this book or it would drive her crazy.

Chapter 13
Penn Who?

Liz turned on her computer and typed *Penn Mitchell* into the Google search bar. Pennmitchell dot com and several book links to Federal Underground appeared at the top of her search results, as expected. But she needed more. If a whistleblower with clandestine knowledge went through the trouble of writing a book revealing top-secret information, Liz would expect that individual to cover the basics such as creating an author website, complete with profile pictures and a biography. *Typical*, she thought. She scrolled down the search results, scanning each entry; mostly reviews, blog tours, videos, and appearances. Not a bad looking kid—dusty blonde, gaunt, cheeky, blue eyes with a mysterious sparkle—comparable to Seattle grunge rocker Kurt Cobain's profile. Finally, she had a face to go with the name. Great. But then she found something she hadn't expected—an unusual headline in the New York Times dated October 6, 2009.

NYU STUDENT MISSING.

Liz clicked on the link and read the article containing Penn's picture. This was definitely the same kid. But could his story be a fake—an elaborate hoax to create an identity that didn't really exist? She continued reading about the college student who was allegedly abducted in broad daylight. There were witnesses but all leads came up empty. The van was unmarked and no one saw the captors' faces. Originally thought to be a prank, days and weeks went by before Penn fell from the headlines. After further digging, however, Liz found the other articles announcing Penn's odd re-appearance on his mother's doorstep, and the missing person's report filed with NYPD and the National Crime Information Center. His return seemed anti-climactic, pissing all over the press' conjectures of foul play or murder. In the end, there wasn't a story, just a kid with amnesia. She wondered if it could've been a publicity stunt?

"That's odd." Liz vaguely remembered hearing something about the case, but was too wrapped up in her own bereavement at the time to really invest much energy into the story.

He's abducted and comes back and writes a book like this? That seems a little weird. Liz tried to wrap her head around the possibility of that happening. It wouldn't be a big surprise if Penn wrote about his abduction, if that's what it was. But an abduction doesn't usually equate to access to government secrets, aliens, and underground government conspiracies, so the term *whistleblower* popped back into her head. It's not as clandestine as the nineteen sixties Deep Throat fiasco. It's the worst kind of whistleblowing—covertly and publicly revealing government secrets. Again, this brought her back to Badger. Why would he get involved? *Impossible. He'd never. And, he's dead.*

Confusion and questions stirred into a flurry of anger and frustration. Liz needed answers, and she was good at finding them. If there was anyone she could trust, it was herself; she had learned that long before Vince came into her life, before the FBI filed down her sensitive edges, or her mother decimated her childhood. Unaware that her mother was narcissistic, she didn't have a clue why she was living life on her own, why Meredith Kingsbury was always so preoccupied with herself, with her art, with her lovers, with whatever it was that brought her pleasure at that moment. Elizabeth cried. She cried often. She grew weary of pleading for her mother's attention, instruction, and friendship. Hell, she'd take the scraps from Meredith's smorgasbord life, savoring every minute she could, snatching what little love she'd find from that lonely table where she picked and nibbled on the crumbs that fell to the floor. Elizabeth learned to cook and clean and fix and mend her broken life all by her lonesome long before her first period. Oh, yeah, Liz could trust Liz. She taught herself what it means to work, what it means to share, to give, and to love. She'd unravel Penn Mitchell's identity with her brain tied behind her back. She'd find answers. She would.

She clicked on the keyboard and logged into the FBI's Data Integration and Visualization System, searching for Penn's personal information. She found everything she needed: birth certificate, high school transcripts, and his computer's IP address, which matched the one associated with his website. If Penn's identity was a cover to hide the real author, someone did a bang-up job. After studying his website's book tour schedule, she pinned down his next appearance at the Blue Bird Bookstore on the lower east side the following morning, Saturday at 11:00 am, an appearance she wouldn't miss for the world. But first, she needed to put in a call to Ted Gilmore.

•••

Ted's cell phone rang and the housekeeper answered. "Mr. Gilmore is outside at the moment. May I take a message?"

"Maria, could you please tell him it's Agent Ramsey?" Liz didn't want to say the next line, but she knew it was the only way Ted would take the call. "It's an emergency."

"They're hitting the piñata right now."

Liz sighed. She'd forgotten about little Betsy's birthday. "I'm so sorry, it really is important."

After a brief pause, Maria said, "One moment please."

Liz sensed the irritation in her voice. She imagined Ted would rip Maria a new one for interrupting the party, but she felt even worse for forgetting the event. Ted made a point to remind most of his underlings that Betsy's birthday was a high priority for him. It wasn't like Liz to forget. She adored Ted's daughter, but that damned book had her so tied up in knots she couldn't think about anything else. She hoped she'd catch him in a good mood, so she could speak freely, and personally, off the record.

"What's going on, Elizabeth?"

That was a good sign. He'd only call her that when they were off the clock. *Stay cool, Liz. Stay cool.*

"Hi, Ted. I apologize for the interruption."

"Well, I was a little surprised that you didn't show up. So what's the emergency?"

"It's a little hard to explain."

Ted breathed into the phone and said, "That doesn't sound like an emergency."

"I'm sorry. That was the only way I could get you."

"For God's sake, Liz. What do you want?"

"It's about a book... but not just any book—" She heard the phone hang up.

"Ted?"

Dial tone.

"Ted?"

She redialed the number.

"Ted, please don't hang up," spouted Liz when he answered. "It's important. I wouldn't call if it wasn't. A possible crack in national security."

She heard Ted's agitated breathing again, but at least she had his attention.

"You've got thirty seconds."

"Thank you," she said, gathering her thoughts. "I've run across a book that I believe has leaked top-secret information to the public. I just finished reading it. It's frightening."

"So you're scared? Is that why you called me in the middle of my daughter's birthday party?"

"Yes... Well, no... It's not like that. I'm not scared in that way. I'm afraid this is the real deal. It's not fictitious, Sir. This is hardcore. Secrets cloaked in a novel; the kind of stuff we don't speak about."

"Tom Clancy hardcore? Or Vince Flynn?"

"No," said Liz, sensing his condescending tone.

"Hmm. I've read them both, and they had me pretty convinced, too."

Not what Liz wanted to hear.

"Listen. Why don't you get some rest? Enjoy the weekend. Or come on over and have a beer. Say hi to Sherri. She always enjoys your company—"

"Ted. Stop!" Liz could feel her heart racing. She wasn't crazy. She knew the difference between fiction and the real world. "The author cites details inside military bases that a civilian wouldn't know about. He'd have to be ex-military, or outfitted with special clearance."

"So he's retired; half a step away from the grave. Nothing new. Guys need to get things off their chest. Happens all the time."

"He's a civilian," said Liz.

"He's imaginative," insisted Ted.

"Writes about things I've heard you and the brass whisper... And..."

"And what?"

"The protagonist..."

"Yes?"

"He's CIA."

"Liz? Really?"

Liz paced across her office floor. "I know, Ted. This is going to sound crazy, but everything about him sounds like Vince; from his death to his work in Iraq, Syria, and Denver."

"Liz... it's a coincidence. Let it go."

"No, it's not. Vince was dabbling in places he shouldn't have been. I didn't know what he was up to, but—."

"If the writer's a whistleblower, let the CIA handle their own mess."

"I can't. I'm afraid Vince is involved."

"It's just a book... a fluke."

"Ted. Listen! The protagonist's name is Badger... I'm the only one who ever called him that."

Ted went silent, his breath pulsing into Liz's earpiece.

"Have I got your attention now?" asked Liz.

"Yes." Ted paused and said, "How soon can you get me a copy?"

"I'll bring it right over."

"Okay," replied, Ted. "What do you want from me?"

"I want to bring the kid in."

"Kid?"

"Yeah. I'm sorry... I failed to mention the author's a student."

"Jesus, Liz."

"Wait till you read it. It's stranger than fiction."

"We'll see about that. Bring me the book. And be subtle about the kid. If he doesn't deliver, you're dropping this. Understood?"

"Understood."

Chapter 14
Thunder Lady

Penn mingled with the patrons in the cozy independent bookstore, and in the process noticed a brunette watching him from across the room. She had hurried in several minutes earlier, wet from the sudden downpour. The shop was small, so the ruckus she created when she entered combined with the thunder that blast as she burst through the door was enough to draw all eyes on her. Later, during a brief moment when Penn stood alone, this *thunder lady* approached him, and he felt his neck heat up, a tic that flared up when beautiful women came within an arm's length. She stood about five seven, an inch or two shorter than his wiry self, and wearing a fitted jacket, black slacks, and white button up.

He glanced at her briskly and drummed up a poem in his head. *The pounding under the floor feels shady. For before me stands the Thunder Lady.*

With a hip, no-nonsense look about her, she wiped drops of water from her eyes and reached out her other hand. "Mr. Mitchell?"

"That's me," Penn said, clasping her soft hand, desperately trying to force the schoolboy grin off his face.

"Hi, Penn. I'm Liz Ramsey." With a book tucked under her arm, she flashed her badge briefly. "I'm with the FBI, and I loved the book."

"Thank you," he said, nervously. "That means a lot coming from someone in your position. I'm flattered… I've never met a federal agent before."

Liz smiled, gaping momentarily. "Well now you have."

Penn grinned, silently admiring the agent's alluring blue eyes until he realized how awkward the moment had become.

"Oh," Liz said, breaking the silence. "Would you mind signing my copy?"

"Not at all," said Penn, reaching for her book. He loved this part. *Wait till Lu hears about this! A smoking red-hot FBI agent tracking me down for an autograph.*

"You know, I was very impressed with your work. It was absolutely engrossing."

"Thank you," Penn said, looking up briefly, smiling, hoping he hadn't said any of that out loud. She had to be the cutest woman he'd seen all day. Between her floral fragrance and enchanting features, he felt drawn to her.

"Badger reminded me of someone I used to know."

"Really?" Penn asked, perking up, genuinely curious.

"Yes."

"Who's that?" he asked, while artfully scribbling his name on her book.

"My ex-husband."

Penn's smile faded, and his brow lifted as he dotted the "i" in his last name. "Oh really?" *So much for floral enchantment,* he thought.

"Honestly, I'd love to talk more about your book here, but I'm afraid we'll have to take it to the Bureau." Her eyes quickly shifted from friendly to something much different, taking Penn off guard.

"Pardon me?"

"The content of your book has some questionable material, information that my superiors believe could pose a national security risk."

"Wha—You're kidding me, right? Is this an FBI joke?" Looking around for a camera, Penn asked, chuckling awkwardly. "Are you videoing this for Youtube? I call prank."

Liz didn't look like a jokester. Her smile had vanished, reminding Penn of a Criss Angel disappearing trick, her eyes stern and penetrating. "Do I look like I'm kidding?"

"Well, no. I guess not," Penn said, a little put off by her flip-flopping tone.

"I have to bring you in for questioning."

"Because of my book? That's the joke of the year."

"I'm not joking, Penn. We'd like to ask you a few questions about the content, about your sources."

Laughing her off, Penn said, "It's not real. It's made up. So there's your answer."

She removed her copy of *Federal Underground* from Penn's hands and cocked her head. Her eyes seemed to be studying his reaction. "Maybe," she said, smiling assuredly as if she knew something he didn't.

"Maybe?" Penn asked. "It's fiction. I should know. I wrote it."

"I appreciate the signature, but when it comes to national security, we don't take any chances."

"National Security?" Penn stopped himself before he raised his voice. He scanned the room, suddenly feeling as if he was being watched, and then whispered irritably, "National security? What are you talking about?"

Liz matched his timbre. "I hate to pull you away from your book signing, Penn. I really do. But I need you to come with me. It'll be painless. I promise."

Penn recalled the moment the lights went out on him in Washington Square Park. He stepped back feeling guarded. "No. No, I don't think so. I've been hauled away before and it didn't go so well."

"I'm afraid you don't have a choice," Liz said, tapping the book on her hand and gesturing toward the front door. "We can do this discretely if you like... Or not."

Hesitating for just a moment, he looked her square in the eyes. She appeared sincere. Sounded honest enough. But she was too hot to be an FBI agent, eyes rich with that girl-next-door appeal. Agents only looked that good in the movies—Demi Moore, Sandra Bullock, Jodi Foster types.

"Can I see your badge again?" asked Penn.

The agent displayed the badge. Penn knew a real agent wouldn't hand the badge over. He examined the taut leather case. She could've been on the cover of Vanity Fair, all cute and in uniform and stuff. The embossed text on the badge looked official: Federal Bureau of Investigation, Department of Defense. The agent's badge number: 4876. Her sidearm, a Glock 22 .40 caliber was tucked firmly in her holster.

"Badge number?" asked Penn, still peering at her identification.

Without looking she replied, "Forty-eight, seventy-six."

Stunned, Penn looked toward the entrance. Rain gushed down outside; the last place he wanted to go at the moment. He felt a rush of emotions: embarrassment, fear, anger.

"I have orders to bring you in for questioning. But if everything pans out, you'll be free to go within a couple hours."

Penn kept thinking, *This can't be happening. She must be joking.* The words replayed over and over in his head, so much so that he wanted to laugh out loud. He thought about his mom, and what she'd think. She'd probably giggle with her little mouse voice, and his Dad would assume it was true, assume the worst in him. The mere thought that he'd created anything dangerous was a joke in itself. *Me? A threat?*

"So you're saying I have to leave? With you?"

"Yes."

"Now?"

Liz nodded. Her eyes spoke truthfully, but Penn couldn't trust his senses; the situation was far too extraordinary, far too unbelievable, too reminiscent of his past. He thought for a moment about his dreams and aspirations, how all he ever wanted to be was a writer, and that all afternoon he immersed himself in the fruition of those dreams. A Sunday afternoon chatting with readers, signing books, and talking about the art of words is exactly what he'd hoped for. His life had finally fallen into place. But the assumption this lady was making put a damper on his little dreams.

No matter how insignificant the book signing was in the scope of things, it meant everything to him. Espionage wasn't his gig. And although he took his stripes early in life, sacrificing his identity to *the divorce*, the book had changed him in some ways, feeding his once malnourished confidence, kudos long overdue. No one would take that away from him.

All of this took him back to the abduction. Could *they* be coming for me—to finish the job? They got away with it once; they could get away with it again. Another three months in the cooler. Lights out. Memory loss. Been there, done that. *But what if it's a trick?*

"And if I refuse?"

"You don't want to do that," insisted Liz.

"Why should I trust you?" Although deep down he knew he could—he just didn't want to. "I don't even know if your badge is real."

"I assure you it is."

"You could be an Annie Wilkes type for all I know."

Penn turned, perusing the Kurt Vonnegut section, demonstrating his unwillingness to simply accept her word, sure that this lady was a head case. He had better things to do.

"I think we're done. Nice to meet you," he said, and he started to walk away.

"Don't move, Penn," Liz commanded.

Penn stopped and noticed a few customers watching the exchange and he felt his face redden and heat up. He could see Liz had placed her right hand near her sidearm. But that wasn't enough to validate his fears. This bookstore fiasco was getting out of control. The joke had gone on long enough. He continued walking, confident that Thunder Lady would end the charade. He took another step and heard the agent shout, "Don't move," and then felt his arm twisting, and his face and chest slamming into the bookshelf to his right. The shock and sting filled his mouth with the taste of blood, immediately sending a rush of anger coursing through his being as a few books tumbled to the floor.

"What are you doing?" Penn asked, hearing voices chattering over Liz's radio. She didn't reply in the midst of the struggle. Cold metal clasped around his wrist followed by the burning tug of his other arm. The agent's knee pushed into his back and he was on the floor, both hands restrained within seconds. Penn heard others rushing in, calling Liz by name, and shouting, "subject detained", "apprehended".

"What the hell are you doing?" Penn shouted, face-down on the green Berber carpeting.

Liz replied to someone on the radio and then leaned down and said, "I didn't want to do that."

Penn lifted his head, shocked, swollen upper lip bleeding. He had intended on giving her a piece of his mind when a smartphone flashed, temporarily blinding him. An enthusiastic fan had bent over to take a picture that would net her about $3,000 paid by check from BVZ Magazine, who gladly published Penn's face on the cover of their next issue with the headline: ABDUCTED YOUNG AUTHOR, WANTED BY FBI?

Chapter 15
The Blue Room

Liz sat on one side of a table in the Federal Plaza field office, 28ᵗʰ floor, room 2819. With a legal pad and her engraved Montblanc pen she'd received for 10 years of outstanding service to the Bureau clutched in her hand, she was ready to take care of business. Penn sat across from her, sheepish in every way imaginable, clearly in shock that he'd been apprehended. She put him up in the Blue Room as it was often referred to, not only because of the comforting color thought to aid in relaxing those questioned, but because of the steel blue, tainted two-sided mirror used for observation.

"So, how did you come up with the story?"

"I wish I knew."

Penn shuffled in his seat, touching his tender lip with a damp cloth Liz had provided.

"No need to feel nervous, Penn. I'm here to help."

Penn looked outside the window and Liz could only imagine what he was thinking. Was he scared? Guilty? Confused? He looked as if he was all three; he could hardly keep his wary eyes on her. He seemed callow, scared.

"Did anyone suggest what to write, or give you ideas?" asked Liz.

"No," Penn said with a chuckle, although his frightened face betrayed his laughter.

"And you wrote the book on your own accord?"

"Yes. One hundred percent."

Liz scribbled a few notes and said, "Do you have any idea what triggered the concept, and or characters?"

"Not the foggiest. After I returned, it... it's hard to explain... I just had to get it out."

"Returned?"

"Yeah. After I was kidnapped."

"Okay," replied Liz. "We'll get to your disappearance later. But what was it? Really? Inspiration? Research?"

"Inspiration, I guess," explained Penn. "Never really thought about it. It's a writer thing from what my professor told me. Some work for their ideas, others trip over them."

"So you just stumbled on Federal Underground?"

"Yep. Pretty much."

"I see," said Liz, writing. "And who is your program counselor at the university?"

She observed Penn a moment and briefly glanced at the two-way glass.

"Professor Harden. Maggie Harden. She's the head of the creative writing department at NYU."

"Okay. Thank you... Now, tell me about Badger. Who is he?"

Penn turned his eyes back to Liz with a sly grin. "He's the hero. My protagonist."

"That he is," affirmed Liz. "How did he get the leading role?"

"I don't know. It's like... it's like he's everything I want to be. You know? Like he's a part of who I am... or what I want to become. After you spend so much time writing about a character, you befriend them. You know? You trust them. I guess there's something about a guy with so much strength, and yet he's weak at the same time. Vulnerable."

"Interesting." Liz knew Vince. He was too strong for his own good, but he had a heart that would melt at the site of a broken robin egg.

"And do you know anyone like this character? Does he remind you of anybody?"

Penn shook his head. "No. I've never met anyone like Badger."

"What about your father?" Liz knew the answer to that. Her research had excavated every detail about Penn. But she needed to put some flesh on the kid, bring the files to life.

Penn turned away, looking back at the two-way glass. "Not hardly."

That's what she was looking for. *The kid definitely has daddy issues. That little tidbit may come in handy later.*

Liz heard a tapping on the glass. *Time's up. Good cop out—Bad cop in.* She stood up and said, "Thirsty?"

Without looking at Liz, Penn answered, "Sure."

"What's your poison?"

"Mountain Dew."

"Awesome," Liz said in good cop fashion, saluting her captor with a smile. "Let's do the Dew."

She tucked in her chair, grabbed her pen and notes and headed for the door. Gilmore would come in, as planned, and take another approach, which concerned her. The kid seemed so green she began to wonder if she'd stepped out of bounds, unable to let go of Vincent. Had she taken this too far? What if the kid was telling the truth? She'd look like a fool and the Bureau would look reckless. Penn certainly didn't have a criminal profile.

"Will I need a lawyer?" the kid asked.

Liz laughed, feeling a little sorry for the wordsmith. "Probably not. But you have every right to have a lawyer present if that's what you want. But like I said, this should be very quick and painless, nothing official."

She opened the door and looked back at Penn. "I'll be right back." She smiled, closed the door and walked away.

•••

After a few minutes, Penn grew tired of sitting still, studying the icy blue walls and two-sided mirror with a video camera whose red flashing light penetrated the reflective glass. He stood up, walked to the door and cracked it open, looking left and then right. The floor buzzed with agents, men and women, all dressed in professional attire, likely preoccupied with interesting cases like money laundering, Russian mob syndicates, Ponzi schemes, and bank robbers.

When he returned to his seat, a framed poster caught his eye.

"The mission of the FBI is to protect and defend the United States against terrorist and foreign intelligence threats, to uphold and enforce the criminal laws of the United States, and to provide leadership and criminal justice services to federal, state, municipal, and international agencies and partners."

To his amazement, Penn found himself anticipating the words before he actually read them. They seemed awfully familiar. He closed his eyes to test himself, and immediately repeated the FBI mission exactly as it read on the poster. "...to protect and defend the United States against terrorist and foreign intelligence..."

Knowing what the poster said even though he'd never read it before freaked him out. He tried to remember if he'd read it in high school or college, but nothing came to mind, so he dropped it. A brain spasm was hardly important at the moment. He had bigger fish to smoke up.

The room was silent and Penn knew they were watching. He could feel their eyes assaulting him. He looked at the red LED in the two-way glass, scoffing at the idea that he was a criminal worthy of observation, interrogation—or hell, for that matter, suspicion. He jammed a finger in his mouth and began chewing his nails incessantly. *Like I don't know what they're doing. Like I wouldn't know other agents are observing my behavior, listening, plotting their next move.*

Penn could feel anxiety building in his chest. This didn't seem like the brief interview Thunder Lady had promised. He started to feel claustrophobic. He looked at the mirror, but wouldn't dare crack a smile. *No need to encourage them by showing my cocky side.* He'd seen enough spy movies to know not to act insolent or frightened. But now that he was being investigated, and they obviously had the wrong guy, it was hard to control his smart-ass self, but it was more difficult to keep from crying like a baby.

The last time he felt like that was in the seventh grade, when he came home with a bad report card—straight D's—every class. He felt like the dumbest kid in the world. But he wasn't stupid, and he knew it. He'd never feel that way again. Something had to change. He'd work harder. Study more. Read often. Write. Penn worked out all the details about his new life as he rode his bike home from school that day—the awards, the accolades, the praise he'd receive next semester for getting on the honor roll—he had it all figured out in a matter of a mile or two, but he still had his father to deal with. Yes, Dad would have a few things to say about Penn's performance, and it wouldn't be good, or helpful, or kind. That's when the anxiety hit hard. Penn's father had a way of transferring his own failures on everyone around him, especially Penn. *No son of his was going to fail the seventh grade, goddamn it.* Franklin V. Mitchell would make sure of that. He'd let that boy know that *only losers get straight D's*, and *Mitchells aren't losers, and they don't get bad marks. Hell no. Pull up your bootstraps, boy, and apply yourself. Focus, why don't you? And to ensure this never happens again, you're grounded for the rest of your life, or until you get all*

A's, whichever comes first. Got it? Good. Now get to your room where you'll feel useless and ashamed and scared and puny!

With a sudden need to check his pulse, Penn put two fingers on his neck. Blood was racing at breakneck speeds. Remembering the last time that he felt small and fearful and anxious seemed so much like the present. But that wasn't the big time. *This* was the big time. He finally had something to write home about. And according to Penn's analysis, the interrogation would only get worse.

Penn didn't like those old memories. The only redeeming—and somewhat comical—aspect was that a federal investigation would stir up thoughts about his upbringing, downbringing, call it what you like. Shit was getting real, real fast.

The only thing he could think to do was run. He'd never really been in trouble before so he didn't have the street smarts to talk his way out of this like some guys, like his buddy Lu Chi. Penn had always been a better writer than talker. Besides, this ordeal seemed so outrageous that he figured it would all be over soon. *Hang on. Just get through this,* he thought. *I'll call mom, and we'll get all of this straightened out. Dad'll call his lawyers and as mom used to say, they'll get this fixed faster than you can butter your bread. Or, I can run. Fast. I'm still young.*

He heard voices outside the door, whispering. He turned, and hurried back to his chair, anxiously waiting to see *Thunder Lady* enter with an ice cold Dew. Alas, that was not the case. When a tall, muscular man sporting a military-style flat top and cold blue eyes walked in, he realized that he was right; this is the real deal. The guy didn't look very nice, not as pleasant as Liz anyway. He had a copy of the book in one hand and a soda in the other, but no smile, no Thunder Lady.

Chapter 16
Brilliant Motherf#¢%@?$

The man eyed Penn distrustfully as he strolled in, took a deep breath through his nose, and exhaled as he placed a copy of *Federal Underground* on the table. He stood about six foot three and had the body of a Cleveland Browns linebacker, professionally dressed, a shade sharper than the younger agents in the hall.

"Hello, Mr. Mitchell," the man said, reaching out his hand. "Ted Gilmore—Special Agent, Violent Crimes Against Children Division. How are you today?"

Penn gripped his hand and encountered the man's intimidating grasp. "Considering my circumstance... not too good."

Gilmore paused, still gripping tightly. "Not good, huh? I thought you were on cloud nine with your bestseller and all?"

"Well, I'm here... obviously. So there does seem to be a problem."

The man glanced at Penn smugly and released his grasp. "If you haven't done anything wrong, you shouldn't worry." He handed Penn the can of soda and turned back to Liz, who was still standing at the door. "Thank you, Liz. That'll be all."

Gilmore picked up the book and opened it, thumbing through the pages.

The door closed and Penn popped open the can of *Dew* and took a sip, thinking, *at least the lady kept her promise.*

"So you're the author of Federal Underground?"

Penn swallowed. "Um. Yeah. That's right."

"I trust Agent Ramsey has explained why you're here."

"Yes, she did."

"Excellent."

The man pulled out a chair and dropped it opposite Penn. He hoisted his right leg up and planted his foot down with one elbow on his knee.

"Agent Ramsey tells me that you fabricated all of this. Is that correct?"

"Yes."

Gilmore squinted, studying his detainee. "You understand that we believe otherwise?"

"I do."

"Great," replied Gilmore, turning to a dog-eared page and dragging his index finger along as he read. "So you think that there are... individuals in the US government that want to, quote, 'destroy America from the ground up'?"

"Personally? No."

"Well, you wrote a pretty convincing novel that tells a different story."

"It's not the first novel with a message like that," snapped Penn.

"That may be true, but you added a unique twist to the premise."

"I'm not sure what you're talking about," said Penn.

"The intelligence. The GPS coordinates. They don't publish that information in Time Magazine."

Penn didn't know how to respond to that. *Why does he care about that stuff?* He wondered. *That is so unimportant.*

"Where did you get the details?"

"What details?"

"The coordinates. The locations of the bases and missile sites?"

"I picked them at random. Most were near a known military base, so I thought that was pretty cool... Why is that such a big deal?"

Gilmore laughed boisterously and smacked the book against his left hand. "Because they're not random, Mr. Mitchell."

Something about his tone sent a chill down Penn's spine.

"Listen, kid. We believe someone—or a group—is working with you, interested in leaking national security details. Obviously, there's more in this book than a few tacks on a map, and that's why I'm here, for now."

"For now?" asked Penn.

"Yes."

Feeling irritated and ready to rip Sergeant Tight Ass a new anus, Penn said, "But you're from the department of fucked up children. Why are you questioning me?"

Gilmore's face turned coal-fire red. He took a deep breath, apparently forcing himself to stay calm. "Agent Ramsey, who you've already met, was the first to encounter your work. It's just a matter of going through the appropriate channels. And seeing how this is a unique circumstance, and we're the first to respond, it's our duty to act as a first line of defense."

The Agent's eyes narrowed. Penn instantly regretted his smart-ass comment.

"If we're not satisfied with what you have to tell us, Mr. Mitchell, the Bureau will hand you over to the Counterterrorism Division in less than twenty-four hours. They, along with several other intelligence agencies will be very interested in what you've published."

Gilmore turned toward the two-way mirror and Penn noticed how casually he strutted across the room.

"Shut it off," Gilmore said to whoever was behind the glass. "All of it," he insisted, with a wave of his hand.

He walked back to Penn with an air of self-control, thumbing through the pages of the book, and said, "I'm here, Penn, because we don't know how much you've divulged. We have a team looking into the book as we speak. So why don't you make this easy on yourself and tell me who helped you write it?"

Penn sighed and dropped his face into his hands. "Nobody. I already told Liz that."

Gilmore moved closer and Penn felt the man's breath wafting across his face.

"It's just me," said Penn, slow and assuredly. "No one else. I swear."

"Okay," said Gilmore, sighing. "Here's the thing..." He spun the chair around and sat down with the back against his stomach. "I have a really hard time believing that."

"Why?" asked Penn. "It's a simple answer."

"It's simple. True. But I read your book and I was shocked. Don't get me wrong; the story itself wasn't anything to write home about. It was okay. But here's the problem, Mr. Mitchell: There are certain elements of our military that must not be made public, particularly outposts that are off the grid. I'm sure you understand that. But you—" Gilmore chuckled. "You just published coordinates to classified missile launch sites and top-secret underground bases, among other details. That's treason, my friend."

"Fake coordinates," insisted Penn. "They're made up."

"No, Penn, they're not. You really need to wrap that around your little head. Our national security may be compromised because of what you've published."

"I don't believe you," said Penn, shaking his head.

Gilmore scoffed, glaring. "Did you serve in the military, son?"

"No." Penn shuffled in his seat.

"Right. Then you see the problem I'm dealing with."

"Not really."

"Well then let me enlighten you. The coordinates... they're not fiction. They're real and the only way you'd know their locations and objectives would be if you had a high-level clearance. And you don't. Never have. Therefore, the only reasonable conclusion is that you've received intel from someone who knows, someone who has an interest in sharing that information with the reading public, or worse yet, our enemies."

Penn sat in the chair holding his drink, thinking about the mess he'd found himself in. Nothing was making sense. His hands were shaking. His nerves wrecked. The Big Agent Guy and Thunder Lady were lying—they'd figure that out eventually. *God, what's wrong with these people?*

"This is extremely serious, young man."

"I gather that," Penn snapped.

"Do you know where you are, Mr. Mitchell?"

"Yes, I do. I'm very in touch with reality, if that's what you're insinuating."

Gilmore laughed. "You're a pretty bright kid; I'll give you that."

"Thank you."

"Maybe too bright."

"Why do you say that?"

"Because I've been dealing with brilliant motherfuckers like you for twenty-eight years now, and the biggest problem with your kind is that you assume you're smarter than everyone else. That's what makes you think you can get away with it. Unfortunately, Mr. Mitchell, that's your weakness."

"I told you... I wrote it alone. No one else was involved," said Penn, hands outstretched, feeling exasperated and a little nauseous. "Why won't you believe me?"

Gilmore crashed his sledgehammer fist on the table and said, "Because what you're saying is impossible!" Perspiration percolated across his face. Veins snaked around his thick neck and his eyes seemed to turn darker, converging on his target.

Penn jerked in his seat. He felt Gilmore's power play as tangibly as he could feel his heart pounding in his chest. Yet, as intimidating as the guy acted, he was missing something. He plucked out parts of the story and not others, an idea that was beginning to trouble Penn. If what Gilmore was saying was true, and if, in fact, Penn *was* involved in a conspiracy to expose classified information, unbeknownst to himself, why wasn't the agent questioning the rest of the book, which is actually far more significant to the story? The coordinates were only mentioned in passing. The meat of the tale had greater implications, a game-changing paradigm that would not only be nightmarish, but devastating to much of Earth's population. As disarmed as Penn felt in that moment, he had to return fire. He'd been bullied before and knew the best defense would be to stand up in spite of his fears.

"You're wrong," said Penn, as boldly as he could, sitting up in the chair and placing the soda can on the table.

Gilmore relaxed his white-knuckled grip on the book. "By all means. Please explain."

Penn's hands were shaking again. He crossed his arms to cover his nervousness. "Okay... Um... If you think I'm a whistleblower, then what about the deep tunnels, rail systems, aliens? What about the abductions? They're part of the story, too. Don't you care about that? Maybe that's the part you're concerned with, so much so that you aren't even mentioning it."

Ted didn't respond.

"So those parts are true?" asked Penn.

"I never said that."

"By accusing me of treason, you're inadvertently admitting that a black government is building a web of underground military bases to protect humanity from an extraterrestrial threat. Or is it conspiring with the extraterrestrials? I forget."

Gilmore's brow bent curiously. "What's your point?"

"My point is, if the military locations I've listed are so top secret, and I've somehow breached U.S. security, then everything else I wrote must be true, because it all came from the same place."

"And that's what we're after..." said Gilmore, pointing at Penn. "...where it came from."

"Geesh! Are you going to frisk my brain?"

"Maybe."

"Okay. The book is about a black government scrambling for control inside a planet that's on the brink of Hell literally breaking loose. There's your answer... So is it? Is that why the book's a problem for you?"

"I'm not interested in science fiction," insisted Gilmore. "I'm interested in facts. In evidence."

"But it's all connected. That's how I wrote it. Point A is connected to point B, and point B to secure point C, and D, and so on. All of the facts are interrelated. If you add up all the pieces, you can see the big picture. Not up close, though; you have to step back and look at everything with an open mind. Only then can you see how everything fits into the story. The military bases play a minor role—the missile sites and outposts immaterial. The real story is what's going on a thousand feet below the earth. So if you think this book is a plot to expose the truth, then God help us all, because this story doesn't have a happy ending."

Ted sat down, no longer puffed up. "I didn't say everything in the book is accurate. There's plenty of conspiracy drivel in there. My only concern is that a terrorist cell will read this crap and kill Americans. Is that what you want? Do you really want innocent blood on your hands?"

"No," said Penn. "Why would I?"

"I'm not asking why, Mr. Mitchell. That's what's at risk when whistleblowers spout off."

"I'm not a whistleblower."

"The hell you aren't!" Gilmore slapped Penn hard across his face with the book, sending him rolling off his chair.

Penn felt the burn and heard a ringing in his ears and a rush of blood to his face. He crawled across the floor near the door when Liz rushed into the room and shouted, "Ted! What are you doing?" She grabbed his arm just before Ted assaulted Penn a second time.

Gilmore shoved her back and shot an incriminating look at his subordinate. Penn crawled away, crumpled into a ball, afraid and in shock. Nothing made sense. The last snapshot he had of Special Agent Gilmore looked like a wild hog with thick, angry jowls and arms swinging. He heard Liz yelling at Gilmore as the two agents walked into the hallway. He pulled himself up and rested, leaning against the wall, wiping blood from his nose.

Ramsey and Gilmore continued arguing, and after a sequence of doors opening and slamming shut, Penn could hear them behind the two-way glass. He realized he was alone, and that got his mind buzzing with possibilities. *I'm not doing this*, he thought to himself. *I can't stay here. These people are delusional*. His eyes toggled from the door to the two-way glass, and back to the door again. He wondered if he could escape before they'd notice. Their shouting match continued, leaving him alone and in the hands of fate, which he knew could bring more trouble upon himself, but he had to do something, and waiting for another smack across the jaw by that giant hog wasn't on his bucket list.

Penn's nose was throbbing, his hands covered in blood, but he could only think of running. He looked at the door again and listened for voices in the hallway. The only sounds he could hear were coming from the observation room. He had to flee. Something compelled him. Although he couldn't explain why, it felt natural to close his eyes and imagine his surroundings, to envision which way to turn, as if he was wired for escape, trained from birth for this very moment.

He knew to turn left because that's the way Liz brought him in, but his instincts went further than that—he knew what came next—the best escape route. He'd run down the hallway and find an elevator after two right turns. Something told him to get to the basement: Level B2.

In a decisive moment, he snapped a quick glance at the two-way glass, then at the table where his phone and wallet lay. *Now. I have to go*, he insisted, and then shot away from the wall, snatching up his belongings and stuffing them into his pockets as he darted out the door. He immediately turned left, running as fast as he could down the long hallway. He could see agents in his periphery as he passed open doors, and heard the clamor that trailed behind— "What's going on? ...Who was that?"

By the time Penn turned the corner to his right, he could hear Agent Ramsey shout his name, followed by the rapid fire of her low-heeled pumps striking the floor. He sprinted thirty feet down the hall, and then turned right again until he came to the four elevators. He hit all the down buttons and waited, sweating, shaking.

"Stop him!" Penn heard Liz shouting, followed by several feet stomping and sliding. Sounded like a mob approaching.

Penn looked for another way out. A stairwell was just down the hall. *There might not be enough time to hitch a ride*, he thought. *And what if there are other agents in the elevator? Oh my God, what have I done?*

"Penn! Stop!"

Penn's heart was throbbing, practically bursting out of his chest, but he wouldn't be deterred. Not now. It was far too late for that. His mind had surged into overdrive and it seemed as if he was running on autopilot. *Turn right. Thirty feet. Right again. Level B2 at all costs*, he heard himself think. *Stairway. Go. Go. Go!*

Giving up on the elevator, he ran toward the exit door labeled with a red EXIT sign. Running again, he realized that he could hear exactly what was going on behind him, completely tuned in to his surroundings. The elevator bell dinged and the doors opened. Liz shouted something to the occupants, who sounded puzzled, but quickly joined in her pursuit.

"There! He's taking the stairs," he heard Liz shout.

Penn shoved the door open and it slammed against a concrete wall. He heard several more feet clapping across the floor, as he gripped the rail, jumping down three and four steps at a time. When he turned the first corner on the landing, he noticed an agent bursting through the door above him, then another, and another.

He sprinted to the next level and heard Liz call his name again, her voice echoing in the stairwell from above. He looked up. His eyes met with hers as she glanced down the corridor.

"Don't move, Penn!" she shouted. "It'll only get worse!"

He couldn't look at her again. Doing so made him want to stop—to give up and turn himself in. But he wasn't about to do that. They had already sealed his fate; already decided that he was guilty, which wasn't true. He wasn't going to let Gilmore beat him into a confession. Liz continued her pursuit, her voice fading as Penn put all of his energy into running as fast as he could, keeping track of each new level.

Nineteen. Eighteen.

When he approached Level Seventeen, the exit door opened and a couple of agents charged at him, but Penn grabbed the railing and flung his legs over, instantly shooting him eight feet down and about twenty steps ahead of the agents. When he hit the concrete steps he felt a burn in his right ankle and knew he couldn't do that again. Youthful agility would only take him so far.

The agents commanded him to stop, but he tuned them out, focusing on the lower levels. Sixteen. Fifteen. When he hit the fourteenth floor, he realized that he could no longer hear Liz or the other agents, so he stopped and looked up the long flight of stairs. They had disappeared, probably regrouped, or planned to ambush him on the first floor. He thought about his next step. There were few options. *Continue, and fall into their hands. Or take a chance, a huge risk.* He could walk out of the stairwell and into the Level Fourteen hallway, hoping to find an unoccupied elevator. *If I'm lucky, I'll make it to B2. But they'd expect me on the main floor, not the basement.*

He was sweating profusely so he wiped his face with his shirt, took a couple deep breaths, casually opened the exit door and walked into the empty hallway. He made his way toward the elevator, trying to look as inconspicuous as possible. *Only twenty feet to go. Ten. Five.*

There were four sets of elevator doors and three out of four were descending. One was going up.

"Come on. Come on."

He hit the down button and within a few seconds, the door began to open. He had fully expected to find Liz or some other agent waiting, but the compartment was empty.

He hurried inside and hit B2. When the door closed, an alarm began blasting: a slow, high-pitched whooping sound.

"Shit!"

He counted the floors as he passed each new level: T*en, Nine, Eight, Seven.*

The elevator stopped between Levels Five and Six.

"Damn it!" *They've shut me down.*

He looked up and realized the only way out was through the light fixture. He'd seen Bruce Willis climb through those in action movies, so he figured he could do it, too. After making a quick assessment of the elevator's structure, he realized he could climb on the stainless steel handrail that wrapped around the perimeter. The space was small enough that he pressed his hands near the controls, jumped up on the railing, and shimmied until he could reach the ceiling. He examined the light fixture and noticed two small levers that seemed to hold the cover in place. He pulled the levers back and the decorative cover swung loose, still attached to the hinges on one side. From there he could see how easy it was to push the fixture housing up for a quick escape.

Although the angle of his body felt awkward, he managed to shove the unit up and out of his way, flinching when the two bulbs fell out of position and onto the floor, exploding into a mess of shattered glass. Driven by adrenaline, he grabbed the edge of the new opening and pulled himself up into the elevator shaft. Emergency lights had turned on, illuminating the passageway, emergency ladder, and doors at each level. Hoping the elevator didn't restart, he hurried down, keeping track of each new floor—three, two, one, and finally, B1. It seemed there were no more levels, which felt odd; he expected one more. He stretched his leg over to the small ledge in front of the doors and tried to pry the sliding door open from inside the shaft and remembered that there was a manual lever at the top of the door, a lever that if pulled in one direction would release a safety mechanism, easily allowing him to open the steel doors.

It worked.

He would need a special key to access the lever from the outside, placing it through a small hole that most people never noticed, but from inside the door, no key was needed. He didn't know how he knew that, but he didn't care. He stepped into the basement level and entered a strange circular hallway wide enough to handle fork trucks and other such equipment. Instead of tile floors and drywall, this level was constructed from concrete, encapsulating the walls, floor, and ceiling. After running several feet, Penn noticed a cargo elevator. There was only one level marker: B2.

He pushed the button and it opened immediately. He stepped inside, the elevator descended one story, and the door opened. This time, the curved hallway had a finished look, much like the upper levels, and exactly like he remembered, although he was becoming increasingly troubled about the intimate knowledge he had about this place.

He turned left, running down the strange hallway that could be better described as a circular vestibule. If he didn't find a way out, he'd end up right where he started. There were a few doors here and there, but for some reason, he was looking for a specific route... on the right. He slowed down at each entry and then looked it over. Each door looked the same until he came to a stainless steel door that he immediately recognized.

This is it. Something about this location commanded him to stop.

He reached for a doorknob, but there wasn't one there. Desperate, he pushed his shoulder into the door a few times, but it wouldn't budge. Like a fly caught in a spider's web, he couldn't leave, stuck in place. For some odd and impractical reason, he was convinced that this was his only escape.

He heard voices echoing in the distance. A pack of agents were rushing into the basement. Doors opened and closed in a fury. He couldn't see their bodies, but he could hear them moving closer, stampeding like a herd of bulls. Voices clamored in the Federal Building's tomb, someone shouting, "Not in here," someone else, "All clear," and others cursing with labored breath.

The herd had grown. The bulls were approaching, and they were coming fast.

He studied the door hoping something would make sense, praying something would stand out when he noticed a brass plaque to the right of the steel doorjamb. The sign measured about eight by twelve inches, sporting an engraved portrait of and dedicated to Dwight D. Eisenhower. Penn thought this was a strange place to dedicate anything to a president, completely out of the public eye. He ran his hand over the cold metal. *That's it*, he recalled. *Something about the plate...* He handled the sign, trying to lift it, pull it, pry it, but nothing worked. When the voices sounded like they were only forty or fifty feet away, he figured they'd finally catch him. Then, like every other detail that rushed into his mind as clear as the day he started writing the book, he remembered, somehow, that the plate slides to the right.

He passed his fingers over the brass, and it moved with little effort, revealing a strange looking device inside the wall. He knew exactly what he was looking at—a retina scan.

I hope this works. The mob was moving closer. *They'll be here any second.*

He put his face against the scanner and a green beam moved across his eyes. The door slid open and a whoosh of stale air blasted Penn's face. Without hesitation, he slipped through the opening, past a light curtain, and into a lion's den for all he knew. Recognizing that the object had successfully entered. The sensor made a switch and a hydraulic cylinder closed the mysterious portal.

Penn stepped into complete darkness, thoroughly spent. His rubbery legs gave way and he slid down the door's interior, panting. He heard a commotion on the other side and forced himself to breathe in silence, listening with an ear pressed against the steel. It was clear that the agents didn't know how to access the door. Assuming Penn wouldn't know either, they moved on, hooves and horns clattering forward in search of their prey.

He rested momentarily, catching his breath... until he heard someone whisper his name.

Chapter 17
The Brotherhood

"Penn Mitchell? Is that you?"

Weary from the chase, Penn opened his eyes but could only see darkness. He was shocked to hear his name. Why would anyone be lurking behind a retina-scanning door beneath the NYC FBI field office and how did he, it, or whatever know his name? Penn jerked backwards, stopped only by the cold steel that hit his back. *Who the hell was that?!* Thought Penn. *Who the effing hell was that?* The voice reminded him of Lu Chi, fast paced and spastic. Lu hardly ever shut up. And neither would this mouthpiece, calling from the dark with his deep baritone voice.

"Come on. Let's go. We gotta get you out of here, kid. Don't have much time."

Penn shivered in the black space, and as his eyes adjusted he caught sight of a rail-thin hand reaching toward his face. Suspicious at first, Penn reached up and pulled back, reconsidering, and then reached his hand out again, gripping the bony meathook. *This is do-or-die,* he reasoned. *I don't have a lot of choices here.* The voice sounded trustworthy—the hand, just a tad creepy, nothing he couldn't handle. The hand yanked Penn to his feet and as Penn stood up, a visage broke through the shadows just inches from his face. The guy's small dark orbs—separated only by his schnoz— glared as the rest of his face appeared. Flat top. High cheek bones. Lips, thin and stern. Older, probably mid- to upper-fifties.

"This way," the man said, as his eyes brightened and his lips widened into a welcoming smile. "We have to leave, now." The guy offered his hand again, this time for a firm shake. "I'm James Donaldson," he said. "My friends call me Truck."

"Truck?"

"That's right... now let's get lost before they figure out where you went."

"Okay, Truck."

If it weren't for the narrow slits of light surrounding the door behind him, Penn wouldn't have noticed the corridor. The man turned and ran. Penn followed, barely keeping up. The passage that he had unwittingly discovered seemed to have a slight downward grade, just enough to guarantee they'd run as fast as humanly possible. When the gleam from the door had vanished, Truck turned on an LED flashlight and the tunnel radiated with a whitish glow.

"We got a long haul ahead of us," said Truck, hardly breaking a sweat. "Hope you're wearing your sneakers."

Huffing, Penn could barely utter a word. "O…kay." He felt his feet flopping on the concrete and wished he'd thought to wear his New Balances instead of his Vans.

"We've been monitoring you," said Truck. "Didn't expect they'd catch on this soon. Don't matter; they've been waitin' for you."

Penn could feel a burn in his legs already. His gut ached. But he had to ask, "Who's... they?"

"Can't tell you that. It's just you and me right now. Just you and ol' Truck, runnin' under New York City."

Yeah, just you and me, thought Penn…. *with the rest of the whackos living in the sewer*. He figured he should stop and ask a few more questions, but the guy could be out of earshot by the time he caught up with him, so he kept moving.

"Where... are we going?" asked Penn, barely keeping pace with Truck.

"Can't tell you... But you'll be safe... Guarantee it."

"Great... Thanks."

The trail had begun to level out and a dim light appeared in the distance. The tunnel reminded Penn of an endless hallway, a backdrop to a nightmare; the one where he'd run all night but never move more than a centimeter, constantly stretching for a hand just out of reach, a doorknob only a spitting distance away. But the light ahead brought the tunnel into perspective. It wasn't endless after all.

"There," said Truck, pointing. "Through that door."

Slowing down, Penn noticed a rusty doorway under the light. The gritty steel and modern fixture contrasted the arched stone walls that looked as if they were bored out thousands of years ago.

Truck stopped first and opened the door, looking in all directions. "Quick. This way."

Penn stopped and bent over, grabbing his knees, catching his breath. His legs felt like rubber. "Wait," he said. "I can't keep up."

"Yes you can," Truck said, assuredly. He helped Penn through the door. "You can rest in here."

Truck shut the metal slab behind him and the latch snapped closed, echoing through the dark cavity. When they were both inside, Truck flipped on a light switch and Penn found himself in a huge cylindrical chamber made of thick rusty steel. The sides were at least twenty feet high giving the appearance that he was sitting in the bottom of a giant empty soup can with no way out, except the way he came in.

"Where are we?" asked Penn.

"A bunker—You okay?"

"Yeah," replied Penn, still recovering from the run. He noticed Truck moving in his direction—a bit too close for his comfort. The man looked Penn over, top to bottom, front to back as he paced back and forth, recovering from the run.

"You're bleeding," said Truck, pointing to his nose.

Penn felt the crusty blood and attempted to wipe it.

"They hurt you?"

"No," said Penn. "Coulda been worse."

"Break any bones?"

"No."

"Did you have counsel present?"

"'Counsel'? You mean a lawyer?"

"That's what I said."

"Um, no. I didn't."

"Darn," whispered the man under his breath. "Anyone know where you were?"

Penn realized he never called his mom to let her know that he was called in for questioning. No one knew where he'd gone, not his family, Lu, his publisher, or his agent. Putting it together, he figured they never really wanted him to make contact with anyone.

"No. I meant to, but things kinda' got out of control."

Truck abruptly ended his visual examination and said, "They wouldn't allow it anyway. Agent Ramsey might've, but not Gilmore. He's on to you."

"Wait. What?" Penn stepped back, reclaiming his personal space. "Gilmore?"

"That's right," said Truck. "Gilmore was bound to find out. We practically put your book in his hands."

"Whoa. Wait a minute." Penn circled Truck, trying to make sense of what the runner had said. "'On to' me? What the hell's that supposed to mean?"

Truck laughed and his voice carried through the vault like a ram's horn. "It's too much, too soon. I realize that. All in good time."

Penn wasn't amused. "Hey! Quit with the bullshit! I don't have any idea what's going on. It's not a game. This is my life… Just tell me why I'm here. Where we are? Anything?"

Truck opened his mouth, pausing before he spoke, turning as Penn circled around him.

"Does this have anything to do with my first disappearance?"

"Maybe," said Truck, shrugging his bony shoulders.

"Did you do it?"

"No. There are hundreds, maybe thousands of us. I'm not sure who abducted you."

Finally. Something. I'll definitely get more out of this guy.

"And who are you?" asked Penn.

Truck sighed and pointed to the concrete floor. "Better sit down. I'll give you the basics after I have a little something to eat. Been down here twenty-four hours now. Got a long trip ahead of us." Truck pulled a smashed peanut butter and jelly sandwich out of a fanny pack and said, "Want one?"

Penn shook his head, sliding his back down the corrugated steel cylinder.

"Better take it. You're gonna need it."

Penn reluctantly reached for the sandwich. He could hardly tell which part was bread and which part was the filling. After opening the sandwich bag and thoroughly sniffing the PB and J, he decided it was edible, and took a small bite to start.

"See," said Truck, talking with a full mouth. "You'll need the calories."

"Thanks," replied Penn, feeling peanut butter stuck in the roof of his mouth. "Talk. Please."

Truck sat down beside Penn. "Well, bub, it's hard to explain," he said, wiping a glob of jelly on his pants. "Probably won't believe it."

"You're probably right. But then again, this is getting pretty bizarre."

The man laughed out loud and it echoed in the room. Then the chamber went silent for a second as if it were anticipating what Truck was about to say. The city above vibrated, penetrating the silence, a gentle hum inviting the spoken word.

"*We* aren't anyone special—a buncha misfits, really. But we're many and we're secretly working together... Gosh, I know this is gonna sound funny... we're working to save the rest of you."

Penn couldn't move. He couldn't speak. *How do I respond to a statement like that?* He almost burst out laughing, but he didn't. So he asked the most logical question.

"Save us from what?"

Truck glanced at Penn, lowered the sandwich from his mouth, and looked away. "I don't need to tell you," he said. "You already know."

Penn didn't understand what he meant. And the man still hadn't answered his first question. "Who are you?"

The guy looked at Penn, revealing his gentle smile. "I'm a heavy equipment operator and I work in a deep underground military base, known as a DUMB. I'm part of the resistance. And you already know what that is."

Oh, you're dumb, alright. "Resistance, huh?" *Great. The fans are taking the book way too seriously.*

"There are others. All walks of life. All over the country. All over the world," responded Truck, his smooth demeanor cooling Penn's nerves. "Some work for the government. Some are contractors or serving in the armed services. And we're building the Federal Underground that you wrote about. We work under the black budget projects with military contractors:

NATO, CIA, NSA, DHS, UN… you name it and they have a hand in it. The Department of Defense is ruling over it all. Everything in your book is real, Penn. We're here to help. I don't know why you were chosen, but I know that every one of us has a gift, a talent, an asset that can be used against the machine."

"The machine? Wait. The military machine?"

"Yes. The military industrial complex in your book. President Eisenhower penned the phrase."

"I know"

"Of course you did."

"Yeah, but… So what does Eisenhower—and the machine—want with me?"

"I don't know. I may never know."

"What about the eye scan? How'd I get through the door?"

"I'm not in a position to tell you that."

"Why?" demanded Penn.

"That'll come later; after I deliver you to my handler. He'll give you the details and answer all your questions. If we can get to him."

"If?"

"This won't be easy, kid. There's a reason why they sent me."

"Why's that?"

"I'm a runner. Been a runner for eight years now. Was an overweight drinker and brawler before I found the truth. When I realized what we're up against down there, I knew I couldn't live like that. I'd be useless. You'll see what I'm talking 'bout. You'll learn. Heck, we'll probably put in four miles before we hit the maglev."

"Maglev?"

"You heard me. Tunnels, caves… aliens, too. Just like you wrote about."

Penn tried to shuffle the scraps of information Truck had given into a full deck, but it didn't happen. Going backward, thoughts raced through his mind: *Truck, military machine, FBI, arrested, Thunder Lady, Federal Underground, writing, nightmares, kidnapped.*

He slumped, silently contemplating for a moment that seemed to last minutes. Truck waited patiently, sitting, dangling his lanky arms between his legs. Penn could sense the runner's patience, allowing him time to absorb it all.

How could he ever put his life back together? It was like he'd been given four corners to a five-thousand-piece puzzle. Impossible to assemble. Everything was spiraling out of control. And at the first sign of guidance, the puzzle goes 3-D on him. *What the hell? Okay, Dad. Where are you? Enough of the "what hurts me makes me stronger" bullshit. You can come out now.* He wanted to pinch himself, to make sure it wasn't a dream, but that would be foolish. It was real. His heart was pounding in his chest—he could still feel his neck throbbing. Oh, this was real alright. Real as shit.

Truck stood up, Penn supposed, to stretch his legs a bit.

Penn watched Truck walk around the chamber, listening as the shuffling of his feet echoed in the soup can.

"Truck?"

Truck stopped walking. From the opposite side of the bunker, he lifted his head and said, "Yeah, kid?"

"Can I just go home?" asked Penn. He wanted to be strong, to show no signs of weakness, but inside he felt like running back to the FBI to call his mom so she could drive him back to Twinsburg and tuck him into bed. Maybe he'd wake up and this would all be a dream, a terrible nightmare.

Truck turned, examining Penn as he walked, and then he squatted a couple feet from Penn. He paused a second and spoke with a voice as gentle and genuine as Penn had ever heard.

"There's no way out, Penn. Once you're in, you're in."

Penn smirked, taken aback. "First of all," Penn said. "I'm not in until I say I'm in."

"Not true," said Truck.

"And if I walk?"

"They'll find you, and feed you to the Serpents."

"Serpents? What? Wait. Why?"

"Because you broke the rules."

"What rules? I didn't know anything about this until today."

Grinning, Truck replied. "There are still rules, Penn. Not knowing them doesn't exempt you from the game."

"What kind of rules?"

"There aren't many."

"Good. What are they?"

"Well," said Truck. "The first rule is that no one's allowed to know what's going on under the Earth. Next, once you know, you can't talk about it. The third and final rule, if you talk, you're dead... Pretty straightforward, huh?"

"Well we're talking about it and I'm still breathing."

Truck laughed. The man's easy-going attitude had begun to grow on Penn. His bony smile felt comforting, like the assurance one gets from a fun-loving uncle, or gentle grandfather. But there were still so many questions. When Penn was about to ask another, Truck put his hand on Penn's shoulder and said, "Ain't no iron fist up there, Penn. Power's down below, controlling, deceiving and manipulating the highest levels of government. That's why we're the only ones who know 'bout 'em. We see 'em every day—work with 'em, building a web of support, a link between the two worlds, and the barriers that keep the rest of y'all up there safe. The Pentagon knows—they're very aware of the underground. The creatures give us what we *want*, and we give 'em what they need. We're the only common folks who know."

"And me? What do I have to offer? Why did you suck me into this?"

Truck stood to his feet and reached down for Penn's hand. He lifted Penn and said, "Other than the fact that you're a storyteller, I don't have any idea. Hell, you can't run worth a hill of beans, and I can tell by the looks of you, you ain't no good at tunneling."

"Well, I've never tried, but that doesn't mea—"

"You ever shot a gun?"

"No."

"Shit," said Truck scratching his nubby hair. "All I know is someone's got your number."

"Who's someone?"

"I wish I knew. I take my orders from one person, and he takes his from another. That's how we protect ourselves. Most of us don't know who's involved except the man above and below himself, and I won't ever give 'em up. It's all about trust. A brotherhood. You understand what I'm sayin'?"

Penn didn't understand. He heard the guy, but it didn't compute. Not totally, anyway. The world in his book was surreal, unimaginable. But on the other hand, if the book, *Federal Underground,* and everything this lanky dude was saying was true, it could only make sense if the world he created in his dreams was actually real. But not just real per se—it had to be reality—an inconceivable reality—a complete re-write of everything he'd been told. He couldn't handle any more questions. Hell, he couldn't handle the answers, for that matter.

Truck lifted the steel plate in the center of the floor using a crowbar he found lying on the floor and said, "Let's go, kid. We've got a long trip ahead of us." The runner pointed his flashlight down the deep tunnel, revealing an endless steel ladder. Truck asked Penn to go ahead, but Penn didn't fully trust the man. The guy could close the lid and leave him for dead. Based on Penn's recent experiences, his sixth sense was telling him that this could be a trap. He refused to enter unless Truck led the way, which he did. Truck grabbed the crow bar and gladly climbed down the shaft, humming what sounded like an old gospel tune.

Penn began his descent and slid the cover over the manhole, thinking about the world he was about to enter. He remembered the creatures from his dreams, and for the first time he began to worry more about what was down there than the man leading the way. After a few rungs he could already feel the drop in temperature, smell the stale, moist air, and practically touch the darkness; it was that thick. He thought of his mother and Dad and Lu Chi while sliding the plate over the hole, and wondered if he'd ever see them again.

Chapter 18
Jaws of Life

Liz circled Level B2 one last time, double-checking that every room had been inspected, every door opened, and every corner turned inside out. Penn Mitchell had vanished. *Gilmore will be furious.* She might even be put on probation—the last thing she needed. Mother would turn over in her grave. *Do you know what I look like as a parent when you screw up?* She heard her say in the back of her mind. *I won't be able to show my face for weeks. I will not have my daughter acting a fool, making silly mistakes.*

Losing Penn was a cosmic error. Mother was right for once. Her daughter left Penn unattended. She was rusty. It'd been too long since she'd worked in the field. He had the answers she needed, and she turned her back while he was alone. *Stupid!* She had to find him; there was no choice. Badger was alive; she could feel it in her bones and that squirrely kid was the only one who knows anything, even if he couldn't remember—and that can be fixed.

There were ways of making detainees talk; drugs to influence recall, and drugs to help them forget. Sodium pentothal for starters, and if that didn't work, a healthy dose of sodium amytal. To counteract the session, she'd jack him up with what Vincent called "Old Reliable"—scopolamine—to block out the memories of the injections. He'd puke out his hippocampus if she had any say in the matter. Besides, if she didn't dispense the barbiturates, Gilmore would; he'd probably take care of everything, but she had a bad feeling about the way he was handling things lately. She'd never seen him so out of control before. Angry? Yes. Brutal? Never.

After checking the last room with agents Bernie "Near Death" Holeman, and neophyte Chase Teagle, she passed the steel door with no handle for the third time. No one could access it and that really bothered her. No handle. No keyhole. "What the hell are you doing in our basement?" she asked the mysterious door. It didn't answer, as expected. She and the other two agents rammed their shoulders against it, again and again. Nothing.

Penn's in there. She could sense it. And she could see grimy fingerprints all over it. *There's gotta be a blueprint somewhere. Someone in this building knows what's behind that door*. She rushed through the hall and ran up the stairwell until she came to B1, where she entered the elevator en route to Gilmore's office; the last place she wanted to go. But then maybe she didn't have to do that. Holeman and Teagle waited for her next instructions, and she knew exactly what she needed to do. Call the Fire Department. *Better to ask for forgiveness than beg for permission.*

•••

The door looked like the side of the USS Stark after it was struck by two missiles. A team of three firemen chewed the door wide open with heavy-duty drills and the Jaws of Life while Liz snagged a flashlight from a maintenance man on B1. After kicking the jagged steel, it fell to the floor. The firemen moved to the side and Liz signaled for her two colleagues to follow. She flipped on her light and stood in awe of the hidden tunnel and recognized the electronics beside the door interior—iris identity authenticator. Her fears where confirmed when one of the firemen slid the brass plate open, revealing the eye scanner. *Holy shit. This kid's in deep.* Shining the beam on the dusty path she saw one set of footprints coming toward the exit, and two moving away. Someone had intercepted her detainee. Maybe he wasn't as innocent as she anticipated. Liz turned around as Agent Holeman cautiously walked through the opening, and she thanked the firemen for their service.

He's not alone, she mused. *And they're on the run. We need to hurry.*

"Come on," Liz said, gesturing for the agents to follow. "They went this way. And they're running."

Liz ran side by side with agent Teagle until they came to the steel door further down the tunnel. Holeman slowly fell behind and eventually gave up, waving for them to continue. Teagle opened the door and Liz stepped inside the underground silo, noting the tracks left behind by the two runners. Their prints meandered throughout the circular room but stopped in the center, right next to a cast iron manhole cover. She didn't have any way to lift it. It was too heavy for either of them. *Damn it. We're wasting more time.* She sent Teagle back to get the firefighters while she called Gilmore, fearful she might not get a signal.

She dialed and her boss answered.

"He managed to escape through a secure door in the basement. Passed a retina check. And he's not alone."

"Jesus Christ, Liz. How'd he clear the eye scan?"

"If I only knew."

"That little prick. I knew it. Part of a goddamned terrorist cell."

"Well, I'm not sure about that, Sir. But he's definitely not alone. They're running through a tunnel system under our building. Maybe they've taken him again? Maybe someone else opened the door... or took him... like before."

"Into a sewer?"

"No. It's something altogether different. I can see their trail because of the dust, but even that's starting to fade. It's man-made. An old passageway."

"I'll get the skinny on the tunnels and have Jack at the NSA locate his phone. If he's still carrying it, we might be able to track him."

"I'll call you when I know more."

"Just bring his ass... [static]... alive... [static]...We need to... the other set of prints..."

"Gilmore?... Ted?... Are you there?"

Damn. I'm too deep.

"Lost the signal."

Liz heard a commotion outside the silo and a beam of light flashed through the entry.

"Teagle, is that you?" Liz said, peering toward the door.

"Yeah, it's me," said Teagle. "We've got a couple pry bars."

"Great!"

Teagle and one of the firemen lifted the manhole, grinding it across the concrete floor inch by inch. When the heavy steel had cleared the orifice, Teagle shone his light down. "Wow!" he said. "I... I can't see the bottom."

"Let me have a look," said Liz. She leaned over, peering into the circular pit. All she could see was a concrete tunnel no wider than three feet in diameter with a steel ladder that seemed to drop to the center of the Earth. Seeing the depth of the hole, her legs started to feel jittery. "Oh, my God."

"What's the matter?" asked Teagle, staring into the abyss.

"I'm not too keen on heights," said Liz.

"Me either," admitted the rookie.

The fireman, initially curious about the caves, picked up the pry bars when another call was broadcasted over his handheld radio. "Good luck with that," he said, as he walked out.

Disregarding the twisting that was taking place in her stomach, Liz pushed past her fears. *This has to be done,* she thought. If Penn was in trouble, she needed to pursue him. If he was truly part of a terrorist cell, the tunnel could potentially lead her to their back door. "We've gotta get down there," she said. "They could be miles away by now."

"Or, they're hiding," said Teagle.

"You think so?"

He nodded. "There's only one way to find out," said Teagle, fearfully glaring into the darkness. "Ladies first."

What a pansy. Liz stretched out her hand and replied, "Go ahead then, Teagle."

The rookie paused, visibly apprehensive, and took a step back. "You know what, Liz, I think I'm gonna pass on this one. I already have a heavy caseload. He's your baby. You can nurse him."

"And you can nurse your mother, asshole. Get down there."

Liz stood in shock for a few seconds, scowling at the rookie. When he actually turned around and walked out of the door, she realized everything about Penn Mitchell had turned bass-ackwards. She knew she needed to climb, to continue the chase despite her fears, but it seemed more daunting than when she first spied him in the bookstore. She thought about her mother and knew there would be nothing but criticism if she didn't go.

She stuffed her flashlight into her back pocket, realizing she hadn't any idea how fresh or old the batteries were. Did she have ten minutes of power? An hour? A minute? She checked the charge on her phone: seventy-eight percent. That would help if the flashlight died. She also put it in airplane mode to save as much battery life as possible and then began her descent.

Rung after rung she plunged into the shaft. On occasion, she'd flash the light down, but the ladder, firmly bolted to the concrete, continued with no end in sight. Her arms and legs were growing tired. She worried she wouldn't make it. Did she miss a branch in the tube? Did she pass an exit to her back when she was concentrating on foot placement? *Damn. Maybe Pussyfoot Teagle had the right idea.* Liz had to stop. She leaned back and relaxed a moment with her back pressed against the concrete opposite the ladder. She reached into her pocket, snatched the quarter left over from when she bought Penn his drink, and dropped it to assess how much further she'd have to climb.

The coin fell, twirling, spinning, knocking against steel rungs and etching the concrete until it finally landed with a splash. Blooop! Took about ten seconds. Seemed like forever. But there was hope. Captivated by insignificant facts, she knew an object would fall approximately 4.9 meters per second, which in this case translated into about 49 meters. *One hundred and fifty feet to go. You can do this, Liz. Deep breath.*

A few minutes later she felt a blast of cool air pummel her back. She grabbed the flashlight to investigate where the draft was coming from. When she turned to look, her right foot slipped, and the jolt and loss of balance caused the flashlight to fall out of her hands. As her body twisted, she caught a brief glimpse of a large cave.

After debating whether to continue or not, she opted to carry out her plans, but refused to let go of the rungs, traversing the ladder without the use of her phone to light the way. Thirty more rungs and she finally touched down in a shallow puddle of water where the flashlight lay in pieces, completely inoperative. She grabbed her phone and turned on the LED flashlight application. The beam of light revealed a vast room several stories tall and equally wide, populated with stalactites, stalagmites, limestone rock formations, and a crystal clear river flowing through the middle of the rocky floor.

"This is definitely the Twilight Zone," she joked.

Certainly nowhere she wanted to stay by herself. With zero supplies and no food or sustainable light source, searching the cave could prove disastrous. She scanned further and noticed there were several tunnels of various sized openings that branched out from the main room where she was standing. Everything was damp and the temperature cool. She was not prepared for this. There wasn't any way she could proceed. No way to tell what direction Penn and his companion had taken. She had to report back to Gilmore and take stock of the situation, regroup, and organize a team.

She shot a few pics and recorded a short video as evidence of her discovery. While filming, she saw something creeping over the mouth of one of the adjoining cave openings—something non-human, reflective eyes glaring. It peeked around a crevice and quickly slunk back into the shadows. Startled, her finger slid across the screen and the flash shut off, leaving only a dull blue light pointing right at her chest—a visual target for whatever was down there. Beyond startled, she blindly reached for the ladder. Liz stuffed the phone into her pocket and hurried toward the top, terrified to her core. She wasn't up for the leading role in a horror flick.

She thought of nothing but *escape*.

She used all of her remaining strength to shove the manhole cover over the hole and then collapsed upon it. Her heart raced like she'd run a marathon. She hadn't felt that scared in years. *Oh, my God. What the hell was that? It looked... humanoid. Oh, shit. It was so fast.*

Breath Pulsing. Hyperventilating. Her mind replayed the creature clambering up the archway in one of the tunnels, practically climbing upside down. *How did it—? What does that?*

Easy, Elizabeth. You'll blow a head gasket, her mother cried from the grave.

Penn was gone, possibly devoured by an albino subterranean creature. *Could've been me. It was only forty feet away.* She'd run out of there like a scared little schoolgirl, which is what she felt like most days, no matter how much she resisted. But that was beside the point, and a fault she'd rather not bring up, especially since her mother was still pelting her with defeatist thoughts. Her fears had no place in this investigation. *Time to move on. Focus.*

She checked that her phone was still in her pocket, the only proof she had of the cave and the creature. As far as Penn was concerned, the only hope she had of finding him rested with the NSA, and they were usually pretty good at pinning down FBI targets with their Bi-Traveler system as long as the mark wasn't using the SerpentPro blocking application. The blocker wouldn't totally hide her mark, but it could delay finding him to the point of uselessness. She wanted to examine the video, but not in the cave and definitely not alone.

Liz rested for several minutes and began the hike back to the Bureau. Thoughts of Penn and his book and the cave rushed through her head. Penn Mitchell had the potential to become one of NYC's most wanted fugitives and it all started on a hunch, even though it seemed unlikely at the time. Yet with each passing minute, Penn was getting further away, probably half-dead. If he was alive, he was becoming more of a threat; not just because of what was in the book, but because what was in the book could be real— or at least partly true, based on the cave and that thing scaling the rock. Fortunately, Gilmore had come around and decided that Penn was worth the investment. *Clearly he sees a larger threat. Typical brass. "Need to know" is getting old. Bet he doesn't know about the caves though. Damn thing's sitting under the New York City field office—come one come all,* thought Liz—*and I just ripped the underground security door open like a can of sardines.*

Chapter 19
Necessary Evil

Bobby Lee Reynolds and his buddy Verl Mickelson had camped in the Navajo State Park near Pagosa Springs in southern Colorado for two days, four-wheeling and "investigating" a mish-mash of local legends. Clear, starry skies wrapped them in a blanket of celestial bliss, and they jibber jabbered late into the night. All that was left of the campfire was crackling embers and smoke wafting across the campsite. Bobby Lee sipped the last of the Jim Beam double-aged bourbon while Verl munched on a bag of peanuts, even though his doctor told him they were bad for his liver. But who really cares about the liver? Verl sure as hell didn't buy peanuts for his liver; he bought 'em for his palate and they worked wonders on that organ. It was the perfect weekend: fresh mountain air, clear skies, comfortable mid-May temperatures. For Verl, it was a much-needed getaway from the craziness of six kids and what seemed like an eternal winter plowing snow for the city of Denver. The late hours had put a strain on his marriage with Becky Ann, but she did her best to understand and even suggested that at the first break in the weather, he and his best friend, Bobby Lee, spend some time outdoors camping and whatnot.

Bobby Lee, on the other hand, had gone through a nasty divorce a few years ago and had made a habit of prompting Verl to blaze the great state of Colorado to investigate cattle mutilations, UFO sightings, and the elusive Bigfoot. He had nothing else to fill his time— no kids, no pets, no wife, *thank God*—so he spent countless hours chasing fringe theories of all kinds. He worked for the city of Denver, too, picking up trash and cleaning up the Mile High Stadium for extra cash on game nights. Got him free seats and a little extra money to buy his toys: big-ass truck, camping gear, night vision goggles, and four-wheelers, oh yeah, baby! Bobby Lee was that guy; the one who appeared to have everything men want: toys, great looks, and freedom.

Bobby Lee had given all he had to Maggie Buchanan Reynolds for three years straight—an all-time record. Maggie was the dispatcher at the dump, as hot as they come in southeastern Denver: blond, not too thin, great bod, and *good to go* as they say in the trucker's union. He married her in Vegas during a drunken company retreat, a poor decision that became achingly obvious when Maggie's roving eye quickly began roaming in all directions. Bobby Lee soon realized her heart was as dry and cold as the tip of

Pagosa Peak in late February. After many unsuccessful attempts to seize Maggie's affections, he gave her one last chance to at least appear to be a dedicated wife, offering to take her on a romantic getaway at The Mountain Landing Resort near the hot springs. But in typical Maggie fashion, she dropped Bobby Lee on his ass for the rubbish District Manager, Danny Flick, who, after making his monthly appearance, asked her out for a drink or two, which was the last day Bobby Lee saw his precious Maggie.

Bitch, whore, slut.

Hence, the toys and search for a deeper meaning to life—although Bobby Lee would never admit that his heart ached if the void crawled out of his heart and severely beat him about the head and shoulders. But oh, how the great outdoors filled the vacancy she left in her wake. Maggie had moved on and left him in a pile of emotional excrement. He was crushed, mowed over, and buried with the rest of the trash.

Verl and Bobby Lee had set up base camp amidst a cluster of Douglas firs they discovered in a flat clearing bedded with a soft pile of needles. Bobby Lee set up his two-man tent on the south side of the mountain base and Verl had gathered wood and kindling for the fire. After a long and unsuccessful day pursuing what Verl thought was obviously bigfoot tracks, they'd finally given up and enjoyed a hearty hobo stew consisting of potatoes, carrots, and shredded beef, wrapped in foil and slow cooked in the hot coals. When the fire waned, they focused their attention on the stars above as usual, hoping to catch a glimpse of a UFO, shooting star, or anything that would entertain their sleepy eyes. Instead, they heard a grotesque sound moaning further down the hill.

Bobby Lee, the younger of the two, jumped to his feet, grabbed his flashlight and Remington 12-gauge shotgun. Without a second thought, he snatched up the loaded weapon and headed toward the noise with work boots untied, t-shirt off, and thick brown hair waving.

"Sounded like a cow," said Verl, grunting as he stood to his feet.

"Holy hot damn!" said Bobby Lee, unable to hide his excitement, plodding through the brush and rocky mountainside.

Something bellowed further down the hill, akin to a sick elephant, and then stopped abruptly. Verl swiped a wisp of hair over his balding head, grabbed the propane lantern, and lumbered after Bobby Lee. Fully aware of the potential for danger, Bobby Lee considered the fact that they could be approaching a mountain lion, bear, or another natural predator. But aside from the risks, his mind was so filled with theories and speculation that his imagination prevented him from thinking reasonably. Dreams of capturing

Bigfoot or a Gray Alien superseded all common sense. Such a find was the end game, the fringe chaser's holy grail.

With his flashlight beaming into the twilight, Bobby Lee saw two white dots staring through the boscage to his right that were far too small to be concerned with, so he raced deeper into the unknown until he tripped over a rock and tumbled down the hill, dropping the gun when he hit the ground. His back and shoulders pummeled the rock-filled terrain and his head plunked down on a stone, splitting the back of his head. He tried to sit up but had to lie down, unable to maintain his equilibrium. He closed his eyes briefly and when he opened them, Verl stood over him, huffing and puffing, sweat dripping off his chin.

"You alright, Bobby Lee?"

Yeah, I'm fine, he thought. Bobby Lee was pretty sure he'd answered his friend, but he was too dazed to know that he'd only blinked and nodded.

"You'll be okay, buddy. Just hang in there," said Verl as he removed his stained white t-shirt. He began to ball it up, Bobby Lee assumed, to place it over the wound or to elevate his head. All the while, Bobby Lee watched Verl scurry around as his vision faded. They hadn't packed a first aid kit or a single Band-Aid, for that matter. *Guys don't need that shit. Got everything we need right in the nature.* So it wasn't a surprise that

Bobby Lee couldn't figure out what Verl was doing, acting all busybody n'such. *Geez, Verl. I'm just a little dizzy's all.*

None of that mattered. A bright light had suddenly devoured the darkness surrounding both men. Bobby Lee squinted from the luminosity, barely catching a glimpse of Verl floating up and into the refulgent beam. In that moment, any sense of realness had vanished. Shadows and light didn't know whether they were coming or going, like a time warp, like a vision that went beyond real—it was palpable. When the figures approached, they moved leisurely toward him as if in a dream. Four creatures, one large and three small, similar to the Grays he'd heard about online and in books. The tall one, in the back, looked different somehow, older, wiser, looming over the others.

Too out of it to get a detailed look, Bobby Lee had to rely on his sixth sense to understand what they were doing. Best he could tell they were sizing him up like a kid studies an ant in the summer sun. He was sure they'd put a lens under the light, as bright as it was, and burn their names across his chest. They could do it—his sixth sense made that clear—and they reeked of malevolence, sending shivers down Bobby Lee's spine. Their large heads and almond-shaped black eyes stared at him with little emotion, exuding what could be interpreted as benevolent curiosity or the strictest science, but his gut was telling him it was sadism—intergalactic pleasure from pain.

Then the cutting began, as if they'd done this a thousand times over.

No anesthetic.

No painkiller.

Bobby Lee felt a burning sensation across his face as his lips were cut from his flesh. Cries of horror ripped through that back of his throat. It was a self-cauterizing cut with very little blood, but the pain was beyond imagination. Then one of the beings ran its arm over his body and he felt a sense of paralysis, somehow numbing the burning sensation in his gaping pie hole. Dazed, he watched Verl ascend further up into the light. His friend's back was arched, his bloated gut facing up, as some kind of antigravity system drew him in. He, too, seemed unable to resist, completely comatose.

There was no blood, but the carnage had happened just the same, with surgical precision. And as Bobby Lee's head rolled to the right out of sheer exhaustion, he noticed the cow lying beside him; the very creature they'd heard grousing in the distance. He'd discovered exactly what he'd hoped to find on the trip—proof that his fringe beliefs were real—evidence that he wasn't crazy, that animal mutilations were a genuine phenomenon. He was right! Aliens exist and his quest for truth had finally borne fruit. But as he helplessly watched the little gray creatures tear and cut and remove the organs and fluids they needed from the beast beside him (For whatever reason—it made no difference as far as he was concerned), he realized how un-entertaining these beings really were. For he had previously longed to meet one, to befriend the mysterious peoples from other worlds in hopes of gaining insight into the greater possibilities beyond Earth. Which is exactly what he got; firsthand, a close encounter of the fourth kind.

Bobby Lee had made the greatest discovery of his life. *They* had come—right on top of him, no less. Working away at his flesh, taking whatever suited their fancy: skin grafts, a few drops of blood, hair specimens and more. He watched in absolute terror as the creatures stuck medical probes in all of his orifices, the experience culminating in dramatic fashion when they inserted an instrument that resembled a melon scoop around his left eyeball. Then, when the appropriate amount of pressure was applied, the inside of his head popped as if an explosion had occurred the moment his optic nerve, blood vessels, and other tissue were snapped or severed, leaving his eye socket in the same condition as his heart, a dark core.

Trembling and in shock, he lay there gasping and watching (with his remaining eye) as the aliens rose up into the large sphere overhead and zipped off toward the mountains. They flew south toward the Archuleta Mesa near that wretched underground base his fellow theorists had always talked about. Some had attempted to sneak in, but they couldn't get past the motion sensors, thermal imaging, and constant surveillance. *A hellhole*, they'd say. It's *a house of horrors,* they'd tell him, where the military and aliens interact daily under the constant threat of friction, and—God help the DoD—the constant threat of exposure. Bobby Lee's sources claimed the system is buffered by black-budget funds, an unimaginable arrangement designed by elite groups within the Pentagon where human needs are exchanged for theirs, promises made on both fronts, and assurances given *not* to eradicate each other as long as all terms are met in a satisfactory manner. One wrong move and we'd kill them, and they'd do the same if given the chance.

The rumors and whisperings he'd sought at the fringe websites and blogs were true. *No mistakin' now.* Were it not for the pain and agony he was feeling, he'd be happy as a tornado in a trailer park. Instead, he lay dying at the hands of his idols, previously unaware of what they really were and what they were really capable of.

With each gurgle, wheeze, and flinch from damaged nerves, Bobby Lee Reynolds suffered miserably. But he found it ironic, as he lay there feeling cadaverous, that an alien craft would haul his eyeball and other vital tissues... [gurgle]... into the Archuleta Mesa, in Southern... [wheeze]... Colorado... [flinch]... and descend into the top-secret Dulce base... [wheeze]... where he'd heard from a reputable source... [gurgle]... that the creatures below conspired with a black government, and although none... [wheeze]... of his friends... [wheeze]... could break in... [wheeze]... he'd managed to infiltrate the complex... [wheeze]... one body part at a time.

Wheeze.... Wheeeeze..........Wheeeeeze................

And with his last breath, his remaining eye caught a glimpse of a lighted convoy far in the distance. One-by-one, a long line of vehicles barreled down the dusty road, speeding in his direction. The sun was on the verge of breaking over the eastern horizon, and a misty fog shrouded the pines, hills and wildflowers as they rose from their slumber. And although his vision was fading fast, he'd swear on his mother's holy grave that the train of vehicles was military, probably coming to investigate and/or collect his remains—a necessary evil to protect the good citizens of America from knowing that Hell and all that is wicked positively exists under the crust of the earth.

Chapter 20
Supersonic

Truck kept a steady pace despite the orange jumpsuit that covered his body. Penn figured the guy could run much faster, but he was obviously being kind, or restrained by the baggy outfit. They were only a quarter mile from the maglev station, and on schedule, according to the runner. With only two hours until Truck's shift began, they'd reach the depot and start blazing under the Midwest in a matter of minutes, as long as Penn cooperated.

Penn had learned a lot from Truck as they coursed through the dark caves and passages that wound under the city. Truck let him know what was above: Lower Manhattan, then Mid-Town, and finally beyond Hell's Kitchen—that's where they'd connect with the maglev. Truck said it paled the depths of The Lincoln Tunnel and put the Amtrak high-speed rail systems to shame. But Penn knew that already. He remembered reading about the magnetically driven trains in a Popular Mechanics magazine at his dad's apartment, giving him just enough information to include them in his story, or so he thought, but he never thought he'd ride in one. Any other details he may have included in the book must've been a coincidence. Had to be.

The gradient fell sharply and leveled out eventually. And the burning in Penn's legs and chest subsided on the straightaways, but they never stopped running. For three or four miles they climbed but mostly dipped down the winding tunnel until the trail straightened for the last mile or so. As they approached their point of exit, the grade dipped down a few degrees and after a sharp turn to the right, the limestone tunnel came to an abrupt end, and they encountered another steel door.

Truck pointed his flashlight at the brass plate that honored President Franklin D. Roosevelt, and asked, "Gonna let us in?"

Penn knew what he was talking about, but he wasn't ready for a fictional tale to become real life; not outside of the dream anyway.

"Better get used to it," said Truck. "You'll be on your own soon."

Penn looked at the runner warily, and slid the brass plate to the side. He knew this location. He'd swear he'd been here before, but he kept that to himself; talking about what he knew still made him feel a little crazy. Then just before he pressed his face to the sensor, he asked, "How does this thing know who I am?"

"They've programmed your retina... You're—."

"Glitched," interrupted Penn. "I have a handful of unique identities linked to my retina. Don't I?"

"A hundred," corrected Truck. "Very good. And those identities are shuffled according to an algorithm that determines the best fit for the location—laborer, telecom, tradesman. Today you're a computer programmer named Dean Jones."

"Dean?" laughed Penn.

"Dean Jones. We have IT guys in the resistance, too," said Truck.

"They scanned my eyes when they abducted me, didn't they?"

"Yes. You're a special circumstance. I'm not sure how or when they did it to you. But seriously, we gotta go," said Truck, nodding toward the scanner. "Open it up."

"Wait. What do you mean, special circumstance?"

Truck suddenly looked uncomfortable. "I've said too much already." He anxiously tapped on the stainless steel door. "Let's go."

Penn stared at the guy for a second, wondering if he should proceed. But then what other choice did he have? Truck turned him and he placed his forehead on the rubber pad so the green beam moved over his eyes. The door slid open and they walked into what looked like a gowning room.

Penn knew what to do. The room was no larger than eight by ten and lined with racks containing an assortment of sealed jumpsuits ranging in color from white, yellow, orange, and red.

"Grab an orange suit," said Truck. "We're going deep."

"How deep?" said Penn, sifting through the plastic bags until he found a suit labeled LG for large.

"We'll land somewhere outside Las Alamos in just over an hour."

"The Laboratory?" asked Penn.

"Yes. That's where we'll part ways. I really can't afford to miss the start of my shift."

Penn opened the bag and put on his suit. "You're leaving me? What am I supposed to do?"

"You'll hook up with Badger."

"Bullshit," argued Penn. He knew Badger didn't exist. "That's a high-security research center. I can't just walk in there!"

"Yes, you can. Just think. What else do you know?"

Penn zipped the long front zipper, irritated that Truck would bring his protagonist into this. "Well, that's where they do nuclear research."

"What else?"

Penn shook his head, feeling his heart race. "It doesn't matter."

"Yes, it does. Think. What are they doing there?" insisted Truck. "What did Badger see there?"

Penn threw the bag in a trash receptacle and shouted, "Would you shut up! Badger isn't real!"

"Yes, he is. He's waiting for you."

"Impossible."

Penn turned toward the door where they came in, ready to exit. *This has gone too far. This guy's a whack job.* "I'm not stupid, Truck. You're obviously deranged."

Truck grabbed Penn's arm and jerked him to a stop. "I can't let you leave, Penn. He's waiting."

Penn yanked his arm free and rushed toward the eye scan, but Truck tackled him to the floor. They scuffled for a few seconds. Penn tried to squirm and punch his way loose, but Truck had been in far too many bar fights. He was solid—he gripped Penn like a boa constrictor.

Truck put him in a shoulder lock, a Jiu Jitsu move Penn had seen on Youtube, and one that was impossible to escape. "Say it! What do they do there?" demanded Truck, their sweaty faces within inches of each other. Penn could feel Truck's hot breath cascading his neck. "Before I deliver you, you have to know that this isn't a joke. You have to be prepared to walk in there and do what you're told."

"And if I don't want to?"

Truck was glaring at Penn, his furrowed brow expressing his frustration. "I can always leave you here, and let you figure it out. But you won't last the night."

Penn stared at Truck, still squirming, resisting, testing his opponent's resolve.

"It's real, Penn. Now answer the question: what do they do there?"

It wasn't a matter of what they say they do. It was more an issue of what Penn wrote about.

"They research nuclear powered tunnel boring equipment, among other things."

"And why do they do that?"

"To connect the dots," spouted Penn, reciting words verbatim from *Federal Underground*. "The dots are hives that house the subterranean race below. Connecting the dots is the Pentagon's way of keeping them under control and pressing our military might over their scattered colonies. The maglevs provide quick access from one hive to the next in case things turn sour."

Penn eyed Truck angrily, struggling to breathe. He couldn't fight any longer. Truck relaxed his grip and asked. "Who are they?"

Whatever makes you happy, thought Penn. *They're just words.* "The Nephilim… They're Serpents."

"And what do they want?"

Exasperated by the ludicrousness of his situation, Penn just let the words roll out of his tongue. "Earth... They want our planet."

•••

Jack Feigner, a geo-location analyst at the National Security Agency, logged into PRISM reluctantly. It was already after 5:00 pm and he had a dinner date planned with his wife and a few friends at the Trattoria Alberto in downtown Fort Meade. But when his old friend, Ted Gilmore from the US Naval Academy, had called up a favor, he had no choice but to stay over, despite his cravings for Alberto's fresh Maine Lobster.

He typed in the basic information Ted provided—name, phone number and provider, home address, etc—it only took a few minutes for the satellite and NYC video data to begin rushing in.

Last seen on camera, Penn Mitchell was apparently escorted into the NYC FBI field office by Elizabeth Ramsey. He then exited the building and headed north/northwest toward the Lincoln Tunnel, according to Liz's estimate, although Jack couldn't find any footage indicating that Penn had traveled on foot, again confirming Ted's story that the young man had somehow escaped through a tunnel system under the building. Sounded fishy, but not completely out of the question. After all, Ted was reliable, upstanding, a fellow Plebe—go Midshipmen!

Looking at the digitized image of New York's streets and bridges, Jack overlaid Penn's trail on top of the city's infrastructure digital blueprint. Unfortunately, the path taken didn't line up with Manhattan's current street works. Jack would have to dig deeper, cross-reference the route with other known pathways and dated maps.

•••

Gilmore had assigned four agents from the field office's Special Weapons and Tactical team to accompany Liz into the tunnels below. Penn and his compatriot were making fools of the FBI. They had already made such an impression that the case had come to the attention of the Assistant Director in charge, embarrassing Gilmore to no end. Questions would be asked. *Why did you detain him to begin with? Have you ever heard the term 'procedure'?*

As it turned out, the Assistant Director was aware of the mysterious door, and knew that it was reserved for the highest security and mobilization operations. He approved the team and immediately began the cumbersome process of attaining a warrant for Penn's arrest, all of his Dialed Number Records (DNR), and a phone tap wherever necessary: family, friends, etc. A civilian trespassing on government property and resisting arrest was only a starting point of the charges that would be filed. As it turns out, the New York

Office may have a genuine sleeper cell parked under their front door.

•••

Fully fortified, Liz and four members of the field office SWAT team had entered the tunnel and had descended down the shaft. When they reached the cave, they set up a base camp with battery-powered lighting, signal boosters, and a tactical headset system to ensure efficient communication. Liz donned a loaned set of SWAT gear that fit a little too loose, but it provided the protection and equipment she needed. The plan was to establish a base camp and hope the NSA would could detail Penn's possible route by the time they were ready to probe the tunnels. They did, and Gilmore had Jack on the line informing Liz to proceed to the tunnel all the way to the west.

"Copy that," said Liz. She clicked on her headlamp and hurried toward the entrance. "We're heading to tunnel number one now."

"Great," said Jack. "I've cross-referenced the information you gave me with our national database and found a tunnel system created under the direction of President Eisenhower. It appears the main tunnel comes to a dead end in three point seven miles from your current location."

"Copy," said Liz, picking up her pace. Five LED headlamps flashed across the sculpted stone and their combat boots pounded over the rough rock. The sound energized Liz, reminding her of her active days of service.

"Watch for forks in the trail," commanded Jack from his Maryland office. "They didn't have satellite back then, so they made a lot of wrong turns."

"Will do." She tapped her headpiece to communicate with the other four agents. Pointing to her left she said, "You two watch for branches on the left." Pointing to the right, she said, "You two look over there. They could be hiding in a cleft or an unfinished wing."

The agent and her four SWAT members continued running and observing every fissure and dimple in the tunnel, with Sig Saur 551 assault rifles oscillating with every movement. Liz thought about the creature she encountered, remembering its speed and agility. She didn't want to run into it again, but if she did, she was ready.

After several minutes of running down a steep decline, she heard a beeping noise in her headset. "Go ahead, Jack."

"Do you have a visual?"

"No, we're still diving. I'd guess we still have another mile and a half to go. Why don't you tag my cell phone so you can keep your sights on us?"

"I'll try. I'll get what I need from Gilmore."

"Copy," she said and then paused. "Wait." She lifted her right arm, commanding the others to stop. "Did you hear that?"

The agent closest to her said, "No."

"Listen..." Liz heard water dripping, and the tunnel drawing its breath. Then somewhere further in she heard voices. "We're getting close. Hurry!"

Liz and the others darted through the passage, their equipment and boots clattering as lights flashed across the rock. The voices grew louder, closer. A dim light appeared far off, and the shadows seemed to be dancing. No, scuffling. *We've got 'em,* thought Liz, imagining how she'd find Penn and his accomplice barricaded like test rats in a maze.

•••

Penn stopped moving—thought he heard something.

Truck's eyes turned toward the dark tunnel.

"Did you hear that?" asked Truck, his face white as a ghost.

"Someone's coming," whispered Penn. Anxiety filled his chest. He imagined Gilmore plucking out his fingernails, or waterboarding him to death.

Truck hopped to his feet, drenched in sweat. "Time to go, young man."

Penn watched Truck expertly insert his face in the eye scanner. Within seconds, a set of glass doors slid open and the runner turned and waved for Penn to follow. Penn jumped to his feet, matching Truck's sense of urgency. He ran through the doorway and entered what resembled a New York subway car, only much nicer and smaller. It looked like a giant pill. Truck charged into a cramped cockpit toward the front and frantically began touching the maglev's controls.

"Sit down and buckle up," barked Truck. "Put a strap over each shoulder. Six-point harness, just like a fighter jet."

Penn knew that and already started connecting the latches. "What are we doing?"

"Getting the hell out of here!" responded Truck.

The seats faced forward. The interior was perfectly cylindrical and finished with polished nickel. It looked exactly as Penn remembered in his dreams.

Truck's skin had turned white, his face sweating golf balls.

"This is bad," said Truck. "They're not supposed to be here."

"That's what I was thinking."

"Well how'd they get through the basement door?"

Penn cocked his neck and gave Truck a *how the hell am I supposed to know that* look.

Truck raced to his seat and nearly fell over, sliding across the floor as he raced to his seat, stopping briefly at the front row. "We have thirty seconds and this thing's gone." He grabbed an aviation helmet hanging on a hook and tossed it at Penn, and said, "Hurry. Put that on."

Penn caught the helmet and pulled it over his head with barely enough time to tighten the strap.

A large digital clock hanging from the ceiling for all the passengers to see began flashing and a digitized female voice began speaking. She had a British accent and counted thirty seconds until departure. "Twenty-eight... twenty-seven... twenty-six"

When the power source kicked on, Penn felt the train lift just a tad– as if it were floating on a bed of air, which is exactly what was happening. Although he didn't totally understand the physics of the magnetic levitation technology, he certainly could appreciate it. But the whole experience felt like déjà vu...only in the book, he called it a leviton. From the looks of things, he thought it was going to shoot like a rocket.

To his left, the maglev door began closing and Penn could hear Liz commanding them to stop and put their hands up.

Penn clasped the final shoulder harness. Liz was getting closer, and she had company—armed SWAT.

"Twenty... nineteen... eighteen..." Penn could hear the power ramping up, screaming outside.

Liz slid her gun across the stone floor and jammed it between the sliding door and the frame, preventing it from closing. The other agents helped pry it open until they made their way into the holding room.

The contoured maglev door closed, sealing Truck and Penn inside. In an instant, Penn felt his ears pop. "What was that?"

Truck latched his belt and secured his helmet and said, "It's an air pressure thing, don't worry about it," and then his eyes opened wide. "Get down!"

Penn followed Truck's gaze. Liz was pounding on the sliding door just feet away from the maglev. She pointed to the eye scanner to the right and one of the SWAT guys shot it several times. The door refused to open, so she commanded them to shoot the glass. The agents backed up several feet and began firing.

Penn could hear the bullets exploding, although the blasts were muffled. Round after round, the 45 cal. ammo pummeled the protective barrier that separated the Agents from the Maglev tunnel until it splintered and eventually broke open.

"Twelve... eleven...ten..."

Liz and her team were immediately blasted by a windstorm that had filled the tunnel due to the difference in air pressure. The female agent pushed through the gale force and trudged over the glass blanketing the concrete floor. She stopped abruptly at the maglev hatch, her face pressed against the thick glass, staring at Penn.

"Stop," she shouted. "Or we'll shoot."

The other agents looked puzzled, like they'd seen a ghost. The confusion in their eyes made them look more like cub scouts than FBI SWAT—mouths gaping—speechless. Penn could relate. The day had become the most terrifying of his life, and it was about to get worse.

Truck waved his arms, trying to warn Liz to back off, but she started pounding on the window with her rifle, warning the fugitives. Inside the train, the British voice said, "Prepare for departure... Six...five...four..."

The floor began to vibrate and Penn could hear a deep hum quickly escalate into a high-pitch resonance. The lights dimmed briefly from the amperage load. One of the agents pulled Liz back from the maglev and into the concourse. She looked determined, arms flailing, teeth grinding. Penn watched her call his name one last time as the howling gale swept through her hair and beat her back.

Penn could feel his heart rattling as the train's energy pulsing through his flesh.

"The magnets are generating thrust," said Truck, gripping his armrest with white-knuckled suspense. "The current's loading... Get ready!"

"Three... two... one..." and Penn was soaring at supersonic speeds.

Chapter 21
Clean Up

From the office of: General Murphy Ward
Simpson
7, March 1945

General Dodson,
After three years of daily interaction
with the subterranean creatures, I've
concluded that they are not what they
present themselves to be. Our men and
the civilian contractors working below
find themselves at odds with them and
many have disappeared after completing
remote assignments. We have signed
multiple agreements with the Grays
regarding boundaries, working hours,
etc., to no avail. Please advise.

   The Grays are rarely satisfied with
their demands and constantly requesting
additional supplies and biological
material above and beyond our current
agreements (see material req. below).
Consequently, I highly recommend that

the US Army bolster its presence here and in the surrounding territories. They consistently prove themselves more numerous than we imagined, more cunning than we feared, and buried deeper under the crust than we thought possible.

Regarding their origins, we are learning a great deal, although I am getting reports of inconsistencies. The archeologists have reason to believe their annals appear remarkably similar to ancient texts they've seen among ancient Babylonians, Mayans, or possibly early Mesopotamians. Therefore, however great our advances in technology coming from these beings, I am beginning to question whether they can be trusted. While the others under my direct authority put forth efforts to glean what they can in their respective fields, I will hone my attention on their virtues.

Please note the following materials that have been requested by General Assur, who is a Gray elder (and much taller than the younger ones, by the way) and scientist of some kind. He has promised to show our engineers how to construct the electric typing board and glass picture maker I sent you. General Assur informed me that the inner workings will prove groundbreaking for our race.

Regards,
General Murphy Ward Simpson

Materials Requested 6, March 1945
32 oz. 2 mm dia. Gold wire
11 oz. 2 mm dia. Aluminum wire
500 lbs. white sand
Additional bottled canisters of Boron, Nitrogen, Hydrogen, Phosphine, Helium, S_1H_4, and A_5H_3.

Davenport had received orders from Kirtland Air Force Base to conduct a ground search near Pagosa Springs. High frequency radar had indicated that an unidentified flying object had traveled in and around Dulce, New Mexico and further up into Southern Colorado. It was possible the Grays had sent out another craft into US airspace without authorization. The Sergeant Major was responsible for clearing every flight in and out of the base, and he'd made a point that they would adhere to all security agreements. The last unauthorized flight ended with a heated verbal exchange and three small Grays in body bags— Davenport's way of saying, "Fuck with me and I'll serve you 'Serpent Sushi'". Another show of defiance would not bode well for the tenacious bastards.

Davenport sat at his desk—mission control— knowing these things needed to be handled with care. The Grays could be dangerous underneath. If an unsuspecting human traveled too far into their terrain, they'd drag the *Homo sapiens* to the depths of the underground and present him or her as an offering to their elders, like worker ants carrying a breadcrumb to the queen. If they'd sniff out a human who'd ventured deeper than Level Four, they'd devour the stinking carcass like piranhas. Davenport knew why they never showed their teeth. He knew what was behind those little slits they called a mouth. Evolution was funny that way. You don't have to show your razor choppers if you communicate telepathically. They waited to reveal the real threat, therefore, after trust was gained.

The tension resembled gang wars: casualties, drive-bys, truces, and urban warfare. When they took to the air, they were making a statement; either they were hungry and the Department of Defense was not meeting their growing quota for human flesh, or they needed more (unauthorized) genetic material to continue their tests—tests that would one day allow their kind to be better suited to life above: to the swings in temperature, and heat from the sun. Their needs were real, and so were those of the DoD, but the daily tensions between species rarely ended well.

Davenport was aware of this. He sent out the same team that had handled the Sandy issue a few days back. Strong men. Capable. Dependable suck-asses. He'd hoped they'd return with nothing, anticipating a false report. Made things easier. A day without tin-foil-hat crazies sniffing around allowed him to manage the construction projects and expanding security needs unabated. But if Chirkoff found evidence of an abduction or mutilation, the team would have to clean it up. They would conduct a thorough investigation, which would inevitably require a face-to-face confrontation with General Zahn, a tall Gray that even Davenport feared.

Yes, a thorough investigation could be required. *But there will NOT be mutiny or dissension inside this mountain,* thought Davenport. *Not on my watch. Not now. I'll stake my life on that.*

•••

Chirkoff and Prevot, both Blackstone security contractors, followed the military convoy to the Pagosa hillside. The satellite coordinates led them right to the incident marked with one dead corpse. Chirkoff had seen this many times over; it was Privot's first. Chirkoff knew the difference between the techniques used in collecting DNA samples and the cut marks that were a sign of indignation. Cutting the lips out, he'd learned, communicated that the Grays had been offended by someone's words, probably Davenport's; the hung-dung cowboy, *glupo kovboy*, who had no idea how to treat the woman.

Having recovered many bodies like this before, Chirkoff felt his emotions progress from cold indifference to an anger stirred by a sense of invasion, an awareness that these visitors should not be here. *Not on our planet, anyway.* But the money was too damn good to not take the job.

Glancing at the scene, he spotted several indicators that something had gone wrong. A shotgun lay in a thicket of grass. The glass bowl on a lantern had shattered and the oil had leaked into a mound of dirt, leaving a dark stain of charred soil. One human and one cow, separated like Shakespearean lovers. Still, the assassination was child's play. He'd seen worse.

Bag 'em and tag 'em. Easy. *No problem.*

Standard procedure dictated that they couldn't report the man's death. *Leave the beast take the boy,* as they say. Even the UN knew that you could never leave a human mutilation in the hands of civilians. They're smart. They'd catch on. Local news would have a heyday. Always confiscate the bodies, craft, and any evidence at all costs. Browbeat witnesses if need be. No one talks. Period.

Chirkoff flexed his bulldog jaw muscles, restraining the bile in his throat, and took at least three-dozen photos of the lipless, one-eyed man lying crumpled on the ground with his pet cow. *Mouth mutilated. Eye Missing. Surgical incisions in all the right places.* The other soldiers collected hair, blood, and clothing samples, eventually erasing all signs that the man had ever been there.

The Russian sniffed. He could smell the aliens and their sulfur cologne. The Grays were here—the ancient race that laid claim to Earth—warriors of the underground. The creatures were scientists, biologists, sadists. Oh, and pilots, too, artists in the craft of anti-gravity. And yet, they were submissive to something else, something worse—mysterious beings that ruled the underworld far deeper than Levels Four and Five and far beyond Chirkoff's pay grade. All he knew was the Grays lived a long time, maybe hundreds or thousands of years. The young Grays were the clichéd little guys with big eyes and big heads. But as they grew older, they slowly grew taller and stronger, their skin grew tough and scaly, and their eyes turned in, giving a sinister appearance. If the elder race told the small Grays to "get us meat," they did as they were told, taking a worker from the underground, or sneaking above and snatching an unsuspecting human. This is why abductees and the military saw the small Grays more often. They were the worker class while they were young. If they survived, they might get lucky and live long enough to sprout up and join the ranks of the fighting class. If they continued in their good fortune, they might live to be a few hundred years old and rule over the masses.

They were here all right, thought Privott, but why they came would remain a mystery. What this man was doing out here alone confounded the thick-boned security professional. Although the closer he looked and the more pictures he snapped, he began to believe there was a third wheel at the *partiya*. Old one-eye lying on the ground like a twenty-first century Pompeiian probably wasn't carrying a flashlight, gun *and* a lantern. Someone was missing. The one-eyed victim had a flashlight in his hand. The lantern was ten or twelve feet away. Someone else went up. Had to. And that someone was probably with the Grays right now. And Davenport would need to know. That missing person could be used as a bargaining tool if he was still alive. *Give us the man*, Davenport would say, *and more of your technology, and we'll keep the nukes at bay, for now*. Wouldn't be the first time—probably not the last.

The body was bagged, and the cow left to fortify the old wives' tales that made the fringe theorists giddy, or drum up the idea that a Satanic cult had reaped the cow's organs for some dark and twisted ritual. Organic half-truths and rumors were always more effective than lies. A swift and tidy clean up— ahem, cover up—that's what Chirkoff did best.

Prevot came running out of the trees, pointing excitedly up the hill. He showed Chirkoff the campsite. There were two men—confirmed. *Bastards drank all the bourbon!*

"Clean it up. Leave no traces," insisted Chirkoff.

Prevot complied.

Davenport would not be happy; not that he cared about the abducted schmuck. He expected everyone to follow his rules to the tee—aliens included. No one was exempt. The Russian understood that more than anyone. He'd experienced his share of Davenport's fear-based leadership—gun barrel in mouth, pinky finger in vise-grips. Chirkoff was a fast learner. Those who weren't found themselves down in Level Five, maybe Six.

When the campsite was cleared out, Chirkoff shifted the Hummer into gear and the line of military vehicles disappeared before the sun had crested the horizon.

Chapter 22
Li'l Vigilante

Liz watched the train propel forward until it became little more than a blur. Then a blast of air hit her with a fury, taking her breath away. When the train had disappeared, she stood in the middle of the four SWAT members, and the expressions on their faces asked the same boggling question: *What the hell just happened?*

Stunned by Penn's escape, she barely remembered to call Jack on the radio. She fumbled for her headset controls; fearful of what Gilmore would have to say about this.

"Where is he, Jack?"

She could only hear static.

"Jack?"

"I… [static]… know…[static]… something's wrong… I… [static]… and can't seem to…"

"He's gone. Are you following him?"

"No," replied Jack. "…do…I repeat… [static]… not have… [static]…visual?"

Liz sighed, exasperated. She clicked the mouthpiece and said, "No. He's gone." Her arms dropped to her side, exhausted. She perused the other agent's reactions. They looked as flabbergasted as she felt. And they didn't know Penn. He was just another criminal to them—a delinquent. They hadn't looked into his eyes and questioned his guilt or innocence. They hadn't seen the honesty in his gaze, his simplicity, and ignorance regarding the world that had filled the pages of his book. Federal Underground was fiction to him. None of this was real, or so he seemed to think. A kid with a freakish imagination is all he was. Or at least, that's what Liz hoped to discover—and Badger, as far as the kid was concerned, was just a figment of Penn's imagination, nothing more than a coincidence. And yet...here she stood, watching the very story Penn had drafted not more than a year earlier play out before her eyes in real time.

The setting was evident—tangible—all of it. The maglev. The caves. The stink.

It didn't seem possible that Badger would have any part in this. *No way.* She regretted implicating her ex-husband in her foolish quest for answers. *Who cares?* She thought briefly. *It's just a book. It isn't real.* That's where her head was while questioning Penn upstairs. What the government does behind closed doors had no bearing on her life as long as it wouldn't affect her and her daughter. You can't stop the occasional oversight or mismanagement in an organization as big as the U.S. Government. She understood that; she wasn't that anal about exacting justice. She had even felt a little guilty for bringing the kid in. And now, looking back, she was better off without the book. She was much happier before Penn Mitchell invaded her life—her Saturdays in Strawberry Fields, when life was easier; eight-hour workdays, an occasional lunch with Angie whenever she would catch a break in her studies.

Life was easier then. Ignorance, bliss. Now everything would change.

She was a mother, and Angie still needed her (didn't matter if she was nineteen), although she'd become more self-reliant after two years at NYU. Nonetheless, she was her baby. How would her little girl handle her return to the Field Agent lifestyle? How would her decision to pursue Penn affect her daughter's studies? Liz wasn't sure if she could bear the weight of such a burden. But then she wasn't sure if she could handle knowing the truth about what's happening underground, possibly all across the United States, without losing her sanity. Could she be that plastic working mother who she'd seen a thousand times on their way to Wall Street, strutting their pretty little asses in their pretty little business suits and Gucci bags, without a care for anything that didn't impact their morning coffee and house on the lake? She'd experienced a new reality that she didn't think possible, already witnessing a small part of the nightmarish truth in Penn Mitchell's fiction. Could she turn away and pretend it didn't exist?

No. She could not.

Liz wasn't wired that way. Never was. Even her mother knew she was more predisposed to fact-finding and law and order than most of her peers. So no, she couldn't live and let live in this case. Meredith Kingsbury discovered Elizabeth Hope Kingsbury's bent toward social morality when she'd received a call from a corrections officer in New York's Department of Juvenile Justice. When officer Sheets called, she had Elizabeth, a feisty thirteen-year old at the time, in custody because she'd hospitalized fifteen-year old, Manny Franklin, and was charged with aggravated assault. Elizabeth claimed—and it was later affirmed by the New York County Juvenile Court system—that Manny had strangled and attempted to rape a young girl behind James Crawford Middle School. Elizabeth claimed to have witnessed the assault as it was happening, and immediately came to the girl's aid.

Apparently Manny had tricked the victim into meeting him between the school's loading dock and trash compactor, where he'd promised to give her a free sample of marijuana. When he didn't produce the weed, she turned to leave, calling the punk ass a few choice names, consequently angering the ambitious drug dealer. Manny proceeded to choke her from behind, with his bare hands, until she passed out. When she, the unnamed party, collapsed onto the filthy concrete, Manny attempted to rape her seconds before Elizabeth showed up.

At that time, Elizabeth was an aid for Mrs. Shanks, the 8th-grade art teacher, and was sent out to discard a cardboard box full of scraps and used art supplies when she stumbled upon the crime in progress. She quickly responded by jumping down into the narrow space between the dock and the compactor, yanking Manny off the victim by grabbing his t-shirt collar and rear belt loop, and repeatedly slammed his face into the commercial equipment, breaking his snout in two places. When Elizabeth released the perpetrator to assist the victim, he fell on his nose after losing consciousness, breaking the cartilage in yet a third location. At that time, a janitor entered the scene and hurried to assist the wounded. Neither of the infirmed could speak, and Elizabeth was the only one standing, so her guilt was assumed at first analysis. However, justice prevailed.

That's when Elizabeth discovered her place in this world. The day judge Branson C. Billbeck declared Elizabeth Hope both innocent and a hero changed the course of her life forever, navigating her education and extracurricular activities toward criminal justice, and ultimately The Federal Bureau of Investigation,

Badger, and her daughter. Everything about her life was birthed from that one decisive moment when she chose vigilance over ambiguity. She rarely told the story, usually because for her that day was traumatic, cutting open some of her early emotional scars (none of which matched those left by her mother's verbal treachery), but she did suffer from a mild case of post-traumatic stress disorder just the same. She rarely told the story because she felt it was equally wrong to brag about her heroism as the crime Manny had committed. So she kept the memory buried, even from Angie; it only resurfaced when she was faced with a similar challenge—to choose vigilance over passivity. She could cut her losses and leave the case in the hands of the DHS or CIA where it belonged. That would be easier. That would be the maternal thing to do, to be available to her daughter and end her career with her pre-retirement desk job that bored the living shit out of her. But could she do that? The underground would nag at her the rest of her life. Not knowing the extent of what existed below would torture her, let alone the fact that Penn's tale (and Badger's role in all of it) appeared to have at least a bit of truth based on what had just happened. The tunnel, the maglev, the eye scanners, and let's not forget that thing she'd witnessed climbing on the rocks, had made a huge impact on her state of mind and on her understanding of reality.

Time slipped away as her thoughts stole her focus. One of the SWAT guys gripped her arm and asked if she was okay. When she snapped back into the moment, she said, "Yeah. I'm fine," and then she made the choice. That quickly, she'd decided to pursue Penn and his story, hoping to find Badger as a consequence. Vincent knew her. He knew about Manny. He knew what she was made of more than anyone else, more than her own mother who'd nursed her as a child. If anything in her life was worth reclaiming, it was Badger, her ex-life partner. If justice needed to be served anywhere, it was here under the soil, where something dark and mysterious transcended everything about who and what we are as humans. And if Badger had to choose sides, he'd choose the side of truth. Liz was sure of that.

"Come on," she said to the men encircling her. "This is bigger than us."

She turned and marched into the darkness, and the men followed her back through the winding tunnels, base camp, and up the ladder. She called her daughter from her office. It was time to tell Angie that her mother was going back into the field.

Chapter 23
Road Block

Penn's cheeks vibrated with the thrum of the train. On occasion, the g-forces thrust his body to one side or the other depending on the direction of the curves in the track, but for the most part, the maglev remained on a linear course. They passed mainly through darkness. Sometimes the tunnel's safety lights flashed through the glass ceiling. Eventually, the hum and vibrations put Penn to sleep, until Miss United Kingdom called over the PA system.

"Emergency stop in ten seconds. Ten... nine... eight..."

"Are we there?" Penn asked, groggily.

"I don't think so," said Truck. He glanced at his watch, and then surveyed the tunnel, peering through the glass windows that lined the sides of the maglev. Penn noticed the concern in Truck's eyes when the old man gripped Penn's forearm. "If anything happens... go with your gut. If the Subterranes find you—"

"You mean the aliens?" joked Penn.

"Aliens, little demons. Call 'em what you want... If they find you, run."

"Hey," said Penn, sitting up. "Why are we stopping, anyway?"

"Something's wrong," said Truck.

The digital voice interrupted, "Four... three... two..." Pneumatic brakes squealed and Penn's body thrust forward. The harness dug deep into his shoulders and groin.

"Warning" touted the voice. "Rail blockage. Call the emergency number on the screen for assistance."

Penn looked at Truck. He didn't move. He looked like he was listening for something. The interior lights flickered off. Red emergency lights flickered on.

"What's going on, Truck?"

"I don't know. Maybe the ceiling collapsed."

"Warning. Rail blockage. Call the emergency number on the screen for assistance."

Penn felt panic rip through his spine. The PA system scratched with static. An alarm blared inside the car, and inside of Penn. "What's blocking the track?" he asked frantically.

Truck unbuckled, and Penn watched his every move as the runner quietly stepped into the cockpit and turned a dial, intensifying the headlights.

"Dear... God." Truck said, his voice trembling.

"What?" asked Penn with a shiver. "What is it?"

Truck didn't respond. He stood still in front of the control center.

"What's wrong?"

"If you're a praying man," said Truck. "...you better get prayin'."

"Why?" Penn unbuckled and raced to the front. "What's up? What are you looking at?"

"Get back in your seat, Penn."

Trucks tried to push Penn away, but it was too late. Penn saw them.

"Wha—what are they?" asked Penn, barely able to speak.

He couldn't move. His limbs felt glacial. His eyes bore through the lighted haze beaming into the tunnel. There were so many—hundreds maybe. The creatures from his dreams had swarmed the maglev tunnel. Penn turned his eyes slowly, avoiding sudden movements, absorbing the terrifying sight. Small Grays and their taller counterparts stood near the nose of the train like a herd of cattle crossing the road. Their ribs protruded through their gray flesh, their stomachs looked tight and convulsing. Large, hypnotic eyes seemed empty, emotionless. Their feeble structure and slender limbs obscured the maleficence in their detached expressions. Penn knew they weren't there for coffee and donuts. Even the little ones—the small Grays Penn wrote about—looked angry. Their four-foot short bodies seemed so innocent, incapable of harming anything. Penn could break all four of their skinny fingers in a single snap, he was quite sure of it. Their oversized eyes were hypnotic, leaving him entranced by their otherworldly attraction.

"I hope to God they scatter," said Truck. "They usually move on."

Penn watched in amazement. This couldn't be happening. The Grays defied the headlight as if some kind of screen protected their eyes. Not one of them blinked. Their chests raised in slow sequence. Their large heads seem to balance miraculously upon their skinny necks.

Penn remembered they needed less oxygen; another reason why the caves worked. They seemed perfectly suited for an underground existence. They looked so pale, so bizarre. And as he stared at the creatures standing before him, Penn suddenly felt out of place, intuitively aware that he shouldn't be there.

"Come out of the train," said a voice in Penn's head.

"Whoa!" said Penn, turning toward Truck. "Did you hear that?"

"Don't listen to them," responded Truck. "They have telepathic abilities."

"Do not be afraid," the voice said. *"We'll help you fix the train. You are safe."*

"Truck? What do we do?" Penn quickly scanned each window on both sides and the small window in the rear. "They're everywhere," he said. "And they're moving closer."

"Do not be afraid," Penn noticed the voice sounded like his father. *"You are safe."*

"They're lying, Penn," Truck said mechanically, "Don't trust them. Never trust them."

"Penn Mitchell. You need to go home. Let us take you there. Your mother is worried about you."

"They're touching the maglev, Truck," said Penn, hands pressed against one of the side windows. "Get us outta here!"

Truck didn't move. His hands lay deathly still on the touch screen.

"Turn it on," shouted Penn. "What are you waiting for? They're all over us!"

"They're lying, Penn. Don't trust them. Never trust them."

"Truck?" Something about Truck's voice seemed off. Penn grabbed Truck's shoulder. "You already said that."

Truck stared blankly at Penn. "Don't trust them. Never trust them."

Penn spun Truck around. The guy's eyes were glossed over, in a daze, hypnotized or something. "Truck! Wake up!" Penn shook his shoulders incessantly. "Snap out of it!"

"Never trust them."

"Bullcrap!" Penn realized he was on his own. He looked down at the dashboard, resisting the voices in his skull. The controls seemed simple enough. *Touch screen.* He knew to utilize the override command. That was in the book. *What else do you know? Think, Penn. Think!*

Start.

"Okay, I got this..."

Continue Trip?

"Yes."

Warning: Track Blockage.

Track Cleared?

Yes or No

"Yes."

Override Alarm?

Yes.

Are all passengers secured?

Yes.

"Wait. No!"

He pushed his zombified friend toward his seat and buckled the six-point lock. Truck's head fell to one side from the weight of the helmet as soon as Penn put it on.

"I don't know what they've done to you, buddy," said Penn. "But you better perk up."

Penn ran back to the cockpit and touched *Yes—All passengers secured.*

Start maglev?

Yes.

"Yes. Yes. YES!" Penn shouted as he hit the screen over and over.

Penn heard a scratching noise. He looked up. The creatures were climbing onto the front window, scaling the inch-thick glass ceiling and landscape windows.

"Oh, my god!"

He ran to his seat and started buckling himself in.

Miss UK started counting. "Thirty seconds until take off. Twenty-nine. Twenty-eight..."

His hands shook so bad he could hardly clasp the fourth latch. It pressed tight into his crotch.

Clunk, clump, thud.

What is that? Penn looked at the ceiling. They were creeping overhead, dead eyes staring directly at him, advancing from all directions. An elder Gray made his way to the top and looked down through the glass. Its eyes were threatening, its smirk menacing. And then it showed its teeth—all of them. The thing slowly opened its broad green mouth, quivering with hunger pangs, salivating at the sight of the young author. Saliva stretched across its teeth and then dripped down on the glass.

Penn peed a little in his pants. His entire body started shaking with fear. The thing pounded with a rock and it felt like thunder booming overhead. Its thin, black tongue lapped its thin lips, coursing over twenty jagged little teeth.

The last latch clicked into place and the creature slammed his fist on the glass again, followed by other peals of thunder that clapped over the entire surface of the train.

Truck finally began to stir.

Apparently, the Grays couldn't multitask—the telepathy came to a stop while they were climbing.

"Thirteen... twelve... eleven..."

The glass broke in the rear of the car and Penn nearly tore through his seat belt. Tongues hissed. Throats clicked as the hungry aliens tasted the air inside the pod with their tongues. Long, four-fingered hands pounded everywhere. Penn was living his nightmare. He strained to look toward the back. An angry Tall Gray's hands stretched inside, groping, tearing at the glass, and shredding the canvas on the ceiling. A sea of dead eyes swarmed each pane of glass like piranhas desiring the fleshy bodies inside the tank.

"Eight... seven... six..."

The electric hum revved up. Red lights dimmed. The train's energy pulsed. Magnets generated thrust and the current hit maximum amperage.

"Come on!" said Penn, hoping time would speed up just this once.

Truck shook his head, blinking, unaware.

Penn looked back at the opening in the ceiling. There were two arms inside and the head was crowning through the broken glass.

"Shit!" Penn shouted. He could see its pale skin. Sharp teeth. It was coming.

"Four... three...."

Serpentine hands pounded everywhere—sounded like popcorn in a kettle. Glass splintered. The aluminum skin that wrapped the maglev beat like an ancient war song. The ceiling dented from drumming footsteps. Large and tiny hands alike stretched through the opening in the back, aching to feed, fighting for position.

"Two... one..."

Something fell inside, landing with a thud. When Penn turned to see what had happened, the maglev thrust forward and his neck whipped back, throwing him against his seat, allowing only a brief glimpse of what had entered the high-speed shuttle. The large Gray fell to the floor, and its arms were bleeding profusely, gashed from birthing through the glass. In an instant he saw a stream of scarlet pour on the malnourished being. After it landed, it lifted its head and immediately turned its eyes toward Penn, but the train went supersonic, and the thing flew against the back wall.

Chapter 24
Caged

Verl Mickelson knew the peanuts were a bad idea. His stomach felt unnaturally painful. It burned and ached so badly that he awoke from a dead sleep and found a gaping hole in his gut the size of a softball. He tried to touch the wound, but felt a tearing sensation in his midsection. His body shivered with fever. Muscles and fat lay open, exposed. Yet, despite the discomfort, he wrapped himself with his arms, instinctively warming himself. It wasn't until he felt the hair on his bare chest that he knew he was naked. The shock of this realization caused him to notice the damp limestone beneath his body. He could barely move his neck. The pain was unbearable. But he turned his eyes. Puddles of water accumulated from the constant dripping that could be heard but not seen. He had no idea the liquid was infected with bat urine. Unaware of the dangers, the urge to drink caused him to dip his finger and wet his tongue.

As he moved, a stone pressed against his hip, and he moaned in agony. He shimmied forward despite the discomfort, grinding over skin and bone. Suffering was the only option. What little relief he felt resulted from exhaling and whimpering. Doing so took his mind off the pain shooting from his innards and bleeding stomach.

In that moment of quiet, after breathing out, and when his voice had gone silent, he could hear others wailing in the distance. Some were close. Others seemed miles away. So when he sniffled through his congested nose and blew out a glob of bloody snot that trailed down his lips and chin, he wept uncontrollably, imagining he'd died and gone to Hell, never to see his family again. The screams were terrifying. Could he be next? What was happening to those poor souls out there in the darkness? Sounded like their skin was being torn from their backs. The screaming, ear-piercing shrills were more frightening than the not-so-distant memory of the aliens carrying him out of their craft and into a mother-ship of some kind. But this didn't look like a spaceship; it looked like a cave.

Must've died out there on the mountainside. Gone straight to Hell's what happened. All those nights at the Gentlemen's Club are finally catching up with me, and God has laid my iniquities upon me just like the preacher said He would. Oh, Lord, what will become of my boys, girls, and dear wife? I never meant to say those awful things. And the sluts at Rockie's Roadside Romp meant nothing to me. Just a cheap thrill's all.

"Forgive me, Lord Jesus!" Verl said, muffled due to his missing lips. *Shoulda listened to the preacher when that revival come to town a few weeks back.*

The world had closed in on the plowman. The stark reality of his condition had brought his life to bear in that cold and lonely moment. His wife and six children were far removed from the dungeon where he lay crumpled in a mass of bleeding blubber. The drop of water had already dried on his tongue and that seemed like a big deal at the moment. But he couldn't help to think of his middle daughter, September, who had recently been dumped by her shit-for-brains boyfriend. Verl began to sob as he lay there quivering, remembering how angry she got when he lectured her about how young she was, and how she had her whole life to find Mr. Righty Pants. He promised he'd be there when that day came, to give her soul-mate his blessing and walk her down the aisle, while autumn leaves fell all around September in the fall wedding she always dreamed of. But that obviously wasn't going to happen unless St. Peter walked down into this dungeon himself and stole his pal, Verl, from the devil's grip.

Verl's man boobs jiggled with each whimper while every one of his children came to mind: Daisy, his precious towheaded two-year-old, who'd never know her father from a squirt of piss, and Lucas, his star soccer player. Mazy, his little eighth-grade Einstein, didn't quite make honor roll, but she sure as hell tried. Frankie, as pitted as his face had become, was still destined to play for the Broncos. September, named after his favorite season. And finally, Juan, an adopted son, but he loved him just the same.

Verl thought of all the lost opportunities he'd had to show them his love. So many regrets. And what about Bobby Lee? What the hell happened to him? The screaming coming from the darkness was sure to drive him nuts. Was Bobby Lee out there? Could he be in Hell, too? The reality of his imprisonment brought him to the brink of insanity.

He attempted to shout, "Help!" with no articulation (because his lips were gone) and blood sprayed out of his mouth while he sniveled and wailed, attempting to crawl to the edge of his cell. Inch by inch, he dragged his sack of bones across the jagged rocks that gnawed at his flesh. He slid closer to the steel bars and his cheeks, shoulders, side, hip, thighs, and feet slunk behind like a wooly worm patiently working its way across a busy street. Body fluids trailed behind, but his eyes remained focused on the crimson streak that passed in front of his chamber. It looked damp—fresh—steaming in the cool air. Chunks and bits of flesh soaked in pools of the vital fluid left behind by someone or something that was probably important to someone else. Like Verl, their life had meaning, a purpose.

How many are there? Oh, Lord, he prayed silently, *help me. Jesus, please.*

Through steel rods and iron bars that formed a square opening no bigger than four feet by four feet, he peered out beyond the bloody footpath and into the vast space he didn't know existed a few seconds ago. With his fingers clinching the gate, he pulled himself closer still and gazed at an endless wall of prison cells just like his, illuminated by hundreds of glowing balls scattered between layer upon layer of gated cubicles equally spaced throughout the monstrous crypt. Looked like the little nightlights Mazy kept near her bed. From his cockroach perspective, the stony coops seemed to go on indefinitely, and he could only assume the same number of dungeons populated his side as well. In cage after cage he saw silhouettes of human bodies, some moving some not, some bleeding, some dead or dying. He wouldn't swear to it, but some of the captives seemed individually contained while others appeared to be stored in groups. Prone to high blood pressure on a good day, his heart began to beat irregularly and that pain in his chest spiked even harder than the last time. When he heard footsteps coming in his direction, he tried to slither backward into a corner, to remain out of sight, unnoticed, but he didn't move fast enough. Whoever approached had stopped in front of his doorway. Verl knew to keep his head down. *Don't look. You know better than that, dummy. You've seen enough horror flicks to know not to look upon your captors unless spoken to.*

What Verl knew and what he wanted were two different things. In the face of assured destruction, he pressed his left eye closed and slowly raised his right. The first thing he noticed was the bloody floor had an orange, flickering glow. Although he dared not look up, he could feel the heat from a torch burning only a few feet away. He heard the cage rattle and then it squeaked open, followed by a splash of something that drenched his face. Whatever stood there threw something on the floor. Probably food. He could use it. Anything sounded good at the moment, although he feared it would literally go right through him. So, as not to offend, he peered at the puddle of bat piss and reached out to grab his meal, but recoiled when he realized it was an eyeball with a tail of tissue still attached.

The gate closed abruptly and Verl's captor silently walked away.

Disgusted, Verl vomited all over himself, gagging and almost drowning in his own puke and blood. After a coughing fit that lasted several minutes, followed by an intense burning in his midsection and throat, his vision blurred and his head rolled to the floor. The last thought he had before he passed out, aside from wishing he'd looked up to see who had opened the gate, was that that green-hazel iris looked an awful lot like Bobby Lee Reynolds'.

Chapter 25
Incoming

Alvarez arrived at the Crossing security office at exactly 1645 hours with plans to meet Dean Jones, the new recruit from New York City. According to his official file, the guy was supposed to be a computer wiz out of Texas A & M, who'd spent a year or so working for the FBI, but had recently been recruited by the Dulce tech team. Apparently, the kid had a secret level clearance. That's what was in the file, anyway. Odd for such a youngster to reach such heights, but it happens. Alvarez would intercept the kid at the Crossing, a maglev junction between Dulce and Las Alamos.

This wasn't an unusual pick up; scientists, engineers, government officials, and dignitaries received private escorts in and out of the underground on a monthly basis. If Alvarez wasn't the direct escort, he coordinated the tours with the bureaucrat's security liaison. On this occasion, he was expected to deliver the kid via underground transport to Dulce upon clearing the first checkpoint, but something had gone wrong with the delivery. The MCC (Midwest Control Center) out of Grissom Air Force Base in central

Indiana had reported a problem in the maglev system. Apparently, the car was on course to the Crossing but stopped for several minutes, which was highly unusual. Not a surprise; accidents happen. Maintenance issues arise without warning. But a sentinel event such as this was never taken lightly.

Alvarez was a regular at the Crossing, located between Dulce and Las Alamos, so he passed through security without any trouble. The process was tedious—stripping down, weighing in, followed by a full-body scan—but they processed him faster than normal because he was a regular.

The electricians were ready to de-energize the track if needed. The engineers in Las Alamos Central Control planned to manually decelerate the train, while the maglev was still several miles away, hoping to prevent a crash near the sensitive nuclear testing grounds. Worst-case scenario, Alvarez would take a team into the tunnel and retrieve Dean Jones by hand. Until then, he remained on a direct phone line with the engineers, waiting for his orders.

•••

"They're traveling much slower than normal," said Luke Martin, an electrical engineer and programmer, who supervised the Las Alamos and surrounding tunnel systems from his wheelchair and large-screen master control.

"Copy that," responded Alvarez, setting his backpack on the ground. "Standing by." He looked at the two dipshit security officers that were assigned to him, Thing One and Thing Two. They were too busy with their smartphones to realize there was a problem. Black slacks, silver ties, shiny black shoes, and a badge on their shoulders was all they had going for them. *Security? Pfft. Hardly.*

"Good. I'd rather stop the mag before it crosses the New Mexico border, but that's probably a little overkill. Don't you think, Alvarez?"

"Right," said Alvarez. "I'm not interested in hiking cross-country."

"What, you don't think I can land the pill on your front porch?" said Luke.

"Depends."

"On what?"

"On how fast it's going," Alvarez said matter-of-factly.

Luke laughed. "I've stopped a mag on a dime going four eighty. I think I can handle two fifty."

"We'll see about that."

"Is that a challenge?"

"Affirmative."

"Well, Alvarez, you can take your hiking boots off. He's only thirty-seven miles out. Be at the Crossing in nine minutes *if* we don't put the brakes on too soon."

"What's it take to get him within a mile?"

"No can do. Gotta shut off power with one minute left. If everything goes to shit, he'll need one hell of an airbag."

"And where will that put him?"

"Probably throw him through the flight deck if I'm not careful. But don't worry. I'll slow him down in the next three minutes, and that'll give me twenty-five miles to park it."

•••

Paralyzed from the waist down, Luke Martin had reversed his career path from Green Beret to a GI Bill-funded Master's Degree in Computer Science circa 1999. His legs, once as strong as a horse's, were now shriveled to nothing inside his blue slacks. His arms and chest remained strong from upper body workouts and wheelchair sporting events with other wounded soldiers. But his intellect remained as sharp and acute as his twenty-two-year-old mind that had played a key role in the electronic and psychological warfare that took place unnoticed during Operation Desert Storm, that is, until a 7.62 mm round shot from that rag head's Ak-47 nipped his upper ass.

Luke and several maglev traffic control experts watched the wall of digital screens with trepidation. Military higher-ups, PHDs, and corporate brass had swarmed the room when they'd heard about the impending crash, making Luke decidedly cautious. A team of Pentagon Generals had visited the site that evening, which wasn't unusual at all. One five-star in particular, General Paul Guthrie, a frail little man, demanded that his envoy have access to the control room. Once inside, he stood over Luke like a god capable of wishing the maglev to dematerialize. His breath reeked of garlic and whiskey, and his perpetual scowl reminded Luke of Juror Number Three in Reginald Rose's *Twelve Angry Men*. He watched Luke's every move, mumbled criticisms to the other Generals, and asked stupid questions like, "Why can't you stop it now?"

Luke thought about saying, *because there's a human in there, dumbass. We don't want to leave him stranded twenty-five miles away, alone with the Grays.* Luke figured the guy didn't have much sensitivity for human life, which was a common trait among DoD brass that spent any amount of time with the terrestrials. Like many of the higher-ups that met with Gray elders in the deepest levels, they took on a completely new tenet that, curiously enough, held the Grays in high regard. Luke assumed the Grays had activated some degree of mind control or had even taken possession of their bodies, but that was just a rumor, and could not be substantiated. He'd seen the change take place in those brought in from the

Pentagon. It began with a tour of the facility, followed by a cavalcade to Level Five or deeper. Luke would observe one or two of the visitors before and after their initiation, as it was often referred. He'd always compared the change in the visitors to one who'd seen a ghost for the first time—pale and tense, but unlike the meager interaction with a specter in the dark of night, these highly decorated military men and women came up from the underground changed to such a degree that one might think they'd lost their souls down there.

Luke would never speak of his observations in public. Those conversations were reserved for the rare meeting with Badger, who would disperse only verified facts with the others on a need-to-know basis. Luke absolutely separated the two worlds in which he lived—worlds that, at times, felt like opposing galaxies. The two worlds consisted of his life as a technical contractor and family man, and an enemy of the Black Budget State, a system that had seized the world by the balls.

Today, the passenger was precious cargo; a top priority—Badger's special project. So when General Guthrie callously instructed Luke to abandon the new employee in the tunnel, Luke said, "That's not possible, sir. We aim to bring Mr. Jones one step away from the red carpet."

"And put the rest of us at risk along with half the state of New Mexico?"

"With all due respect, General," said Luke, while turning from the screen. "I have full faith in my team. We've handled issues like this before without a hiccup."

The General dispensed yet another scowl and turned and whispered something to a member of his entourage.

If Luke didn't time this right, he'd have a seriously explosive issue on his hands. If he didn't get the maglev to slow down, the window required to cut the track's power would be dangerously slim. Sixty seconds isn't much. With so many silver-stars in the room, Luke's career, let alone his life, could be at stake if he screwed up. But his priority was Dean Jones' safety. If his team couldn't save him, they'd have to cut their losses and do whatever it took to prevent the train from crashing into the Crossing. An emergency stop was their last resort. The fact that the Crossing was miles away from the Lab made no difference. Shockwaves from Texas, Utah, or Arizona could impact sensitive instruments, so every detail about this delivery had to be managed with the greatest of care. Fortunately, he had a firm grasp on the situation, a covert operation that had been repeated several times over.

Luke loosened his tie. As much as he liked toying with the visitors, the stress was getting to him. The last nuclear explosion in New Mexico occurred in 1945 at the Trinity Site as part of the Manhattan Project and that stirred up a literal hornets' nest with the Grays. The shock waves damaged some of the hives across the state and crippled the US Army's relationship with the terrestrials to such a degree that it took years to re-establish formal negotiations. It was the last thing he wanted on his conscience. Two patches of sweaty pits had already bled through his shirt. Luke took a sip of coffee—black—and picked up the hand-held radio. "Is my electrician still on line?"

"Yes," answered Sandy Fedlesworth from the maglev powerhouse.

"We've got eight minutes and," squinting at the digital screen, Luke added, "and thirty-nine seconds until possible impact. I'm taking control of the maglev in less than three minutes. If I can't slow it down any sooner than one minute before impact, you have to shut off power. Do you understand?"

"Understood," replied Sandy.

"Please confirm that you're standing at Edison Panel 371."

"Confirmed."

"Please confirm that you're ready to pull main disconnect ML-34."

"Confirmed."

Luke turned toward the controller watching the clock and said, "Start the countdown."

"Yes, sir.... Seven minutes and fifty-four seconds... fifty-three... fifty-two..."

"Let's sync your watch, Sandy."

"Ready."

"Okay. Set your time at Seven minutes forty-six, forty-five, forty-four ..."

"Seven minutes forty-three, forty-two... Got it, Captain."

"Perfect. Thank you, Fedlesworth. We're counting on you."

"I won't let you down, sir."

General Guthrie grunted. "Was that a female?"

"Yes, sir," replied Luke. "She's one of the best men we've got."

"Let's hope so," grunted General Guthrie.

Luke picked up the phone. "Alvarez, you still there?"

"Yes, sir, I am."

"Excellent. Don't go anywhere."

"Yes, sir. Standing by."

The traffic controller looked at the clock and with a voice as dry as the desert plains outside said, "Six minutes and fifty-nine seconds until impact."

•••

Penn felt as if he was falling from the sky. His lungs felt icy from the cyclone swirling around every inch of his body. His ears burned from the shrill noise created by air blasting through the splintered glass, but mostly from the thirty-nine-degree temperatures produced by the wind chill. He'd tried to cover his face, but the force prevented him from moving. He could only hope that the creature behind him was in the same predicament. He prayed the thing would bleed to death.

If the maglev stopped, Penn would face a new problem. And by the look of Truck's condition, he wouldn't be much help. He didn't move. Didn't blink.

•••

Everyone in the room gasped when the red dot on the screen kept moving even after Luke had given the maglev a decelerate command. The thing was traveling over four miles every minute. Luke sat in front of a computer screen that was an exact replica of the maglev's cockpit. He tapped the *Reduce Speed*, touch-screen command, but nothing happened. Then gliding his hand over a virtual throttle, he attempted to decrease the train's speed by proxy. Still, the maglev remained on course.

"There's obviously a problem with the ship," insisted General Guthrie.

"It's the communication system," said Luke. "A common issue." He took a deep breath and tried to block out any and all stupid comments. He continued tapping the screen, hoping to find error messages that might help him troubleshoot the problem, but nothing showed up.

"It's as if the main board has crashed," Luke said, frantically tapping on the screen. "Nothing's responding."

One of Luke's controllers asked, "Is it possible the mag is inactive?"

"Not likely," said Luke, although his response had a hint of doubt. "The locator box is mounted in the rear, but if communication's shot, there's nothing I can do."

"Could it be a glitch?" asked another traffic controller.

"Yes," replied Luke. "But we'd need the passenger to reboot the system, and since radio contact is broken, that's out of the question."

"Can you reboot it from here?" asked General Guthrie.

"Not without causing an immediate stoppage and that could be deadly," replied Luke.

"So nothing's working?" asked the general.

Luke hated to say it, but there was no other choice. "That's correct, sir. We're running out of options."

"One hundred and twenty seconds until impact." shouted another member of Luke's team.

Luke picked up the phone. "Alvarez, clear the terminal. Now!"

"Yes, sir."

"Well is someone going to stop that thing?" asked the General, practically pushing against Luke's seat to get a closer look.

"Ninety-three seconds until impact."

Luke swiveled in his chair, reaching for the radio, but the General bumped into the wheelchair's armrest, knocking the radio to the floor, followed by his half-empty cup of coffee. Luke let out a couple expletives under his breath.

"Eighty-five seconds until impact."

Luke grabbed the sticky radio and wiped it on his slacks. "Do you copy, Fedlesworth?"

Silence.

"Fedlesworth? Do you copy?"

"I'm... sir."

"Sandy? Get your hand on the switch."

"I can't... sir... static... repeat?"

"Get ready to pull the switch."

"Sir... trouble.... hearing..."

"Impact in seventy-six seconds."

"Did you hear that, Fedlesworth? Impact in seventy seconds... sixty-nine... sixty-eight..."

•••

Paralyzed by the cascading winds, Penn remembered seeing a sign posted above a small box near his seat that read: FOR EMERGENCY USE ONLY. He hoped for a bright red ax near the emergency exit like the kind he'd seen in action movies, but he wasn't that lucky. It was just a stupid first-aid kit with a red cross on the front.

He closed his eyes, realizing there was nothing to do but wait for destiny to reveal its sick plan. He thought about his mother, knowing she'd be worried sick about him. He hated that. She didn't deserve the heartache she'd lived through. The idea that a sheriff's deputy would show up on her doorstep and explain that her son was eaten alive by a Martian made Penn ill. Dad would be confused. He wouldn't understand how his son managed to create such a buzz. Would take some serious balls to take on the government. Nah. Not Penn. Kid's a daydreamer, a momma's boy, not a doer.

Then, like waking from a nightmare, the maglev came to a sudden stop. Penn's body thrust forward about a fraction of an inch until it was stopped by the full-torso restraint. Brakes squealed. His head jerked forward and back, followed by the sound of a roll, bang, and a thud. The Gray had crashed into the back of his seat.

Chapter 26
Retrieval

Alvarez watched the digital numbers on his watch change from 1:00 to 0:59. He looked up, bending an ear toward the phone. When the call didn't come, he stepped out of the glass-walled security office and into the maglev terminal. The two security officers cautiously dawdled in the opening. With the terminal empty, Alvarez expected to hear a hum like when he used to listen to the train tracks when he was a kid. He expected to feel the floor vibrating, but it didn't.

He stepped up to the yellow safety line painted at the edge of the track and looked into the expansive tunnel. There was no light approaching. No horn blaring. He could only feel a slight breeze across his face. He closed his eyes to concentrate, waiting to get a sense of what had gone wrong when the breeze quickly turned into a gust that nearly stole his black beret. The wind tore through the depot like a haunted hurricane. It came and went in a matter of seconds, leaving nothing in its wake but an odd silence.

Without a second thought, Alvarez returned to the office and called Captain Martin.

"What happened to the mag?"

"I don't know," said Luke. "I lost contact with Fedlesworth and spilled coffee on my radio."

The General had stepped back, silent after his clumsy flub.

"Well, it didn't come through here," said Alvarez. "I felt a draft, though. Guess that means it stopped somewhere close."

"We can only hope."

"If that's the case, it's go time for me and my homeboys."

"Now, Alvarez... They're trained professionals, remember?"

"Oh, my bad. I forgot these flunkies hadn't seen a lick of combat."

"Enough of that. Pack your shit and retrieve the boy," barked Luke. "If my figures are right, he's only two miles from the Crossing. Your lucky day."

"Two miles, huh?"

"Give or take."

"Now I understand what you meant when you said you could stop on a dime—one mile per nickel."

"Seriously. Go get him. He could be injured."

"On my way... Just do me one favor," asked Alvarez.

"What's that?"

"Don't let anyone turn the track back on."

"Copy that," said Luke. "And Alvarez?"

"Yes, sir?"

"Be careful."

"Will do."

Alvarez reached into the red cabinet, grabbed a first-aid kit and tossed it in his backpack. He made damn sure his M-16 was locked and loaded, reached down to confirm that his ankle knife was strapped in, threw the pack over his shoulder, and started out of the office and into the tunnel. The other two guards lagged behind, but that didn't surprise him.

He hopped down onto the track, knowing that ultimately he was alone; that this could be one of the most dangerous assignments he'd ever accepted.

Alvarez looked straight ahead, hoping the two losers behind him would turn back, even though they would make excellent alien fodder. Having them tag along was protocol, not necessary. The only thing about keeping them around was that he couldn't talk out loud; he had to keep his thoughts to himself. His thoughts returned to his father. He'd be proud. What Alvarez was about to do would be one of the most honorable things he'd ever accomplished. Knowing that made him smile, and smiles rarely happened in his gung-ho world. East L.A. ground smiles away a long time ago. But there was always honor and faith.

He pushed the backpack up into a more comfortable position and let his mind drift momentarily to the darker possibilities of what he'd find in the tunnel. The dark trails within the Earth were always filled with surprises. Sinkholes. Floods. Creepy sounds. Wall crawlers. Stray things that escape from Level Four, where biological experiments and black budget money ran rampant. But then he remembered the power of faith and performed the sign of the cross after taking his first step into the abyss. "Dios bendiga a nuestro joven héroe," he said, thinking of the young man he'd set out to retrieve. *God bless our young hero.*

Chapter 27
Dancing with the Devil

Penn reached for his belt buckle but for some reason, the buttons wouldn't depress. He felt like he was in a B-movie where everything goes wrong for no good reason. *Of course the buckle won't open; this is a real-life horror film.* At least he had enough sense not to run down a dark alley or corner himself in the abandoned house where there's no place to run except a closet. No. He'd never do that. Writers can always find another way. Besides, there were probably air vents somewhere on the track—vents that would lead him out.

And there was Truck. Sleeping. Unconscious. *What the hell, Dude.*

"Truck," Penn said whispering, trying not to disturb the creature lying on the floor behind him. "Truck. Wake up." He continued fidgeting with the latch. One buckle unlocked, the second and third came loose as well. The fourth button wouldn't depress.

"Stupid harness."

An odor wafted, rising up and around Penn. Smelled like sulfur, or what they called skunk water back in Ohio. "Come on, latch." The smell was putrid, reminding Penn of something Mom would say when he'd commit violent crimes against the toilet, *Horrible. Just horrible. The plumber can't fix stanky.*

That thing behind his seat reeked. He gagged. It smelled so inhuman.

Never mind the smell. How did it... how did they get on the track? What is it? How many are there? Can't be the creatures in the book. Can't be! If it's true... Oh, my God. Truck's right about all of this. Federal Underground. The Serpents. Hell on Earth. Government deals. All of it.

The lights had gone out—no power at all. Penn sat still and listened while he quietly worked the latches. It was perfectly silent and deceptively dark. Shadows seemed to appear out of nowhere, but Penn knew that it was just his eyes playing tricks on his mind. He could hear himself breathe, and Truck would let out an occasional snort. At least he was alive. *Thank God.*

The final two latches broke free.

What's in the box?

Penn got down on his knees and reached for the emergency kit, but he froze when the creature stirred on the other side.

The thing hissed and clicked, gasping for breath.

Penn slowly rose and shook Truck's chest. The man's head bobbed, but he didn't respond.

Get the box.

He reached back under his seat and felt the latch. It snapped open easily enough, releasing the first aid kit from the metal strapping that held it in place. Penn snatched the container and ran through the pitch-black shuttle toward the front of the maglev, blindly bumping into the seats. He could feel a small latch in front. With a slight tug, he pulled it open and everything inside fell to the floor.

The creature clicked slowly, probably sniffing out its victim.

Penn thought he heard the creature pressing down on a seat as if were trying to stand up. Seconds later, the weight of a footstep pressed against the floor. Penn panicked. *It's coming. It's so dark. I can't see anything.*

Something slid across the deck, probably the other leg, followed by another thud.

It's stirring. Dragging a wounded foot.

Penn knelt down and rummaged through the supplies that had scattered everywhere. Papers. Bandages. A tube of something. Boxes of assorted first aid strips. Tape. Scissors.

Scissors!

He crouched down, gripped the small medical device in the palm of his hand, and edged back against the door leading to the helm. The squeaking floor exposed the Gray's location. Each slow and calculating step plotted its movements. Penn could tell it was walking around his seat, getting closer to Truck. But he couldn't let it devour his sleeping companion. Listening to that thing eat Truck would be just as terrifying as if Penn offered himself as a snack.

In Federal Underground, the Large Grays were the military class, the oldest terrestrial creatures among the dwellers. Some lived hundreds of years and it is rumored that some have lived *thousands* of years underground. They personify the reptilian brain in all of us—the natural desire to breathe, to eat, to survive at all costs. Penn recognized this while his own fight-or-flight instincts surged through his veins. Knowing that he had to survive wasn't enough. If he were going to save Truck, the Gray would have to die. Or, Penn and Truck would die trying to kill it.

The clicking intensified, getting faster as it approached Truck. Penn knew it was sniffing out its prey. Too dark to see exactly what was going on, Penn connected the sounds the creature was making with his memory of the shuttle's interior.

It had to be close.

He imagined the tall creature stooping down to keep from hitting its head on the ceiling, hunching over Truck, ready to spring forward and strike. Its spine spiked out of its back, a robust nervous system that contributed to its unnatural strength. Penn had dreamed of these beasts for months. He knew them well. They had shaken him with night terrors so often that it was as if he'd battled them all his life. He was well aware that their razor sharp teeth could sever a limb. Clothes were unnecessary except when meeting with human dignitaries, and even then, the beasts looked foolish and unnatural.

Penn sat still, listening, shaking, nearly paralyzed with fear, knowing that he must battle the Gray terrestrial, a flesh and blood manifestation of everything he feared. He stood up and lifted the weapon in his hand, fully aware that it was a paltry implement. His best offense would be a surprise attack—a blade in the spine.

The hissing and clicking paused.

Penn remembered how strong and tall the big ones could become. His heart hammered so loudly that the beast could probably hear it pounding in his chest.

The thing inhaled and exhaled with a hiss. It clicked, and clicked again, probably catching Penn's scent with its tongue. Penn imagined the thing lifting his head, bothered that the first bite of the slender kid had been delayed. He had to explode like a bolt out of a crossbow before it took another step. Before it made another move.

Sightless, yet intuitive, Penn anticipated the thrust and lunge required to injure the ancient enemy. So he burst into the darkness, blind, with duel blades leading the fray. The smell and clicking told Penn he was close. He drove the scissors forward, hoping to draw first blood. He struck. The blades went in deep. The alien let out an ungodly shrill from its throat, a high pitch gurgling. It swung its arms wildly, throwing Penn across the shuttle. He hit the curved outer wall, his back taking the brunt of the blow, his chest aching from the force that struck him. Dazed, he awkwardly fell between two rows of seats. His head hit the floor. The scissors fell at his side, and his feet came to rest on a seat in the back row, and he wondered how the thing could be so strong.

Truck called from further down the aisle, his voice groggy. "Penn! What's happening?"

Penn didn't answer. He lay still, hoping the creature would die a quick death. Instead, the creature clicked from the back of its throat and stepped in Penn's direction. One foot pressed heavy on the metal floor while the other sounded like it was sliding. These things could get as tall as eight feet. They were the Nephilim from ancient days; though highly advanced, they were serpents in the Garden of Eden, deceivers that God had warned men to avoid according to some ancient texts. The myths were no longer fantasy. The legends, as Penn wrote in his book, were based on actual historical records. How could we miss it? How could we be so foolish? How could we be so arrogant to assume the writers of the past were simply portraying creatures from their dreams—a simple representation of man's fears? They were real: the cave drawings, the ancient texts, the beings described in Sumerian and biblical writings. The evil things that go bump in the night were actually living under the earth. Penn remembered quoting Genesis 6:4 in his book, thinking it added a supernatural flare to the concept, never imagining it was based in reality. It fit so perfectly. *"And the Nephilim were in the earth in those days and also afterward"*. Mentioned only one other time in all of scripture, the elusive creatures remain a mystery to this very day. Talking serpents? Penn had laughed at the idea. How foolish the writers of scripture must have been, but what a fictional concept it would be. Serpents don't talk, and if they did, they'd have to be a lot bigger to be feared by the human race. Something was obviously lost in translation. Yet Penn couldn't deny the reality of that ancient text because one of the bastards was coming after him and it was a lot bigger than he had imagined.

Penn was a half-mile underground, balled in a twisted mass, thrown across a rail car by a descendent of an ancient and mysterious race. The idea was ridiculous, possibly irrational, definitely horrifying. He heard Truck unlocking his seat belt. Was it possible that Truck hadn't seen the creature fall into the shuttle?

Oh no. Truck.

"Truck. Don't move," whispered Penn. "One of them got inside."

The floor squeaked again and Penn ached, not physically, but from an intense desire to understand how and why he knew about these beasts. For this reason alone, he had to survive. Penn knew he'd entered a world that was never meant to be encountered—a boundary sealed long ago by the ancients. They knew better. They knew the risks. By order of their God, the Israelites killed them off and any people that indulged their needs, or so they thought. Driving them underground, however, would be a more accurate statement. They'd battled the creatures for thousands of years. Pushed them back. Drove them underneath, where they belonged. Yet in our arrogance, modern civilizations have engaged, trusted, and indulged the filthy Grays in exchange for technology and power.

It sounded great…in a book. But now, Penn was sharing a futuristic human transporter with a Gray, a serpent, or something worse. It pissed him off. Infuriated him that he knew how real the creature truly was, and yet his body raced with fear of what the thing might do to him.

The Gray's feet pounded across the shuttle. It was coming for him. He pushed back against the floor, feeling for the weapon, quickly assessing his options. *Die. Fight. Run. Scream.*

Penn felt for the scissors and gripped them tight in his right hand. Looking up from the floor, a shadow blossomed in the darkness, emerging before his eyes. Penn could feel its energy moving closer. He could smell the odor, hear its clicking, and feel the heat discharging with each puff of air. Desperate to act, he sprang up and shot his arm straight out, spearing the thing in the eye. Penn felt the creature's bony breast and thick skin with his bare hand, it was that close. It screeched and hissed and grabbed Penn's neck. Penn tried to outmaneuver the thing, but it was too quick, too strong, and completely immobilizing him.

Penn couldn't see an inch beyond his nose, but he knew the creature's teeth were coming straight at him. Forced to his knees, the creature's other hand gripped Penn's shoulder, shoving him flat on the floor, preparing the main dish. Truck would be dessert. The thing pressed down, and its feet gripped Penn's legs like a vise.

He felt something wrap around his wrists, then squeezing tight at all four extremities. Its feet were double-jointed, acting as a third and fourth hand.

Powerless, shaking and hyperventilating, Penn could barely speak until one word escaped out of his mouth.

"Truck!"

"Penn? Where are you?"

Penn could sense the fear in Truck's voice.

"Over here," answered Penn, knowing he'd die soon.

The thing bit down on the meat of Penn's shoulder, taking a shallow bite, and it burned with the heat of twenty daggers. Penn screamed. He could hear the thing licking its lips.

The overhead red lights turned back on and the Gray turned away from Penn. Blood dripped from its mouth, sending the young writer into a panic. Then like a dream, a silhouette of a man appeared and he shoved his foot into the creature's jaw. It whipped back a hundred and eighty degrees as it dropped Penn, its black eyes glaring menacingly inches from Penn's face. Big eyes narrowed and its tongue flicked rapidly over numerous razor teeth. It grinned mischievously, revealing its sinister urge to hunt and strike terror into its prey.

As the Gray turned toward Truck, Penn plucked the scissors out of its eye, and just as quickly shoved the weapon into the back of its neck, plunging it over and over as quickly as he could. The monster recoiled and rolled across the floor, yelping in pain. Truck reached down and grabbed Penn's arm, hoisting him to his feet.

He gave Penn a key to the cockpit. "Get in there and lock it," he said, turning back to the creature.

Penn shook his head, panting, and said, "No way. I'm not leaving you."

The creature flopped against the outer wall. Blood sprayed from the wounds and splattered against the glass. Its head twitched and its eyes grimaced with hatred.

The red lights flickered.

Truck looked back at Penn, his face replete with fear. He disappeared every time the lights dimmed. "The emergency batteries are dying," said Truck. "We have to gut this thing *now*."

Truck vaulted toward the weapon that Penn dropped on the floor beside the creature. He grabbed it and stabbed the thing in the face and chest until it stopped moving. Penn added several kicks to the head to finish it off.

Exhausted, Truck released the scissors, panting; his face was sprinkled with blood. He lowered his head and said, "Others will be here soon."

"How do you know?" asked Penn, bent over, gasping.

"They have a collective conscious."

"Like a hive mentality?"

"Exactly." Truck turned toward the cockpit and took a deep breath, seemingly collecting his thoughts. He pointed to a messy stack of colored jump suits once stacked neatly on the shelf beneath the controls. "Grab another one of the orange suits and put it on."

"Why?"

Truck glared at Penn impatiently. "Do I have to remind you?"

Penn sighed sheepishly, recalling the color codes required for underground access.

"Wipe the blood off your face, too, and make it fast."

Penn did as he was commanded and considered that maybe Truck wasn't an insane fan, but rather, a legit underground worker on the down side, and possibly telling the truth on the up side.

After several failed attempts to open the sliding doors, Truck hurried to the cockpit. "Through here," he said, waving for Penn to follow. "It's got a breakaway window." He turned and pointed at the jagged opening where the Gray broke through and said, "You don't want to climb through the hole up there." He kicked the cockpit window until it shattered and tore away from the outer seams. Then, like climbing over the nose of an airplane, Truck slipped out, crawling on his belly. Penn did the same, guarding his shoulder as he slipped away. The glass splinters and minor cuts were of little consequence. Penn ran alongside Truck as fast as he could, unaware of what lurked ahead or behind.

Chapter 28
Interception

The hike wasn't physically challenging at all; it was the unknown that made it so treacherous. The two jokers behind Alvarez remained close only because they needed the security of their supervisor's headlamp, which lit the circular tunnel about as bright as a candle on a foggy night. At fifty-five degrees, the chill was a stark reminder that non-human creatures dwelt among the tunnels. He remembered how dangerous they could be. The sad eyes masked the evil behind the Grays' duplicity. On one occasion, he returned a small Gray to its hive that was found wandering on Level Two, which was strictly a human work zone. After going through a battery of formalities, Alvarez was permitted to hand the little guy over to its superior—a tall Gray—the equivalent of his own position, Director of Security. His prisoner, the cliché big-headed, four-foot tall would-be alien, remained mostly silent during its captivity, a time period no longer than four hours, with the exception of a few squeaks and grunts that sounded like a kitten purring.

Alvarez was still new to the facility and the warnings he'd received didn't quite sink in. For most of the security team, it took an actual encounter to truly grasp what was down there. Knowing the creatures preferred the dark, Alvarez locked the thing in a viewing room. For the first three hours it sat still, crouched down in a corner as if it were in hibernation mode, or in a state of meditation. In the final hour of its captivity, the thing began to shift in place and its hands began to shake. A half an hour later it began to pace around the room, twitching, blinking frantically, and talking to itself. Alvarez was not monitoring audio, but it was clear the being was growing agitated. In the final ten minutes, it ravaged the furniture with its sharp teeth, running wild through the room as if it was in the final stage of rabies. Its skin showed signs of spotting. Its heart raced, its mouth foamed, and its peaceful mien had lost all sense of sanity. A rookie security officer at the time, Alvarez entered the room before learning that the small Grays needed to feed every three to four hours, and encountered a beast like he'd never seen. It immediately attacked him, climbing up his torso, aiming straight for his face. It snapped its narrow jaws like a feral dog, barely missing his nose. Alvarez forced the thing back, nearly kicking it into a coma.

Several facial punctures and lacerations later, the young guard seized the Gray and bound him with fetters until a guard with several years of seniority was finally brought in to assist. He fed the creature a few mice, and it was satisfied. Although they were flesh and blood, they were soulless creatures. The young performed the digging and gathering. Unfortunately, they needed to be fed often, and when that didn't happen, they were driven by their needs. This served the tall Grays well, but it was a problem for the Department of Defense. The fertile landscape surrounding New Mexico and Colorado and other areas coveted by the U.S. military couldn't sustain both humans and those living under the earth indefinitely; hence, the truce between our government and theirs. They continued to share their age-old knowledge in antigravity, free energy, and DNA modification, and the DoD agreed to keep them hidden, safe, and their laboratories and bellies full.

They preferred small rodents. They could barely digest large game. Deer, elk, and fowl were cancer-causing. Human flesh, however, was a delicacy reserved for special occasions, or so they said. They didn't want to undo their benevolent   des. As much as they despised the likes of Alvarez, they needed humans to sustain life on Earth, to breed with them and participate in their genetic research, so they rarely killed the men who provided their needs. Alvarez learned the shocking truth that day, and it changed his way of thinking. The creatures that were once giants, gods to the ancients, men of renown according to the scriptures, had genetically engineered themselves into a frail insect-looking race, capable of surviving inside the Earth's crust; although always on the brink, they were no longer capable of surviving above, not for long periods of time, anyway. Turns out, they had genetically downsized by mistake, or arrogance, or foolishness. Didn't matter, really. They still had their strong points, mainly tens of thousands or even millions of years of ancient knowledge, knowledge that humans had lost through wars and destruction and terror and fear. And the most critical knowledge lost above ground was of who is dwelling beneath it.

The Marine (once a Marine always a Marine) walked near the maglev tracks, listening, preparing himself for anything. The world he knew was a lie, and the kid on the train would help the world know the truth. The trip felt comparable to walking through *The Hole* in East L.A. at night. He felt alone and vulnerable. Anything was possible. He gripped his M-16 tight enough to fire at a moment's notice, yet loose enough to respond effectively. He stared straight ahead into the gloom, centered, ready. Limestone formed the circular tunnel. It looked like glass from the high-temperature equipment that bored into the Earth's foundation, giving the walls a glossy sheen. Each step required careful placement. The floor was constructed from concrete and layered with drain pipes, power cables, and tracks; there were only a few feet on either side of the rail making it extremely dangerous if a maglev drove through. This far in, there were no overhead lights, so he couldn't see more than twenty yards away.

He heard voices. The fools behind him were chattering but it wasn't them that pricked his ear. Two distinct male tones were coming from the tunnel ahead, and moving fast. Alvarez quickly assessed the nearest service entrance—one every thousand feet for the first five miles of each maglev station. He quickened his pace to a jog.

"Someone's up there," he said to the other two.

Two shadows appeared in the haze. Two men. One was wounded and his arm resting over the shoulder of the other. Both were covered in blood.

"Alvarez. Is that you?" said one of the men.

"Yes... Do you have the kid?"

"Barely. He's hurt. We ran into a hive and one of them got in the mag."

"Oh, shit," said Alvarez, assessing Penn's wounds. "Get him on the ground. We have a first aid kit."

Truck helped Penn lie down. Alvarez adjusted his light, exposing the severity of Penn's injury. Alvarez could see the teeth marks, reminding him of his first encounter with the Grays, and filling him with rage. He opened the kit and began cleaning skin and dressing the bite.

Truck directed the two guards to secure the track. They appeared leery of taking orders from a civilian, so Alvarez gave them the command as well. One kept guard where he stood. The other checked out the wounded as he passed.

"Did you kill it?" asked Alvarez.

"I think so," said Truck.

Considering the herd mentality, Alvarez said, "They'll come looking for it."

"I know," said Truck. "What do you think we should do?"

Alvarez wrapped gauze over Penn's wound and said, "We stick with the plan."

Truck looked tired. He handed Alvarez a piece of medical tape. "And lead the serpents straight to Badger?"

"We don't have a choice."

"There's always a choice. How far are we from the terminal?"

"Almost two miles."

"Great. What about the hives?" asked Truck. "We're right on top of them."

"We'll need military support." Alvarez looked at the guard keeping watch. "We can send those two jokers back."

"And then what? Tell the brass we've pissed off the ET's by bootlegging a kid into the underground?"

Truck paused, staring blankly at the scissors. Alvarez noticed the dazed look in his eyes. *He's post-traumatic. Must've been worse than he let on.*

"You okay?"

Truck shook his head and peered at Penn's wound. "They're hungry. I've never seen them like this before."

"All the more reason to get to Badger," said Alvarez. "We need to tell the others. He may want everyone to back off a while, stay shallow until the brass settles them down."

Truck turned away. "Something's not right."

Alvarez noticed the fear in Truck's eyes, something the runner rarely showed. "What about the kid?" asked Alvarez, while dressing the cut on Penn's shoulder.

"He's my package," answered Truck. The look on his face betrayed his steely tone. "I'll deliver him as promised. You just clear the path."

"We're a quarter mile from the next service door. Back where you came," said Alvarez, nodding. "You up for that?"

Truck turned around and beads of sweat rained down his forehead. "You want the truth?"

"No," replied Alvarez. "That's not necessary."

"Well then," said Truck, sneering. "Let's get to the door." He knelt down and inspected the bloody gauze on the kid's shoulder. "How you feeling, little buddy?"

"I've been better," said Penn.

Alvarez helped Penn sit up, noticing that the color was returning to his cheeks. He handed both men a bottled water and protein bar from his pack. "You're gonna need this. We're still in the nest zone."

"Nest? W-what do mean?" asked Penn.

Truck looked at Alvarez with that *who's gonna talk—you or me?* look on his face. Alvarez nodded, giving the runner permission to speak freely.

Truck looked at Penn, all joy removed from his face. "Ever see an ant hive?"

"Like an ant farm?"

"Yeah. Just like that."

"Sure," said Penn. "Had one when I was a kid."

"Okay. Well, that's what we're dealing with here. Only the colony consists of several hives that bridge Colorado, New Mexico, and Arizona. We're right above them. They're everywhere: Canada, Europe, South America, the Middle East, Australia."

Penn's face went pale again and he lay back down. He covered his face with his hands in frustration and said, "Remind me again why I'm here?"

"To show you," said Alvarez. "So you can tell the world in your books."

"Well I don't want to," replied Penn. "I already told Truck, but he wouldn't listen to me."

"We knew you'd resist," said Alvarez. "That's why I'm here. To make sure you get to Badger."

"Fuck Badger!" said Penn, clambering to his feet. "I don't need Badger to tell me shit. I've seen enough... Take me home."

"We can't do that," said Truck.

"Then take me to Las Alamos!" said Penn, hobbling toward the rear guard.

"No," said Alvarez. "If we bring you there, they'll kill you... make you disappear. But we can keep you safe."

"This doesn't feel very safe," Penn said sharply.

"I know," said Alvarez. "But you have to see it first—all of it. Then we'll take you wherever you want to go."

"And then what?" asked Penn, painfully slipping his arm through the strapping. "Hide for the rest of my life?"

"No," said Truck. "You just need to write."

"Uh… no," said Penn. "I don't need to do anything but eat, sleep, and shit."

"The people up there need to know what's going on down here," said Alvarez. He could feel himself heating up. This point always worked him into a tizzy. "When you see what's going on, you don't have a choice."

"That's right," interrupted Truck. "There's no turning back, Penn. You've just seen the beginning. There's much more."

"Hey!" called the guard on the inbound side of the tunnel. "I think I hear something."

"Aw Hell's bells!" said Alvarez. "Come on. We gotta go." He grabbed Penn's hand and lifted him to his feet. "Can you walk?"

"I suppose."

"Can you run?"

"I'll do my best."

"Okay then." Alvarez started down the tunnel, waving impatiently. "This way."

The guard to the rear looked surprised. "Hey! Where you goin'? We're supposed to bring Mr. Jones to the base."

Truck grinned and saluted the guard. "In due time."

The guard pointed toward the Crossing. "But it's that way."

Truck never looked back.

"Hurry!" said Alvarez, "I hear them."

"Hear who?" asked Penn.

Truck nudged Penn and replied, "More of our friends."

Penn stumbled forward, and Alvarez heard him cursing under his breath.

Alvarez pointed to the guard up front and said "You. Come with us," and then he pointed to the guard behind him, "You, go back and tell the brass the serpents are coming. And tell Davenport, too." The guard turned and blazed into the gloom, and Alvarez sprinted to the front of the group. "Hurry! They're fast."

•••

Penn could hear the stampede charging ahead in the tunnel. Sounded like the New York City Marathon—feet pounding like war drums. Alvarez's headlamp rocked back and forth, the beam of light swaying with his stride. Every step echoed. Every click and hiss that resonated in the cave taught Penn what hungry under-dwellers sounded like, a lesson he would rather have avoided. His shoulder burned with each painful step, another exercise he could do without.

"We're getting close," said Alvarez.

That didn't make Penn feel any better. That was like hearing mom and dad tell him he was "almost there". That was never true.

"Better get there soon," said Truck. "I can hear them."

Penn looked ahead. He could barely keep pace. Saw a curve in the tunnel ahead, but no door. "Where's the service entrance you keep talking about?"

"Around the bend," assured Alvarez.

"They're coming!" said Penn. "I can smell them."

"Better say your prayers," said Alvarez, performing the sign of the cross. "This is it."

Penn's legs burned. Every part of his body felt bruised.

"A little further, kid," said Truck, turning. He looked as scared as Penn felt. One hungry Gray was enough. But an army? They didn't stand a chance.

Alvarez turned the corner with his light beam. For a moment, the tunnel went black until Penn made it around the curve. He could see the door a few feet away on the left. Ahead, the terrestrials formed a shadow that moved like a black cloud, drifting forward, thundering. The creatures were only fifty feet away. Alvarez flipped off his gun's safety switch while slowing his pace. The guard did the same.

Alvarez lifted his gun, pointing at the beasts and said, "Get him in the door, Truck. Penn, stay with him."

Penn stopped. He couldn't move. There had to be hundreds of them. The Grays boldly marched forward. Six or seven small Grays circled each Large Gray. If Penn hadn't written a book about them, he wouldn't have known they were slaves to the taller, older beings, some of which stood in the back like Kings and noblemen—their faces wrinkly and large eyes shrunken, watching their much younger, much smaller breed perform their duty. That's how Penn described it in Federal Underground, anyway. *This is exactly what I dreamed about*, he thought. But this definitely wasn't his imagination. He could smell this nightmare; their stench wafted across his taste buds—a mixture of sulfur and urine.

Alvarez knelt down and positioned his M-16, eying his first target through the scope. "Come on, Truck. Get the kid in there!"

Truck grabbed Penn's arm and pulled him sideways. Penn knew he should move, but his legs resisted. "Hurry, Penn," shouted Truck. "Every second counts."

The creatures stopped in unison and Penn felt drawn to them. They were already working on his thoughts.

Alvarez shuffled in front of Penn, pointing his gun. "Don't move," he said to the beasts. "I don't want to kill you, but I will." They hissed and clicked, communicating to each other in their ancient language. Truck reached for the door and the creatures took a step forward.

"Truck! Get him in there, now." shouted Alvarez.

The runner pulled the stainless handle and motioned for Penn to get in. He took a step and the Grays did the same, as if *he* was what they were after. Keeping his eyes on the black-eyed Grays, Penn moved closer to Truck, inch by inch, but the bigger Gray standing at the front of the pack snarled furiously, hissing and rousing the others.

Penn looked at Alvarez, curious how he could be so brave. The Marine tightened his grip, positioning the cross hairs on his target.

While Truck yanked Penn through the service entrance, Penn watched the leading Gray let out an angry hiss, spooking the guard standing beside Alvarez. The guard shot a burst of rounds into the crowd of creatures and they came running, shrieking and hissing.

Chapter 29
Tracking

Liz sat on the edge of the NY tactical aviation team's UH-60A Blackhawk, watching the GPS monitor, while Pennsylvania's Blue Ridge Summit zipped by under her feet. The target hadn't moved for hours. Penn must've stopped to rest.

There were days she cursed technology for its intrusive devices, but this wasn't one of those times. She knew if anything ever happened to Angela, she'd be able to find her as long as she kept her phone on her person, and that gave her a sense of connectedness to her daughter. She wouldn't see her for days, maybe weeks now that Penn Mitchell had intruded upon her life.

The target had stopped in Indiana, but Gilmore received a report that the maglev could have had continued west toward New Mexico where it could split off to one of several underground bases. When they reached central Indiana, the Blackhawk stopped at Grissom Air Force Base to refuel, allowing Liz and the SWAT team to investigate Penn's last known location. Upon landing at the Air Force refueling base, they were greeted by Lieutenant General Dick Lawson, who guided them into a drab conference room for a debriefing.

"All I can tell you is that there's a special team investigating the crash."

Liz couldn't believe what she was hearing. "I didn't travel all night to hear that I can't go down there. I'm assigned to that kid. He's my mark. If he's in that tunnel or whatever you call it, I have a right to access."

"Not presently," said the Lieutenant General, tapping a handful of papers on the walnut table. "I don't have clearance to go down there... Neither do you."

"I have a warrant. Full access," Liz said boldly, failing to state the warrant only covered Penn's personal residence and digital records. She handed the Lieutenant General her paperwork, hoping he wouldn't read the fine print.

He opened the papers and perused its contents. Liz knew he wasn't reading. His eyes scanned the pages a little too fast. Still, he grew increasingly agitated with every turn of the page.

"You'll need a warrant from a Federal court if you want to rummage through Federal property."

"This is a matter of national security. Why are you being so resistant?"

"It's not me, little lady," he said snidely. "I take orders, too."

"From who?"

"From my commander, a four-star, who takes his orders direct from the Pentagon."

"What's his name?" Liz opened a notepad and prepared to write.

"General Fritz Bowser."

Liz smiled respectfully. "Thank you for your cooperation." She jotted down the General's name and stepped out of her seat. She walked into the hallway and called Gilmore with her cell phone.

"I'll see what I can do," responded Gilmore.

"Thank you," said Liz. "But I'd like to know how the Pentagon's already involved in this?"

"You and me both," confessed Ted.

"It's only been twenty-four hours since he's escaped. Surely they understand the meaning of investigative continuity."

"They do. But we're bordering on a terrorist threat. There's a chance they'll pull you out of this anyway, and hand it over to the Counterterrorism division, Homeland Security, or God help us, bury it inside the DoD."

"...Where Penn Mitchell's case will never see the light of day," responded Liz.

"That may be the case," said Gilmore. "And if that happens, you'll have to let him go."

"And if I can't?"

"I expect you to be professional."

"When have I not?"

"Well..."

"Never. Ted. That's the answer. Besides you know this isn't about me."

"I know, Liz. I know you *believe* Vincent is involved, but—"

Gilmore's voice trailed. She recognized his cheeky tone but refused to pursue his biases. *Never back down,* she thought. Those three words aptly spoken by her mother stuck to her like glue, bonding all of her broken pieces.

"What are you trying to say?"

"Liz, I... I think you're seeing what you want to see."

Liz shook her head, rejecting his assumption. She couldn't drop it. She couldn't turn away. She wouldn't back down. If there was an ounce of truth in Penn's book, and she'd already discovered that there was at least a pound, then she had to believe that Badger was a central character. The odds were too great for his role to be coincidental. And she wasn't wired to walk away from anything... or anyone.

"Fine. I'll keep you posted."

She hung up and headed to the Blackhawk. The bird was flapping its wings and the four SWATs were standing around waiting for instructions. The sky was clear and the sun kissed their boots and gleaming flight helmets, but dark feelings crept into her mind. She needed to let off some steam. For just a moment she imagined punching her fist through the side of the helicopter. Gilmore's face would've felt better, but she'd take what she could get.

Screw Gilmore. If there was even a slim chance that Penn took the midnight train to Las Alamos, she needed to get there, fast. Kids do tend to lose their cell phones. And if he ditched it in the Indiana tunnel, or if it slipped out of his pocket, she'd let the DoD team head up that wild goose chase. *She* would go where the train was heading. She had a sneaky suspicion that's where she'd find Penn.

Liz buckled up her helmet and told the pilot to take her to Las Alamos National Laboratory.

Chapter 30
Duke's B & G

Sandy Fedlesworth drove her Jeep Wrangler down the dusty road to her cabin two miles south of Dulce. The kids would get off the bus by three twenty-five, and her husband Jake would arrive around four-thirty. After a long night, she was tired, usually processing her daily responsibilities at home. Her twelve-hour shift ended at noon and it was a long drive from the Colorado/New Mexico border, where the company bused three-dozen other workers to and from the base. The filthy dashboard reminded her how much dirt would blast through her hair out there in the desert, but she didn't give it a second thought. That didn't bother her like it usually did. She couldn't stop thinking about the shuttle, where Alvarez, the kid, and Truck were inside the red zone. She was safe and on her way to her cozy cabin. But they were down there among the demons.

She drove past a roadside bar and almost stopped. She could use a stiff, double-barreled bourbon. But she couldn't do that to her team. She needed her head screwed on straight. Then again, the further she drove away from the bar, the more she thought about how useless she was, and how fucked up she felt about Davenport.

Maybe she'd have one drink. Just one to take off the edge. Calm her nerves. She'd done her job as best she could—pretending that she couldn't hear the captain—cutting the power to the maglev. That was classic. Leaving the last sixty seconds shrouded in mystery heightened the tension and realism. She wanted to bust a gut back there in the powerhouse. And knowing she actually had work orders to get it done made it that much sweeter. She should win an Oscar for that. Still didn't fix what Davenport did, or stop the nightmares and panic attacks. Those scars would always remain. The only comfort she took in that bastard's existence was that he was his own ticking time bomb.

T' hell with it.

She turned the vehicle around, pulled into Duke's Bar and Grill, and sat with the truck idling. Dirt swirled into a twister and flanked across the passenger side door. She gnawed on her fingernails for a minute, second-guessing her decision. It'd been three years since she'd stepped foot in there. The stress of ten years working in the Dome had finally gotten to her. It didn't feel like they were making any progress. Everything felt more stressful since Davenport. Every switch. Every wire. She felt dirty and stupid and couldn't stop asking herself *Is it worth it?* That was the million-dollar question. She didn't have an answer.

She stepped out of the truck. She didn't want to think. Things were better three years ago.

Truck had lost so much weight back then. He really was an attractive guy. She always told him that, even before he shed the pounds. She recalled how she'd stumbled out of Duke's and drove down country roads, hoping she'd land at home before she came across Truck's house. But she didn't. He was sitting on his front porch drinking green tea in his boxers and sandals. Her headlights were so bright that Truck thought the Good Lord had stopped by to pay him a visit. She stumbled out of her Jeep and staggered up his front porch steps. She knew she looked awfully damned hot in those jeans and blouse. She knew Truck couldn't possibly resist her. All the overtime had put a strain on her marriage. She and Jake hadn't had sex in months, and she sensed that her husband was falling out of love with her. Sandy needed intimacy. She needed to think about something other than work, and fixing dinner, and sleep—or lack thereof. Truck lived alone; at work, they were best buddies. At the time he gave her the attention she needed and deserved. He listened to her and they laughed frequently, unlike her tense life with Jake.

She tripped and landed on Truck's lap. The world was spinning. His eyes looked warm and his smile sent flutters through her chest and further down. The whiskers on his face scratched her hands when she brushed them across his cheeks. She knew she was drunk. Her face had melted and her words came out wrong, but when she wrapped both hands around his neck and pulled herself up to kiss him, she expected to feel his lips press against hers. She expected him to respond with animal instincts, to maul her with his hands and tell her that he always loved her.

She'd misread the signals. Truck dodged her advances, lifted her to her feet, and carried her inside. He sat her down at the kitchen table, poured a cup of coffee, and listened for hours while she cried and shared her struggles at home and her feelings of inadequacy as a mother and tradesman.

Sandy walked toward the entrance knowing that things were far worse now than they were three years ago. Jake didn't want anything to do with her since Davenport raped her. Not that he had a problem with Sandy at first. He wanted to kill that sick fucker. He wanted to follow him home and return the favor with the barrel of his shotgun, but Sandy wouldn't have it. She wouldn't even report it to the police, and that's when Jake shut down, completely closed off. He could handle the long hours. He could handle the fact that his wife made considerably more money. But he didn't like all the secrets that came with her job, and this thing with Davenport had tested his patience.

She stepped into the rustic roadside pub and hopped up on a barstool. Duke Banks, a large man in height and girth, was stocking liquor bottles behind the bar and turned around.

"Afternoon, Sandy," he said, hiding a smile under his thick white beard. "How you been?"

Sandy forced out a grin. "Not bad. You doing alright, Duke?"

"Can't complain. Can't complain a bit." He closed a box, set it under the counter and leaned forward, giving Sandy his full attention. "What brings you by this early in the day?"

Sandy tried to keep it together but inside she felt like bawling. *Toughen up, girl*, she told herself. "Been a long week, Duke. Just need to loosen up."

Duke chuckled and said, "We can help with that."

"Figured you could."

The barkeeper grabbed a glass. "Jack?"

"Double. Three rocks. Hold the Coke."

"That bad, eh?"

"Yeah. That bad."

Duke fixed her up and left her to her thoughts. He always knew when to leave her alone. And that's exactly what troubled her. She was alone, not just physically, but emotionally, and spiritually. She couldn't tell anyone about her work and what they were doing under there. She'd seen friends lose their wives and husbands and children because they couldn't keep their mouths shut. No one knew who was ultimately responsible. There were too many players—the military—the contractors—the fucking Grays—contract security—those weird guys with the black suits. The underground was run by a who's who of individuals that never existed. Check on Davenport and all that comes up is a soldier who died in Vietnam. Look into Truck and his social security number doesn't even exist. *No wonder they can get rid of us without anyone ever noticing.* Their budget wasn't just black; it was a black hole. They could do anything they wanted to do. They could hire, fire, shoot and maim anyone that got in their way and no one would know whom to blame or point their finger at.

Blame the government and all she'd get is ridiculed and suspicious looks, as if she were some kind of conspiracy theorist whack job. Contact her congresswoman or state senator and they'd never respond. Call a private investigator and he wouldn't get within six miles of Dulce or Black Lake or Las Alamos or Area 51. All she had was the resistance, and she didn't even know who most of them were. Her world had grown increasingly smaller; the underground was closing in on her. And now Truck and Alvarez were down there, too, trying to bring this kid that she knew nothing about, or why he was so damned important, into their world. They were putting everything on the line for him.

Duke set the glass down on the sticky walnut counter and walked away. Sandy picked up the drink and swirled the ice around a few times, hypnotized by the performing cubes as they danced through the golden whiskey. She took a sip, then guzzled the rest. A few minutes later her face felt numb, which was exactly what she was hoping for. She laughed when she thought of her girls, cried when she thought of Jake, and slammed the glass down and asked for another when she thought of Davenport. In between the tears and the buzz, she thought of Truck and Alvarez. Needed to loosen the bolts to get a handle on everything. In the process, she determined she was tired of playing it safe. She could do more. She should. She would… after another drink.

Chapter 31
Fire in the hole

Penn's ears were still ringing from the security guard's rifle when he and Truck burst through the door. He didn't recall hearing Alvarez giving the order to fire. In an instant, all Hell broke loose. The creatures were pissed. They attacked, screaming and hissing, climbing over each other to get at the men. Alvarez and the soldier remained on the other side. Their automatic weapons fired like jackhammers on New York City streets.

Truck told Penn to keep running. He said he'd hold the door until the other guys made it through, but they were taking too long. As he ran, Penn could hear Truck yelling frantically, cursing at the Grays and shouting for the soldiers to get inside. Penn wanted to obey Truck, but the stress of the gunshots and hissing and clawing was eating at him. So when he heard a blood-curdling scream, he had to go back.

He turned around and found Alvarez fighting his way through the door, and Truck lying on the floor, bleeding out. Truck's forearms were shredded from repeated clawing, and his eyes stared blankly at the ceiling, mouth gaping, and body thrashing. A stream of blood flowed across the floor, making it difficult for Alvarez to maintain his footing. He was desperately trying to close the door, but the security guard's arm was stuck between the door and jamb.

As soon as Penn noticed the guard's hemorrhaging fingers, the creatures on the other side pulled the appendage through and it was gone forever. Almost immediately, several four-fingered hands, some with claws, some not, reached through the gap, hoping for a taste of more meat. Their vile voices sent a shot of terror through Penn's heart. He scrambled to the door, and pulled Truck's limp body out of harm's way.

Alvarez slammed the butt of his gun into the Gray's bloody hands and the creatures shrieked on the other side. Penn rushed to his aid, pushing against the steel door with all his strength, relieving Alvarez just enough for him to smash another hand clawing through the gap. The pressure increased like steam in a boiler, bubbling over with each new serpent pushing against the door. Penn could hardly breathe. He couldn't hold them back. Alvarez shoved his back against the bloodstained barrier, straining so hard the veins in his neck were about to explode. His face was filthy and splattered with red bits of Truck and serpent blood. He turned to Penn and said, "Push!"

"Okay," Penn cried unnervingly, sensing the urgency in the man's voice.

Penn bore down with all his weight, carefully protecting his wounds. Alvarez pointed his gun into the widening gap and unloaded the rest of his clip. Pop, pop, pop, pop, pop! Bullets penetrated their target. Some ricocheted, flaring into the tunnel. Penn felt like someone had covered his head with a tin bucket and set off a dozen M-80 firecrackers inside. His ears rang as he watched the frenzied hands fall away.

"Cover your ears," insisted Alvarez as he pulled a grenade from his utility belt, pulled the pin, and tossed it into the tunnel. When Penn heard the grenade hit the floor on the other side, the hissing and clicking came to an abrupt stop. Then Alvarez kicked the door shut, turned the deadbolt, and pulled a steel bar that pivoted, dropping horizontally on a latch.

The grenade detonated, followed by the clatter of falling debris and shifting girders. Everything rattled, including Penn's teeth and bones. The blast threw countless bodies and limbs against the door. Thin lines of dust blast through the cracks surrounding the door and pieces of concrete fell from the ceiling. The pressure shocked Penn so intensely that he lost his balance and slipped on Truck's oozing lifeblood. He caught himself mid-fall, but a sharp burn zipped up his arm like he'd twisted a nerve with a pair of vice grips.

Alvarez helped him to his feet, but Penn still slid clumsily over the blood, totally freaking him out.

"Sorry, Truck!" Penn said apologetically looking at the older man, incapable of recognizing the seriousness of the man's injuries.

"Let's go," said Alvarez.

"What about Truck, and the guard?" said Penn, pointing.

"We have to leave them."

The runner was sweating, shaking, and bleeding profusely as he lay crumpled on the floor. Penn grabbed his arm and tried to pull him over his shoulder, but the dead weight was unbearable.

"There's too many, Penn. They'll break through soon enough," commanded Alvarez, pulling his gun's shoulder strap over his head. "We have to run. We have to meet Badger at Dulce."

Penn crouched down and tried to lift Truck again. A ribbon of blood washed across the ground as his arm trailed over the concrete, and Penn was forced to surrender. Truck mumbled something as Penn's ear rubbed across his whiskery face, but Penn couldn't understand what he said, so he pulled back, hoping to read his lips.

Weary and barely breathing, Truck whispered, "Let... me... go."

Penn felt hysterical, like he'd lost a limb and he needed to pick it up and stick it back on. Everything felt crazy. He couldn't understand why Alvarez was staring at him. He couldn't understand why Truck was just lying there.

"Run... Penn. Save... yourself," said Truck.

Penn shook his head. "No way," he insisted, jostling Truck up on his shoulders. Truck's one hundred and seventy pounds weighed Penn down, aggravating his already wounded shoulder. He slumped to his knees and Truck collapsed to the floor.

The runner's face was losing all color. His eyes could barely stay open.

Penn slapped Truck in the face, panicking. "Truck. Come on. Snap out of it."

"Get out of here," wheezed Truck.

Alvarez knelt down. "We have to go, kid."

Penn glared at him. "We can't leave him."

"They'll kill us, Penn... Kill both of us," replied Alvarez.

"No!" cried Penn, as knots twisted in his stomach.

"Now!" commanded Alvarez, gripping Penn's orange sleeve. "We don't have time."

Truck's breathing slowed. His eyes rolled backward and his head rolled to the side. He took one last breath and passed on.

Penn had never seen anyone die before. He didn't know how to respond or what to say. For a moment, everything around him disappeared. All he could see was Truck's pale face, silver whiskers, and blood-splattered hollow cheeks. He felt his chin begin to quiver and tried to control it, to master it. But watching Truck waste away was too much. Tears welled in his eyes, and he knew it was over. Penn stared, war-weary, tears pouring out. His only redeeming thought was that Truck had a cross dangling from a leather band. It had made its way out from under his shirt, revealing the man's faith in an extraordinary fashion.

At least there was that, thought Penn. *At least he had faith in something,* something Penn thought very little about. Penn wiped his tears with a dirty sleeve and felt Alvarez tugging. He heard a scratching at the door. The hissing, clicking, and pounding had begun again, shocking Penn back into reality and into survival mode.

The security bar rattled and then bowed when the door boomed forward. Alvarez pulled Penn's sleeve. "Time's up, Penn. We have to run. Now!"

Torn from Truck's lifeless body, Penn was forced to his feet. Alvarez reached into his backpack, grabbed a gun, and handed Penn the pistol. He took hold of Penn's shirt again, twisting it with a balled fist, pulled him close and said, "Aim for the head." Breathing heavily, Alvarez had never looked so fierce. He unlocked the safety and checked that the gun was loaded. Satisfied, Alvarez said, "Do you hear me?"

Penn nodded, overcome with terror now that he'd snapped back into reality.

"Their skin's high in carbon. Hard to get a kill shot." Alvarez pointed between Penn's eyes. Right here. Got it?"

Penn nodded feverishly and said, "Okay…. I will."

It was like Alvarez had turned on a switch, activating something ferocious within. His eyes, darkened from spattered blood, were on full alert. Every motion blistering, his once gentle voice, now commanding. He loaded another clip in his gun and said, "Stay in front and don't stop running."

Alvarez nudged Penn forward and they took off. As much as Penn feared what the Grays would do to Truck, his thoughts veered to the tunnel ahead. The walls were built of concrete and painted white. An endless line of yellow tape on the ground pointed the way. The familiar scene reminded Penn of his book— the battles, and the escape routes. It seemed Truck and Thunder Lady were right. This was not fiction.

As they came to a fork in the trail, Penn had to make a decision: turn left, toward the closest maglev, or right, through a tunnel that neither Penn nor Alvarez were very familiar with. Penn knew Badger's place was near Las Alamos, but the directions were fuzzy. Penn remembered that most of the resistance only knew how to get there above ground; the path underneath was a different story. If they could get to the closest maglev, they'd be at Dulce in no time, probably rolling right under Badger's mountainside barn.

Penn knew where to go. They ran about a half-mile until they came to another service tunnel. "This way," he said, "We can take another maglev to the Dulce caves."

"You sure?" asked Alvarez.

"Yes. I mean… I think so."

"I think you're right," said Alvarez. "Good work."

They entered a secondary maglev staging area. Penn took control via Alvarez's command. They put on their harnesses and helmets and zipped off. The 125-mile trip took eighteen minutes without a hitch.

They offloaded the maglev and re-entered the tunnel system. Alvarez unpacked a spelunking headlight and fastened it around Penn's head. They had a couple more hours of travel in the tunnels, but Penn didn't complain, thinking of Truck.

"More caves?" asked Penn.

"Yes," said Alvarez. "This won't be easy. We're in their territory now."

"Their territory? I thought we're in federal territory."

"I wish. This is their home. We're trespassing."

Chapter 32
War Room

After refueling in Oklahoma City, Liz and her tactical response team landed at Las Alamos National Laboratory in New Mexico. Liz hopped out of the bird and onto the hot tarmac. Las Alamos seemed like a ghost town, but when the site's leadership heard Liz was pursuing Dean Jones—aka Penn Mitchell—their superiors were curious about what she had to say, giving her crew permission to land. A soldier escorted her into a meeting where military and civilian leaders had gathered.

A young soldier led her into a plush conference room, opened the door and said, "They're in here, Agent Ramsey." He smiled graciously and said, "Have a pleasant day." She thanked him and entered the room.

The first thing Liz noticed beside the table of men was the outside wall made of glass panels—floor to ceiling—a third-story view of the site's tarmac. The three interior walls were painted light blue, adorned with pictures of past presidents, generals, and other military heroes. The American flag stood proudly on a flagpole beside a framed picture of the current President of the United States.

A tall man in uniform, chest covered with medals and stripes, and shoulders shielded with four silver stars, stood up, and said, "Hello, Agent Ramsey. Please have a seat." He gestured toward the last available chair at the opposite end of the table. Twenty or more seats were filled with officers and a few men in suits, including Luke Martin. They stood up like gentlemen, nodded, and smiled courteously. She sat down first, and the others followed.

After a few perfunctory introductions and welcome to Las Alamos bullshit, General Johnathan Smith asked her what she knew about Dean Jones.

"I don't believe there is a Dean Jones," Liz answered matter-of-factly. "We believe his name is Penn Mitchell, an NYU student, and author of the book, Federal Underground."

"What's your connection to Mr. Jones... eh, pardon me, Penn Mitchell. Did I say that correctly?" asked the General.

"Yes. It's Penn, as in the writing utensil, only with two n's." Liz chuckled along with a few others.

"And why do you believe *Penn* is posing as Dean Jones?"

"Sir, with all due respect, I believe there's a network of military and civilian terrorists manipulating

Penn Mitchell, selling him as a programmer to get him underground. I don't know why, exactly, but the fact that he has a military clearance to enter one of the country's most secure sites proves that the network has infiltrated your computer and security systems."

The officers whispered amongst themselves.

"And what does this young author want?" asked one of the brass seated near General Smith.

"I don't know," said Liz. "I don't think he wants anything."

"Then why is he down there?" asked a stiff looking officer with three gold stars.

Liz shrugged. "It's complicated. I can give you the long story if you want but—"

"We'll take the short story," said General Smith, "if you don't mind."

"Okay. The short story: He wrote a book that you'd be very interested in—lots of top-secret goodies. I read it, and reported it to my superior, Special Agent Ted Gilmore, because I didn't think a young college kid would know about stuff like that—aliens, details about the underground rail systems, nuclear launch sites, and coordinates to top secret outposts. He described this very place like he was standing here painting the colors and smells of the decades-old tobacco smell, the flag, and every one of your heroes on the wall." Liz watched the men shuffle in their seats. There was no nameplate or placard on the door that she could remember, so she asked. "Is this the War Room?"

General Smith leaned forward, appearing curious. "Maybe."

"It's in the book," answered Liz, pausing while they whispered again. "Anyway, Gilmore read Federal Underground, doing his due diligence, and came to the same conclusion I did. When we apprehended Penn to ask a few questions, he denied any knowledge of military secrets, and passed his book off as fiction."

"Do you have a copy of the book?" asked a young officer sitting to her right.

"Not here. But you can find it in every bookstore across the country."

"So, tell us," said General Smith, as he poured water from a pitcher into a clear glass cup. "How did Penn end up in the maglev?"

"Things got out of hand. There was a foot chase, and we lost him. He completely disappeared underneath the New York Field office. We couldn't find him anywhere. After tracking his phone with the NSA, we pinpointed his location—in *your* underground rail system. And I have reason to believe someone intercepted him and is aiding his escape."

"Any suspects?" asked Luke Martin.

"No," responded Liz. "It's just hard to imagine that the kid could survive down there, let alone control a train."

"It's a maglev," said Luke. "And the touch screens aren't really that difficult to figure out." He rolled away from the table in his wheelchair, approaching Liz. "Maybe he got scared, snuck into someplace he shouldn't have been, and stumbled upon the tunnel. The touch screens are duck soup."

The officers shifted their gaze from Luke to Liz expectantly.

"I don't think so," said Liz, noticing their confusion. "Here's why. When I first read the book, I was convinced that it was his way of whistleblowing. But after questioning him, I started to believe him; he was just telling a story. Said the tale was banging around his noggin and he needed to set it free."

"And you believe him?" asked General Smith.

"Yes and no. I believe he *thinks* it was just a story. But I think he knows more than he thinks."

Luke rolled next to Liz and said, "And that's why you think there are others involved? That he's just a pawn?"

"See... that's where it gets tricky. That's why I need to find him... why *we* need to find him. If there are others assisting Penn, manipulating your computer systems and plugging top-secret information into some random kid's brain so he can write a book unbeknownst of its origin, we're dealing with something bigger than a sleeper cell. We're talking a total collapse of the Department of Defense security."

"I wouldn't call it a total collapse," said Luke, snickering. "A bug in the system, maybe. A collapse? Not hardly."

"The kid cleared numerous military retina scanners," said Liz. "What would you call that?"

The room went silent for a few moments before General Smith stood up and walked toward the large pane overlooking the tarmac. He looked through the glass and said, "What makes you think someone brainwashed him?"

"I didn't say brainwash."

The General turned toward Liz. "You insinuated. Why?"

Liz looked away, realizing they didn't know about his abduction. She gripped the arms of her chair, feeling pressured. They weren't asking the superfluous questions she assumed they would. "Well," she said. "That's why it's more complicated than the short story. There's more."

"Go ahead then," said the General. "We're listening."

"Okay. He was abducted several months before he published the book."

The officers grumbled. "Abducted?... Why didn't we know?... Why was he...?"

"It was all over the news—The Times—Fox—CNN—Yahoo," said Liz, "He was gone for a month. Came back with amnesia, headaches, nightmares. He even dropped out of college for a while. Was a shame, because he had a full ride."

"And this book?" asked the General. "What's it about?"

Liz looked at the men surrounding her. She sighed and said, "It's about us, about all of this. It's about everything happening right now."

Luke rolled back and addressed the General. "That's ridiculous."

"It's not likely," said Liz, "But every minute that passes by I feel like I'm living the story. And the kid's imitating the life of the main character, Badger, a Central Intelligence agent who finds himself in the underground on the run from the Feds, and facing the perils of the government's biggest secret."

"And what's that?" asked General Smith with a haughty grin. He walked away from the glass toward Liz, peering at her quizzically. "What is the government's greatest secret, Agent Ramsey?"

Liz immediately thought of the wall-crawler, and the creatures Penn wrote about. "The ET's." She assumed they'd laugh out loud and disregard her. "The secret, according to the book, is the government's treaty with a civilization that's lived under the earth for tens of thousands of years. The secret is that the DoD uses vast sums of black budget money to keep them hidden, to assist in genetic research, to re-engineer their technology, and to block Earth's real history. In exchange, they receive protection and cover when the U.S. Government parks their ass on top of their hives, safeguarding them from anyone who might discover the truth. Oh, and the DoD provides for their food so they don't have to sneak out of their crypt when they get the munchies. That's what's in the book, sir."

Liz could've continued, but the chuckling and laughter grew too loud.

One of the officers seated on the left in the center of the table tried to hush the jeering taking place. The white-haired middle-aged officer stood up and asked Liz what they eat. He seemed sincere, his voice calm and reasonable.

"Rodents, among other species."

"What other species?" asked Luke, glaring as if he already knew the answer.

Liz looked the men over, imagining how they'd fare in Hell Hall on Level Seven in the Dulce Base. Part of her hoped it was all a joke, totally fiction. Part of her feared for her life.

"Us," she said. "They eat us, gentlemen...according to the book. According to Penn Mitchell, they are the Serpents who tempted Eve in the Bible, the Nephilim mentioned in ancient texts. They are the personification of evil that we fear, and their fiery home, Hell, is real and it's underneath us. As unimaginable as it may sound, they are the mystery behind secret societies, in The President's alleged Book of Secrets, passed on by Masons who first cut into their dwellings and raving scribes who documented the encounters. Those who survived an encounter passed them off as evil spirits and demons, or they chose to keep the knowledge to themselves."

The room fell silent. Liz felt a little foolish. Their silence could mean so many things. Hearing herself didn't help. It did sound crazy. But then she remembered Badger and the creature she saw down in the cave. That was real. She knew she wasn't crazy.

They could've made her feel a little nuts, but then she told herself to n*ever back down... especially not now.*

The men sitting before her could be part of the solution, or part of the cover-up—if one really existed. There wasn't any way to tell. She didn't know who to trust. She'd have to navigate her way through these brass barriers—just her and the SWAT guys, and she wasn't sure how committed they'd be if things went sideways.

General Smith walked closer to Liz, crossed his arms and said, "So you're hoping *your* Penn Mitchell is *our* Dean Jones?"

"Yes."

"And if he is?"

"Then we all have a real problem on our hands."

General Smith laughed and stopped a few feet short of Liz, and looked over her shoulder. Liz followed his gaze. The soldier who escorted her was standing at the door. He saluted the General, and said, "I have an urgent message for you, sir."

The General walked to the door and the soldier handed him a piece of paper. He read the memo and turned around, his face grew flush as his eyes revealed his irritation. He peered at a few select officers, and said, "Meeting adjourned." He rushed down the hall and the other officers quickly stood up, pushed their chairs in, and hurried out of the room. Only Luke Martin remained.

Luke rolled his wheelchair next to Liz and said, "You've stirred up quite a hornet's nest."

Liz sighed. "They must think I'm an idiot."

"I doubt that."

"Oh really?" said Liz, snickering. "Why did they leave? Was it something I said?"

"I don't think so... I expect the hunt for Dean Jones isn't going so well."

Liz stood up and walked to the door, hoping to see where the officers had gone. The SWAT team had gathered outside the room, waiting, and turned their attention to her when she stepped through the doorway.

The pilot leaned his shoulder against the wall next to the door and joked, "What have you done?"

Liz sneered. "Made a fool of myself."

"You sure?" replied the pilot.

Liz narrowed her eyes and asked, "Why?"

"Something's going on. They got troops gathering, red lights flashing, and I don't think it's a tornado drill."

"Are you serious?" she asked.

"I wouldn't lie to you, Liz." He motioned her to follow. "Come see for yourself."

Luke rolled past the agents. "Wait," he said. He spun in a quarter circle to face them. "I'll take you. I know exactly where they're going."

Chapter 33
They all Float

Sandy called Truck's cell phone but it never made a connection.

He's too deep.

"Damn it!"

She asked Duke for a cup of black coffee to go. When he handed it to her, he asked again if she was okay. "Just fine," she said with resolve in her voice. Something had clicked over in her, and it wasn't just the alcohol.

"Thanks for everything," she said, nodding at Duke, grateful for his non-judgmental establishment.

She dropped a twenty on the bar and headed to the Jeep, barely cable of steadying her coffee. It spilled on her denim shirt, while she dug through her purse for her keys, so she set it on the roof. After finding the keys, she revved the V-8 and backed up. The coffee splashed across her windshield, and the cup rolled across the hood. Cursing her absentmindedness, she turned on the windshield wipers and drove away.

Not my day, I guess.

Sandy made it home in record time, at least an hour before the girls would step off the bus. She barely missed an old Apache woman pulling her donkey on the side of the road and barreled sideways into her dirt driveway. Dust billowed and the crunching gravel sounded like a landslide. She hopped out of the Jeep, walking right through the dirty cloud and into the cabin. The sun gleamed over Mount Monero to the west but it would disappear in just a few hours, blanketing her homestead with a mammoth shadow. All of Dulce would lock their doors, count children, and barn up livestock if they had any. Many of the residents lived off the grid. They conserved energy by turning off unneeded lights, making the town and countryside nearly black after sunset. She'd leave a note for Jake and the girls, telling them what to make for supper and a list of the things she'd usually take care of. *Can't forget to set out a half pound of ground beef. And by God, Jake better not forget to bring in the retriever before bed.*

Sandy gathered water bottles, loaded the spare fuel tank, and tossed some extra clothes in a duffle bag. She thought of her route: east, away from the Monero Mountain range and then south on State Route 84, merge into Route 30 and then Rural Route 502. The almost two-hour trip south would get her close to Los Alamos Laboratory before dark, but then finding Badger's place was another story altogether. She always got lost when she hit the White Rock area.

That's where dirt roads bled into the desert and rattlesnakes were mistaken for winding trails. And when the sun goes down... *Flashlight! Damn. I almost forgot—batteries, too.*

She stuffed a fresh pack of Duracells and a headlamp in her bag, and then inspected her crossbow. Made damn sure she had plenty of bolts. Thankful that Jake talked her into joining him when he went hunting, she took off her work clothes and threw on her Gore-Tex camouflage and hiking boots. She wrapped a belt around her waist, slipped on a holster and packed her pistol in case things got ugly. She threw everything in the Jeep, including matches and the two-man tent and then drove toward Las Alamos.

•••

The drive was long and White Rock was growing dim as the Jemez Mountains swallowed the daylight. Distant stars began to emerge, and that was always a sign that it was time to turn in. But not tonight. She needed to find that unmarked road at the edge of Highway 4, where the skull-shaped boulder sat beside the Native American jewelry shack. She took a hard right and then three miles back north on a road that was barely visible in the light of day.

When she made the turn, she could've sworn she saw a shooting star to her left. But that was probably her imagination. She needed to concentrate—to focus on the task ahead. Truck needed her, and she had a roundabout responsibility to get Penn Mitchell safely to Badger.

The edge of the road was lined with Buffalo Junipers, Burr Oak trees and Austrian Black Pines, but they thinned out the further she drove. This was the road, no doubt about that. But it didn't look like anyone had traveled it for years. Sandy figured that's the way Badger liked it. He lived close enough to White Rock to snag the Internet service and buy life necessities, but far enough off the grid for anyone to notice he was there. When she brought Truck into the fold, it was her responsibility to introduce him to Badger. That was only the second time she'd been there; this was the third.

The Jeep jounced up the dirty road. The rocks grew bigger as she barreled on, remembering she needed to endure the discomfort until she came to the twin boulders. That's where she'd park the vehicle and carry her gear another half mile up a winding path until she arrived at the barn. Positive she was getting close, she slowed down and turned off the radio.

Then it happened again.

She thought she'd seen another shooting star to her left. She turned and looked around. The crescent moon barely graced the Earth with its light. Everything looked black outside except her beaming headlights.

She leaned forward, hunting for the twin boulders when something landed on the hood of the Jeep. Came right out of nowhere. She slammed on the brakes and the Jeep's light filled with foggy dirt. Her arms locked and her head jerked forward. She looked like a pile of rags. The junk didn't move; neither did Sandy. She wondered if someone had dropped a ball of supplies from a plane or if it was waste from an airliner. *Talk about being in the wrong place at the wrong time.* She opened the door and pulled out her loaded pistol— pointed it forward and then left and right, searching in all directions. *Did I hit someone?* Then the thought that she hit Badger raced through her mind and practically destroyed her. She didn't remember seeing anyone on the road. Not even a deer or possum.

There weren't any tracks near the Jeep; not a footprint. There were no sounds that alerted her, no smells to guide her senses except the stench coming from the clump on the hood. *What the hell is that?* Sandy stepped closer and poked the wad of clothing with her gun. It didn't move. She jabbed it again— harder. Nothing. With her arm outstretched, she used the barrel of her gun to lift the material but quickly released the damp mess. The clothes were soaked in red fluid, and smelled of decaying flesh. Some of it was dry and crusty, most of it was wet and sticky. Whatever it was, it *wasn't* living anymore.

Distraught by the idea that she might have killed Badger or any human besides Davenport, she reached for the bloodied rags, disgusted, and pulled it off the hood. The remains hit the earth with a splat. *Didn't sound like a human body. Not very heavy either.* She lifted the edge of what looked like a T-shirt and found more bloody clothes: jeans, running shoes, and in the center, a pile of human bones. Not a shred of entrails or sinew remained. Sandy stared—eyes wide open— knees buckling. Her heart raced. She forced the bile in her throat to stay back where it belonged. Her mind ran wild with questions. *Who could it be? How'd it get there? Is there a murderer nearby? Is he toying with me?*

In the midst of the terror coursing through her being, she realized there could be a wallet or some form of identification. She pushed back her fears and rummaged through the clothing, sickened by the blood, unraveling the fibrous puzzle until she saw something glimmering among the rib bones—a leather band. She reached through the collarbone and grabbed a necklace, hoping she wouldn't recognize it.

When she saw the tiny gold crucifix tied to the leather, she shrunk back in horror. She knew who it was; she recognized the pendant. She held it in her blood-soaked hands and studied it, hoping that her mind was playing tricks on her. But it wasn't. The pendant belonged to Truck. Then from somewhere high up, a light beamed down. She sprung back and the light followed, widening until it completely engulfed her. The beam was blinding. It was warm. Electrifying. Whatever hovered above her didn't make a sound. With one hand blocking the glare, she pointed the gun and blasted a warning shot. The light went out, but she knew the object was still there. She grabbed the leather and cross from the bloody mass and sprinted toward Badger's barn on the hill.

Whatever was up there followed her silently overhead. They had killed Truck and were coming after her, too. It seemed to be stalking, silently waiting to subdue her under the blanket of darkness. She could feel the foul intentions of those inside—kept her looking over her shoulder every few seconds. Still she ran, pushing back the hopeless feelings that tried to rise to the surface. Badger wasn't far. He could help. *Just run*, she thought. *Just keep running.*

Sandy looked up to her left, racing through the brush and dirt and rocky terrain. The thing looked like a round shadow, a dark sphere camouflaged by the night. And when the moonbeams glowed just right, it looked metallic, like a living, breathing ball of chrome. She knew what it was. She knew who they were. She reached back and shot two rounds, knowing full well the act was futile. But it felt good to shoot. The light beamed down, honing its ray to a thin line, slowly moving closer to her. She gripped the crucifix tight in her fist, scrambling toward the barn. In the distance, she could see an orange glow through a window in the loft. She shot her gun at the UFO, aiming while she continued running. Didn't matter if she missed; she needed to warn Badger, rouse him up, get his attention. She could only imagine how many locks and bolts the guy needed to unlatch before he'd open the front door.

The ray's trajectory was within several feet. She called for Badger, shouting his name. She saw someone inside the upper windowpane. The silhouette moved, peeked through the glass, and disappeared. She prayed he'd come to the door. Looking back, she could see the beam illuminating the undergrowth like a plasma cutter. She knocked, pounding desperately.

"Badger! Open up!"

He didn't answer and she couldn't stand there waiting. The beam was coming closer. She ran around the barn, hoping to find a loose board or open door somewhere around back. When she turned the corner, she sprinted to the rear but was quickly reminded that the barn was built on the side of a mountain. The dirt and rubble inclined sharply, bringing her closer to the roofline with every step, and closer to the craft.

She turned back and slipped under the overhang. The beam had disappeared. It must've lost her in the shadows.

Refusing to waste a single breath, Sandy pounded on the barn walls, rounded the corner again, and continued calling Badger near the entrance. She could hear locks sliding, unlatching behind the door.

"Badger, hurry! It's Sandy! Help me!"

She pounded on the door over and over, looked up and saw the sphere circling above the gable. The door started shaking, the barn siding rattled, and the roof clattered overhead. The entire building sounded like it was going to fall apart. The beam shot straight down, severing the moonlight, etching the crusty earth toward Sandy.

She heard another clasp slide and the door finally opened. She looked up and fired her last round at the orb.

"Fucking demons!"

Badger grabbed her left wrist and squeezed. "Get in here," he commanded, tugging her arm.

Then just as she took her first step into the doorway, the beam of light caught her feet and she felt its warmth penetrate her bones. She screamed and pulled the trigger, click after empty click, while Badger pulled seemingly against her will. Fully in shock and frightened for her life, she turned away from the sphere and stared at Badger as if she'd seen the face of God, unable to move. But she didn't think about running, she could only think about the mound of blood and bones back there in the dirt.

"Truck's dead," she said, "They killed him."

She handed Badger the necklace, cupping it in his hand.

"He's gone," she said, her voice cracking painfully. "There's nothing left of him."

The light enveloped her legs and she felt its paralyzing heat. Overcome with a weightless sensation, the gun fell from her hands and she gripped the left side of the doorframe. Her feet started rising off the ground. Undeterred, she reached out to Badger and he gripped her forearms with the leather cord and cross dangling from his hands. He tugged as hard as he could, but he couldn't overcome the antigravity technology. And although she didn't understand it, she felt a sudden urge to let go, but she resisted.

"Pull!" she screamed through the wind that'd begun stirring the dust. Her legs lifted horizontally, then high above her head. Her nails dug into the old wood as she attempted to claw her way inside the barn. Badger's hands slipped, wet from perspiration, sliding down her forearms and making their way to her fingertips. They were both screaming. The barn was shaking. Debris from the ground swirled all around.

Resigning to her fate, she looked up and felt oddly captivated by the light that had engulfed her. Badger's words grew empty, his fingertips barely grasping hers. Although his teeth were clenched and his body valiantly deployed, Sandy knew it was over. She watched him as if he were performing in slow motion—a beautifully choreographed, futile show of selflessness. His black hair and beard whirled around his face while he helplessly witnessed her abduction. The loss and pain were apparent in his eyes; that she could see, clearly. But the beam devoured her body, reeling her away from Badger and into the blazing light.

Badger's voice grew faint. He called her name and she could read his lips—*Sandy... I'll find you... Don't give up...* She knew what he said, but there was no sound except the turbulence of wind and energy buzzing through her ears.

She hovered over Badger like a hummingbird. Vertigo prevailed. She felt nauseous, lightheaded. Her body floated up, and she thought of Stephen King's *IT* "they all float down here" scene. *But where was "here"? Is that where I'm going? Down there? What about the girls? And Jake? They need me.* She levitated ten, twenty, thirty yards above Badger and everything about her life became nothing more than a distant memory. Her thoughts of her children, work, and the resistance faded as she entered the belly of the craft. Badger vanished in the light. She swam in it. It felt warm. It felt relaxing... It felt amazing *up here*.

Chapter 34
A River Runs Through It

Penn pumped his arms, trying to ignore the burning in his shoulder. He gripped the pistol, hoping he'd never use it, and ran as fast as he could through the dark passage. The tunnel zigzagged, sinking deeper with every stride, lighted only by his headlamp and the dim beam coming from Alvarez's light. The air was damp and cool, reeking of eggy sulfur. He was thankful for the fresh draft that breathed through an occasional chasm or shaft drilled from above the surface. He couldn't help but wonder how far down he really was. The path was steep at times, slippery and sharp, but he and Alvarez kept running until they entered another chamber.

As the tunnel opened, Penn stopped abruptly, nearly falling into a hole in the moist floor. He looked down and his headlamp revealed a raging river under the perforated stone. Looking ahead, it seemed as if a large bridge had formed into a mesh-like structure. The stony latticework clung to the outer walls like a spider's web. Below, the current had eroded the rock to its bare bones, forming a floor that resembled a ribcage: the water below, its blood; the open chamber, the lungs. An occasional stalactite hung from the ceiling, kissing the webbing, stabbing the bony ribs as water splashed up through the car-tire sized cavities in the floor.

"What is this?" asked Penn, breathing hard, noticing Alvarez' confused look.

"It *was* a solid floor. We're supposed to meet Badger in a cave on the other side," said Alvarez. "But this is new. The water must've cut through the stone in the last few weeks."

Penn stepped closer and felt a gush of air pushing through the openings in the cave floor. Sounded like a giant seashell. The deluge boomed throughout the cavern, splattering tiny droplets on his face as it sprayed.

"What do we do?" asked Penn, shouting over the teeming water, stepping back from the edge. "It's too wet to pass over. If we slip, we're done."

"We have to cross it," insisted Alvarez.

Penn evaluated the gaping holes and he felt butterflies flapping in his gut. He could only imagine how deep and far the water traveled.

Alvarez studied the cave and then looked over his shoulder. "It's our only way out."

"You think it can handle our weight?" asked Penn.

"Doesn't matter. They'll eventually get through that door and there's no way we can kill 'em all. They won't stop until they catch us, or they'll communicate with the closest hive. One or the other."

Penn canvassed the floor and noticed a wider path that snaked its way around the holes, well supported by stalagmites. "See that trail?" he said, pointing.

Alvarez observed the path. "Yeah. I see it."

"What do you think?" asked Penn.

"Can't hurt, can it?" said Alvarez, kneeling down and reaching into his backpack. He pulled out a rope and handed it to Penn. "Here. Tie it on to the stalactites every chance you get."

Penn flung the neatly wound rope over his shoulder and took his first step on the spindly rock. He turned back for a moment, doubting if this was the right move. Alvarez watched Penn carefully, nodding encouragingly. Penn focused on his footing although his nerves were shot. He took a few steps, balancing between the gaping holes and tied the rope on the closest stalactite. When he pulled the double knot tight, he hugged the calcified pillar and took a deep breath. Peering into the nearest hole, the water looked dark and foamy in places. This was no bubbling brook. One wrong move and bye bye, Penn.

"Tie the other end around under your armpits," said Alvarez. "Just to be safe."

Penn did as he was told, trying to ignore the pain in his shoulder. Feeling like a worm on a hook, he felt his shoes slip after taking his first step. Alvarez warned him to be careful.

Penn's heart raced and he did his best to steady himself.

"Move carefully but quickly," instructed Alvarez. "We don't have all day."

Still hugging the rock, Penn nodded and took a step forward.

"If we get to the other side, we can destroy the stalactites. Maybe it'll collapse."

Sounded good to Penn. He never wanted to see another Gray again. He recalled the story his mother used to teach him about the serpent in the Garden of Eden, and how the devil slithered up that tree and deceived Eve. Used to give him nightmares. And even then, the thought sent a chill up his spine. *Could these things really be the serpents spoken of in the Bible?* Distracted, he took his eyes off the floor and lost his balance, narrowly clutching the rope.

"You okay?" asked Alvarez.

Penn rested a moment, catching his breath and planting his feet.

"Yeah. Barely."

"Good. I'm right behind you."

Alvarez shuffled over the rock and the two traversed the slick stones, navigating over the webbing when Penn heard a rumbling in the distance. He snapped his head back in the direction where the noise came from and lost his footing. Alvarez snagged Penn's arm and together they fell awkwardly to the floor with a grunt. Penn slipped feet first into the water. Alvarez landed on his side, barely gripping the rope. The water felt ice cold and flowed much faster than Penn imagined, drawing him into the current.

"Alvarez!" cried Penn, clasping the rope with his right hand as his body slipped deeper into the river. He tried to inch his way up the rope, but he didn't have the strength.

"Don't let go, Penn!" shouted Alvarez as he scrambled to get closer.

"I'm trying...but it's pulling me in."

Penn felt the cold rise to his chest, water filling his jumpsuit. His arms were slipping on the wet rock, splashing like a child frolicking in the ocean.

Alvarez dropped his backpack and lay down on a stable part of the floor near Penn. He wrapped the rope around his hand and wrist, reaching for Penn's arm.

The current was sucking Penn's legs under the rock and the limestone floor cut against his chest like a guillotine. He was afraid it might cut him in half. The pressure against his ribs made it hard to breathe.

"Pull me up," begged Penn, straining for air. "I'm slipping!"

"I need to reposition," shouted Alvarez, as he spun around.

"Hurry!" said Penn.

Alvarez reached down with both hands and grabbed Penn's forearm with one hand and the back of his jumpsuit with the other. He pulled from the back and Penn could feel that it was making a difference. The water sprayed his eyes and face, making it difficult to breathe.

"I can't see," said Alvarez. "The water's beating the shit out of me. I have to get behind you!"

Penn felt the water yank him back the moment Alvarez let go. When he started pulling again, Penn said, "It's working." But then Alvarez let go and reached for his bag.

Penn looked back in dismay. He felt the water breaking over his shoulders and said, "What the hell are you doing?"

Alvarez pointed toward the path where they came from and said, "Look!"

Penn couldn't see past the water pummeling his face—there were only shadows.

"They're coming!" shouted Alvarez.

Penn turned his head and wiped his eyes at the risk of getting sucked in. His headlamp reflected in the water and beamed a shimmering light across the walls. Further in the distance, he could see the shadow of a hundred bodies emerging, and it was approaching rapidly, silent against the raging torrent.

Chapter 35
The Barn

Badger slammed the door shut and locked the deadbolts. "Damn it, Sandy!" He ran upstairs, looked out the loft window and watched the craft shoot toward the north. There was no question in his mind where they were taking her or what they could do. He'd seen it before—from the human storage facility to the biological experiments and a machine that made human smoothies. What he didn't understand was why they'd come after Sandy. There was always a reason. Abductees were usually taken intentionally. Either she'd pissed off an elder Gray, or was given over to them by a human authority figure. So Badger figured there could only be one explanation—Davenport.

Davenport wasn't known for making hasty decisions—cruel decisions, yes—not hasty. He'd built a reputation on his strict adhesion to policy, so using the Grays as a weapon against the resistance could pose a new—and serious—problem. The military generally performed internal investigations where uprisings were concerned, and the Grays managed their own as well. It was the difference in how they dealt with rebellion that separated the two life forms.

The military began with an investigation, court martial, or a simple dismissal of civilian contractors. The Grays would start by throwing the accused into the liquefier—guilty upon accusation. *Sink 'em and drink 'em* was the phrase used to describe a Gray's fate if it betrayed the will of his race.

Badger knew full well how the Grays handled discipline. They offered to punish any of the men and women on the human side, if needed, but that was usually an unacceptable solution. The Department of Defense generally resisted offering their soldiers and tradesmen as food. The CIA and other agencies could find plenty of human waste around the globe suitable for the Grays. Homeless. Schizophrenics. Hookers. Dope heads. Runaways. Starving children in Africa—when young blood was required to satisfy an offense. The powers that be couldn't control global population—not without an elimination factory, anyway. So they got rid of the rubbish with kidnappings, abductions, and allowances made through treaties with the Grays that later developed into human trafficking to meet the needs of wealthy deviants acquainted with the DoD's dirty little secret. After all, silence comes with a price.

But the Grays needed to eat, too. And they needed to perform biological experiments. Experiments they hoped would return their race to the prominence it once knew when they were demigods to those above ground. This was the core of Badger's theology, a theology handed down from Bruce Warnill. Badger's work in the CIA aroused his curiosities when he experienced the corruption and whitewashing regarding abductions and disappearances of innocent lives. It wasn't until he met Bruce that he learned there was more to the story, a story literally covered up long ago. In a moment of sheer honesty, Badger questioned Bruce about the cover-ups and weird goings-on. Bruce replied with utter frankness, entrusting the agent with a sizeable portion of the truth.

The terrestrials had retreated underground thousands of years ago, quietly snatching their sustenance. The creatures were lost to history with little more than myths and legends that scarcely proved their existence. But then in 1942 when the Army Corps of Engineers discovered the hive near Dulce, New Mexico and started dropping nukes out west, everything changed. Human technology had awakened the age-old sleeping giants under the earth. When the War Department learned that the military and the Grays had mutual interests, they found a way to meet each other's needs. Within a few years, reports of Gray aliens were popping up everywhere because "permitted" abductions were increasing exponentially. The "aliens" were given freedom to take to the skies, a strategy that would discombobulate the human race to no end, further concealing the true origins of the serpent race.

With Bruce's knowledge of ancient cultures, Badger learned the full truth. According to Bruce, the Israelites attempted to eliminate the serpents and the peoples they had infected by order of their God, Yahweh. The Rephaim (giants), Amorites (slayers), Jebusites (polluted), Hivites (serpent men), Emim (terrible ones), and the Nephilim, who devoured the inhabitants of Canaan, were tainted morally and genetically due to the spiritual corruption of the fallen ones—the angels. The evidence was out there waiting to be found in every culture around the globe. And it all boiled down to genetics. By studying ancient symbols, Bruce discovered that genetic tampering was commonplace throughout the ages, indicated by the frequent display of the rod of Ascelpius, a winged staff with double-helix serpents created by ancient cultures who worshiped serpents and the demigods that tampered with human genetics. It was the serpent race, known today as the Grays, that tainted the genes by breeding with humans; hence the serpentine double-helix, the very symbol established by modern medicine long before DNA was introduced into our modern vocabulary. Although there were many occult uses and theories regarding the symbol, Badger knew its true origin. And he knew that their genetic tampering had slowly transformed their historically serpentine appearance into what is known as the twenty-first century Gray alien.

Badger and Bruce were convinced the ancient knowledge must be exposed. Some believe the gods were simply mythological. Some believe they came from distant planets. Others, like Bruce and Badger, held a firm belief, based on the recurring presence of wings on these demigods seen in Egyptian, Babylonian, Mesopotamian and other ancient artifacts, that they were the descendants of the fallen angels detailed in the Bible. These angels, in their ultimate disdain for God, had sex with women to intentionally corrupt human DNA. According to ancient texts, some of the fallen ones were so corrupted that they not only had sexual relations with humans, but animals as well, hence the Centaur, Chimera, Cyclops, Dragons, Medusa, and many of the heroes in Greek mythology. They also seemed responsible for biblical giants such as Goliath, Lahmi, Og, Sihon, and many more. The corruption of the human genome is why God needed to destroy the world, and rid humanity of the serpent race and the other contaminated crossbreeds. And yet somehow, the serpents—the Grays—survived.

The strength of their genetics dwindled over time, and the seed continued to deteriorate. Yet it was this seed that God proclaimed he would be at war with when he told the serpent, "I will put enmity between you (serpent) and the woman, and between your seed and her seed."

Badger knew the evil that existed in this world came down to a simple passage in scripture. It was all about genetics. The battle for good and evil came down to a wicked strand that not only persisted in the underground creatures to this very day, but also within strands that exist in human DNA. And those who carry even a smidge of the serpent genes carry the secrets— the knowledge of good and evil, the story of their origin—and they will do anything to keep that knowledge to themselves. Badger could hardly believe that the human race was infected with the same genetics as that age-old serpent from the Garden of Eden, but Bruce assured him it was true, and that the DNA connection is why the secret has been buried for so long. Those with the serpent gene pass the secrets down generation after generation, and as their influence has grown, so has the size of the cover-up.

Elizabeth had almost caught on. But the wool was still pulled over her eyes. Had she only looked into the two men from her breakout case back in 2006, she might have discovered that the two abominations were employed by the CIA, and were responsible for hundreds—if not thousands—of abductions connected to the underground. Badger couldn't prove it, but he believed the genetically tainted humans were completely under the control of the Grays, either brainwashed or possibly part of the Gray's collective conscious. Either way, there would never be an indictment, because shit runs downhill in the federal government, and the hybrids, as they were called, were everywhere, or so it was believed.

Had Liz dug a little deeper she might've found the answers to important questions: *Who are they? Where'd they come from? Who hired them? Who performed their background check? How'd they get a high-level security clearance? What's their blood type?* One name would lead to another and another, and pretty soon you'd have half of the Department of Defense indicted on charges of a conspiracy so unfathomable, so impossible, the case would be dismissed on grounds of sheer improbability—global abduction, kidnapping, murder, torture—crimes against humanity to such a degree that the world would come apart at the seams.

But that's water under the bridge. The world was just beginning to get a taste of it with Penn's book. They needed to be told about the federal underground in a subtle fashion. First, the idea had to be planted in their minds with the use of fiction and then film. Then, when they had been warmed up to the concept that there was no such thing as aliens from outer space, but the Grays are actually an ancient race living beneath us—eating us, devouring our loved ones—only then would they be ready to accept the truth with their own eyes. It was a brilliant idea. Penn had begun to accomplish exactly what Badger had imagined.

But today was a bad day in the larger scope of things, with Sandy gone, Truck dead, and no word from Alvarez.

Badger had dealt with trouble like this before—rogue Gray sects, militant traditionalists—but the DoD would nip it in the bud. They'd make concessions, guarantees, and so forth; whatever it took to keep the serpents underground and out of sight. But Sandy's abduction was blatant, targeted. He rarely encountered aggressive Grays. The last time that happened was about five years ago when they were digging a tunnel into Level Four. Badger and a few members of the resistance had planned to break through the wall in midday when the Grays were sleeping, but for some reason one of the small Grays wandered through the adjoining cave, hungry and scavenging for food. Badger remembered how it got that crazed look in its eyes and charged his team with its mouth wide open and teeth chomping. Badger shot it and they quickly disposed of the body in a lava pit no one in security knew about. Turned out the tall Grays monitored each of their little ones with a microchip embedded in the back of their head—monitored emotions, vital signs, etc. So when they discovered the little one had vanished, an army of tall Grays marched up to Level One, ready to kill.

Badger, Truck and a few others managed to seal the hidden tunnel with false rocks. When they returned to their stations, the presiding Sergeant Major Dunlap was gone, superseded by Sergeant Major Davenport. New treaties were set in place and the DoD managed to get the Grays to lay down their weapons in exchange for more bodies.

Lately, there were rumors that the Grays were tired of treaties, a growing concern for the resistance and DoD alike. They wanted too many bodies, and there's no way the CIA could comply with their demands without arousing public suspicion. All signs indicated they were taking matters into their own skinny little meat hooks.

Badger leaned against the wall beside the window and considered his options, which were limited. There wasn't time to manage from the helm; he needed to get back into the field. He turned and peered across the loft, marveling at the many crucifixes mounted on the walls and hanging from the rafters: Latin, Eastern Orthodox, Celtic, Patriarchal and St. Anthony crosses.

They had kept the creatures away until now, but the religious artifacts didn't save Truck or Sandy.

Something was amiss.

The extreme aggression didn't fit the Grays' normal behavior. Without his full team, he'd have to go in and find the boy himself. No way Alvarez could bring him to the barn alone. They'd need his help if they were going to survive in the nest below.

Fully determined to retrieve the kid, he ran his hand over the crosses and rapped the suspended crucifixes as he walked down the stairwell. They tapped each other like bamboo chimes, clanging and pinging as dust drizzled downward like a morning mist. He stroked the iron cross, the simple wooden crucifix, and the brass image of the Savior, a full-scale model of Jesus Christ crucified, bolted to the wall.

The crosses were more than art to Badger; they were an obsession, a fixation that started when Truck had carved that wooden crucifix he had kept around his neck. They inspired him to continue the work that Bruce had started all those years ago. Seeing the crosses reminded him of the enemy, spurring him on in the battle for the souls of men.

He looked at the giant crucifix and made an honorary sign of the cross in memory of Truck. As he did, he thought of the burly biker who landed flat on his face in a drunken stupor the night before he crossed over. Badger remembered how Truck used to be such a badass, never admitting that he was afraid, never allowing a single soul into his heart. Bearded, bloated, and mentally on the verge, Truck woke the next morning in Sandy's care. She made coffee and for the first time, Truck openly shared how the creatures below had challenged his belief systems. He told Sandy what he'd seen down at Level Five—the human cargo, the Homo sapiens/animal hybrids, the liquefier and stream of human juices that flowed to the lower levels. He admitted that he hated himself for taking the job, for remaining silent, for protecting those wicked creatures. And that, he told Sandy, is why he was eating and drinking himself into oblivion. He wanted to die. The money wasn't worth it anymore. That's when Sandy told him about the resistance and about their origin. And that's when Truck turned his life around—found his purpose.

At the bottom of the stairs, Badger ritualistically read open copies of The Book of Enoch and The Bible resting on a display table. He read them daily, reminding himself of the passages that had always confounded him...

"The Nephilim were in the Earth in those days, and also afterward..." (Genesis 6:4)

...and his favorite from the book of Numbers, after Moses had sent his twelve spies into the land of Canaan (2000 years after the flood).

"We saw the Nephilim there (the descendants of Anak come from the Nephilim). We seemed like grasshoppers in our own eyes, and we looked the same to them." (Numbers 13:33)

Badger needed to know what the Nephilim were, why they were here and manipulating human biology, how they survived the flood, and why there was so little written about them, even though there are drawings of serpent-like humanoids on every continent throughout history. The cover up was massive, but masterfully hidden by the most reticent of organizations.

Badger recalled how his choice to join the CIA was the best decision he ever made. The missing persons and human trafficking operations were only a small vein in the river of secrets that flowed through Washington, the Pentagon, and black budget operations. Blood spilled in the name of national security, and it ran underground, feeding the demons below, satisfying the terrestrial beasts; they had the capability of destroying nations if they were free to roam and conquer.

Badger knelt down and kissed the Book of Enoch, the first in recorded history that documented these creatures. Discarded by the church long ago, not for its lack of authority, but for the truth it revealed. Badger opened the book and began reading.

"To Gabriel also the Lord said, Go to the biters, and destroy the offspring of the Watchers, from among men."

Badger closed the book and kissed the leather binding, inspired to continue. *The world will know the truth. Penn will reveal the biters. If anyone can bring the underground to life, Penn Mitchell can do it.*

The leader of the resistance stood up and quickly made his way through the barn. The rickety shelter seemed humble enough at first glance—weathered barn-wood walls and cast iron fixtures barely capable of holding the building together. But there was a secret buried below, a high-tech operation that had taken years to complete.

Badger filled his canteen with water from the old-fashioned hand pump in the kitchen and hurried down into the cellar where he loaded his weapons and stuffed a few rations into his backpack. *Never use explosives in the caves if you can avoid it.* That was his modus operandi. He tried to convey that to the team, but each member had to use what he or she felt comfortable with. Slip in quietly and undetected, he instructed. Use a knife, machete—whatever kills quickly and quietly. But in this case, he also packed his trusty FN Browning semi-automatic pistol and another handgun. He threw the pack over both shoulders, slid a wooden shelf (that posed as canning storage) away from the foundation wall, and stepped into the control room. A concealed cavern with its own server and mainframe linked to the resistance: Ariba S & T, Los Alamos, Area 51, NORAD, Fort Collins, White Sands, Carlsbad, Groom Lake, and Fort Huachuca. The resistance ran deep. The Penn Mitchell operation was a pet project, shared only with a select team. Penn was Badger's baby.

The room was dark, carved out of the rocky mountain, and purred with the sound of amplifiers humming. Directly behind the computers and control screen that displayed the location of each member of his team, the room narrowed and formed a dimly-lighted tunnel that led to a maze of passages and caverns unknown to the DoD even though they ran parallel with their most secretive military posts.

This was the work that Bruce Warnill had started long before the CIA recruited him. As a young officer supervising a small outpost of soldiers responsible for monitoring the Gray's movements, it wasn't hard to enlist the first recruits in the resistance. The soldiers back then were battle-hardened from the war, unwavering in their patriotism. Not one of them understood why their government, who by 1949 knew well and good that the Grays had a thing for human flesh, did nothing to stop the massacres and abductions. If the government wouldn't put an end to the wholesale slaughter of the human race, Bruce and his recruits would. The serpents had to be annihilated. And Bruce had a plan—a plan that would take time and vast resources to be effective.

Before Badger began his search for Penn, he texted Luke. He needed a status update. Luke replied:

Liz n troops pursuing Alvarez n Penn in tunnel. Heading to Dulce.

Confident that Alvarez would link up at the appointed time and location, Badger clicked on his headgear and headed toward Dulce in his personal maglev.

Chapter 36
Cornered

Liz followed Luke Martin as he wheeled his way down the hall and into an elevator reserved for *Authorized Personnel Only*. The SWAT guys remained on the third floor, keeping watch and ready for a quick escape. When Liz stepped inside the elevator, Luke hit the "close door" button before the others could get inside.

"What are you doing?" asked Liz. "I need my team."

"In good time, Agent Ramsey."

Livid, she reached in front of the Captain and hit the stop button.

"You don't have any right to separate us. We're a unit."

Luke spun the wheelchair around toward Liz, his eyes staunch. "Stand down, Agent Ramsey."

She couldn't believe the nerve of this guy. Who was he to cut her off from her backup? *Why would he?*

"We're trying to help you," insisted Liz.

Luke grinned and scratched his balding head. "You don't have any idea what you're doing. How can you help us?"

Liz eyed him angrily. "I do, in fact," she said, stepping back assuredly, trying to figure out what this jerk was after. "I think Penn is innocent, and I need to get him back to New York where we can straighten all of this out. It's not that complicated. I think he's a victim here. But I think there are others involved—others deeply entrenched and more dangerous—."

"Stop!" said Luke as he slammed his hands on the wheelchair's armrests. "Stop. Please."

Liz had to catch her breath, offended by his crude unprofessionalism.

"I'm sorry?"

Luke glared at her with an intensity surpassed only by Badger when he was holding his ground in an argument and replied, "Exactly what I said."

Liz swallowed her pride, holding back her irritation for the time being. "Fine," she said invitingly. "Explain."

"First of all, if I really cared for your safety, I'd have you escorted out of here. I can't believe you made it this far."

"What's that mean? Is Penn in danger? Do you know about the terrorists?"

Luke laughed out loud and said, "Of course Penn's in danger. We're all in danger, you and me included."

"Why? What in God's name is going on?"

"It's simple... If they get to Penn before you do, they'll kill him. And rest assured, they'll kill you before you set one foot out of New Mexico. Engine trouble. Cardiac arrest. Pilot error. Whatever it takes. It'll all seem legit by the time they're finished. And after that, they'll go after your family and friends, in case you've contacted anyone."

"Why?"

"Because you weren't supposed to find out about this place."

Liz shuffled her feet. "Everyone knows about Las Alamos. What's the big deal?"

Luke nodded and pointed to the elevator buttons. "Hit B2, if you don't mind."

Liz nodded slowly and pushed the button hesitantly. "Okaaaay?"

"Sound familiar?"

"Yes," she said. "That's where Penn—"

"I know... B2. New York Field office. There's a lot of crazy around here, but we're used to it. We play the game. Smile and nod. Do you understand?"

"No. I'm sorry," said Liz. "I don't get it."

"Listen. Las Alamos was built here for a reason. They're not just developing weapons here. They're developing micro nuclear power stations, anti-gravity craft. Covering it up. Literally."

"Sounds conspiratorial," Liz said flippantly.

"It is. But it's not a conspiracy theory contrived by citizens about the government, it's a conspiracy contrived by the government against the people."

"You're losing me, dude."

"Didn't you read the book? They've made deals with those things down there. And if they tell the American people what's underneath, panic will ensue. If they tell the truth about those gateways to Hell, they'll look foolish or evil, depending on how you look at it. They have no choice but to keep it under wraps."

"What do you mean by 'gateway to Hell?' You're not talking about "Hell" as in Heaven and Hell are you? That's just rhetorical, right?"

"Listen, Elizabeth. Everything you know about aliens is a lie. They're not extraterrestrial. They're *terrestrial*, and they've been here longer than we have. They're genetically altered beings and their origins, we think, trace back to what we refer to as the fallen angels. But who or what they are is immaterial at this point. Whatever they are, they're not human, and they're not friendly. They despise us and no one knows how many there are."

"Then why are we protecting them?"

"We're not protecting them... we're... we're restraining them."

"From what?"

"Destroying us... completely."

Liz couldn't decide whether to laugh or throw up. The guy seemed sincere. He had to be telling the truth...or completely off his rocker. But then she remembered the wall-crawler back in New York City, and everything in Penn's novel. The book was a little fuzzy on some of the details. So maybe Penn only knew so much.

"What's the point?" she asked.

"In?" responded Luke.

"In restraining them."

Luke turned his eyes down. "They're extremely powerful. They let us see what we want to see. Today it's Gray aliens. Yesterday it was serpents. And once upon a time their predecessors were giants, gods: Zeus, Aphrodite, Apollo, Baal, Enki, Jupiter, Osiris, Ra."

"Are you for real?" asked Liz. "You're freaking me out."

Luke leaned back in his wheelchair laughing, shaking his head. "You think the ancients made that shit up? They didn't have television to rot out their brains and excite hyperactive imaginations. They wrote what they saw—they documented what was real to them, not some silly tale that helped them understand the trials of life. Mythology is total bullshit. Penn's book is based in reality, and now that you're in the federal underground, you are a mark."

The elevator bell rang and the door opened to a dark, steel constructed tunnel that seemed to go on for eternity in both directions. Luke spun the wheelchair in front of Liz, blocking the door. "They're already going after Penn," he said, pointing down the hall.

Liz peeked out of the elevator door after hearing boots trampling. "Who are they?" she asked, watching a platoon of soldiers running deep into the tunnel.

"Central Security Services—CSS—Special Forces, some UN and NATO elites. They're privately contracted by the Las Alamos National Laboratory, and they're funded by the Department of Energy."

"So why are they using non-US military to secure the backbone of our nuclear program?"

"Cost savings is the official reason. The Department of Energy pays the bills, but that's not the point. The point is that Las Alamos is a ticking time bomb. If the terrestrials get out of hand, the Pentagon will light this place up."

"Why?"

"Because they'll do anything to keep the serpents a secret. It's like when an abusive husband keeps his victim secluded from her family. He can better control her when no one knows what he's up to. So blowing up a nuclear test site in the case of an emergency could easily be explained as an unfortunate and heartbreaking accident."

"Okay. Not sure I buy that. But why are they going after Penn? He's just a kid."

"It doesn't matter how old he is. He knows. And so do you. If the soldiers find him, they'll hand him over to a couple of Men in Black, and that'll be it."

Liz leaned against the elevator's steel wall, thinking about that statement and wondering about those two men back at the De Carver Youth Center.

Luke pushed the button to close the elevator door. "We need to get you out of here, and back to New York as fast as possible. Take a long vacation. Spend time with your daughter. Relax. But until then, play the game."

"Wait," said Liz, cautiously moving away from Luke. "How do you know I have a daughter?"

Luke lifted his hand revealing something that resembled a TV remote and said, "We know a lot about you, Elizabeth." He clicked the remote and the lights went out. Liz felt a slight disruption in the elevator's movement and then just after it started going back up again, the lights turned back on and the elevator door opened. Luke was gone. Her SWAT team stood in front of the elevator door, forming a semicircle, and Gilmore stood in the center of them all. He looked at Liz and said, "We've got Mitchell." He seemed so excited that she wanted to puke. If he only knew what that meant.

Confused about Luke's vanishing act, Gilmore's words muddled her thoughts.

"H-h-how?" she stammered, still confused about Luke's disappearance. "Where is he?"

"They know where he is... I overheard one of the brass talking." Gilmore motioned for her to follow him. "Come on, Liz. We've been assigned to a special unit that'll handle him once they get him out of there."

Chapter 37
Whirling

Penn felt his hands slipping on the rock. Alvarez crawled across the wet floor and checked the clip in his gun and snapped it back in place. "Grab my hand," he said.

Penn clawed for his hand but the river pulled him in, making it impossible to pull himself out. The only thing keeping him from getting sucked in was the rope tied around his torso.

"I can't!"

"Try harder," said Alvarez, pointing his gun at the shadows, finger on the trigger.

Penn felt water rushing over his ear and across his face as he sunk deeper. The shadows grew larger by the second.

"They're almost here," said Alvarez. "Hold on."

Phantom figures took form as the bodies entered the lighted cavern. They weren't creatures. They weren't aliens. They were soldiers. A platoon of what looked like American soldiers rushed into the cavern.

"Thank God!" said Penn, gripping the rope with his last bit of strength. He wondered why Alvarez was still pointing his rifle.

"Don't move!" shouted one of the soldiers. The man was surrounded by two-dozen soldiers wearing dark uniforms, still obscured by the shadows.

"You're on Federal property," he said.

Alvarez steadied his trigger finger.

"Stay back," shouted Alvarez. "The rocks are unstable."

"We just want the kid," replied the soldier.

Exhausted, Penn looked at the men with gratitude. "Thank God."

•••

Alvarez put his gun down. "Thought you were the Grays. Bastards are everywhere."

"We know," declared a soldier as he emerged from the shadows. "You don't have to worry about them—we've secured the area." He wore a black camouflaged uniform, black beret, and a strange patch on his left shoulder. From a distance, Alvarez thought it was an American flag, but as he moved closer he realized it wasn't an American flag at all. The patch was new; one he hadn't seen before—a rectangular patch featuring a gold star in the center of the flag with gold wings shooting out each side. The rest of the triangle was lined with ten alternating stripes—five white stripes and five black stripes. There was no doubt that the leader was a Captain; the two silver bars made that clear enough. Alvarez knew to check rank, but this captain was not an enlisted US military soldier, UN, or NATO.

At that moment, Alvarez realized that he'd only been involved with the front end of Dulce's security group, guiding delegates, visitors, and staff. He'd never been involved in the other side of the Federal underground—the removal, purging, and disposal— the group that made people and evidence disappear. He could only guess that they were the purgers—the militarized Men in Black.

The soldiers had come within feet of the perforated floor, and they all wore the same badge—or flag, as it were. Releasing Penn to these guys was not going to work, but they were within striking distance, so he had to act fast. He had to be proactive.

He glanced at the kid. He was barely hanging on.

"Looks like the water ate through the floor," remarked one soldier.

"It's unstable and very slippery," said Alvarez, waving his free hand as a warning. "Don't come out here." He reached down and grabbed the rope and made the appearance of pulling Penn out.

The Captain said, "Looks like you could use a hand." He motioned for a couple soldiers to help.

Alvarez looked at Penn, afraid of what they'd do if they got their hands on him. He thought of all the work Badger and the team had put into getting Penn in the underground, and all that'd be lost if he disappeared. *Federal Underground* would be pulled off the shelves and Penn Mitchell would go down as a one-hit wonder who lost it all because of a drug overdose, or some other fabricated demise that would discredit the book and author. But what would really happen is beyond imagination. They'd feed him to the Grays and the creatures would savor every bite—sweet revenge, considering the numbers lost as a result of that damn kid. Alvarez couldn't let that happen, but he couldn't run, either.

The two soldiers crept across the wet rock like two kids trying ice-skating for the first time. Alvarez strained to keep Penn afloat. He thought about his father and knew that he couldn't fold under pressure. He had to stay the course. He had to redeem his family name.

"Take the rope," he said to the soldiers, noticing that the Captain was watching him closely. "When I get a hold of him, I'll tell you when to pull. Got it?"

The soldiers nodded as they stood with legs braced, scarcely able to maintain their balance. They looked like cookie cutter soldiers, fresh out of boot camp, hair buzzed and scared as piss. They pulled the rope and it sprung tight. When he was ready, Alvarez signaled for the men to pull, and then he reached down and very quickly removed his knife from his ankle sheath. The

Captain shouted something to the men, but Alvarez was too busy slicing the rope to understand what he said. As the blade cut through the braided strands, he watched the look on Penn's face turn from relieved to terrified. Penn reached for the rock, gasping and screaming, but the current had already pulled him into the raging river below.

The two soldiers fell backward, tumbling to the ground, and the entire platoon took up their arms. One of the soldiers fired and Alvarez felt a burn when the bullet clipped the tip of his right ear. He wanted to grab it, to dull the pain, but there wasn't time. With most of his body submerged, Alvarez reached into his backpack and grabbed a M-67 grenade. While holding the lever tight to the grenade, he removed the safety pin, followed by the pull ring with his index finger, and then tossed the grenade toward the platoon, knowing he had four seconds to grab his pack and swim away. Better to die at the hand of nature than shady mercenaries.

•••

A bullet zipped through the water and Penn's headlamp revealed the bubbly trail left in its wake. Overhead, he heard rounds ricochet across the stony floor and cavern walls, followed by a rumbling that sent shock waves through the river and the marrow in his bones. Blood escaped from his bandage and swirled in the water like a crimson ribbon dancing in the wind and for a split second, he contemplated how pretty it looked until he realized it was *his blood*.

He spun and twisted in the drink like a dirty sock swashing about as the water flowed this way and that, hurling him with extreme indifference. Then he dipped and dipped again, his head popping in and out of the water long enough to steal a gasp of air, and the stirring and plunging continued.

Sure that he'd die before it was over, he experienced a brief moment of anger and wondered why Alvarez let him go. And just as he turned his thoughts back to breathing, his body slammed into a boulder the size of a small pickup truck. Pain ripped through his bones from head to toe and he started spinning, circling round and round and round.

As he realized he was caught in a whirlpool, his head burst out of the water, allowing a quick gulp of oxygen before the water sucked him back in.

Chapter 38
Lava Pit

Badger ran through the caves and tunnels bored out decades ago, hoping to intersect Alvarez and the kid. Whatever happened, he knew he could never do anything like this again. In retrospect, Penn was just a boy victimized by his own ambitions. Using children as a weapon was weak, a tool used by terrorists, and he was no terrorist. He was a freedom fighter, an emancipator. Penn was just a kid. Badger wouldn't rest until he knew he was safe.

He'd arranged to meet the trio (Alvarez, Truck, and Penn) at the lava pit later that night and then retreat back to The Barn to re-educate Penn, but now everything was off. The timing was skewed. Who knew when they'd make it, or if they'd survive at all. He didn't anticipate a disaster. That's not how they operated. All he could do is follow the plan and expect Alvarez to come through. Details would come later. *What happened in the maglev? What were the circumstances that brought Liz to Las Alamos? How much does she know*? There were too many unanswered questions. The calculated margin of error had totally failed.

The tunnel narrowed, and Badger knew he was getting close. He crouched down and walked until he had to crawl. Soon he was flat on his belly. He tied his bag to his feet and pulled it along until he arrived at the designated meeting point. The tunnel opened up into a large chamber that he'd stumbled upon while digging a random passage to serve as cover in case of an emergency. About one hundred feet in length and width and height, the Grays came within a few feet of mining into this unique cavern. It was a perfect hideaway. A crevice in the rock breached the crust above and offered a continuous influx of fresh air, which was necessary considering the toxic gasses that bubbled out of the small, campfire-sized lava pit in the center of the room. It emitted a beautiful red glow, lighting a circular portion of the space, giving the appearance of a fiery snow globe. Although sitting around the lava pit alone left one to wonder about the black corners that eluded the blaze. It wasn't a place you'd want to remain alone for an extended period of time.

Badger set his pack down and waited by the fire.

Chapter 39
Cascade

Penn had nearly passed out when the river plummeted forty feet into a pool of crystal clear water. He tumbled down the thick spray of frothing current, free falling until he landed. He swam up through the water, blackened by the darkness above, his surroundings visible only by the lighthouse effect created by his headlamp beaming forward. When he burst out of the water, he took several large gulps of air, desperately grasping serendipity.

Alvarez splashed a few feet away, followed by his backpack. When he rose to the surface, Penn wasn't sure if he wanted to hug the man or punch him in the gut. He barely had the strength for either choice. But the smile on Alvarez's face made his decision for him. They swam to a shallow area, embraced and laughed. Penn relished the moment, feeling a sense of freedom and escape, although he knew they were far from safe. The creatures would find them. And help was even further away.

Penn pulled back, remembering that he was angry. He said, "Why'd you do that? We were good to go, man."

Alvarez shook his head, throwing the sopping pack over his shoulder and said, "We were good *as dead*, Penn. They weren't there to save you. They were there to get rid of you."

Penn frowned in disbelief and walked away. "Yeah, right."

The cavern was dark, gripped in the echo of crashing water. He turned and the light revealed another cliff. Thirty feet up, the walls followed the curvature of the pond about three hundred degrees and then dropped out of sight. There appeared to be another drop—a waterfall flowing over the edge of the final sixty-degree arc that lined the pool (about seventy feet), but the water lacked the intense current that pulled him in, so he waded close to the edge through waist-deep water that glowed when his lamp flashed in front of him.

"Be careful, Penn," instructed Alvarez.

Penn could hear the former Marine splashing toward him, but he was tired of being watched over. Something had to change. Their journey into the depths of the underground seemed pointless and stupid. He still didn't know why he was chosen, and he couldn't care less. He began to question everything all over again. Badger wasn't anywhere in sight, as if that mattered. What could Badger possibly say that would make him feel better about being down there? Penn sighed. *Nothing.*

He wanted to go back to his old home in Ohio; back to his old school, start over, and pretend none of this ever happened. He even missed his dad a little.

"Where are we?" asked Penn.

Alvarez stood near the edge of the pool as water ran over his hands. "I'm not sure," he said. "This is new to me."

Staring at the vast empty space, Penn's eyes began to adjust to the darkness, revealing what looked like Space Mountain, the indoor roller coaster he remembered riding at Disney World when he was a kid.

"Whoa!" said Penn, nearly falling over the cliff. He looked down and there seemed to be an endless pit below.

"Do you see that?" asked Alvarez.

"Yeah... They look like stars... Millions of them." Entranced, Penn felt drawn to the lights that danced in the darkness. He looked down and the *stars* seemed to go on forever. He looked up and they were there as well. The site was stunning, but impossible.

"They can't be stars," said Penn. "Can they?" He walked through the water with his right hand stroking the smooth edge where the water spilled over.

"No. They can't," said Alvarez with a hint of uncertainty in his voice.

"Aren't you supposed to know where we're going? I thought you were my guide."

Alvarez didn't respond.

"Alvarez?" Penn turned around and found Alvarez leaning over the edge.

"What is it?" asked Penn.

Alvarez turned and his face looked white as a ghost. "Look," Alvarez said, pointing.

Penn leaned over and saw more stars along the cliff—thousands, perfectly aligned. He lifted his head and looked back at the stars in the distance and noticed for the first time, as more of them came into focus, that they, too, were evenly spaced, row after row, column after column, their alignment masked by the sheer darkness and enormity of the fractured earth.

"Are those lights?" said Penn.

Alvarez nodded.

"Is this where they live?"

Alvarez shook his head.

"What is it, then?"

Alvarez didn't respond.

"Hey. Did you hear me?" Penn shook Alvarez's arm.

Alvarez turned slowly and looked at Penn. "The lights… they're lamps."

"Lamps for what?" said Penn. "What are they doing down here?"

"They're lighting the chamber room... I... I know where we are now."

"Where?" asked Penn, relieved Alvarez knew something.

"I can't be sure because I've never seen it from this vantage point before. Th-there's a process. A procedure. We only saw a very small portion when we were down there."

"Who's we?"

"That's not important. The important thing is to show you." Alvarez started circling the edge. "Walk that way," said Alvarez, directing Penn to go in the opposite direction of the arc. "Look for a way down. A stairway. Anything."

Penn slid his hand across the edge of the pool, sliding it through the cool water. The edge dropped straight down and the lights glimmered behind the watery curtain and continued on both sides. If he stretched his neck out far enough, he thought the cliff out there circled around to the other side, but it was too massive to know for sure. There didn't appear to be any way down. He came to the edge of the drop where the cliff started up again and turned around. Alvarez was waiting for an answer. Penn lifted his arms and shook his head. "Nothing."

"Keep looking," said Alvarez, as he wiped blood from his ear. "They got me. Barely. But they got me."

Penn grimaced at the sight of the bright red tip of Alvarez' right ear. Alvarez shrugged it off and Penn turned away, looking over the edge of the drop off. And then he thought of the waterfall. From a writer's point of view, it would be cliché, but possible nonetheless. He waded through the water and began swimming when it was too deep. The falls splashed and percolated beautifully, forcefully pushing Penn away as if it were trying to hide something. But there beyond the streaming deluge was a slab of stone, arcing forward.

He sloshed through the shoulder-deep pool, through the outer edge of the raging water, and climbed up on a smooth floor of calcified limestone where water dripped through small cracks in the stone above, filling puddles that ran over the edge. Although the small cave looked vacant at first sight, his headlamp revealed far more. He saw hieroglyphs on the wall and a large stairway that spiraled downward. The images resembled ancient depictions of man and beasts and blood sacrifices. Penn's headlamp shone on a serpent demigod that stood a head and shoulder taller than the humans bowing at its feet. Dressed in a purple gown and covered with gold and symbols that one would find in a Masonic Lodge, the Serpent King held a bludgeoned lamb in one hand and a bleeding baby in the other. Its mouth dripped with crimson fluid and the line of groveling humans went on indefinitely. He'd seen this image before and he had described it in his book. And the stairway… he knew where it went.

Penn turned and called for Alvarez. Feeling a little afraid, he hoped what he thought he'd find at the bottom of the stairs was just his imagination, because what was in the book was terrifying. He looked through the wall of water and imagined it flowing with blood, streaming over the edge and for the first time, he wanted to meet Badger. He no longer felt angry about his abduction. He didn't want to run away. He needed answers. That's all. The bloody depictions on the cave wall were unbearable to look at, practically incomprehensible. They defied his understanding of history, of life, of truth.

There was no mention of these beasts in school. No mention of them in history books. They were products of our imaginations, invented within the distorted minds of tinfoil-hat crazies, or so he was told.

Alvarez sloshed through the water and climbed into the cave, gazing with awe.

"I see you discovered a piece of history."

Penn moaned. "If that's what you want to call it. Looks like a warning to me."

Alvarez put his hand on Penn's good shoulder. "It is."

"Let me guess," said Penn pointed toward the stairway. "We're going down there?"

"You got it."

Looking at the hieroglyph, Penn said, "Are we standing on an altar?"

"Probably. Blood sacrifice is spiritual to them."

"I don't think we should stay here. We should go."

"I agree," said Alvarez, adjusting his pack on his shoulder. "I didn't know where we were at first because I lost my bearings in the waterslide. It wasn't until I noticed a dark spot out there that I knew exactly where we are."

"What do you mean, 'a dark spot'?" asked Penn.

Alvarez tugged on Penn's arm. "Come on. I'll explain."

Penn turned, glad to get out of the death chamber, and followed Alvarez. They hastened down the stairs and Alvarez explained. "The dark spot is where our elevator is located. There aren't any cages there, so it's dark. I've only been there once. Davenport gave me a guided tour once as part of my training, but we didn't come this way."

"Wait," interrupted Penn. "Cages? For what?"

Alvarez stopped and looked at Penn, inches from his face. "Humans. This is a storage facility, Penn. All the lights. They mark the trail. And every light marks a cage where someone's son or daughter or husband or sister is stored—"

"—for food and research?" interjected Penn. "Or genetic experimentation…"

Alvarez looked at Penn with the concern of a big brother. "Yes…I… thought you knew that."

Penn turned away, feeling a little embarrassed. "No. I mean… I *knew* it, but I refused to *believe* it."

"Even after the Gray attacked you in the maglev?"

"No. I… I was in shock. It's not that I didn't believe at that point. I just didn't trust any of you. It was too much, too soon. But now, after seeing what those things did to Truck, I feel differently."

Penn ran his hands through his dripping hair and felt a painful reminder from his shoulder. The burning sensation caused by the bite sent a proverbial chill up his spine.

"Check that out," Alvarez interrupted, drawing his attention to the inside of the stairwell. It opened up into a large, cylindrical, open aired chamber where a narrow stream of water poured down the center of the spiraling staircase into an abyss of darkness. Huge limestone pillars supported the pool above and the stairway circled the glistening water as if it were to be worshiped as much as blood.

"This has got to be an important place. I don't think we should be here," said Penn.

"I think you're right," agreed Alvarez. "I know a way out, but we've got to pass a lot of cages first. Are you up for that?"

"I don't have a choice, do I?"

"No. Not really."

"Looks like the stairs go down several more stories before we'll see any cages. What then? I dropped my gun."

"Me, too, but I've got more goodies in my bag." Alvarez reached into his pack and pulled out a blowgun and a leather pouch filled with darts. "Take these. The poison on the tips will drop the small Grays in a second."

"What about the big ones?"

Alvarez shook his head. "They're immune."

Penn grabbed the tube and pouch and studied the ornate carving in the wooden blowgun. A serpent twisted around a pictorial storyboard that told the tale of Adam and Eve. The image reminded Penn that from temptation to banishment, the serpent ruled their world, tempting them day and night. Glaring at the dart gun, Penn realized how literal the biblical passage really was.

"Where'd you get this?"

"It was a gift from my grandfather. He was a religious man." Alvarez said proudly. "He loved carving things."

Penn put the blowgun to his mouth and gave it a try, imagining the damage it'd do. "What else have you got in there?" asked Penn.

Alvarez pulled out a miniature crossbow. "We need to be quiet down there. Don't want to attract any attention to ourselves."

"That all you got?"

"No," replied Alvarez. He reached into the pack and pulled out a Swiss army knife. "Never leave home without one of these." He peeked into the bag. "I've got more bolts and an extra flashlight—if it still works."

Penn looked across the cavern and the sheer number of cages gave him a brief sense of hopelessness. But then he tried to remember the goal: to meet Badger, get answers, and find his place in the resistance; a thought that seemed odd if not altogether wrong. But he'd seen enough. It was time to *buck it up, soldier,* as his father would say.

"Alright," said Penn. "Let's go."

Chapter 40
Lost and Found

After waiting an hour past the scheduled delivery time, Badger decided to take action. It was hard to leave the comfort and warmth of the lava pit, but he had a bad feeling about the kid. For all he knew, things had gone from bad to worse. They could be in the tunnels fighting for their lives, or already dead. There were other passages that would intersect their trail if they were still en route. He picked up his gear and hurried through the tunnels.

•••

Badger peered through the small peephole in the stone. Decades of carving had taught the resistance to dig from the center, carve outward, and then back to the center because you never knew what was on the other side. In this case, when the miners broke through the stone, they decided to use the small hole as an observation point.

He knew there was trouble the second he looked inside. A group of soldiers, *Black Flags*, as he called them, had set up a reconnaissance camp in the cavern. They appeared to be investigating what looked like an explosion of some kind. As Badger examined the scene, he noticed some of the soldiers were missing limbs, some dead, some lifting the infirm on portable gurneys. They had set up battery-powered lights and were taking pictures and examining a charred hole in the rock formation.

That's new, thought Badger, as he detected something strange near what was obviously an explosion. Several holes appeared to have been corroded in the limestone floor, and although it was difficult to see at first, he thought he saw running water passing underneath. He reached into his bag and pulled out his binoculars. He was right. A raging river was flowing under the very trail that Alvarez and the kid should've been traveling on.

"Damn it," he said, cursing under his breath.

Could they have been involved in whatever happened down there? Alvarez is prone to using any and all means to survive. Although it went against protocol, it was likely that Alvarez would resort to using hand grenades. And by the look of things, it could be that they were cornered by the Black Flags. Maybe Alvarez didn't have a choice. The other possibility was they could've fallen in the river, or, escaped through it. That could be disastrous.

Badger pictured the map of caves and tunnels in his mind, contemplating the most efficient route possible to catch up with Penn and Alvarez. And there were many. But there was only one direct route—down the river. To accomplish that, he'd have to slip into the cavern and then into the river, unnoticed.

He crawled backward through the dark, narrow tunnel until he came to what appeared to be a dead end, but it was a false rock. He lifted a latch from the right side of the cave and opened the hinged rock with extreme caution. God knows what creature could be on the other side. When the rock was fully opened and it was clear to step down, he hopped onto the cave floor and closed the stone door, wedging a thin piece of stone in the gap to keep it closed. He adjusted his pack over his shoulders and started running.

When he came near the side of the tunnel, opposite the Black Flag base camp, he noticed two men working near the blackened hole. They couldn't possibly know where the water led. No one knew about the *waterslide*, as Badger called it. That was one of those secrets he kept to himself. If they fell or jumped in as a desperate attempt to escape, they'd end up in the storehouse, and that would be bad news. Alvarez knew how to get out of there, but he'd end up in a dangerous area within Dulce's most dangerous levels, and that wasn't an acceptable option. Badger would have to retrieve them himself.

If he had a smoke grenade or flash bang, he could distract them long enough to slip in the water. But he didn't have either of those things, so he reached down and grabbed a handful of rocks. After choosing the best one for throwing, he crept as close to the cave opening as he could without being seen. The water was flowing harder than he remembered. He'd have to play this out very carefully. So when a couple of soldiers disappeared into the tunnel on the far side of the cavern, he threw the rock as hard as he could. Unfortunately, it landed on a tent and was barely noticed. One of the medics looked up and probably figured something had fallen from the ceiling. Badger threw another stone and the rock cracked against the stone floor, attracting the two investigators' attention. They and several others turned cautiously toward the noise. As they walked with their backs turned, Badger rushed to the river unnoticed. With the soldiers preoccupied, he dropped in and was washed away, surging through the current, spinning through the whirlpool and crashing into the waterfall below.

When he landed in the pool at the base of the falls, he walked out, dripping wet, and hurried past the sacrificial chamber and down the winding stairs.

Chapter 41
Radiation

Penn raced along the path overlooking a steep cliff that seemed to go down to eternity. Tiny lights that looked like pale blue LED bulbs, precisely centered over each cell, illuminated the trail. He passed cage after cage, each one holding a prisoner. The captives looked human: Caucasian, Black, Asian, Native American, large, small, young, old, and everything in between. Most didn't speak because their lips were cut out. They just moaned and grunted. Some were children, filthy, naked. They looked like dirty bones wasting away to nothing. Others appeared to be alien/human hybrids. Half man, half Gray. Some of the prisoners had extra limbs or digits or tails. Human freaks, yet human just the same.

Penn slowed down and eventually stopped at one of the cages. He felt nauseous. He felt powerless and incapable of saving just one, let alone all of them. He looked inside the cage, gripping the rough steel bars. A woman lay in the fetal position. Her hair mopped over her face, but dark eyes peered through the mess. Penn started when their eyes met. She was too weak to make any sudden movements. Her hand stretched across the damp floor, reaching, tugging on Penn's heartstrings. His light beamed on her face. Her lips were still intact, but she didn't speak. He shook the gate. It was solid— not going anywhere.

Turning toward Alvarez, who was at least twenty yards away, Penn whispered, "We can't leave them here."

Alvarez stopped. His shoulders slumped. "We can't save them all, either. There's not enough time. We don't have the resources."

"They're human, Alvarez… most of them anyway."

"And there are thousands of them."

Penn turned back at the girl in the cage, making note of her appearance. "Where do they come from?"

"All over," said Alvarez as he walked carefully between the cages and cliff. "Come on, Penn. Hurry up."

"No, seriously. There's so many. Do they abduct them all?"

Alvarez paused and turned. "Not all. We think the CIA gathers them up as much as the Grays."

Penn's heart sunk. "I was afraid you'd say that." That's what he wrote in the book, but he thought it was so outlandish that it made for great fiction, not fact.

"Now let's go" said Alvarez. "And walk softly."

Penn caught up with Alvarez and the guide reminded him that the prisoners were part of the ongoing biological endeavor to strengthen the Grays' ability to dwell on Earth and build tolerances to our ever-changing diseases and thermal conditions. The intact men and women in the cages were the lucky ones. Most had a purpose that required a living, breathing body for breeding, mind control, or soul snatching. The rest were thrown in the liquefier and served to hungry terrestrials further down.

Penn vowed to return and set them free. He thought of the families that had been searching for their loved ones in vain, and the heartbreak the parents must've felt when they came to terms with the fact that their babies were never coming back. If they knew where they were, if they knew what was happening to their loved ones, they'd go ballistic.

Alvarez led the way, walking past multiple cave entrances, looking for a familiar symbol. He told Penn that he couldn't recall exactly how far they'd have to go until they found the passage that led to the upper levels of the Dulce base. Each entrance into the hive was marked with a unique symbol carved in the stone over the passage. The language meant nothing to Alvarez. As far as he knew, Davenport was the only one privy to the ancient language.

"I'll know it when I see it," said Alvarez. "Looks like a capital C, or something like that."

Penn followed, watching his footing and stealing an occasional glimpse into the cages. He passed a blubbery man lying on the floor holding an eyeball and almost threw up. But he pressed on, fighting everything that told him to stop and help. They needed to stick together. He had to focus on the trail and listen to Alvarez' commands. "Stop. Clear. Forward." It was hard enough blocking out the moaning captives. Their weeping and bawling were deafening. Sounded like bitter souls crying in the pit of Hell. And maybe that's where they were—running through the caves of Hades, Sheol, Gehenna, or Tophet. There were a hundred names for the Netherworld, but the one that stuck with Penn was the Abyss. The holding tank seemed endless. It was a never-ending pit created and forgotten about thousands of years ago. *Could this be Hell? Could this be what cultures around the world refer to as Hell on Earth?*

Alvarez stopped, and Penn bumped into his backpack.

"This is it," Alvarez said, pointing at the carving shaped like a crescent moon. He turned the corner and Penn followed. "If we make it through here, we'll end up at my home base."

"And if we don't?" said Penn.

Alvarez smirked, "We'll wish we did."

"That doesn't sound very promising," replied Penn.

"We'll be fine… as long as we don't end up in the blender." Alvarez clicked on his headlight. "I'd rather be in one of those cages than chopped into mush."

Penn certainly understood that. Alvarez started into what looked like a deserted cave, and Penn said, "If you're lucky, you might end up rooming with that cute chick I saw a ways back there."

Alvarez stopped dead in his tracks and turned abruptly. "What chick?"

"I don't know," said Penn. "She wasn't bad looking. And she was sort of out of it, like she'd been drugged or something."

"What did she look like?" asked Alvarez.

The intensity in his voice was cause for concern.

"I, I don't remember exactly," stuttered Penn. "She… she was short… cute… brown hair… wore cargo pants. I don't know why that stands out to me. It just does."

"Jesus!" Alvarez turned around, narrowing his gaze.

"What's the matter?" said Penn.

"I don't know… maybe nothing."

"Do you know her?"

Alvarez paced nervously. He double checked his pack and counted the bolts. "…five, six, seven," he said to himself.

"What are you doing?" asked Penn. "We aren't equipped for a rescue, remember?"

"I don't know," said Alvarez, as beads of sweat rolled down his forehead. "If I walk away, I wouldn't be able to live with myself."

"Are you serious?" said Penn. "We were lucky to get out of there the first time."

"I know," said Alvarez. He brushed past Penn and started walking. "She'd do the same for me. You can stay here if you want. I'm going back."

Penn sighed. As much as he wanted to save every human in there, he knew it was risky. But then…the trail seemed quiet enough. He turned and followed Alvarez, feeling the burn and exhaustion in his legs, glad they'd save at least one prisoner.

"How far back is she?" asked Alvarez, searching each chamber as he passed.

"Not far," said Penn. "We're getting close."

"Good."

"What are you going to do?"

"I don't know. Pick the lock. Tell her we'll come back."

"And what if she isn't there when you return? You can't promise anything."

"Not worried. I'll deal with my promises."

Alvarez stopped again, and Penn slammed into him, almost falling off the cliff.

"That's her," said Penn. "That's the girl."

Alvarez knelt down and gripped the bars. "Sandy?... Sandy!"

The woman moaned and rolled her head. She could barely open her eyes. Alvarez looked at Penn and said, "I know her. Look at her neck."

Penn peered at the girl. He didn't see anything out of the ordinary. A leather necklace, pale skin. Penn turned toward Alvarez, confused. "I don't know what you're talking about."

Alvarez reached into his olive-green t-shirt and pulled out a leather necklace that looked remarkably similar to the one around the lady's neck.

"I made that for her. She's an electrician. She's one of us."

"What is she doing here?"

"I don't know. They must have just taken her. She was working this morning, and—"

"Did you hear that?" whispered Penn. "Someone's coming."

Both men looked toward the crescent moon entrance and saw two small Grays, one with keys in his hands. They stopped, startled. Their large almond eyes glared in a state of confusion. When Penn stood up, the Grays ran away, taking short, hurried steps. They didn't stand a chance if Penn ran after them.

Penn could hear their voices clicking hysterically, and the fearful squeals that emanated from their throats.

"Crap!" shouted Penn, turning toward Alvarez. "They saw us. What do we do?"

Alvarez looked at the Grays running away, and then back at the cage. "I'll be back, Sandy," he said. "We'll get you out of here. I promise."

The prisoner could barely make a sound, but Penn knew she heard what Alvarez said.

"Come on, Alvarez. Let's go." Penn started toward the crescent moon gate.

"Hang on," replied Alvarez, reaching into his pack. He loaded a bolt into his crossbow and quickly took aim. The weapon engaged and the bolt disappeared with the whooshing sound.

One of the Grays fell and rolled off the cliff, taking the keys with him. The other Gray ran toward the loading station, disappearing into the darkness.

Penn didn't wait for Alvarez. He continued running toward the crescent-moon gate. As he turned a corner, he felt wet stone under his feet. Then, before he could brace himself, his shoes skated across the rock and he fell on his side, tumbling near the edge of the cliff. He looked down and almost rolled off when he saw the endless drop, revealing a thousand caves with a thousand innocents waiting for a Savior. Looking back, he watched Alvarez running toward him. But something was following both of them.

"Alvarez! Behind you."

Alvarez looked over his shoulder just long enough to see something behind him. He ran full bore, reached into his bag, and grabbed another bolt. When he turned the corner, he stopped and pointed his weapon back at the figure that was chasing him, taking careful aim at its head. He wouldn't fire until he saw the gleam in the creature's eyes, but the shadows emerging from the lights made it hard to focus.

"Hurry," shouted Penn. "Kill it."

"Hang on, kid. Not yet…"

"What is it?"

"I don't know."

Penn watched nervously.

Alvarez narrowed his gaze, held his breath and relaxed his shoulders. When the target came into view, he dropped his weapon and exhaled.

"Thank God," said Alvarez.

"What is it?" asked Penn.

Alvarez turned toward Penn and grinned. "It's Badger."

Badger? Penn got a glimpse of the man and his heart raced with nerves, but when he came into view, Penn heard a loud bang coming from the area near the elevator. Sounded like industrial lights kicking on. He turned and noticed the dark spot by the elevator had suddenly lit up with a purplish glow, like a stadium-sized black spotlight. The purple rays touched everything, including Penn's jumpsuit, turning the orange material into a bright green in the same way a black light makes white objects glow.

"Damn it to Hell!" shouted Alvarez as he ran inside the crescent moon entrance. "They've tagged us."

"What does that mean?" asked Penn, following close behind.

"The light… It's marked us… imprints a nano-code on everything, like a tracking device. It's on our skin, hair, clothes. Will take a while to get rid of it."

"What about Badger?"

"He'll catch up. Keep running."

Just as Penn entered the tunnel, a high pitch alarm sounded. It wasn't deafening, but it hurt his ears. He stopped, looked out at the storehouse, and watched purple lights turn on at every cave entrance, including the one right above his head. The light blinded him for a second. He stopped moving, rubbing his eyes. It was so hot he could feel the heat radiating on his skin. When Badger arrived, he shoved Penn into the cave.

"It'll burn you," insisted Badger. "The lights are radioactive."

Penn stumbled a bit. When he regained his balance, he stared at the bearded man.

"Good to see you again," said Badger.

"I... wish I could I could say the same," said Penn, reminded that he was abducted and Badger was the abductor.

"I understand," said Badger. "And we'll discuss that later."

Looking over Badger's shoulder, distracted by movement stirring in the distance, Penn noticed something rushing out of the cave entrances throughout the cavern. The rocks looked like they were alive—like they were moving. He narrowed his gaze. Black lines—no—shadowy beings poured out by the tens, hundreds, and possibly thousands. Dark bodies swarmed out of the caves like an army of ants starting up the trails and cliffs, heading straight for the trio. Penn's eyes widened, and Alvarez shouted, "Run!"

Chapter 42
Swarm

Penn raced with the two men through the tunnels, running as fast as he could. Badger led the way and Alvarez protected the rear. The Grays' tunnel emitted a purplish glow that responded to their presence, lighting the rock as if it were activated by a motion sensor and going dark seconds after they passed.

Penn's legs were so weary that the least obstruction caused him to tumble to the ground. His jumpsuit was wet and worn and covered with holes in the knees and elbows, his face blackened with soot and debris. Badger egged him on, helping him up when he'd fall. The old guys seemed to enjoy the thrill of the chase as if they knew everything would be okay. Apparently they didn't care about being chewed to bits by an army of Grays.

The trail was steep and slick at times. With the Grays coming, they had to go up, which was much more taxing than the trip down. They could hear clicking and hissing as if the creatures where right there with them. It scared the crap out of Penn, but Badger assured him that the Grays had set up some type of audio warfare meant to scare anyone off who happened to venture into the caves. Penn affirmed that it was working on him and continued on.

The tunnel narrowed and they had to climb over a pile of boulders that had recently collapsed. They crawled on their bellies, whereas the aliens would probably slip right on past in quick sequence, one right after each other. They were far more adept at crawling. The thought reminded Penn of the Bible verse where God told the serpent, "You will crawl on your stomach and eat dust all the days of your life."

The delay left Penn with an even greater sense of urgency and dread. His mind flashed back to the nightmares that inspired the book. He recognized the fear rising in his chest. Fight or flight was not the question. *Don't let them eat you* was the predominant notion that kept him moving forward. Not that his mind wasn't racing with other thoughts like, *could I escape again?*

No.

He wasn't that lucky. He'd never been lucky. Why he hadn't already been chewed up or swallowed whole had become a mystery that baffled him, and yet, it motivated him to run faster than he imagined he could.

Badger assured Penn that they were close to the base and that everything would calm down eventually, reminding Penn to breathe, to keep pumping his arms.

"Hurry," commanded Badger. "We can make it. You'll see."

Badger sounded like Truck. Or maybe it was the other way around. Had Truck learned from this guy— the keeper of secrets? Badger, it seemed, had the answers he was searching for. But he'd never know the truth if they were killed. He could only hope they'd survive. As far as he could see, they were minutes away from a grisly death. For now, the goal was to live—and run, run as fast as he could. The swarm was approaching. He could hear the rumbling footfall swelling like a tsunami.

Chapter 43
Landing Pad

Liz, Gilmore, and the team were soaring toward Dulce in the Black Bird. She anticipated that the military wouldn't hand Penn over to the FBI until after they investigated him thoroughly. Then she'd get back to researching the real story behind the book. Liz was convinced there was more going on than Penn realized, and the fact that they were chasing this kid a thousand miles from New York City only a day after his arrest was enough evidence to confirm her assumptions and at least some of the facts in Penn's book.

The helicopter buzzed over the scenic mountain range, once part of an Indian reservation, and slowly descended upon a hidden landing pad. The place didn't look anything like a military base. The pad was camouflaged with a dark green triangle in the center of a light-green circle painted to look like tall grass. The base's entrance was built into the side of a mountain with pine trees painted and textured on the large metal doors that prevented conspiracy theorists from locating the entrance from afar. If the pilot hadn't remained in correspondence with someone at the base, he might have missed the mark. There were no buildings. No traditional tarmac. No landmarks. As Liz tried to make sense of the unorthodox base, she wondered if the guy in the wheelchair was right; maybe this was a setup, and they were the mark.

The Helicopter landed, and Liz hurried out of the bird after the pine tree-painted doors opened. When a man in a black uniform escorted them into the side of the mountain, Liz immediately knew something was wrong. The black patch on his shoulder looked like a mockery of the stars and stripes. As they prepared to walk through the mechanized door, Liz made a gesture toward the flag on their host's uniform. Taking notice, the SWAT guys circled Liz, assuring her safety.

She had heard whispers of a black budget military force developing outside of congressional oversight, but laughed it off. The idea was a ludicrous, fringe conspiracy theory—or so she thought. But then in *Federal Underground,* it was all about protecting the secret and planning for a New World Order, one that could no longer be contained, a world where dark men who've embraced those living under the Earth would control and mold a new existence.

The idea was so farfetched that Liz had almost put the book down, nearly laughing off the entire premise—a soulless Draconian government conspiring with an alien species. Ba ha ha! Introducing the global community to "visitors from outer space" (although she knew they were terrestrial) would enthrall humanity to such a degree that they'd easily forgo their traditions and faiths. They expected "radicals" to resist, but radicals were easily extinguishable when they stood in the way of progress. The world would hate them, and see their primitive religious ideologies as insane in the face of the reality that life exists on other planets. "We are not alone," they'd say. "We are not special," they'd insist. "We are but a humble race in the brotherhood of diverse and random life forms in a universe that has evolved by chance, without God, and on our own accord. We are the masters of our destinies. We are the deities of this world, they'd say—and humans can be like gods, too," a message as old as... well, the first encounter with the serpent in the Garden.

The book changed everything for Liz. Badger, the maglev, the creature in the cave and the man in the wheelchair had caused a cataclysmic shift in her world. And now she stood face-to-face with the notorious soldiers that Penn wrote about. The soldier who'd guided them into the mountainside, whoever he was, said something about a Sergeant Major Davenport and waved them forward into a cave that was as mysterious as the book that had altered her life. The way things were unfolding, she'd have to change her focus from retrieving Penn Mitchell to saving him, and very likely, saving herself.

Chapter 44
Sh## Storm

The Grays were moving in large numbers. The war horn blared. Red warning lights flashed throughout the facility. Apparently Penn and Alvarez had committed a grave sin by trespassing on the ancient temple, one of many forbidden zones. But it was all part of Penn's enlightenment. He didn't understand why he was chosen, and as much as he hated being caught up in it, a part of him felt privileged to know the truth.

The mystery of human origins was awash in contradictions and millennia of lost documentation, of which the most ancient records available were from the Sumerians, and their records were too often interpreted figuratively rather than literally, creating a gap in early man's actual experience. Were there actually gods among us? Giants? Hybrids? The Bible and every religion on Earth seem to think so, and yet the US government was doing everything they could to hide the facts. No matter what their true origins were, no matter when and where the Grays came from, there was so much to learn, so much to hate and fear about the deceitful beings underground.

Penn could hardly focus on his fears; armies of serpent-like beings were chasing after him, hoping to erase his very existence. He bounded over the very rocks that had witnessed tribes and primeval cultures swallowed whole by the ancient race, lured to their death by the deceptive creatures. Some vanished without a trace, like the Anasazi. Others left cave drawings of "ant people" and "serpent men", misinterpreted by scientists unwilling to accept the explicit evidence emblazoned on stones and holy places everywhere.

The rock beneath his feet helped him along, giving him strength and speed to elude the Gray terrestrials, despite his debilitated state. Alvarez waved him on, brandishing his war face. Badger charged forward, guarding his protégé with his life. Penn's breath labored, his heart thumped hard in his chest, and his eyes focused on the endlessly emerging path ahead. Step by quickening step, they fled the hive as it transitioned from the ancient tunnels into the military zone.

The prisoners' faces flashed through Penn's mind's eye and he practically shed tears over their plight. The children. Sandy. The man holding the bloody eyeball. Someone had to free them from the phosphoric stink below and the cold captors that brought them there. The fates that awaited were too terrible to imagine—

biological and genetic experimentation, sexual probing. They couldn't be left behind. If ignorance was bliss, knowledge was hell. Something had to be done and Penn could not live with himself if he turned his back on the thousands of humans down there. He followed Badger, knowing he'd come back. He had to. He had no choice in the matter.

Badger turned and looked at Penn as if he could read his thoughts. The man slowed and pointed to a door that surfaced in the darkness. "This way," said Badger. He opened the rusty entry and held it open until Penn and Alvarez passed through. Then he locked it, securing the steel crossbar, warning Penn that the large number of creatures would easily break through.

Penn put his hands on his head, momentarily catching his breath. Badger lay a hand on Penn's shoulder and said, "Time to warn the others."

"It's eighteen-hundred hours," said Alvarez, looking at his watch. "Shift change."

"Right," agreed Badger. "Let's go."

After running a short time, they entered a much larger tunnel carved out of stone, illuminated by lights dangling overhead. It looked like a work zone with mining equipment, muddy boot tracks, and the smell of gasoline wafting in the air. Penn noticed jackhammers and electric work buggies parked on the side of the trail, which grew wider and wider the further they ran. The lights were bigger, too, like the kind in a gymnasium, and the equipment in the area was much larger. Cranes. Earthmovers. Bulldozers. Workers—lots of them. Soon the tunnel no longer resembled a cave. It had opened to a vast dome-like structure rumbling with heavy equipment vehicles and humans being transported to and from work sites scattered throughout the underground.

Penn looked at Alvarez to get a handle on his mood. Were they safe here? Really? There were so many people busying themselves with work, and it was so noisy from the machinery they couldn't possibly warn everyone, let alone save them from what was coming.

Penn watched Badger stop every so often and whisper in a random worker's ear, then another one, and another. They clearly knew him, and responded to his murmurings, passing on the horrible news to everyone within earshot. Some of the individuals Badger spoke with stopped what they were doing and turned toward the center of the dome, looking in the direction where the trio had come from. Then Penn heard the squawk of a megaphone. He turned and watched Badger hop up on top of a people-mover, adjusting the volume on the battery-powered device.

"They're coming! Everyone, listen! Take up your arms! Take up your arms! The Grays are coming and they're hungry!"

Some of the workers ran off to warn the others further in. Others stopped cold; their faces stoic and determined. Like a chain letter on steroids, the silent whispers grew into a roaring thunder as civilian and military personnel gathered their weapons—shovels, pipes, hammers, guns. Some had a look of fear written on their faces, others snarled with anger. Many seemed familiar with the war cry.

As Penn watched the workers and military personnel become warriors, he could feel the ground begin to vibrate. It was gentle at first, increasing in intensity with every second. A few of the workers ran out of the dome, away from the fight. The rest prepared their weapons. They loaded clips. They unlocked the safety mechanisms. When the vibrations had grown into thunder, a cloud of dust began to emerge from the mouth of a single cave, followed by other entrances that intersected the dome. Penn climbed up the side of a bulldozer to get a better look. His heart sank when he saw the hordes of hellish creatures advancing from the darkness. The miners surrounding Penn knew what was coming. Their courage was as palpable as the resolve written on their faces.

From a distance, Penn watched Badger and Alvarez instruct the heavy equipment operators to circle in front of the human army, to lead the fight with their machines. When the workers and soldiers appeared ready, Badger flagged Penn down and instructed him to follow.

Badger rushed Penn out of the dome and into a storage area that housed an assortment of mining tools. He handed Penn an eighteen-inch prospector's pickaxe and said, "You're going to need this."

Penn gripped the pickaxe in his hands, wishing he'd had the implement when he was trapped with the large Gray in the maglev.

"I know you didn't ask for this, Penn. None of us did. But this is the world we live in. Pretty soon, everyone'll be clutching a pickaxe."

"I'm ready," said Penn, gritting his teeth. "I hate them."

"With good cause," agreed Badger. "They need to be extinguished."

The tools hanging on the wall nearby began to rattle and the workers were shouting and banging their weapons together, taunting the approaching Grays.

Badger placed his hands on Penn's shoulders. "Stay close to me and you'll be okay."

Penn didn't feel very comforted until Badger reached into his backpack and retrieved two Beretta

92s, and even then, the guns seemed rather meager. "They want to eat your face," said Badger, handing one of the guns to Penn. "Aim for the head or neck."

Penn nodded, hoping he was man enough to handle the horrors that awaited.

"I can try."

Badger looked Penn over with approval and said, "You were a good choice. I can see that."

Penn turned briefly when the workers let out another massive roar. The time had come for him to join the fight, whether he wanted to or not. He was bound by blood—Truck's blood and the blood of everyone trapped in the cages. He gripped his weapons, ready to enter the fray, but then he stopped. He needed to know why he was there in the first place.

After taking a step forward, Penn looked back. He had to know the truth. Despite the adrenaline surging as the herd of Grays approached, he looked Badger in the eye and asked, "Why me?"

Badger took a deep breath and Penn clenched his fists, crazy scared about what the answer would be.

Badger looked Penn over, assessing his choice. "I chose you, Penn, because I knew you could write a bestseller."

The answer took Penn off guard. He almost laughed. "What?... You're kidding, right?"

Badger furrowed his brow. "Is that not what you expected to hear?"

"No… I… not that we have time…But…"

Badger glanced at the clashing armies as another roar swelled through the dome. "Listen, Penn. I knew you were the one when my daughter, Angela, was a senior in high school. She'd been working on an essay for weeks for a big scholarship. I couldn't see her or talk to her, but I always knew what was going on in her life.

"Anyway, she was so excited about the contest because she loved writing and telling stories. She'd been writing since she could hold a crayon in her hands, for Pete's sake. I used to read her work when she'd stay with me. She was very talented. Had all the confidence in the world she'd win. But she didn't…you did," said Badger, pausing. "I can't explain it, but I knew then and there you had a place in the resistance. I know how to abduct, and brainwash. I can make people remember or forget just about anything. So when you beat my daughter in that writing contest, I knew I found the author of *Federal Underground*, and I knew I could put the story—or at least the idea of the story—in your head."

"That's why you kidnapped me?" This was not what Penn was expecting to hear. Totally threw him off.

"Yes. I wish I could say I was sorry. But it had to be done, for the greater good."

Badger gently knocked on Penn's head with his knuckles and said, "We filled that jelly donut of yours with images, and maps, and pictures that you'd never forget. And you'd never know you were brainwashed. You'd think you were inspired. You'd use your gift to express the story we planted in your mind, which by now I think you'd agree isn't a far cry from the truth."

Penn didn't respond for a moment, although plenty of expletives ran through his mind. What could he say that would change anything? He shouldn't be surprised that this insanity had started with such a ludicrous idea. Besides, talk would only delay the inevitable.

"Well I guess you were right," Penn said shrugging and stepped forward. "We should go. They need our help!"

"Hang on, Penn," insisted Badger, holding Penn back with his hand on his chest. "They're not the only ones who need you. You need to understand something; without you, the world was getting a story planted in their minds, too. Problem is, it's a lie. This is truth. Just look out there..." Badger turned and pointed at the ensuing battle. "The underground. The Grays. These are the greatest stories of our lifetime, Penn. What's happening right here, right now, is the result of what's not being told up there. Wouldn't you agree?"

Penn shrugged his shoulders. Sweat streamed down his forehead. How could he argue with the man? Wouldn't do any good if he did.

"Look, Penn. You had to see it with your own eyes. It was the only way. But you'll have to continue the story, outside of here, because it's not over yet. Far from it."

Penn turned, distracted by the roaring that had escalated in the big room. He looked toward the dome and watched the heavy equipment charging forward, leaving billows of smoke and dust in their wake, plowing down the first wave of aliens. Shots were fired. Weapons clanged. Then the reality of what he was about to do finally hit Penn in the gut.

He looked at Badger, feeling a bit nauseous, and said, "I'll do it. I promise."

Nodding, Badger said, "You're a brave man." He put both hands on Penn's shoulders and whispered something like a prayer, followed by the sign of the cross, and then he gently shoved Penn forward. "Now, let's fight!"

Penn never felt more scared and courageous at the same time. He gripped the pickaxe and the gun, took several deep breaths and marched forward, staying close to Badger as instructed.

As he entered the dome, Penn watched a tall Gray overtake a stout bulldozer driver, ripping into his neck just before a Black Flag Soldier shot him in the head. The creature fell on the track pads that pulled the thing under the machine, rolling it over without the least interruption in its progress. Subsequently, two smaller Grays leapt upon the driver and finished him off, stuffing their faces with his meaty flesh. The sight sickened and infuriated Penn. He raced into the conflict, shooting as the biters crowded around him, while some of the civilians ran out of the dome screaming in horror. Many of the fighters were part of the resistance. Many were not. All that mattered to Penn was freeing the humans below, and every Gray he killed would bring him one step closer to that end. He squeezed the pickaxe tight in his left hand and the gun in his right, and started in on every Gray, tall or short, that he encountered. A small Gray hissed as it sprung toward his face, only to be met with a bullet in its eye. Another ripped at Penn's jumpsuit, tearing away his sleeve, but it encountered the tip of the axe in the side of its neck. When he gripped the Gray's head to pull the blade out, its carbon flesh felt icy against his skin. Its razor teeth continued chopping like a wind-up toy long after it fell to the ground.

Penn lifted his blood-splattered face and watched a sea of terrestrials storm the human roustabouts. And as the Grays entered the realm of man, the stink from the underworld forced its way into the Dome. Bulldozers charged forward, blowing angry fumes. Rock crushers plowed over the aliens, grinding them to bits and spitting them out their asses. The Grays that escaped the mechanized cavalry chewed the unarmed and vulnerable like scavengers on roadkill, leaping from one target to the next. Some of the humans stopped fighting and turned their weapons on themselves, unaware that the elder Grays had taken their minds captive.

Crippled by government deals that eliminated their use of laser technology, the Grays were forced to use their natural weaponry—teeth, telepathy, and claws. Tens of thousands of years could not change their basic urge to sink their teeth into the keepers of the Earth. Seeing the savages in their frenzied state stirred Penn's fears, adrenaline and survival instincts, so he swung away. Badger pushed forward, firing round after round. They had to die—every last one of them.

Chapter 45
The Illusion

Liz and her team were caravanned through a series of large tunnels big enough to fit a semi-truck, deep into the mountain, to an area buzzing with frenzied military personnel. Liz sat cattycorner from the driver in a six-passenger transporter. He turned and watched her frequently. An alarm whooped loudly and she covered her ears with her hands. She shut her eyes and breathed deeply to prevent an anxiety attack. The tunnel began to close in on her. She took several calming exhalations, thought of a time when she and Badger and Angela were still happy together, and for a moment, the whooping seemed to tone down.

When she opened her eyes, she passed by what appeared to be a hanger carved out of stone. Enormous steel doors were rolling closed, but she could see the commotion inside the storage facility. Black Flag Soldiers were frantically attempting to strap down and cover dozens of odd-shaped craft with parachute-sized tarps. As the vehicle sped past, Liz craned her neck to scan the room. She glared inside, wondering why the vessels were underground. And then it hit her. These were not airplanes. They looked cylindrical, cigar-, and saucer-shaped, and polished to a mirror finish. Some were small, about the size of a luxury sedan, while others were much larger, the size of a private jet. As much as it pained her to admit it—they looked a lot like the clichéd *UFOs*.

Flying saucers. Here? Underground? Oh, my God. The guy in the wheelchair was right.

Red lights flashed and dozens of soldiers zipped past in Humvees, moving deeper into the underground, driving at breakneck speeds. The whoop-whooping made it hard to think. When the electric vehicle stopped, the driver quickly hopped off and hurried into an office built into the side of the rocky walls. Seconds later, the driver walked out of the office accompanied by a tall and stout officer in uniform. Liz quickly noted his name and rank: Sergeant Major Davenport, U.S. Army. She knew details would be important if she should survive.

The two men spoke under their breath, occasionally glancing at Liz and her team. Their conversation grew heated, partly because Davenport kept being interrupted by frequent calls on his portable radio. He often pointed in the same direction that the armed soldiers were traveling, instructing the driver to "listen closely", "find the kid", "all eyes above and below", and other such commands that were cut short from either the alarm blaring or another truckload of soldiers driving past. When the conversation seemed to come to a close, Davenport started walking away, but then looked back at the driver with a menacing look in his eyes, and said, "On second thought, keep them here. The kid's marked; I'm sure of that. Finding him won't be a problem," and then he stepped onto his chauffeured personal transporter and drove away.

The driver immediately instructed Liz and the other agents that there was a security breach and that the grounds were off limits and extremely dangerous. He escorted them into the Sergeant Major's office and demanded they remain there until they receive further instructions.

Liz could only imagine what the soldier meant by "security breach". Surely all the commotion wasn't on account of Penn Mitchell. He couldn't possibly be a threat in a place like this highly secured underground base. But then the only alternative, Liz realized, was the type of chaos Penn wrote about in *Federal Underground*: Alien rebellion, genocide, or mutiny from the civilian population. None of those comforted her.

She sat down in a chair by Davenport's desk, quietly contemplating how bizarre all of this had become. She thought back to the strange behavior Vincent demonstrated before his passing—the secrets, the lies, his unexplained death overseas. If Vince had anything to do with Penn, or whatever was going on in this hellhole, there could be a real chance she'd run into him, and she wasn't sure she was ready to face him. The thought caused her already racing heart to spasm. Life was easier when all she knew was the lie. The truth, she realized, was so much more painful than the illusion she had believed all those years. She watched the soldier close the door, and wondered if she'd made a mistake pursuing Penn all this way into the mountains. But then she had a fleeting thought that Gilmore was right. Maybe, it wasn't Penn she was after. Perhaps it was Badger all along.

Chapter 46
The Fray

Penn swung his pickaxe over and over and over, slaughtering a small Gray that had leapt onto his back. It clawed at Penn's eyes and bit at the top of his skull until blood streamed down Penn's face, awakening a new bat-shit crazy that Penn never knew existed inside himself. He reached up and around and yanked the damned thing to the ground and bashed its head in until it more or less resembled a smashed muskmelon. The Gray's veiny skull lay broken in pieces in a mash of blood and brains and strange white juice that oozed out of the top of its skinny little neck that now resembled a bloody golf tee missing its veiny, gray golf ball. Penn's heart was pounding so fast it felt like a speed bag thumping inside his chest. He looked down at the creature, eyes blazing with fear and furry, then looked up and around, naturally taking a defensive position. Small Grays surrounded him, but they fell as quickly as they attacked. They were either beaten to death by one of the human combatants, or shot dead by a distant sharpshooter. With a moment to spare, he wiped the blood from his eyes and caught his breath.

To his right and about thirty feet away, Badger was busy fighting a large Gray. The beast threw him to the ground with ease, poised to attack when Penn aimed his pistol at the seven-foot terrestrial. It must have known what Penn was going to do, because it whipped its head in Penn's direction, hissed, and sprang at him like a giant grasshopper with claws. The thing's large almond eyes glowered as it vaulted forward, but they suddenly glazed over when Badger sliced its Achilles tendon with his tactical knife. As the serpentine elder Gray staggered to the ground, Penn fixed his sight on the creature's forehead and pulled the trigger, finishing it off. It convulsed and screeched as its vital fluid poured out of the back of its head.

The humans had been outnumbered at least three to one, but with the heavy machinery, they were winning nonetheless. It would've been a different story if the Grays had access to their anti-gravity craft and laser technology. But given the Gray's current handicap, the humans had the advantage.

Penn shot several small Grays in quick sequence. There were so many, it was nearly impossible to miss. After an hour of relentless fighting, Penn thought to check on Alvarez. He stood up on an enormous rock that naturally stair-stepped up about six feet and canvassed the dome. He couldn't see Alvarez anywhere. Badger cleared the area with his pistol, taking down several small Grays that made their way through the machinery. Blood sprayed. The sounds of weapons hitting skulls clanked everywhere. Heavy equipment roared and guns raged through the dome as more and more of Davenport's men showed up. Bodies piled up like termite mounds. A human lay half-eaten for every half-dozen Grays that had died in battle. Still, the terrestrials kept charging into the dome like a swarm of army ants.

Seconds later, three small Grays scurried through the masses and chased Penn down from the rock and through the crowd, cornering him into what he thought was a dumpster turned on its side. Panic rose back into his torso. He looked left, but the metal box was pushed all the way against the cave wall. To his right, a huge crane barricaded him in, practically guaranteeing his end. There wasn't anywhere to run. The Grays lunged forward, showing their piranha-like teeth before they pounced. When one came too close, Penn shot it in the head with his last round and it flew backwards, hitting the stone floor with a thud, clicking its final words as its body shut down.

The remaining Grays looked at their fallen brother and then charged at Penn, snarling with depravity in their eyes. Their arms retracted and their faces leaned forward, teeth first. Penn kicked the one on the right in the stomach, and swung the pickaxe at the other, tearing into its face. The Gray with the axe wound screeched and shuddered, pausing briefly to touch the laceration. Penn didn't hesitate. He swung again. He connected. He didn't like killing anything, but when he felt the squish and thud of the over-sized brain, he howled at the thing with frenzied eyes and gaping mouth, gloating in his victory.

When the third Gray recovered from the kick in the gut, it ran on its hands and feet at least five feet up the arched stone and sprang toward Penn with its choppers snapping. Penn yanked on the pickaxe, trying to pull it out of the dead Gray's head, but it was stuck.

Penn spun defensively when he saw the thing springing from the wall and thought he'd pissed himself, although there was no time to be concerned with that.

The Gray landed on the writer and they collapsed into the metal box. The young Gray kept chomping its teeth, while Penn held it back with both hands gripped tightly around its neck. The damned thing was stronger than it looked. As they grappled, the metal box started shaking and rising off the ground, startling both Penn and the Gray. In a nano-second Penn realized the box was a large bucket hanging from the massive crane, suspended by heavy wires and hydraulic hoses. When the Gray looked up, presumably to figure out what was happening, Penn punched the thing in the face. He reached for his pickaxe, only to remember it was on the ground in that second Gray's skull. The Gray's face flung to the right, and when it turned back, it ravaged Penn's forearm, one bite after another. Penn roared and watched his arm drip with blood. Filled with horror and adrenaline, he wrenched the Gray's tender neck, wobbling it back and forth. He figured he'd overtake the thing with ease, but the creature's four limbs were all working against him, tugging with the power of two aliens. It entangled Penn's hands with its digits, and when Penn broke free, another hand or foot took hold of Penn's arms. The damned thing was so fast up close, it was like he was fighting a four-foot squirrel.

In the midst of the struggle, the heavy equipment operator buzzed his horn in a very distinct pattern—three quick beeps—and Penn knew he was going to open the bucket's jaws. He punched the Gray in the face again and it staggered backward. Penn immediately broke free and mustered enough strength to climb up the side of the metal scoop so that when the opposing buckets opened like entwined fingers spreading apart, the Gray grasped the slick surface with its nubby hands, and its legs started falling through the gap, slipping down the slick steel. The driver capitalized on the opportunity, closing the buckets with the powerful hydraulics, severing the

Gray in two. Its lower torso fell to the ground, while its arms jerked hysterically until they finally recoiled into a ball like lifeless spider legs. The thing let out a series of brain-dead clicks followed by a sickening gurgle. Penn watched as milky eyelids closed over the Gray's eyes and white foam oozed out of its mouth. It belched its final groan, reminding Penn of an evil spirit he once heard in a horror flick—growling, vile and fiendish. And in that moment, he remembered that the serpent race were soulless creatures and that when they died, they became the abhorrent spirits known to the Greeks as *daemons*, or demons, malevolent beings found in every culture. Enemies of God, they had nowhere to rest until they were cast into the fires of Hell on judgment day.

Penn wasn't sure if he made that shit up or if it was another fact Badger planted in his head. Either way, he witnessed a grotesque transformation of a doe-eyed Gray into a horrible spirit.

The driver lowered the bucket and Penn hopped out. When his feet hit the ground, he noticed a bloodied Badger staggering near the base of the crane.

Penn remembered that he was bleeding and tried to cover the puncture wounds on his arm with his hand, but all he accomplished was smearing the blood. He stumbled toward Badger, knowing that he had very little strength left. His breath felt labored and his legs could hardly hold him up, but he managed to limp forward.

Badger, too, was breathing heavily, and bleeding badly. When their eyes met, the Dome suddenly quaked with heavy gunfire booming in the distance. More Black Flag Soldiers had arrived, and they were pulverizing the Grays with MK-14 fully automatic machine guns and M2 50 mm weaponry mounted on their vehicles.

Badger cradled his right arm with his left hand. It must have been obvious that Penn looked concerned about Badger's condition. Despite the uptick in decibels, Badger shouted, "Don't worry about me. I'll be fine."

Penn perused the surrounding area but didn't see any Grays approaching. The soldiers were pushing them back into the tunnels.

 Badger winced and stepped away from the base of the crane. "It's time to go, kid!"

"No," argued Penn. "I want to stay and fight."

"We have other plans for you."

Penn shook his head. "I'm not leaving."

"If you don't get out of here now," said Badger, nodding to someone behind Penn. "...they'll kill you. And I'm not talking about the Grays,"

Penn turned around and Alvarez was standing there, his face sprinkled with blood and his chest thumping. Alvarez shoved his knife back into the sheath strapped to his belt. Penn noticed the blood covering his hands and the bites on his collarbone and face.

"We'll take care of the fighting," said Alvarez, huffing out every word. "You... you take care of the writing."

"I can do both," said Penn, pleading, and then he flinched when he felt a burning in his arm.

"Not if you're dead," said Badger. "Besides, I need you to deliver something. Something very important."

Important? Penn could do important.

Alvarez looked around, loading a bolt in his crossbow, watching for Grays.

Badger handed Penn an envelope and said, "I need you to give this to Elizabeth."

"Thunder Lady?"

Badger looked confused.

"Never mind," said Penn. "Long story. You mean Agent Ramsey?"

"Yes," Badger said, nursing his arm.

Penn had never put it together. But come to think of it, she did seem awfully interested in his Badger character.

"Penn, please. I need you to hand deliver it."

"The Agent who arrested me? Why would I go back to her?"

"Don't worry about that. When she reads this, she'll know what to do."

"What about all the people down there? When are you going to save them?"

"Soon. I have a feeling it's going to happen sooner than we anticipated."

Penn looked over Badger's shoulder. The battle waned. The soldiers continued pushing the Grays further back into their nest.

Alvarez nudged Penn's good arm. "Come on, poco hombre. Davenport'll be here soon. We gotta get you outta here."

Penn handed the unloaded gun back to Badger.

Badger wouldn't take it. "Keep it," pushing the gun away. "You'll fight again. Maybe sooner than you think." Badger grabbed a loaded clip from his belt and handed it to Penn. "You may need these where you're going."

Penn wiped an itchy glob of blood off his face and took the clip. "Thanks."

Badger looked Penn over and said, "Your job is to tell the world what's going on down here. Understand? Make 'em believe it. Paint it in full color."

Penn nodded. He could do that. Reluctantly. But he'd do it, if that's what Badger wanted.

Badger reached his hand toward Penn. Penn stretched his arm forward and they firmly shook hands. Penn wanted to hug him, but that felt kind of awkward. He'd only known the real Badger for a couple of hours, although Badger, the character in his book, was much like a hero he'd known all his life. They both stood for a cause that he could get behind. He felt like he could conquer the world down there, deep in the underground where Hell runs wild. He felt strong, confident, and important; a far cry from the little-boy feelings he'd felt in New York City. He was nobody up there. But he had a purpose in the underground, and the idea puffed him up more than anything he'd ever done in his life.

After Penn and Badger said their goodbyes, Alvarez led Penn to a passage out of the mountain where he'd avoid detection. The trail was an abandoned mining tunnel that would be safe to travel as long as the rest of security was tied up with the Grays, who were retreating deep into their caverns.

As Penn crawled through the tunnel, he knew that a battle could ensue at any time. Terrible creatures could come chasing after him without a second's notice. Lives would be lost. Men and women would make the ultimate sacrifice, protecting the rest of the world from an enemy that officially didn't exist, an enemy that would be denied as long as they could be hidden from the public. And it was at that very moment Penn realized who he was. He was no longer a momma's boy. No longer chasing the wind. No longer suffering from daddy issues. He was a writer *and* a warrior. It was always in him. He was always a storyteller. But without the passion that emerges from skidding on the sharp edge of death, the gift would've remained dormant, waiting to rise up like the burning summer sun. Without Truck, Alvarez, and Badger, Penn would've been lost forever.

Badger was right; the world needed to know the truth, and Penn would deliver it like nobody's business between the covers of a book. He'd seen it with his own eyes. He fought the serpent race with his bare hands. He saw the evil in their eyes. Penn heard their lying voices hijack his thoughts. The underground was real. This was no ordinary story. It was not a fable, myth, or allegorical fairy tale of days gone by. *Federal Underground* would unveil the secret history of mankind, unravel our fabricated past, and honor the silent valor of those who gave their lives to protect the human race. And Penn Mitchell, a hero wielding little more than a pickaxe and a pen, would warn the world with his stories. And there are plenty of tales to tell about the Federal Underground.

The End of Book 1... Prepare for more...

DEEP UNDERGROUND
Penn Mitchell's Ancient Alien Saga
Book 2

Chapter 1

A cave near Dulce, New Mexico

Penn Mitchell's lungs burned as he ran up the dark and musty mineshaft from the depths of the federal underground. Dirty hands scraped the edges of the rocky wall, caking his fingernails with decades of filth. Every step injected a cold chill into his chest and every breath thrust him beyond the point of exhaustion. His raggedy orange jumpsuit smelled of the underworld; it was dank, reeking of his own urine and the blood of battle. Penn stopped running for a moment and rested against the earthen wall.

His heart pounded mercilessly, thumping from the pangs of war. He could barely stand. Every one of his limbs trembled with terror and his arms and shoulder caked with crusty blood. The twenty-year-old glanced deep into the mineshaft. The horrors he'd seen raced through his mind like a night terror, the kind that wakes you up with cold sweats in the darkest hour. But this wasn't his imagination. This was real—too real, in fact—the bite marks were proof of that.

His legs felt like liquid tissue, jellifying beneath his skin. When he put his hands to his chest, he could feel his heart firing like a machine gun. But he couldn't stop moving. He had to get as far away from there as he could.

But then what? Where would he go? They'd surely find him.

That damned book he'd written had taken him to Hell and back and he had no idea if he'd ever escape. And if he did, they'd find him and end his life without a second thought. The climb through the abandoned mineshaft had become his last hope of escape. The tunnel would take him outside, finally free from the stink and malevolence below. Alvarez had showed him how to escape, which paths to take, where the secret doors were and such, "But after that," Alvarez said, "Run. Run as far and as fast as you can."

Sweat flowed down the creases of his face like a river, washing away dirt and blood collected from a thousand feet below the surface of the earth. He wiped rivers of perspiration from his eyes, but more continued to flow like a muddy river. Resting cooled the ache in his lungs and stiffened his muscles. He felt dizzy. *Just breathe*, he thought. *Keep breathing… keep moving.*

He briefly looked back into the darkness and stumbled forward. *They'll kill me if they find me.* The thought was enough to push him forward. With sore hands supporting his withering frame and a headlamp lighting his way, Penn lifted his eyes, inhaled the smell of dusty death and noticed a faint glimpse of daylight further up the passageway. The light energized him. A rush of whistling wind strengthened his resolve.

Air. Real air. Thank God. He'd forgotten what it tasted like, what it smelled like.

He took a reenergizing breath and looked back one last time. His eyes wrinkled and his throat swelled with a fearful lump as he recalled the last forty-eight hours—two days that would forever change his life.

He stepped forward, climbed over a pile of fallen timbers and quickened his pace. The light drew near, shimmering through what looked like a tiny crevice in the distance. The air felt thinner, smelled fresher, tasted cleaner. Tiny rocks and rubble shifted beneath his feet. He could hear the wind blowing, and see the dust stirring ahead.

I wonder what I'll find out there? A mountain range? A forest? I don't care, anywhere is better than here.

He covered his eyes, guided by the sunshine that had begun to stream between his fingers. He could taste freedom on his dry tongue. His feet pounded, heavy from exhaustion. He couldn't think straight. After everything he'd seen, a storm of confusion imploded his understanding of the universe. *What the hell am I going to do now?*

Penn's filthy body burst out of the tunnel into a shower of light. He felt like a jet blasting through a blanket of clouds at twenty thousand feet. Booosh! But he was quite sure he looked more like vomit spewing from the mouth of a barfly.

Gasping for air, he sucked in the fresh oxygen and fell to his knees. Dazed, nauseous, and dizzy, tears welled up as the sun blinded his vision. Liberated from the cave, the joy of his deliverance was cut short by the sound of a *click*.

A click? Here?

He felt as if he were being watched. Still on edge, he opened his eyes and squinted into the blur of light and shadows. Then, without warning, an angry chorus of voices shouted, "Federal Agents! Get on the ground!"

Confused, he peered at the blurry figures, lost in the daylight and openness of the vast blue sky. Anxiety filled his throat and chest, and his head began to throb.

There must have been ten shadows clicking and shouting.

"Federal Agents! Get on the ground!"

"Get on the ground! Now!"

"Now! Get down! Now!"

Their bodies came into focus in that fraction of a second. They were human. *Thank God!* They had guns. *Oh, shit!* Their faces looked jumbled, but the desert-like mountains, pines, and shale cliffs in the distance began to take form. He was in the Archuleta Mesa. He knew where he was, even though he'd never experienced the "above" terrain there until that moment.

Before he lifted his eyelids, he felt a brief sense of joy. He felt like weeping. He felt like laughing. And then his face slammed into the rocky ground with a thud.

Powdery dirt stirred around his body and entered his mouth as the shouting continued. The weight of three men pressed hard against his spine, head and legs. One of the men twisted Penn's arms behind his back and zipped a stiff vinyl Ty-Rap around his wrists.

One by one the men backed away, whispering as their feet shuffled over the ground. All Penn could see were the mountains far off in the distance, a drop off where a dirty gravel trail came to an abrupt stop, military boots, camo, a few dress shoes and navy-blue slacks.

Penn coughed up dirty phlegm and forced his head upward, hoping to catch a glimpse of his captors. The dark figures gathered around and huddled in groups of two or three, snapping pictures and taking notes on their handheld devices. One of them looked familiar. When his eyes connected with hers, she took a few steps forward, bent down and stared. He knew her face.

Although the woman remained a blur, she called his name. "Penn?"

Her voice seemed to blow like the mountain breeze. "Peeeeennnnnn?"

God, I'm dreaming again. He blinked his eyes trying to focus, feeling weak and dizzy again.

Clouds engulfed her face, and the sounds coming from her mouth began to fade. "Penn Mitchell?"

Her shadowy figure stooped closer, reaching out for him in a moment that seemed to last forever. Thunder Lady had found him. Or was it the other way around? Didn't matter, really; Penn was just glad to be free from the underground. He could give Badger's note to Agent Ramsey, and immediately make good on his promise. But the shadow figures blurred, and each breath grew heavy. A wave of nausea rushed through his throat, and his face felt like melting wax. Then, despite his best efforts to remain conscious, everything went dark.

About the Author

Jeff Bennington is the author of four Amazon #1 category bestsellers *(Reunion, Twisted Vengeance, The Secret in Defiance, Creepy: The Full Collection)*, and the founder of The Kindle Book Review. He lives and creates in Central Indiana with his wife, four amazing children, and two hairy beasts that bring as much misery into his life as they do joy.

You can follow Jeff's adventures on Twitter @TweetTheBook, on Instagram @WriterRunner, Facebook, and his newsletter. But whatever you do, enjoy this crazy thing called life by experiencing it vicariously through Jeff and his crazy characters. And there are many more to come.

Acknowledgments

I would like to extend a big thank you to those who have helped me over the last few years as I formulated this series beginning with my gun guys, Steve Hovermale, Bill Crawl, and Brad Doke (a voracious Sci-fi fan) who offered valuable feedback to this horror/supernatural writer. I'd also like to thank Katherine from Streamlined Editing for the multiple read-throughs. Your careful eye is much appreciated. And how can I forget the thousands of readers who nominated this book in the Kindle Scout program. I am eternally grateful for your support and faith in me, and this book. I can't tell you how much I don't want to disappoint you! Likewise, I owe a huge debt to the Kindle Press team for taking this book on. And finally to Amber, Caleb, Levi, Asher, and Anna, you give me so much joy when we're just hanging out and living life. My crazy life would be mighty dull if I didn't have you. I love all 5 of you.

If you enjoyed Federal Underground...

If you enjoyed Federal Underground: Book 1, I promise I'm working diligently on the next book: Deep Underground (Book 2). In the meantime, would you do me a huge favor and write a review, talk about it with your reader friends, and share the Amazon link? Writers like myself could not do what we do without your continued support. So don't delay, go to the Federal Underground Amazon book page and post a review right now while the book is still fresh in your mind.

THANK YOU!
Jeff Bennington

Do you like supernatural thrillers?
Try Jeff's other books.

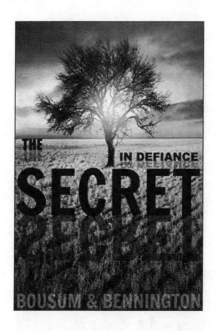

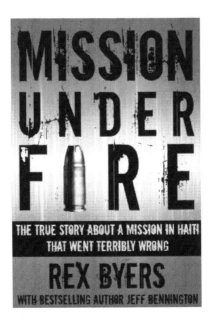

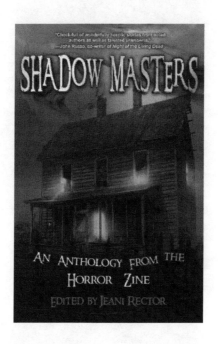

Made in the USA
Middletown, DE
16 January 2024

47973809R00250